Quick Pick

Quick Pick

DAN MORRIS

iUniverse®

QUICK PICK

iUniverse books may be ordered through booksellers or by contacting:

iUniverse LLC
1663 Liberty Drive
Bloomington, IN 47403
www.iuniverse.com
1-800-Authors (1-800-288-4677)

ISBN: 978-1-4917-4253-2 (sc)
ISBN: 978-1-4917-4254-9 (e)

Library of Congress Control Number: 2014915079

Printed in the United States of America.

iUniverse rev. date: 09/03/2014

Chapter 1

Jonas Jackson was not a content man. In fact he was at odds with the entire world as he knew it. More precisely, he was an angry man heavily burdened with his share of regrets and disappointments. Most surely, if contentment was on one side of his life's scale it would ride weightless against the disappointments that had been thrown his way.

His traveling experience had been primarily limited to his short military service. It had been a rewarding adventure for the most part. Like others with a history of some venturing about, he was now reduced to spending his idle hours dwelling on his more significant memories; both good and bad.

Distressingly, this day was not unlike most of his current days; it was joyless with little promise of anything uplifting. Squirming under his blanket provided nothing in the way of relief or comfort for his tormented and worn body. For him, the smallest exertion tended to add to his physical and emotional discomfort. Furthermore, there was no promise for a brighter future. In fact, his world had closed in on him, smothering his expectations for any sign of improvement. He had been robbed of his family and old friends. His life had been pillaged by Mother Nature. Now, he was forced to redefine the meaning of why he was here on earth in such a hopeless condition.

Each morning, the sunshine of a new day arrived without hope, only to serve as a reminder that he had to battle the world around him just to maintain his meager existence. That was certainly deplorable by anyone's standard. His whole life was a bitter imprisonment as he struggled for survival. He was at war with not only himself, but the entire world. This was a war that he had no weapons with which to fight.

There was nothing in his foreseeable future that glimmered with encouragement about his present situation. In fact, his life had continued to spiral downward for several years now. However, this was one of the times when he would cope by clinging to some of his nearly forgotten and better memories. With vivid clarity, his mind allowed him to recall 1964 and those white sandy beaches of the Caribbean. Life back then had been full of promise and limitless possibilities. His health had been good and his mind and heart had danced with visions of a good life; one filled with happiness and a prospect of a modest prosperity.

His life in the U.S. Navy had always been structured. The emotional and environmental perks of the U. S. Navy had always been gratifying and positive. As a boatswain mate, he had enjoyed sea duty and to this day his thoughts were always drawn back in time to a place where gentle ocean breezes and clear blue skies had soothed his soul and warmed his heart. He had graciously enjoyed the occasional interruption by a cool cleansing storm. It had been a good, healthy and robust life. Sadly, those days were gone, lost to changing times, and circumstances beyond his control. Men and women who believe that people create their own destiny fail to understand the power of Nature. Fate had a way of destroying the best of intentions regardless of how well a person planned or how hard they worked. This was the reality of life for the rank and file and even for the privileged for even they had no immunity to fate.

He had religiously kept a crude journal of his navy life; travels and adventures had been plentiful and nearly always rewarding. Without that tattered old journal his memories would surely be lost and irretrievable. Every seafarer knows the anguish and despair brought on by forgetting the details of all of his or her adventures and misadventures so it was not unusual for Jonas to cling to his journal as if it was the Holy Bible. His life had always included a variety of inner spiritual thoughts that he could seldom adequately express in everyday words. However, his hand-written entries never failed to prompt his old emotions to rise above his circumstances. Like most people, the good things in his life had always been felt on a deep emotional or spiritual level and were rarely openly expressed for others to inspect and judge. They were private matters and they were all he had left. The writings and ramblings in his journal were the only things that could put a smile on his lonely and aging face.

He rolled over on his back and pulled his frayed blanket up under his chin. The lone tear that trickled down his face gave him pause to wonder if he was now weeping over sins he had committed or sins he had yearned to commit during moments of spiritual weakness. Tear or no tear, he was keenly aware that he had not caused all the tragedies in his life so the blame was not all of his own making. Life was usually too complex to blame every event or catastrophe on any single source, especially if that source was one's self.

Jonas accepted the truth that God was aware of all his sins and evil thoughts. Over and over, he had asked God to forgive his sins and he believed that God's forgiving grace could be counted on for forgiveness; all in good time according to God's plan. As a child, Jonas' mother had told him that God often tested His followers and when He was satisfied with their faith, many blessings would rain down out of the heavens and fill those once-lost souls with spiritual gifts. No matter how bad his life got, there was no way he could dispute his mother's faith and wisdom.

In spite of the way his life had turned out, God, or his understanding of God, was very much a part of his daily regimen and thoughts. One thing Jonas had learned from a Navy Chaplain was that God didn't make anyone do anything. People were not puppets with strings that God manipulated. God's job included guiding and influencing people and rendering a final, eternal judgment. God gave us many gifts and the greatest one was that of a "free will." However, God does take a great deal of interest in what we do with our "free will" that He so graciously gave to us. By our own thoughts and actions, we all determine our own eternal demise and whatever path we choose for our journey through life; it represents our exercise of "free will." Yes, sometimes we pay high prices for the way we live, and at other times, we receive rich rewards. Maybe God does, at times, exercise His power to influence who gets what. But, for the most part, He leaves most decisions to us.

Every human being is born into this world destined to endure as long as he or she can and then they simply relinquish their souls to face new challenges or profit from wonderful spiritual blessings. Mankind also can suffer from leading bad lives. The big question for Jonas was what he deserved from how he had lived his life? Sitting up and leaning back on a brick wall, he looked at his surroundings with a sense of wonder in his eyes and a puzzled expression on his face. Why were some people blessed with physical wealth and emotional contentment while others had to endure a shattered life full of poverty and despair? Would he ever unravel the truths and realities of his life? Would he ever be able to face his eternal destiny with a warm and content heart when it was time for him to draw his last earthly breath?

Some mornings he greeted his day wallowing in contempt for his life and at other times he was optimistic enough to believe that better days were waiting for him. He had too much pride to ask for sympathy, but, he did not have too much pride to keep him from asking for a helping hand from a passer-by or for praying to God for things to become better in his otherwise miserable life.

At the height of his service in the U.S. Navy, he had served on LST-1175, a 445 foot vessel known as the USS York County. On this very morning, in a blurred daydream, he was able to conjure up one of his favorite memories dating back to August of 1964. The

USS York County was a favored vessel for amphibious operations by the United States Marine Corps. They had picked up the Marine Corps' 3rd Light Anti-Aircraft Missile Battalion at Morehead City, North Carolina and transported them to the coast off a Puerto Rican island named Isla de Vieques. The island was a tropical paradise and the name translated into English as: Small Island. By Caribbean standards, it was certainly a small island; being only 21 miles in length and 4 miles in width. The white sandy beaches and crystal clear water were breathtaking and vacant of tourists because it was used as a U. S. Navy gunnery range. However, there was a small village on the island called Isabel Segundo and the island's population totaled less than 10,000.

The plan was to run the bow of the York County up on the beach and drop its ramp and then off-load Marines and their vehicles. There was a good reason for that day to be seared into his memory and that added some excitement to the morning air. The excitement quickly mounted as he recalled standing on the deck peering down at the ramp as it dropped into place on the beach. The first vehicle down the ramp was a jeep pulling a small trailer. A young Marine officer was sitting in the passenger seat urging his driver to drive off, down the ramp, through some water and onto the beach. Unknown to the Marine officer and driver, there was a large hole in the sand at the end of the ramp. The thing that happened next would provide many years, even decades, of laughter for Jonas and his shipmates.

The jeep and trailer disappeared into the water, completely submerged. The driver and young officer quickly surfaced, thrashing their arms wildly until they were pulled out of the watery hole; a rescue that left them standing on the beach. They looked like angry wet rats. Many sailors cheered while many more heckled the Marines. For Jonas, days like this made life worthwhile. Those were good times. It was too bad that he couldn't return to that day and relive his life up to the present day.

One of the worse things he had ever done in his life was to get out of the Navy. Like many young men who went off to serve in the military, he had missed home. New Orleans was where he had grown up and that was the place he had so begrudgingly missed. Family, friends, familiar streets and the sound of jazz music was what he remembered of home and to him those memories were not replaceable.

Like other black youths from New Orleans, he had walked down Bourbon Street a thousand times if he had done it once. The soul-caressing sounds generated by saintly grey-haired jazz musicians had floated on stale air out of Preservation Hall. That music would always echo in his mind and stir his soul and it would always call to him like a siren from a mystical Greek island.

Sadly and unfortunately, there was no going back; no replaying of his life. Hurricane Katrina had intervened. It is one thing to think about going home, but, it is quite another feeling to know that his home, as he remembered it, was no longer there; not the way it had once been. Now, he was in Dallas, Texas and people who only a few months ago had warmly and caringly called him a displaced person were nowhere to be found. He had spiraled downward to become what local citizens knew as a homeless person; a street person. He was a man without means and with little hope. If he had only stayed in the Navy, he would now be a proud retired enlisted man and everywhere he would go people would thank him for his service. Now, people of means only looked down on him; some with pity and others with scorn. His presence was nothing less than an urban eyesore. He had somehow joined the ranks of the unwanted and unworthy. If only arrogant people with wealth and good health could experience his predicament, just once in their lives, they would have a different and better understanding of other less fortunate people. Anyway, that was one of his opinions concerning life. Surely, somewhere out there, there were people who had been down and out only to pull themselves up by their own bootstraps. But, how does one start that process when he has nothing?

Arrogance was a disease of the well-off; while poverty and despair were the diseases of the homeless. Hopefully, if he would someday become better-off, like those who were always driving by and gawking, then he would possess enough humility to understand that not all homeless people were degenerates. Although, he had to admit that there were degenerates, emotionally unstable, and people predisposed to crime out there among the homeless. Conversely, there were also criminals and psychopaths among the rich. Yes, for every blessing in society there is also a curse lurking about somewhere. The rich usually do a better job of covering up the dark aspects of their lives, and of course they dress and eat better.

Hurricane Katrina had blown out the guiding light that had once been lit to shine the way for him to achieve the American Dream. That awful storm had destroyed all of his dreams and claimed the lives of his wife and son. The howling wind and thrashing rain from Katrina had been the sounds of God slamming the door shut on his whole life. His only hope was that the same God that had sent Katrina would open another door for him to escape through so he could put this horrible nightmare behind him. A minister in a homeless shelter once told him that through prayer, a man could knock and knock, for years on end, on God's door until his knuckles bled before God answered. The message had been clear; never give up or lose faith because God is aware of each of us and will work according to His own timetable.

Jonas looked at the backs of his hands and imagined he could see scars from his years of knocking through prayer on God's door. Still, he believed that God was the way and the truth. Jonas had only one question for God: Why did You take my wife and son instead of me?

The sleeves on his shirt were threadbare with a few tears and they were also too short for his long arms. He hadn't shaved in weeks and his beard was altering his facial features. The sadness in his dark brown eyes was becoming more pronounced with the passing of each day. His hair and beard were now turning white. At least his teeth were withstanding his hard life because they remained white as ivory.

Struggling first to his knees, he finally stood with a complaining grunt. As was his routine, he pulled a knit cap over his dark balding head. Any man that could stand had the capacity to take on another day; there was no other choice. When he could no longer manage that, he would know that the end would be near.

Purpose was what he was lacking. He needed a meaningful goal; something to drive himself toward; something more than the nourishment he could gain from food; his goals had to possess emotional power. There had to be something that was measurable in some way; something self-gratifying. The good things in life had eluded him in a merciless way. Earlier in his life he had been blessed with having a loving wife and a strong son to care for, and a home. Although meager, his home had been his castle. Now, he was the only person he had to care for and that responsibility was something that he could hardly meet.

His wife had been a devoutly religious woman who was meticulous at keeping their home clean. Whenever foul language was used in her presence, she would lecture everyone within ear shot. As for his son, Jonas Junior, there was a deep sense of pride. The boy was industrious and had a way with money that astounded anyone who knew him. A family friend once said that Junior once squeezed a dime so hard that he could hear it squeal.

Junior had tackled his homework with a fierce devotion and his grades reflected his tenacious effort. He was not athletic enough for any kind of sports scholarship, but, he was a fit lad. He went about earning his way in college the old-fashioned way; he worked as a crewmember on various shrimp boats in the Gulf. He would work a year and then attend college a year until; at last, he was in his junior year of college. This was the year he had applied to become a New Orleans Fireman. He had been accepted and was waiting for a spot in the academy when Katrina struck.

A month had passed before Jonas learned that his wife and son had both perished in the storm. Jonas was at a shelter in Dallas along with other displaced people from Katrina when he learned the fate of his family. He never got to attend a funeral or properly say goodbye to the ones he loved more than life itself. He was shocked and emotionally paralyzed for weeks. The weight of his devastation had pushed him to the lowest of depths.

Once a man hits bottom there is nothing to do but look for a way back. In the meantime, he would have to adapt until he figured out a way to get back up and stand proudly. Without a purpose, a man only exists as an empty shell. Jonas needed, and wanted, something to live for. Escaping through cheap alcohol was not a real way out and it was destroying his body and mind. Seeing life through a drunken stupor was not the proper way to cope. Becoming an alcoholic was a dead-end goal; it was part of being on the bottom. It was part of the trap. Like a trapped wild animal he had to free himself.

The last thing Jonas wanted was to pass the point of no return. Looking up at the morning sun he broke down and started to cry. Between uncontrollable sobs he once again prayed to what he understood to be a merciful God. Also, he was praying and crying for a sign, any sign, that there was still hope for him. He was ready for whatever God had in store for him.

The squeaking sound of a discarded shopping cart's wheels caught his attention. The rusty cart was brimming over with old garments and assorted treasures plucked from inner-city dumpsters and cluttered streets. The middle-aged white lady pushing the cart was Gertrude O'Malley who Jonas affectionately nicknamed Gerty. Her skin was weathered; sunburned, tough, looking like leather and wrinkling ahead of its time. Bloodshot, her eyes appeared worn and nearly lifeless. Her grey hair was straggly and nearly reached her hips. Life on the street was hard enough for men, but, it took a harsher toll on women.

Jonas admired the way Gerty trudged along every day, without complaining, except on rare occasions.

Gerty's jeans were faded with both knees torn. She was wearing a new denim blouse and new tennis shoes which Jonas figured she had picked up at one of the shelters frequented by street people. Through chapped lips she asked, "You want a touch of this?" She held up a bottle of cheap wine and offered it to him.

Still dwelling on the importance of acquiring some intermediate and meaningful goal or purpose, Jonas embraced a new idea. "No Gerty, I'm on the wagon. I'm trying to get myself together, if you know what I mean." The idea to stop consuming alcohol was something that would surely please God while showing proof that he could stand on his own when it came to being tempted by the devil. He was encouraged by his own actions and that hadn't occurred in a long time.

Jonas genuinely cared about Gerty and worried about her health and wellbeing. Like all homeless souls, she had her own story and it was filled with darkness. Gerty, and many others like her, knew that life was an educational endeavor. The school of life served up many gifted students who learned their lessons well and their stories would become great talks at church meetings. Of course, those that failed in the school of hard-knocks would fail miserably. Sadly, the streets are one of the worse dumping places for a human being to end up at.

Twenty years ago, Gerty had been a loving wife, mother of two, and a dedicated nurse. Her mother had been a psychiatrist and her father an electrical engineer. She had everything going for her; that is until she took a tumble into the world of prescription drug abuse followed by a reckless life with addictive recreational drugs. Her addiction had been too strong for her to fight off. The deeper she fell the more she destroyed her life. Her dependency became her daily norm and any means of acquiring those illicit drugs was tolerable and justifiable.

Like many who had found themselves entrenched in the drug cult, she was only able to begin climbing out because of a lengthy prison sentence. Her family had disowned her and they were all getting along just fine without her in their new lives. Yes, in spite of having an out of control mother, Gerty's children were blessed by having the good fortune of living productive and meaningful lives with their grandparents.

As an ex-convict with a history of drug addiction, she was barred from the nursing profession. To her credit, she had at least been able to break the tether that had once held her prisoner, like a ball and chain, to the drug culture. However, the bondage of her emotional scars was still there and strong enough to cause her to give in to alcohol; a legal drug that was openly tolerated by society. Life had stacked the deck against her and that had occurred with her cooperation.

Gerty's new life on the streets as a homeless person was not easily tolerated by her. The transformation had been increasingly unbearable as she faced each new day with disappointment. Alcohol, as a coping remedy, was working out for her, even though she knew it was not what she wanted out of life. After all, she was a realist. People in any emotional and economic state are still members of the human species and that means they are prone to socializing; albeit on their own level. Confined and restricted by circumstance, she had no choice but to socialize with those living in her environment. Her adaptation to her surroundings and social network included Jonas Jackson. He had become a close friend who would not judge her. She liked the fact that Jonas was quick to encourage her whenever she mentioned doing nice things like attending religious services at one of the homeless shelters.

She was not offended when he declined a drink from her bottle of cheap wine. In fact, she respected his newly found strength and wondered when her day would come; a day when she would take a meaningful lunge toward sobriety. She walked around her shopping cart and hugged him. "Good for you, Jonas. If anyone can make it, it will be you."

"Gerty, honey, today is the day I start taking on the devil. My purpose in this life is not to see how much I can drink. Somehow, I'm going to start over. When God sees fit to give me a new mission, I'm going to be ready for it." He looked up at the sky as he articulated his pledge. God was up there somewhere and listening.

Jonas knew he could count on Gerty as he began to struggle with whatever it was that was beginning to gnaw at his soul. He only hoped that whatever it was that was welling up inside him wasn't one of the same old chains that had dragged him down before. Bad things can come back at a guy under new disguises and the devil was always there, pointing in the wrong direction.

Looking around at his deplorable surroundings, Jonas concluded that by declaring his vow to stop drinking alcohol made the morning appear brighter and clearer. Yes, the morning was beginning a new day with rays of bright sunshine.

With dark eyes that shined with a new brightness, Jonas studied Gerty for an extended moment. Yes, he knew that his life had been inundated with many periods of darkness, but Gerty was not a part of any of those times. She was one of the bright lights in his life. He liked to think that they would have been friends even if their lives had turned out differently. They went together like salt and pepper; him black and her white. They were both creatures of God.

Jonas smiled as a thought crossed his mind. Maybe God was about to trust him with himself. Another comforting and reassuring conclusion popped into his brain; there is nothing permanent except change. Some new change had to be on its way to him.

The sound of Gerty's voice snapped him back from his hopeful thoughts. "Come on, Jonas. Let's walk the streets together on this beautiful morning."

There was a strange fancy growing in his mind as he accepted her invitation. Somehow, Gerty was part of the change that was coming his way. She was not some cold-mannered and callused woman that looked down on him. She was his friend. She had left a positive lasting, indelible imprint on his otherwise disgusting life.

For the homeless, urban streets and alleys can be a hellish place. The morning was too lovely to waste it on walking about in hell. So, slowly and deliberately, they made their way out of downtown. Comfortable with each other's presence, they lapsed into silence, each wrapped in their own thoughts.

There are three classes of friendship; need, pleasure, and pain. Their friendship did not involve any aspect of the flesh; it was based on pain with a bucket full of understanding. On they walked until they found themselves walking along Greenville Avenue. Their sense of hearing had tuned out the squeaky wheels of Gerty's cart.

Chapter 2

Frank McLaughlin, Private Investigator, with occasional exceptions, lived a life not unlike those of other people. Thankfully, as a bachelor, his life was less complicated than most people he knew. For instance, unless he had been out late at night working on an investigation, his morning routine was fairly standard. Actually, being a habitual early riser was one of the routines he felt fortunate to have developed. He would rise early with the morning sun to acquire a sneak preview of what the day would be like. After that, he would fix breakfast for himself, then tend to his cat, Leo, and finally catch up on the news via a local television station. The latter, he accomplished by channel surfing while eating or petting Leo.

On this particular morning, while running through the channels, he caught a few minutes of a documentary on the environment and global warming. Like the average Joe, Frank could not make up his mind when it came to what the alarmists were always squawking about. There was just too much information and not enough proven facts on whether global warming was even occurring, and if it was, could the phenomenon only be part of the natural planetary scheme? Scientists unanimously agree that there is adequate evidence to support the existence of past ice ages, thus, there had to be intermittent periods of global warming as part of the cyclic nature of the planet's climate. He, like most people, tended to view the world as it appeared at the moment. Even the earth's sun has periods of warming, thus, the earth can warm as a residual effect like often happens on Mars. Drawing conclusions without all the facts, he knew, was a trap that many people often fell into. And then there were those who used the fear of global warming and climate change to advance their political agenda and war on the energy industry. Frank was sure there would be no end to the controversy.

The biggest question for him was whether man's relationship with the planet was bringing about some catastrophic interference with nature? Perhaps, things will have to get worse before civilization will know the true impact that modern life and industrialization are having on our planet. In some small way, he wanted to do something positive for the planet so he had planted some trees and shrubs in his yard. He realized that his efforts would have virtually no impact on the planet, but, it made him feel better. Switching to the news was just as disconcerting as the documentary on global warming and the environment.

Probably the 1950's generated a more comforting feeling for average folks if they were alive during that time and old enough to have an idea of what was happening. Those were the days, and in Frank's opinion, that era was worth reflecting on.

His youth had been filled with optimism, confidence, peace, and mediocre prosperity. Luckily, he had been too young at the time to grasp the reality of the Korean Conflict. Korea aside, the 1950's was a time when the light of hope shined brightest for his generation. There were jobs for those who wanted to work and the family was the nucleus that bound people together; not the government. The majority of aliens back then were in legal status and they wanted to be part of a vibrant, healthy, and growing society; one that embraced freedom and liberty. Aliens, with their eye on citizenship, embraced the values that the U.S. Constitution guaranteed. In many cases, they were escaping the stranglehold of some oppressive and restrictive country. America was their hope and they didn't mind the effort it took to come here legally.

Now, and unfortunately, there are way too many aliens here illegally and many openly declare their disdain for our country and its heritage. Why on earth would they want to change America? Immigrants were once the back bone of our country instead of a burdensome liability.

Frank did not truly understand why the once strong moral fabric of America was now under attack from enemies the world over; even from subversive forces within our borders. Frank concluded that, without any doubt, our government was at the root of our country's ills. Soon, the progressive liberals that had infiltrated our government would become our masters. Their debilitating efforts were setting America up as a ripe target for any country or movement to tear us asunder. If his current views were aligned with conservative views, then he was obviously a conservative. The country was losing its way. Ironically, he figured the new forward should be a return to the past. America's founding fathers had it right. If he had a magic wand, he would wave it with all his heart and resurrect and bolster the past.

Frank shook his head in disgust. He wondered who would save us from ourselves. It will be a sad day when liberty is snatched from our hands, only to be replaced by a bigger and more powerful government. Once our souls are commanded by others who are more aligned with evil, rather than by God, our country would be lost or close to it.

He had to switch off the television before he burst a blood vessel in his head. Hopefully, enough people were noticing what was happening to America and they would unite to restore her to her original splendor. Healing would not come easily and would never be permanent and that was the nature of politics; yes, the fight would be a never-ending one. Additionally, fixing the rest of the world and the environment would often have to be placed on the back burner until our nation is restored to its original greatness; the best among the world community.

Leo pounced on his lap and drew him back from his thoughts and worries over a country running off-course. Frank bent his head and smiled at his yellow feline companion while running his hand down the cat's back. At the moment, Leo's affection failed to fully satisfy what Frank's heart hungered for, but the cat was all he had as a comforting distraction. As a side thought to his growing concern for America, Frank's heart also ached for the comfort of a woman; a mate to share his life with; someone to share his views with. How could a man feel such emptiness at this stage in his life?

Oh, there had been women in his life and any of them could have made him feel full and loved. Yes, his head was filled with fond memories of good times and of women that he had loved and lost. Now, he was a private investigator married to his work and a loner by most men's standards. He was also afraid to risk loving another woman again.

Emotionally, his life had been painful. Over the course of his life, he had been an adventurer and a wanderer and that meant he lacked stabling roots. The closest thing he had to a firm grounding was a few nearly-forgotten memories. He had always wanted to live in another time where he was not restrained by domestic responsibilities. For some undefined reason he always drifted toward the vague realms of an unconventional lifestyle. The way his life had played out was painful because he had been unable to adjust to the peace and calm of conventional life. He was an admitted adventure addict who never seemed to get his fill.

A long forgotten and youthful sensation stirred in his heart. No matter how hard he tried to block it out, the feeling kept returning, especially during the holidays. He came from a broken home and he had no family to return to and no prospect for creating a family he could call his own. He had managed to lose himself in a crowded world that was forever changing and that was stressful.

Sometimes he thought his life was like playing a card game with the devil and the devil was cheating. Laughing grimly to himself at his analogy, he gazed at himself in a mirror hanging on his living room wall. His furrowed, shadowy face reminded him that he was getting older; traveling on the down side of life's journey. Time was surely running out, that was for sure. Was this that defining moment in his life where he had to confront the demons in his life and change his misguided ways? Somehow, he had to visualize and attract a better life for himself. A new question was now beginning to nag at him: Why wasn't he focusing on what he wanted instead of what he had? No wonder he wasn't attracting those things in life that he hungered for; he wasn't asking the universe for those things he truly wanted. Wallowing in self-pity was hardly a good goal. Simply put, there was no clear destination for him to focus on as he was closing in on life's end; his journey was lacking a clear focus and direction.

He had lived his life by making choices, and at the time he had made them, he had believed he knew what he was doing. His memories and history had been of his own making and his life's rewards had been many. Sadly and ironically, the rewards in his life were now nothing but weightless buoys that allowed him to drift without direction. However, he realized that it was not how long a person lived that counted; it was how well he had lived. One consoling result was apparent; he had run all the races in his life without cheating. This concept alone was what kept melancholy away.

The cool, crisp morning air nipped at his face as he walked out onto his patio. Steam swirled up from his coffee cup as he looked around at nothing in particular. He liked being outside, close to nature. Wild birds splashed in the birdbath, a squirrel jumped limb to limb in his large Arizona Oak. He enjoyed moments like this when he could look, listen, and feel. The vast world of nature had always been a mystical thing to him. The power of nature was incalculable and never fully understood by most men. His reverence for nature was something he felt more than he understood.

At last, the time for morning reflections faded. There was work waiting at the office and he had bills to pay.

He left his house enthusiastically prepared to take on a new day. There were only two insurance cases to wrap up at the office so his day had the prospect of being easy. On most days he was grateful for the solitude that came with working alone. However, there was a down side to too much solitude.

Driving east, the morning's sun was nearly blinding. It was a Thursday morning and only a week before Thanksgiving Day. Squinting to take in the scenery, he was surprised that there were hardly any people walking along the sidewalk. Normally, at this time of day there were people scurrying about on their way to work or to some appointment. On other mornings, he was struck by how the police would drive right past the many homeless souls that were still curled up under park benches and trees or in the dark confines of an overpass. The police somehow didn't care if these people were alive or dead unless some concerned citizen called in wanting the police to do a health and welfare check, thinking someone was lying about, sick or dead.

Maybe the police were exhausted from an early morning struggle with drunken revelers, settling early morning domestic disputes, or dealing with other crimes of a more violent nature. Serving and protecting the public did have its share of ugliness. Frank had no particular interest in what the police were doing, and after living in the big city environment, he had gotten over seeing the homeless in their deplorable condition. Callousness was now his accepted state of mind, thus, he crouched behind his disinterest. Besides, no client had ever wanted to investigate the plight of the homeless, except in the case of: "The Runaway Mom" that he had worked in New Mexico.

A school bus rounded the corner and he had to smile as it passed by in the other direction. The windows were filled with sad frowning faces, staring blankly out of steamed windows as they headed to school. A couple of kids noticed his interest and ventured a half-hearted wave at him. When he waved back there was a chain reaction of waving little hands in response to his acknowledgement of them. For them, this was the highlight of an otherwise boring ride to school.

Frank wondered what his children would have been like if he had had any. He guessed that they would have been happy, loving, and well-adjusted kids because he would have been deeply involved in their lives. He liked to think that he had the capacity to love children and the temperament to be a good father.

He slowed up a bit; not because he was approaching his office driveway, but, because he noticed two pedestrians making their way along the sidewalk on Greenville Avenue. They stood out because the woman was pushing a shopping cart. Their dress and un-kept appearance singled them out as being among the city's homeless ranks. The scene was common in any large metropolitan city. A common sight or not, Frank began to consider what he was observing. His mind was suddenly whirling with a keen new interest.

At first glance, the element of race was a distinguishing characteristic of the couple. The man was black and the woman white. Their approximate ages was even more defining. The man was much older than the woman; perhaps he was in his sixties with the woman appearing to be in her late forties. The woman's hair was graying but not yet white. As expected, her face had a rather weathered appearance. However, it was always a person's eyes that interested Frank. A person's eyes always had a story to tell.

Eyes have a way of partially reflecting a person's life story; although not in any great detail. Also telling, to some degree, was the way a person stood, walked, and moved. Frank always paid attention to body language, especially during conversation. Slowing his vehicle, Frank tried to make some eye contact in a manner that would not appear too intrusive. The couple had just as much right to the public sidewalk as anyone. They also had, and rightly so, some expectation of emotional and intellectual privacy. Frank was confident that they were also used to being gawked at.

The man was quick to notice Frank's interest. Even though the man was in the company of the woman, he still somehow looked pitifully alone in his surroundings. He was tall, well over six foot in height, and as expected, thin in stature. His eyes were wide, bright, and absorbing. The man's eyes met Frank's and it was clear that they were somehow strangely and mutually interested in one another. There was no exchange of intimidation or anger between them. Little did either of them know, at this moment, that these first few seconds of eye contact would turn out to be the foundation for some future trust and friendship?

Frank's interest in the couple, to his dismay, generated the realization that he had been on the cusp of stereotyping them. Like the general populace, his first instinct was to avoid homeless people, thinking they were most likely filthy degenerates and the notion of interacting with them was repulsive. Most people feared that most homeless people were mentally deficient and emotionally unstable. Actually, that assessment was sometimes accurate.

The more Frank studied the couple, the more he knew that there was a great story behind their current status. Whatever their situation, the couple didn't deserve to be looked down on and shunned. There were secrets here that needed to be uncovered in order to understand their predicament. Yes, the couple's secrets were probably worthy of uncovering, but, they were also none of Frank's business. The urge of wanting to uncover secrets was a curse to Frank's character. However, his curse was what passionately drove him to be a student of life. What skills did these two have to master in order to make their way through each day? What kept them from giving up? What were they like on the inside?

Frank sped up and dismissed the exchange as anything that would ever end up impacting his life in any manner or fashion. Of course, Frank's life and emotional makeup had never been anything akin to that of the average man. His fate and destiny had rarely been the product of careful planning unless it was part of some significant investigation that demanded careful attention to detail. During every important investigation, he had always made himself acutely aware of the actual risks and factors he was facing, and based on his assessment, he had gone all-out to painstakingly plan and execute every move. These were some of the traits that made him a successful investigator. Unfortunately, it was the little off-course jaunts and inquiries of a private and personal nature that were daring and risky, thus, rewarding on another level. Whenever he didn't know what he was getting into he felt the tinge of challenge and that thrilled him, even prodded him on.

Frank never grumbled about working boring insurance cases. He enjoyed not being idle. The prospect of diving into two new cases was stimulating. Tirelessly and patiently, he went about resolving all the issues he knew his clients wanted clarified. Three hours passed before he wrapped up the last case. All he needed in order to withdraw from the solitude of work was to stand, stretch, and yawn. The process reminded him of a butterfly wriggling out of a cocoon.

Frank went to the front window of his office, and while looking outside, a low whistle slipped from his lips which were unconsciously pursed. He was giving a genuine reaction to what he understood about life in general. After all these years of muddling through life on his terms, he still wasn't sure what was real and what was staged. Each time he had reacted to what he had seen or done, he was not sure if what he was experiencing was real or staged to give the appearance of being meaningful. He knew he didn't have to explain or justify his feelings or reactions to anyone but himself. He was in the business of explaining facts, not feelings, and that pretty well summed up what he was feeling at the moment: "To thy self be true."

He stood there for a while watching the parking lot. The light breeze of early morning was strengthening into a stiff wind. Perhaps a cold front was on its way. Dirt and sand began to wave across the parking lot mixing with falling leaves from an old oak tree on the north end. The sun was ducking behind some newly formed clouds.

If only the fax machine would kick in with a new case. Something, anything, had to happen before boredom sat in. Frank was not like some men that were well-suited to idle time. For him, idleness was nothing short of a death sentence. Finally, the solemn spell was broken when he looked at his wristwatch and saw that it was lunchtime. At any rate, it was an early lunchtime and it was arriving at the right time.

He grabbed his windbreaker and headed out the door. Since he wasn't hungry enough for a full meal, he decided to grab a sandwich from a deli somewhere. After driving about for five minutes or so, something caught his eye.

The homeless couple he had seen on his way to the office was trudging along oblivious to the rest of the world as if consumed in their own thoughts. Frank couldn't resist another opportunity to study them for a minute. He pulled into a parking lot and parked as inconspicuously as possible. The longer he sat there, observing, the more his curiosity began to well up inside. His interest in the couple now equaled his hunger pangs. He always liked eating more when the weather was beginning to cool. Also, the seed of a new adventure was beginning to take root in his mind.

An idea, a great idea, had popped into his head. Surely a homeless couple wouldn't be offended if he offered them food, hot food, in exchange for conversation. He needed a cover story, though; a good reason for offering them what was an obvious handout; in other words, "bait." Naturally, he didn't want to appear condescending when he approached them.

With a plan clear in his head, Frank sped out of the parking lot. Within a few minutes he was wheeling into the parking lot of a nearby Kentucky Fried Chicken. He ordered three meals to go and was on his way in a flash.

Spurred on by the prospect of a new adventure, he pushed the throttle of his little Nissan Pickup. His eyes searched the sidewalk up ahead as everything else whizzed past in a blur. He was in luck; the couple had settled on one of several park benches and they were having a discussion of some sort. Frank surmised that they were talking about finding something to eat.

Frank had rehearsed his scenario in his head and was ready. He pulled his truck up sharply in front of the couple and jumped out. In the most sincere tone he could muster, Frank addressed them: "Please excuse my interruption," Frank began. "I was supposed to have lunch here at the park with two friends and they just called me on my cell phone and cancelled. Would you two like to join me? Lunch is on me; it's my treat." He hoped his boldness would not be taken the wrong way.

Frank opened the plastic bag so both of them could see inside at what he had to offer in the way of lunch. They craned their necks to get a better look inside. When they looked up, their faces broke into wide smiles. The expressions on their faces indicated that they may have bitten on his bait; hook, line, and sinker. At this point, the only communication from the couple was the looks on their faces and their smiles were all the encouragement that Frank needed to press on.

Nonetheless, before any initial contact with unfamiliar subjects, there is always that brief moment of apprehension. At least if this encounter suddenly crumbled away there would be no real loss or harm done other than the cost of the food. The most well-intentioned venture always came with a risk. Frank was fully aware that initial impressions could deliver either favorable results or disappointment.

During the few split seconds while he waited on the couple's response, Frank's nose was bombarded with the overwhelming scent of alcohol that was coming from the woman. It was a combination of cheap wine and nicotine. The same sense of smell also told Frank that the man was in need of some personal hygiene; a bath and clean clothes. Oh well, what could one expect when confronting a homeless couple.

Frank took the safe route of not displaying any emotion that would project any semblance of annoyance. Some people can become easily offended when a stranger shows too much interest. For instance, is an unfamiliar person smiling at you because of your apparent poor circumstance or social position, or are they simply displaying sympathy, or better yet, empathizing over your unfortunate situation? Predicting a person's perception of you is not always an easy thing to do. He knew that it was always best to keep a stranger guessing if you didn't want to jeopardize your goal.

Suddenly, the man's face beamed with approval to Frank's offer. "We sure do appreciate your offer, mister. As you can see, we're a little down on our luck." The man's eyes blinked quickly several times as an indication of his nervousness as he spoke.

"I'll second that." The woman chimed in. "My stomach could use some nourishment right about now." She patted her stomach.

Frank sensed that the man was assuming more of a role in the conversation so he extended a hand to him first. "I sure do appreciate you joining me for lunch. I don't really relish the idea of having to eat alone. Honestly, I was afraid that you might turn me down."

Not wanting to lose the momentum, the man continued. "Let's just chalk it up to good old-fashioned southern hospitality. Besides, you're picking up the tab and something like this doesn't happen very often to the likes of us; you know what I'm saying?"

When Frank took the man's hand to shake it, he couldn't help but notice his worn and tattered shirt. Frank's mind flashed to his closet and all those old shirts of his that he had intended on donating to charity. They were all still in very serviceable condition, unlike the shirt on the fellow he was talking to. Frank figured that the man was at least worthy enough for some hand-me-downs. There was no question in Frank's mind about the man being the recipient of some really bad breaks in his life. Next, Frank turned his attention to the woman. At this point they deserved equal attention.

Frank had, through some conscious effort, willed himself oblivious of the passersby driving out on the street. Most of them probably were wearing "yucky looks" on their faces which he equated to being a bit on the pompous side.

Suddenly, Frank's face broke out into a smile as if he was remembering something. "I'm sorry. I haven't introduced myself. My name is Frank." He took hold of the woman's hand, gently, as he spoke.

In a somewhat cocky and exaggerated manner, she responded by sheepishly smiling and stating: "My name is Gertrude. They call me Gerty for short. My friend here is Jonas. He's a southern gentleman, through and through. Me, well, I'm a Yankee, a damn Yankee." She laughed at her own banter to further demonstrate that she had a sense of humor. Once her hand was withdrawn from Frank's hand, she quickly folded her arms and glanced theatrically down at the food as if to say she was ready to eat. Frank concluded that under more acceptable circumstances she would be the life of a party.

Frank didn't have to put the couple at ease because they were putting him at ease. Who would have thought that the homeless had the capacity to be pleasant? Yes, the wall of awkwardness was crumbling nicely and that meant Frank was in for a pleasant visit.

Behind the park bench was a large oak tree in a little cove of shrubs. Jonas beckoned to Gerty and Frank to move over under the tree where there would be less wind and more privacy. They sat in a circle 'Indian style' with the food spread out between them. Frank regretted not having some sort of picnic cloth to spread out on the ground. Oh well, he was sure the couple had eaten in less accommodating conditions.

Frank zeroed in on her when he picked up on something she had said. "Gerty, just so you won't feel like the Lone Ranger here, I'm also a Yankee. I'm originally from Ohio."

She quickly bounced back. "I was born and reared in the Windy City; Chicago. You can't tell it by looking at me now, but I came from a good family; a professional family. My mother was a psychiatrist, a successful one in every respect except when it came to me. I was always the thorn in her side." Gerty was full of quilt and regret and her tone made that clear.

Frank knew from experience that the shortest distance between two people was courtesy. "Sweetheart, I fully understand where you're coming from. I doubt if I was the gem in my neighborhood. Although, I think I was important to my mother. All we had was each other. Had I been a girl, I could just as easily be right where you are in life. Every time I turned around I was in trouble. If I hadn't joined the military, I think I would have ended up in prison and who knows what would have happened after that." Frank was trying to send a message to Gerty. He wanted her to feel comfortable talking to him. But, most importantly, he wanted to convey to her that he could listen with an understanding heart and an open mind. It seemed to him that, like everyone else, he had some kind of a cross to bear; some crosses are just heavier than others. At least he wasn't homeless.

Many times in Frank's life someone had reached down to him and helped lift him up by his bootstraps. One thing he had learned from all his tough experiences and hard knocks was that he had a duty to others to give them a lift up. Otherwise, too many good people become trapped on the bottom and that is a very lonely place.

Jonas was not missing a word of the exchange between Gerty and Frank. Setting there, listening, Jonas' mind was taking in everything and doing its best to comprehend. Messages from God, often hidden or disguised, tended to come from strange places and at times they arrived at unexpected moments. There was no telling where their conversation would take them or what they would do when they got there. Jonas wasn't sure of the outcome, but it couldn't be all that bad. Maybe God was about to answer one of his door-knocking prayers.

The mere thought of God reminded Jonas that they couldn't eat until grace was said. He didn't want to be rude, but, he had to interrupt. "Excuse me; we need to give thanks to God before the food gets cold. Come on, let's all hold hands."

Frank answered first by saying "I'm sorry. I guess we got carried away. Having a good conversation has a way of getting me side-tracked." He took hold of Gerty's hand and within a second or two they were all holding each other's hand.

When Jonas bowed his head Gerty and Frank did likewise. Jonas cleared his throat and then began. "Dear Lord, we thank Thee for this daily bread that will strengthen and nourish our bodies and fill our souls with love and understanding. Lord, as we eat please protect our sailors at sea. Watch over them wherever they might be and keep them from harm's way. Protect our soldiers while at war with those who oppose peace and uphold evil. Guide us as we search for our own peace while doing our best to follow Your path. Shine your heavenly grace on our souls as we make decisions about our lives. Let us remember the wars and hardships that have passed and learn from them. As we eat this food you have provided, hear our prayers of thanks as we think of those who have nothing to eat. In the name of Jesus Christ, our Lord, accept our gratitude. Amen."

Gerty and Jonas immediately began to eat. Frank, on the other hand, paused to think about the words that Jonas used when saying grace. There was one element that Frank wanted to clarify. Jonas had been too quick to mention sailors. Did Jonas ever serve in the Navy? Did he have family members that served? There had to be a connection.

Frank grabbed a drumstick and bit off a piece. He spoke as nonchalantly as possible when he prodded Jonas for information. "Thank you for mentioning the military during grace. Myself, I'm retired from the Army. Did you, by any chance, serve in the military?"

Jonas swallowed a bite of food and then replied. "I sure did. I was in the Navy for four years. Those were some good years. I wish I had stayed. That was a long time ago, but I'll never forget." He stuffed another bite into his mouth.

Frank avoided eye contact with Jonas as he considered not only what he had said, but the tone he used when saying it. There was some underlying and stressful feeling thrown into the mix by Jonas, and Frank wanted to put his finger on it. Maybe the Navy was where Jonas' story really began. Frank would hold on to his hunch until he learned more.

When Frank pushed back from his thoughts and looked up, he caught Jonas studying him. It was an odd moment as they sat there, engaged with one another without saying a word. Jonas stared, eyes blinking, dazed like a man who stepped outside into the bright sunlight after being in a dark room. Frank had to admit that Jonas had a remarkable face; bold brown eyes; thick grey hair in need of grooming; a square, projecting chin tucked inside a nearly white beard; and thick chapped lips. If properly groomed and appropriately dressed, Jonas could easily pass as a learned college professor. However, that was a far cry from what he actually was. Appearance only gives us a hint of what makes a person who he is on the inside and that is rarely a complete and accurate description.

At this point, and unlike Gerty, Jonas had not displayed any sense of humor. His mind was dealing with more serious things than having a good time during his lunch. He was a man trying desperately to figure out what his mission in life was. All the answers to his questions about life were linked to the secrets and mysteries he was keeping locked up inside.

Not knowing the magnitude or substance of what was going on inside Jonas' head; Frank asked himself, silently, what key would be needed to unlock the secrets of Jonas' past?

Frank realized that their lunch would soon come to an end. Somehow, he would have to construct some pretext for setting up another encounter. Gerty began tidying up their mess by stuffing everything into the KFC plastic bag.

When it came to Jonas, Frank had to break the spell of the moment. He had to bring Jonas back as he teetered on the brink of melancholy. An idea flashed through Frank's mind and he seized the opportunity.

"Jonas, I hope I'm not picking up on a bad vibe here. I hope I didn't say something that offended you. You look like someone just stole your puppy. You said you were in the Navy and I told you that I had been in the Army. It's not that old Army/Navy rivalry thing that's got you upset with me, is it?" Frank was using a pleading tone.

Jonas sat there a few seconds as if considering what Frank had said to him. A hint of embarrassment spread across his face and then Jonas responded. "No, it's me. I'm mad at myself. I guess you could say that I'm a little, no, a lot, jealous of you. You stuck it out in the Army and retired. You have benefits and a pension. You also have pride. Don't get me wrong, I'm sure you earned everything you're getting. I have failed myself, over and over. On top of everything else, Mother Nature took from me what little I had managed to put together in my life. Hurricane Katrina took my wife and son and all my belongings, even my home. Once I hit bottom, I gave up. I've been here too long and now I want out. I want what's left of my life to account for something."

Now, it was Frank's time to sit and stare, and consider what Jonas had just dumped on him. Gerty began to speak before Frank could respond.

"You know, Jonas quit drinking today. I offered him a touch of my wine and he turned me down flat. I really think this is his time to begin crawling out of the sewer. I saw it in his eyes this morning. Someday, my time will also come. Anyway, I hope it will. The hardest thing about getting out of all the shit we are in is to come up with a plan that we can work with. Jonas is my friend and I want him to make it. If he makes it, then I know there's hope for me, too." Gerty meant what she had said. Her eyes seemed to flash with hope and her jaw was set with determination.

Now it was Frank's turn and he was aware that their eyes were set on him in anticipation of his words. This was definitely a time to take the higher road of encouragement. He leaned back on the huge oak tree and then delivered his message with as much wisdom as he could find on such short notice.

"Jonas, I think you are thinking in terms of money. I hope you don't think that I'm rich, because I'm not. One thing I do try to accomplish is to enrich the lives of others by helping out whenever and wherever I can. I try to keep a positive outlook and encourage others to make the world a better place. For there to be an end or an outcome, there has to be a beginning. Several times in my life, I had to start over; to begin anew. Each time I failed, I learned something. No, I won't win the Nobel Prize for peace, but, I will feel good about myself each time I am aware that I helped others find some peace in their lives. I want everyone to become the best person they can be." Frank was ready to turn this opportunity into a lecture of sorts; one filled with encouragement.

"I think you keep looking into the past and end up playing the blame game. There are probably things in your past that you would like to change, you know, do them over. You can't do that. You might be able to go back and fix some of the things that you have done or didn't do and that's okay. However, the biggest thing you have to do is to fix what you can with respect to the present while keeping an eye on the future. Yes, you are going to have to challenge yourself if you expect to make progress; life is rarely easy. You're also going to have to learn to deal with failure because there will always be setbacks. The answer to finding your way out is inside you. Sometimes it is buried deep and sometimes it's not. Sometimes your path forward is so close that you can't see it. Nevertheless, there is always a way out for all of us. Looking in the right places with the right attitude is the hard part.

"No matter what you want to do with the rest of your life; you know, all those things you want to change for the better about your life; there is one thing you will always need; that's courage. There will be times when you will have to look fear in the face and beat it down. Jonas, you can do this. I know you can. When you said grace before we ate lunch, I realized that you haven't given up on God, and that shows me that you have strength. When you need courage, your faith is a great place to find it. I have one last thing to say to you, Jonas. As you go about clawing your way out of the mess you're in, don't do it by hurting or destroying others. Our karma has a way of finding all of us. Make your karma good and enjoy the blessings."

Jonas hung his head for a minute before reacting. He was thinking and weighing his options, which were not plentiful. "I have my long-term goals set in my head. I just don't have a short-term plan for getting to where I want to be. Look at me. I'm a mess. I haven't shaved in months and I haven't had a shower in a week. My clothes are full of holes and until this morning, all I wanted out of life was to get drunk on cheap wine that I bought after begging from well-intentioned strangers at intersections."

Frank listened to Jonas and realized how fortunate he was. "So, Jonas, what happened this morning that made you want to take this giant leap?"

"The strangest thing came at me this morning. I woke up having a dream about a good time in my life. It is unusual to have nice thoughts and memories when you are in the biggest slump of your life and everything seems so hopeless. This morning was all different. It's hard to explain. Look at me, I'm old and worn out. I have never been afraid of hard work. Right now, I think I would sell my soul if I could get work. But, my biggest job that I want to do is to go back and take care of some things that I screwed up. I just can't die with my heart filled with guilt. Didn't you ever have something in your past that you left undone? Don't you have any loose ends that you want to take care of before you die? God, I hope I'm making sense here. I hope I haven't finally gone crazy."

Frank shot Jonas an encouraging smile hoping it would help put him at ease. "No, you're not crazy. I don't know what it is that you want to do with regards to your past. But, I do believe that having a positive goal of any kind is a healthy thing. I know that you are sincere or we wouldn't be having this conversation."

Jonas smiled for the first time during their discussion. Together, Frank and Jonas looked over at Gerty who was totally mesmerized at the depth and course of their interaction. She was not used to such a discourse in the underworld of the homeless. In recent years, she had not witnessed anything like the way Jonas and Frank were interacting. Inwardly, she wanted to be part of what was happening, yet, she was not sure she was ready for it.

The only words that Gerty could think of to contribute to the moment were: "We are all loose ends that need to be connected. Since all of our days are numbered, I guess this is as good a time as ever to begin cleaning our lives up. This is one lunch that I will never forget."

In spite of the foul body odors, smell of stale cigarettes, and the retched smell of cheap wine, the three of them gave a group hug to solidify the moment.

They all released their embrace while feeling the beginning of a new chapter in their lives. Frank was encouraged by what was happening, but, he also knew the situation for the couple was far from changed. In fact, it was extremely fragile.

The only one present with any means was Frank. He liked embarking on new crusades because it gave additional purpose to his life. Knowing the ball was somewhat in his court, he would have to take the lead. At least leadership was something he knew about.

Now taking the initiative Frank asked; "Can you two meet me back here for lunch again, tomorrow? Lunch will be on me again. Also, I have some ideas about how to kick things off. Here, take these." Frank opened his wallet and handed Jonas six one dollar bills.

After taking the money, Jonas studied the bills for a minute and then handed two of the bills to Gerty and two back to Frank. Getting two of the bills handed back to him was a bit puzzling for Frank.

Jonas quickly clarified what he was doing. "I want you to buy me a lottery ticket, make it one of those big ones for a lot of money; a two dollar quick pick. Make it a cash option, I feel lucky today."

Frank laughed at Jonas' gesture. "Man, don't you know that you have ten more chances at being struck by lightning than winning the lottery. Why don't you take this money back and use it wisely."

Jonas shoved the dollar bills away with the back of his hand. "I know winning the lottery is nearly impossible. But, think of it this way, how much of a chance do I have of winning if I don't even have a ticket? Please, make sure you get one of those 'quick picks' because I don't have any lucky numbers that I know of."

Frank folded the two bills and stuck them in his shirt pocket. "Well, I can't argue with your logic, Jonas. You guys will meet me back here tomorrow, won't you?"

"Yes, we'll be here at the same time tomorrow." Both Jonas and Gerty waved as Jonas spoke. They ambled along back toward the inner city.

Frank climbed back inside his pickup and watched his new acquaintances in his rearview mirror. Instead of starting the engine and driving off, he sat there collecting his thoughts about the couple and the conversation. He had a lot to think about.

The couple was homeless, rootless by fate and circumstance, frivolous people who lacked any semblance of attachment to society at large. They were stranded in their own society that was rampant with despair, poverty, and crime. They were obvious outcasts from ordinary life. Sadly, for far too long, their only allegiances had been to survival and to some extent to each other.

Frank had to ask himself exactly what he owed to the couple. In truth, he knew he didn't owe them anything. Although, there was an understanding that he would somehow help them and that was binding enough for him. Frank had to search within himself for self-control. Yes, he knew that he had to forcibly restrain his mind from wandering endlessly in circles with no sense of clear purpose or a set destination. He had to reel his thoughts back or become frustrated.

Searching through all of his thoughts that were occupying the moment, there was one daunting thing that he realized. He had experienced this initial feeling before and like the other times, he would work through any glimmer of reluctance and proceed without knowing if it was, or was not, the right thing to do. Like the other times, the driving force behind his motive was self-serving and it certainly was not born out of necessity. His real motive was to quench the thirst of his own curiosity. In the beginning, the motive driving each of his ventures had seldom been altruistic.

Questions! There was always one important question that topped the list. What would he do once he learned all the secrets that Jonas was guarding? Life is so interesting and Frank knew he was a devoted student. Lastly, wherever his involvement ended would certainly help define his karma.

He started the engine and drove back to the office to see what new cases had come in on the fax.

Chapter 3

Jonas lagged behind Gerty, preferring solitude to conversation. He needed time to reflect on a wide variety issues that were weighing heavy on his heart and in his mind. Detaching himself from Gerty's company required some willpower since she was not only his best friend, but probably his only true friend. Right from the beginning when they had first met on the streets, they had enjoyed hanging out together in a comfortable and quiet friendship.

Her intellect and social graces tended to hover above others on the street. She had been the product of a past with elevated social stratus; a concept that was slowly narrowing and fading in a forever growing depressed economy. However, for a number of reasons, she had fallen from its clutches, finding herself with no path on which to return to the status quo of middle-class society. To Jonas, there was one thing that Gerty was not, and that was a snob; as if there was such a thing as a snobbish homeless person. She was down to earth, level-headed, and that allowed her to adjust smoothly to the homeless environment and develop a streetwise savvy with a pace that few in her shoes could match.

For a few moments Jonas watched Gerty meander her shopping cart between streaks of shadow and shards of bright sunlight. The further she moved away from him the more his thoughts turned to other matters; matters of the past. One particular dark spot in his history haunted him, begging for a resolution that was unlikely to come.

Jonas' life had been built on the graves of people that he had respected and loved. The crushing reality was that his life was now in the throes of tragedy and it was still crumbling further because he had no way of turning it around. The only consolation he had was that the tragedy in his life was not the result of him bloodying his own hands. The closest exception to that fact was when he failed to act and follow up on something that he knew, in his heart of hearts, was not right. This was one matter that time would not be able to heal. This was a cross that he had been carrying for over four decades and it did not involve his wife and son.

Saddened by his past failures, he found himself imprisoned in a state of despair that would linger for the rest of his life unless he could somehow come to terms with it. Until he gained sufficient resources, he could only make silent vows to someday return to a time and place that left a dark blemish on his soul. He had to somehow rectify that critical moment of inaction. He had not been a friend when he should have been. Perhaps he could not have done anything at the time to have made a difference; in retrospect, he would never know for sure. The questions that haunted his dreams would have to be addressed and resolved if he was ever to find peace.

In some unexplainable way, on this day, he found himself encouraged. His old goal to learn the truth behind a four-decade old event had, once again, been resurrected. So there it was, clear as day, right there at the forefront of what remained of his otherwise miserable life. For the time being, he would keep this goal to himself because it was an extremely long-range goal; if not an impossible one.

Jonas knew that God was the only honest dealer in the card game of life. In the case of his life in the Navy, Jonas was convinced that he had neither won nor lost the game. God, as the supreme dealer, had simply swept all the chips off the table and placed them on a shelf until the game could be taken up again.

When Gerty became aware that Jonas was no longer walking with her, she looked back to see where he was and what he was doing. She saw that he was walking alone; apparently wrestling with some issue that he was in a quandary over. Jonas had placed his hands in the frayed pockets of his tattered trousers and the expression on his face was stoic, as if he had fallen into a trance; a symbolic swirl of dry leaves that were being blown about by one of life's harsh breezes. The poor man had become a habitual and natural worrier about things that were out of his control. Anyway, that was the way she viewed her friend at this moment.

She instantly knew that she had to somehow lift his spirits. So many times she had seen members of the homeless community slump into deep states of depression. She had experienced way too many occasions when she had found herself in the same emotional state and it had always been painful. Spiritual and emotional scars cut just as deep into the fabric of one's life as if it had been done with an actual knife cutting one's flesh. Jonas was her friend and right now he needed to be rescued from his slump.

When she reached him, she placed a hand on his shoulder. She smiled warmly and then slipped an arm around his waist. Her mere presence warmed his spirits and he couldn't help smiling back at her. Her words and tone were reassuring. "Don't let life get you down, good buddy. In time, this too shall pass." Reassurance was all she could offer, but it seemed to be enough.

Because of his advancing years, Jonas was not a stout man, nor was he emotionally stable. His fear was that he would die before having a chance to make amends for his past. At present, optimism was his primary tool for dealing with life; repairing broken intentions, and pushing back the guilt he had inherited.

Gerty's face glistened with a sweaty sheen as a result of the long afternoon walk while pushing her shopping cart. Similarly, Jonas realized that his body was foully damp with perspiration. He was tired of being a public spectacle and figured it was even worse for Gerty; a female and former nurse. She certainly knew the importance of proper hygiene.

The sun was making its way to the western horizon and that meant the temperature would soon drop. The wind began to pick up and fan their faces cool and dry. Strands of long hair began to blow across Gerty's face and the affect caused her eyes to squint and slightly tear up. Jonas waved away strands of her long hair from her eyes and somehow he knew things would get better for both of them. He now had a hunch; a gut feeling. It was the prospect of hope.

"Here, let me push that cart for you. It has been a long day. What do you think of this guy, Frank?" Sooner or later, he knew they would end up talking about their new acquaintance.

For a drawn out minute she thought about what Jonas had asked and then said, "I think he's for real. It isn't every day that a stranger takes to the likes of us. There seems to be something caring and gentle about him so I don't think he wants to exploit us in some manner. I'm not sure how to express it, but, there doesn't seem to be any meanness in him. I did get the impression that there is a sense of loneliness about him, though. I think he has had his share of tough times and that means he may have some trust issues. But, don't we all have some trust issues? I guess we'll know how serious he is about his desire to get to know us if he shows up tomorrow, like he promised."

Jonas thought about what Gerty had said. "I wonder if Frank ever hit bottom as far down as we have."

"No telling." She bounced back. "One thing I can say for sure is that he knows a lot about life and he didn't come by that knowledge easily. I think he gave you some really good advice back there. You don't get that smart about life without a lot of ups and downs. At any rate, I'm keeping my fingers crossed." Her jaw was set when she ended her position on Frank.

Each afternoon when the sun began to set, it opened the door for the arrival of the criminal element. Youthful criminals often preyed on the homeless. It was common knowledge that the homeless often successfully begged for money on street corners and used the money to either put food in their stomachs or satisfy some craving for drugs or alcohol. Jonas and Gerty were always vigilant of those criminal elements because they were potentially harmful to anyone that appeared weak or infirm; and that targeted group included them.

As the shadows of evening began to creep around them, they began looking for a suitable place that would provide shelter from the weather and a safe place to sleep. Others in their loose knit community were busy doing the same. Homeless men were already congregating around entrances to deserted alleys and around niches of concrete behind old dented dumpsters. The routine rush among the homeless was now under full sway.

Since Jonas and Gerty planned to meet with Frank the next day, they decided to conveniently share the same spot. They were making their way under an overpass with an eye on a crawl space up high when they noticed a young black man approaching. Without saying a word, they braced for a possible encounter.

Gerty remembered that she had found an old ball peen hammer on the street a few days before and that it rested within easy reach among her belongings in the shopping cart. She was not about to give up the two dollars Jonas had given her when he split the money Frank had given to him. The young man continued to close in on them.

They were collectively and acutely aware that their situation was about to change for the worse. Neither one of them was about to give up a single dollar without a valiant fight. Money, in any denomination, was difficult to come by for them. More often than was fair, homeless people sometimes lost their lives for an amount of money that would be trivial to other more fortunate people. People with more means would think it would be madness to fight to the death over a couple of dollars.

Sadly, death and crime are a noteworthy reality of those living on the streets.

Gerty bent over and pretended to sneeze and used the deception to stuff her two dollars into her bra. Jonas placed an arm around Gerty and stuffed his two dollars down into his underwear. The youth was now within arm's length of them.

The man appeared to be about seventeen or eighteen years of age, lean, muscular and soon he would become aggressive. He first faced off with Jonas. "Hey pops, you holding any money? Come on give it up, it ain't worth bleeding over."

The youth held a knife in one hand while he frisked Jonas with his free hand. He tugged and ripped Jonas' shirt and trouser pockets. Angered over not finding any money, the assailant began slapping Jonas with an open hand, eventually knocking him to the ground.

With Jonas out of the way, the youth turned his attention to Gerty who was attempting to move away from the altercation. "Hey bitch, where you think you're going?" He grabbed a hand full of Gerty's hair and jerked her around until they faced each other. "You're about an ugly old bitch. What you holding?"

"I'm not holding anything, asshole." Gerty spoke defiantly, not wanting to demonstrate any degree of fear. Young gangsters seemed to respect a little attitude when properly applied. However, that did not prove to be the case this time.

"You got a mouth on you, bitch." He smacked her to the ground next to her shopping cart. "What's in the cart, bitch?" He shoved the shopping cart over next to Gerty's side and began grabbing some of the contents, tossing them aside.

Jonas had now sat up with his knees drawn to his chest. In an effort to draw attention away from Gerty, Jonas displayed his own bit of attitude. "You're a real tough guy, aren't you? If this was twenty years ago, I'd have you on the ground coughing and spitting up blood. You're nothing but a smart-ass little punk."

Gerty seized her opportunity as the assailant turned his attention back to Jonas. She spied the handle to the ball peen hammer and snatched it up in her hand. Her movement went unnoticed by the now agitated young man. With an overhead swing of the hammer, Gerty smashed the young man's foot, repeatedly. Gerty recognized the sound of splintering and shattering bone. Screaming in excruciating pain, the man dropped his knife and fell to the ground holding the smashed fragments of what was left of his foot.

Jonas was suddenly towering over the man and kicking him in the ribs. "How's it feel to have your ass kicked by a woman and an old man, you sorry piece of shit?"

A crowd of other homeless men and women had now collected around the scene. Apparently, the youthful assailant had at some time assaulted and robbed all of them. The ensuing attack was like a frenzy of sharks going after fresh meat. They were all viciously attacking the downed man. The hunter had now become the prey.

Jonas mumbled to himself, but loud enough for Gerty to hear. "That jitterbug doesn't have the sense that God gave a gnat."

The comment drew Gerty's attention. "Why did you call him a jitterbug? I thought a jitterbug was a dance from back in the late 1930's and 1940's."

Jonas was quick to provide the answer to her question. "That's true, a jitterbug was a dance. But, in the Deep South it has another meaning for black folks. A jitterbug is what we call a wild and out of control young man, a troublemaker. Remember the other day when we saw a bunch of young black men congregating on a corner and we took the long way around the block to steer away from them. Well, they were nothing but a bunch of jitterbugs."

After taking a few seconds to process what Jonas had said, Gerty commented. "Well, I'll be damned. I just learned something. Don't be surprised if I use that word sometime."

It would only be a matter of time until the police descended on the scene so everyone involved faded into the outer realms of urban structures just as quickly as they had appeared. Now, the attacker's pockets were ripped and emptied; someone even took his knife. Obvious to all involved, the heart of evil was truly depicted by violence. Acts of violent criminal activity was always a high-risk enterprise and not to be undertaken lightly. Vigilante and mob rule often is the only court available to the homeless. Life on the streets is a hell of its own making. For Jonas and Gerty, rescuing their own lives had as much merit for them as if they had rescued the entire world.

Gerty had the benefit of both a formal university education and years of hard knocks; life on the streets. Still, she struggled to draw from her academic accomplishments and moral depository of real-life experience to organize life into some meaningful perspective. Even though she had been raised in a family grounded in religious beliefs, she still had her doubts. Perhaps it was a lack of faith on her part or a warped understanding of faith, but she couldn't help but think that God had failed way too many people on way too many occasions.

Shaking her head regretfully, Gerty concluded that, yes, God had somehow failed to create the paradise that people were led to expect, where people would be free of disease, ignorance, and needless death. The irony of God's message seemed to be: instead of delivering his people from evil, He had somehow delivered them to it. She recalled how ministers in religious-based shelters had preached their sermons of eternal damnation. Her understanding of the Christian concept was that God continually threatened the non-believers with destruction; an apocalypse of some sort such as nuclear conflagration, death by pollution, or the likes of disease epidemics and leprosy. She wondered if these threats reflected the true face of God. Should that be the case, then it gave credence to the need for alternative religious movements. They were forever popping up all over the world; most notably the New Age movements she saw during her college days. Why was God sending so many mixed signals to the afflicted and down-trodden? Are not these the very people who need Him the most? Gerty could only conclude that she was tired of being a victim, whether by her own hand or by a higher hand. Jonas was right, it was time to escape and that meant finding a way out of the homeless cult. The ripeness of her despair was nothing short of overwhelming.

These thoughts bounced around inside her head like a volley of ping pong balls as she and Jonas stuffed her belongings back into her dilapidated shopping cart. As he busied himself with

Gerty's things, a single thought reverberated in Jonas' head: 'My biggest battle is to conquer myself.'

Each of them, in their own way, wanted desperately to make something good of what was left of their lives. Without exchanging any words, they thought meaningfully about the beauty and love that they had once had and deserted. They both had good memories of a loving and nurturing childhood where they had good parents and friends. They also both had their own reasons for getting "off-track." How to get back "on- track" was the big question?

Jonas looked up beyond the confines of neon lights and tall buildings. Stars were beginning to come out and pepper the blackening sky. Somewhere up there in heaven were the jewels of his life; his wife and son, and their memories were shinning brighter by the minute. His memories were so vivid, so real. He recalled how he and his wife had strolled along with their son through the French Quarter on Sunday afternoons. He would always appreciate the magic of what they had shared.

Suddenly, his whole body shuddered and he found himself back in the present; a homeless man wandering the streets of Dallas seeking shelter with his only friend; another lost soul. Trembling as if a dizzy spell was coming on, he fought off the urge to sit down on the curb and cry. However, this was not his new style; now he was a fighter; he had to be.

"Stop shaking, Jonas." Gerty's voice was sharp and demanding. "You look like a scoop of jelly in a storm. We need to get moving."

Chapter 4

Back at Frank's office there were no new cases nestled in the fax tray. Boredom quickly began to turn Frank's mood somber and his mind dull. There was simply no reason to sit there in his office waiting on work that may not be coming his way on this particular afternoon.

Luckily, there were other things that needed attending to. On the way home he would stop and purchase the "quick pick" ticket for the Power Ball Lottery. Wouldn't that be something if Jonas' ticket actually won? He could see the headlines on TV and in the newspapers: "Homeless Man Wins World's Largest Jackpot." Hell, it would even be something great if he won one of the large secondary prizes. Prospectors in the Klondike probably had the same sort of dreams. Dreams give us all two kinds of experiences: They either give us some expectation of "good" like a day of sunshine or they hammer us down like a nightmare on a dark rainy night.

Jonas, a homeless man, was no different than the rest of us when it came to hope. Whether in the long run, or for the short haul, hope was either an inexpensive illness or a universal cure for what ails us. At first glance, the logic of this thought was a bit baffling to Frank because it was not something he would normally think about. After dwelling on the matter awhile, Frank concluded that hope was really some sort of cosmic lie for those men and women who were desperately in need of help. Since hope was never a well thought out plan, a person should never apply too much veracity to the concept. However, when a person has nothing else, why not let a person cling to something, anything that has some optimistic value. Hope aside, there is more power in creative thought than there is in something un-measurable such as an inward cry, out of desperation, for things to get better. The real problem is where to begin.

Frank turned out the light and walked outside, locking the office door behind him. His immediate priority was to get that darn "quick pick" lottery ticket so Jonas would have something to pin his hopes on even though the prospect of winning was more than remote. In reality, it ranked right up there with impossible.

Once inside the convenience store, Frank listened to other customers as they talked about the lottery with much enthusiasm. All these people were waiting in line with paper money clutched in fidgeting fingers. He couldn't help commenting to a heavy-set elderly lady standing in front of him. "I never realized so many people played the lottery."

She smiled and accepted the question with a tone of energy that Frank did not expect. "You know, I have been on the same job for nearly forty years and I only earn ten dollars an hour. Like any other working stiff trying to carve out a meager living, winning the lottery is my only hope."

"There must be a lot of working stiffs that shop at this store." Frank exclaimed. As he spoke, his eyes scanned the long line he was standing in.

The woman fired right back. "Either you are really rich or you just haven't heard. The cash option for tonight's Power Ball Lottery is nearly Four hundred million dollars. In my world, that's a hell of a lot of money and worth taking a chance for."

At that moment, Frank knew that he would also purchase a quick pick ticket for himself. Jonas did have a good point when he said a person can't win if he doesn't have a ticket. He pulled out four crisp one dollar bills; two for Jonas and two for himself. He was now officially of the same mind-set as all the other working stiffs in the world. Becoming common may or may not be an improvement.

Once he was back inside his pickup, he pulled out a pen and wrote on the backs of the two tickets. On one he wrote his name and on the other he simply wrote "Jonas." There, that was that. On the deepest level he possessed, he knew that neither ticket had a snowball's chance in hell of winning.

The drive home was one of those blank events of a day where nothing was noticed or thought about. There were no philosophical pondering, thoughts of work, or consideration for newsworthy current events. He had simply reached into his mind and found that special box that contained nothing at all. When he pulled into his driveway, he recalled one thing from his past. A woman once told him that men were experts at being idle and devoid of thought. How else could a man simply set for hours with a fishing pole in his hand and stare at a plastic bobber?

Once inside his home, Frank decided to place Jonas' lottery ticket into an envelope and seal it. Tomorrow, he would give the envelope to Jonas when he met him and Gerty for lunch. He felt good about this way of doing business because the Power Ball Lottery drawing was not until the next night. This was a big precaution for something that had no chance of a positive result. Still, there was that one-in-a-million chance of winning.

He looked out the patio door and saw that the sun was sliding down in the western sky, searching for rest after a busy day. There was no doubt in Frank's mind about the way he viewed the world, even things as simple as the sun setting. For him, everything in this world had some emotional interest. His propensity for analyzing everything allowed him not to miss things that others took for granted. Investigators were a strange breed; that was for sure. So many times, the simplest things had been the crucial key to solving some monstrous mystery.

He went about opening a few windows in the house to allow it to air out. After removing his shirt, he tossed it into the laundry hamper and then went to the mirror. The breeze from an open window was cool and soothing on his back. The face that stared back at him was haggard with noticeable stubble and his eyes gave notice that he may very well appear tired and worn not only from the length of his life, but also from the way he had lived it. Yes, "Old Man Time" was claiming him.

He took a shower in lukewarm water rather than one of those hot steamy ones that left a person sweating. Then he slipped into some house slippers and a sweat suit before making his way to the kitchen to fix dinner for him and Leo. That was when he realized that he had not seen his cat since returning home. Leo's saucer and food dish still held the big fur ball's breakfast. Something was not right.

Leo had to be in the house somewhere, it was just a matter of where. Frank began a thorough search that included spaces under furniture and on window sills. Every niche and cranny was checked. Finally, he made his way into the last room; his bedroom. Leo was curled up on an old folded throw rug in the closet. He made no effort to get up when discovered.

When Frank scooped Leo up into his arms, his little pal meowed loudly indicating he was in pain. "Hey little buddy, are you under the weather? Have you come down with something?" Frank's tone was as reassuring as he could make it under the circumstances.

Frank carried Leo out into the living room and sat on the couch with the overhead light on so he could examine his companion. His abdomen was swollen; hard, and sensitive to touch. It was way too late in the evening for a trip to the vet. Frank promised Leo that he would see the vet first thing in the morning.

In the meantime, he would do his best to keep him as comfortable as possible.

Frank spoke softly and soothingly to Leo who remained stretched out on the couch. The fireplace was rarely used, but this was a good time to build a nice roaring fire. It was also a good time to turn the radio on and find the station that played classical music. Once all this was done, he heated up a can of vegetable soup and poured a glass of milk.

After washing the dinner dishes, Frank decided to sleep on the couch with Leo. Cats, like most of God's gifts to the animal world, provide their owners with years of comfort, amusement and companionship while not eating you out of house and home. Leo was all the family Frank had, and that made the cat unique. The average person doesn't really care where pets come from as long as they warm our hearts and comfort us during trying times. In Frank's case, Leo was the center of his life.

Frank's sleep was fretful because of Leo's condition and he woke up several times during the night to check on him. At 6:20 a.m., the sound of thunder broke the silence in the house and that took Frank's mind off of Leo for a moment. However, the lightning veining across the sky did not even faze Leo in the least.

Frank decided not to eat breakfast. Instead, he quickly showered, shaved, and dressed. Then he went about setting up the pet carrier for Leo's trip to the vet. Leo could not be enticed with a saucer of warm milk, a clear sign that he was no better than he had been when Frank came home yesterday afternoon. He did not put up the slightest bit of trouble when Frank put him inside the carrier. Leo's conduct was alarming to Frank because he hated the carrier.

When Frank opened the front door, the morning's dreariness remained daunting. The rain poured down from the heavens like a thousand fountains and that matched the morning's forecast on the kitchen radio.

Leo projected a lost, lethargic stare as he peered out through the carrier's wire door. His scared eyes were glassy and that told Frank that Leo was in a great deal of pain.

Frank drove directly to the vet's office taking great care not to swerve through traffic; the ride was as gentle as he could make it. Since he did not have an appointment, he would at least be the first client there when the vet opened his door for business. The thick black clouds overhead blocked the sun and the morning couldn't have been more gloomy or dismal unless he had parked in the middle of a funeral procession.

At 7:55 a.m., three vehicles pulled in to the parking lot in succession. Frank recognized the vet, Dr. Shaw, along with his assistant, and receptionist as they all made a mad dash through the rain to their office door. Frank followed leaving Leo in the pickup until he was sure Leo could be worked in. Due in part to the weather and the early hour there was no problem having Leo examined immediately.

Dr. Shaw had no problem getting Leo out of the carrier. After a few questions about how long Leo had been sick and about what he had eaten, Dr. Shaw said he would need to do some blood work and an ultrasound on Leo. Leo would have to remain there at the vet's for the morning. Dr. Shaw promised to call as soon as he knew enough to make a prognosis. The time would give Frank the leeway he needed to take care of other things that required his attention.

Frank did not go to his office. Instead, he returned home, and, with the aid of his microwave, he prepared hot oatmeal for breakfast. Then he tackled the task of sorting through his closet, culling out all the shirts and trousers that he no longer wanted. These were things that he would pass on to Jonas. He also put together a grooming kit of sorts, consisting of disposable razors, shave cream, after shave lotion, a toothbrush and some toothpaste. He also gave up one of his belts and a few pairs of socks. In less than an hour he had put together a very substantial care package for his new friend.

There was nothing in the way of clothing or toiletries in his home for females except a toothbrush and more toothpaste. Frank was glad he had purchased such articles in packets; bulk purchases. That had been his way of reducing the number of trips to local stores. When it came to Gerty, he decided he would take her to a thrift store and allow her to purchase a few articles of clothing so she wouldn't feel left out. Frank was not sure if Gerty and Jonas were a couple in the traditional sense, but he was sure they were a team of some sort. Even though Jonas was the focus of Frank's interest, he did not want to risk losing Jonas' confidence by driving the smallest of a wedge between the two.

Realizing that it was still too early to purchase food for their luncheon, Frank decided to throw everything into his pickup and head to the office. Besides, with all this rain there was a chance that there would be no luncheon. At times, the rain slackened in intensity without ever giving in to a full stop. Between the weather and Leo's illness, the day was turning out to be a challenge.

Upon arriving at his office, Frank decided to remove the pet carrier and care package from his vehicle. Following this task, he turned his attention to the office fax. He was encouraged to see that there was a stack of paper in the tray. Sitting down at his desk, he began thumbing through the pages. He had three new auto accidents to investigate for one of his insurance clients. If everything went without a hitch, he would wrap the work up in a day or two. At three hundred dollars a pop, his cash flow needs were met for the week.

There was a message on his answering machine. He listened to it with some skepticism. It was from a woman who wanted her husband followed to see if he was having an affair. She said she was on her way to his office. This type of case no longer interested him because they were simply no longer profitable with the arrival of no-fault divorce law. He would be a good listener out of politeness; but there was little chance that he would take the case. He preferred other types of cases.

He had been waiting for almost two weeks on a case that did interest him, though. A trucking company authorized its safety officer to hire a private investigator to help find out who was hi-jacking some of their trailers. The project was nation-wide and resulted from the failure of the FBI to even identify a key suspect.

Trucking company officials also wanted a study done to expose the methods the perpetrators were using so they could design prevention programs. This case came with an element of intrigue, the potential for risk, and it was intellectually challenging. Also, trucking companies were able to pay his higher than average fees; more profitable than common auto insurance accident cases. Hopefully, the hi-jacking case would come to fruition.

Frank had built his life and career on challenge and it was one of the driving forces for his existence. With challenge came a need, no an essential requirement, to push beyond one's normal limits. When a man's purpose demands that he goes beyond his normal limits to achieve results that are normally denied to others; then he learns what he is truly made of; he defines and strengthens his mettle. Frank thought that every man and woman should, once in his or her life, turn something seemingly impossible into a reality. And those who achieve this realization on multiple occasions within a lifetime will close their careers on the highest of notes. Frank noted sadly to himself that too many of our country's youths were choosing roads that were less than challenging, thus robbing themselves of the exhilarating rewards that came from beating the odds. After all, if the challenge wasn't big, the win wouldn't mean much; that's part of a great work ethic.

The sound of his office door opening pulled him back from his thoughts of working a challenging case. Frank looked up and saw a slender blonde, wearing way too much makeup, approaching his desk. If there was any natural beauty in the lady's face, it was surely cosmetically concealed. Sizing her up further told Frank that she was probably attempting to hide her age with layers of makeup.

When she extended her hand, Frank caught the smell of alcohol on her breath. It was mixed with an overpowering sickening sweet aroma of some exotic perfume. "Hello. I'm the one that left the message on your answering machine this morning. My name is Roxie. You must be Frank McLaughlin. Do you have a few minutes to spare?"

First impressions are critical in any encounter and Roxie was a perfect example of how not to impress. "Good morning. I am Frank McLaughlin. Please have a seat." He pointed to an empty chair in front of his desk. "What can I do for you?"

Not smiling, she responded. "Like the message I left on your answering machine, I think my husband is cheating on me. I want to find out who his slut is and then I want to take him to the cleaners. My husband is well off and I'm willing to split what I get out of this with you when I win in court." She was removing her raincoat as she spoke.

She threw her wet raincoat on the floor before taking her seat. Her attire was even more revealing than her demeanor. Like most men, Frank's eyes went directly to the woman's chest. She was wearing a bright red blouse that was open at the top. Her cleavage was deep and her breasts huge compared to her petite body. Frank wondered how much she had paid her cosmetic surgeon for her symmetrically perfect round breasts. Perhaps, her money would have been put to better use by having a face lift so she wouldn't need all that makeup on her face.

She was wearing jeans that were so tight they looked like she had been poured into them. The boots she was wearing were shiny black leather and went nearly to her knees. In Frank's humble opinion, she was a spectacle among the fairer sex.

Frank addressed her opening statement and not her appearance and demeanor. "Let me get this right, Roxie. You are asking me to take this case on a contingency basis?"

"My husband has a truck load of money and real estate all over town. In other words, he has deep pockets and I want to empty them." She had to know that she was on thin ice when it came to hiring a private investigator. Leaning forward so Frank could get a better look at her cleavage, she launched a flirtatious smile; an invitation.

It was all he could do to contain himself. If he had been watching Roxie's performance on a live stage, he would be in the isle holding his side in uncontrollable laughter. Inwardly, he asked himself if life had just thrown a dumb blonde joke at him to cheer him up on such a dismal day!

Roxie leaned over even more and was about to place her hand on top of Frank's when a clap of thunder shook the room. Frank took the distraction as a divine interruption at the most appropriate time. Silently, Frank spoke to himself, "thank you Mother Nature."

Frank recoiled and then stood up. "I'm sorry, Roxie, but, my policy is a strict one. I never take a case on a contingency basis. Compared to other investigators in town, my fees are quite high and when it comes to surveillance, I require a five thousand dollar retainer, up front. I'm sure if you shop around long enough you'll be able to come up with an investigator willing to work something out with you. Besides, I have a lot of work on my plate right now so I can't really take on any new clients." Frank was using the most officious tone he could muster under the circumstances. Properly turning down a client was an art in itself.

"Thank you. I appreciate your time." Roxie sounded disappointed as she put her raincoat back on. She turned and started to walk toward the door and then stopped and turned back to face Frank. "You're not wearing a wedding ring so I guess you are not married. When this is all over and I'm single again, would you like to have dinner with me sometime?"

Not wanting to hurt her feelings, Frank bounced back with. "I think that's a long time off for you, Roxie. I don't make promises that far in advance. I'm sure you have a lot of men waiting on you. Good luck." That was the nicest way Frank had of dismissing her.

Frank watched Roxie disappear into the pouring rain and in a sympathetic way he hoped her life would turn around for the better. He also felt sorry for her husband, even though he had never met him. They were lost souls on a fast track in the big city.

Looking out the window at the pouring rain, he couldn't help but wonder about Jonas and Gerty. What were they doing on such a dreadful day? They were probably hovering under a bridge somewhere trying to stay dry. The wind had picked up and was becoming stiff as it thrashed rain against the windows and bent tree limbs on the far side of the parking lot. Rivulets of water with small sticks floating in them were running down the street and pouring into storm drains wherever possible.

He couldn't put it off any longer; a decision had to be made concerning Jonas and Gerty. The agreement he had made with them had to be honored or addressed in some way. The least he could do was make some meager attempt to find them. Should he accomplish the task, he would volunteer to feed them once again, even if he had to bring them to his office in order to avoid the weather. The work in his office was not anything that could not be put off for a few days. He grabbed a raincoat, locked the office, and dashed to his pickup. His search was now officially under way.

After driving around for the better part of forty-five minutes, he found himself driving slowly under an overpass. The thought of giving up his search was gaining strength along with the hunger pangs that were growing in his gut. More often than not, it was during some last-ditch effort that something broke for either good or bad.

His eyes drifted up high to the darker realms of the overpass and it was there that he discovered the object of his search. Luckily, under the overpass, the pouring rain had been reduced to a mist and that significantly improved visibility.

The thing that caught his eye was enough for him to pull off to the side. There they were, up high, and huddled under a single blanket looking glum as ever. Although, without question, he had to admit to himself, most homeless people looked glum at any given time. Gerty's shopping cart was lying on its side next to them.

From their vantage point, Jonas and Gerty had no trouble recognizing Frank. In unison, they began waving at him. Their effort was an encouraging sign and that pleased Frank. The couple's acknowledgement was a clear sign that they were still interested in cultivating his acquaintance. However, there was still a ways to go before they could consider him a real friend.

As a learned reflex, Frank scanned the area under the overpass for any signs of danger or interference. The three of them had the area all to themselves. He pulled his pickup onto the service lane where he felt comfortable to park temporarily. He trotted across the street and made his way up the cement bank. His breathing was noticeably a little heavier by the time he reached Jonas and Gerty.

Between breaths, he realized that he hadn't given any thought to what he would say or do. Before he could engage his mind and speak, a blinding flash of lightning shot through the dark sky and lit up everything within sight. Sure, the lightning startled all of them, but, that wasn't the half of it. Guided by nature and physics, the lightning found its mark; a transformer mounted high on a pole at the nearest intersection. The ensuing fireworks resembled a Fourth of July celebration.

Jonas and Gerty both moaned in awe, and just as quickly, a sense of disappointment followed. With a tone of concern, Gerty put forth her best effort to explain their situation. "The cops, fire department, and the electric company will all be here soon. Sure enough, the cops will hassle us by asking questions and running checks for warrants. Eventually, we will be rousted out of our little nest here and forced out into the rain. I hate this shit. Oh well, that's life out here in never-never land." She stood and began collecting her things.

Before Frank could say anything, Jonas started to fold the blanket that had been keeping them warm. As for Frank, he was feeling a bit un-needed and like another obstacle for the couple he was attempting to befriend.

Not wanting to stand out as someone meddling in their business, Frank chose his words carefully. “Hey guys, I hope we’re still on for lunch on me. As far as all this rain, we can eat and hang out at my office until you figure out what to do. Does that sound like a plan?”

Gerty took control of the conversation knowing that whatever she wanted to do would be okay with Jonas. Jonas was usually a follower. “Well, Mister McLaughlin, of all the offers we have had so far today, yours sounds like the best.” Her tone was a mix of sounding factitious and sarcastic. Once her point was understood, they all gave a sigh of relief. Frank figured it was a good try at humor on a dreary day that had a chance of turning even worse.

Frank saw Gerty eying his little truck and realized that she was worried about her shopping cart and belongings. “Don’t worry, Gerty. I have a tarp and some rope so your things won’t get wet. As for us, I think we can all squeeze into the cab.”

As they made their way down to the street, Frank did the gentlemanly thing and took control of the shopping cart. Between the rough surface and the wobbly wheels, he felt like he was trying to herd a bunch of cats. He nearly lost his grip when he slipped on a piece of wet paper. Luckily, they reached the truck without a disastrous incident.

By the time the truck was loaded and the shopping cart was secured, and they were all stuffed inside the cab, the first responder was arriving for the blown transformer. Within seconds there were red, white, and blue strobe lights shooting through the rain. Frank saw a fireman placing orange safety cones out to block traffic. Frank did not envy those who had to work in such conditions. He made a U-turn and watched the scene disappear in his rearview mirror.

The breaths of three people cramped into the little truck quickly caused the windshield to fog over. Frank turned on the defroster full blast so he could see the road. "Since we had chicken yesterday, what do you think about some deli sandwiches for lunch?" Frank was anxious about moving things along.

It had been an eventful morning so far. However, it had not been all that productive; especially when it came to Leo. Frank was getting a bit edgy over why it was taking the vet so long to make a diagnosis.

The visit to the deli went without a hitch and even without much in the way of conversation in the tuck. Finally, they made it to Frank's office no worse for wear. He could tell by the looks on their faces that they did not know what his line of work was. Their gaze was transfixed on the printed lettering on the front door that read: "Frank McLaughlin, Private Investigator."

"Don't let my title bother you. I make a living at it, but, I don't get rich. I was in Counterintelligence when I was in the Army so I'm a natural snoop. Besides, I like being my own boss. When I screw something up, I don't have to put up with some idiot jackass of a boss yelling at me. All I have to do is learn from my own mistakes. Another important thing for me is that I really feel grateful to the world for being able to do something I enjoy and it's just more icing on the cake when I get paid for doing it. Can you think of anything more interesting than watching other people and solving their riddles? That's it in a nutshell."

Jonas labored in thought for what seemed like an eternity, even though it was actually for less than a minute. Thinking about surprising things for such a short time was harder work for him than wandering all over town in a single day. At last, he looked Frank in the eye and simply said, "You must be a pretty smart guy with a lot of tricks up your sleeve."

"Thinking, like work, is a process. Sometimes we are good at it and sometimes we aren't. All and all, there are still a couple of ingredients that are needed if we are going to sort out the good from the bad of human behavior. Those ingredients are training and experience. The thing that brings everything together for a quality investigative product is a sharp imagination and a willingness to take risks. But, enough of that; let's get inside and get some grub in our stomachs." Frank jumped out into the rain ahead of his guests so he could get the office door open for them.

Gerty grabbed the food while Jonas went to fetch her shopping cart, fearing that the truck bed might fill up with water and soak her belongings.

Some of the things in the shopping cart did get wet and Frank told them to spread the damp articles over some of the office furniture to dry. Within minutes the professional appearance of Frank's office was transformed into what looked like a clothing thrift store or a scene from Sanford & Son. Fearing the arrival of a client or potential client, Frank locked the door and closed the shades.

In no time all of them were digging into their food as if it could be the last time they would ever eat. Frank ate his food a little slower because he was engaged in thought. He was thankful that there was no noise and no amount of work nipping at his heels that demanded immediate attention. He also thought he was on good enough terms with Jonas and Gerty to do a bit of prying into their lives and their pasts.

There was absolutely nothing to suggest that either one of his guests were either dull or ignorant. Hopefully, they would be forthcoming in telling their stories. This was a good opportunity for Frank to be himself. Whatever dialog took place, Frank would avoid any temptation for sounding cynical. He would be the epitome of a great listener.

Frank knew that Jonas and Gerty were both harboring a lot of fears that were adding to still older ones because of the fatigue and loneliness they had acquired by being homeless. They had learned to be tough with their environment, but, could they learn to be gentle with themselves? Hopefully, there was a way for them to get past the drudgery of their circumstances while making sense out of their broken dreams and aspirations. When a person is analyzing the experiences of their own lives, they tend to focus on the drama, and that can be worse than anything seen in a horror movie.

So, how does a person accurately measure his or her life while trying to make sense of all the things that were thrown at them at the worst of times? Well, maybe for some people there is no value to dwelling on the past. Instead, they should look to the present since that is the place where they can choose their new beginning. Unfortunately, a person's life sometimes tends to begin somewhere on the other side of despair.

Considering all his internal philosophical jousting about life, Frank decided this was as good a time as ever to open things up with a relevant discourse based on his own life. Besides, Jonas and Gerty were now a captive audience and subject to his reflections and subtle inquiries.

Chapter 5

Frank's counterintelligence experience taught him a lot about interviewing. However, it was his nature and personality, as a caring, yet naturally inquisitive person, that taught him to be sensitive to others and their situation. He was certainly aware that this was not an official investigation where it was necessary to apply pressure. The circumstances in this instance required him to treat his two guests with care and prudence. The last thing he wanted to do was to erect any emotional barriers between him and them. After all, he was only searching for some root cause behind why either one of their lives had spiraled out of control. It could be because of a certain incident or it could be because of various influences over an expansion of time. Their addiction to drugs or alcohol were only by-products or symptoms of things that went deeper.

Finally, he decided to use a hybrid of an interviewing technique known as a "cognitive interview." The technique came into vogue in the 1970's, however, many investigators chose not to use it because they couldn't, or wouldn't, stray from the old techniques such as direct questioning using the standard format of: Who, What, When, Where, Why, and How. With the older traditional technique, investigators just went down their standard list of questions missing a lot of things that influenced a subject's behavior. Besides, as an investigator and experienced interviewer, the last thing Frank wanted to become was a traditional fact-finder that embraced officially-toned rote questioning. Naturally, ultimatums and challenges were off the table.

Frank was confident that he would glean from them the incidents that impacted their decision processes. Yes, he was interested in their motives, and perceptions that were not obvious on the surface. He didn't want piece meal, he wanted the whole enchilada; a complete picture. On one hand this exercise was a game and on the other it was a challenge to his ability to satisfy his own curiosity. Without question, one of his primary goals was to hone his interviewing skills to keep them sharp and effective while he was learning something about human behavior.

His method was simple. He would identify the major incidents that had toppled their lives and careers and then he would proceed both forward and backward in time until he understood who they were and how they arrived at where they were.

Since this approach is designed to be an open-ended exercise, there was no telling where it would take him as an interviewer or where it might take Jonas and Gerty. All he knew was that he would be able to, in some abstract way, put himself into their shoes, emotionally. Yes, the cognitive interview was the way to go; it would produce significantly more information and insight than what would normally be needed in a simple case of who did what to whom.

Frank decided to ease into the interview by talking first about himself. He wanted to convey to them that they were all similar in many ways. "There's a little chill in here because of all this rain. Can I interest you guys in having a cup of coffee with me?"

Not looking forward to the possibility of leaving in the middle of a rainstorm, they both opted for the coffee by nodding their heads.

Once everyone had a cup of hot coffee in their hands, it was time for Frank to kick things off. He leaned back in his chair and began. "You know, I have had my share of being down and out. In the military, I had to make decisions that ended in death for some of my comrades; many had been personal friends of mine. That's a tough thing to live with. But, it was after I retired that I hit bottom, emotionally. I was head over heels in love with a lady and I failed to properly assess a situation we found ourselves in. I'm not going to go into any detail other than to say that I didn't stop her from taking a risk and she ended up dying in my arms. She was shot by a madman." At this point, he fought to hold back tears because what he had said was, in his mind, not only an awkward moment, but, something that had tormented him for a long time. He had just made a cursory confession to two strangers.

"Death is a permanent outcome and there is no way to make it less traumatic for anyone. I'm sure the two of you have also had some heavy crosses to bear. Myself, I don't have to experience someone else's tragedy to learn from it. What do you think?" He had opened the door and invited them in to share their experiences. He couldn't have been any more subtle with his words.

Gerty was quicker to step forward than Jonas. "I don't see any harm in sharing my past and poor judgment. God only knows I talked enough about it when I was in counseling. Like other wives and mothers, I quarreled with my husband. At first, I blamed everything that went wrong on him. That included the little things that every family dealt with. Even though I was a nurse with a college education, I was extremely immature; too immature to have children. My husband, Carl, was an okay guy most of the time. The more I confronted him and argued with him, the more I pushed him away. I think we were both too proud to ask for professional intervention; counseling. It's tough admitting that you have a problem."

Frank wanted to keep her at ease so he agreed with her on the surface without attacking her. "I think all of us have had periods of being so emotionally frail that we lose our objectivity. It's easy to act out and rebel when you feel your world is closing in on you."

"You hit the nail right on the head, Frank. In my case, I worked in a hospital where I administered prescription drugs to patients. I thought I was smart enough to control my cravings. At first, I skimmed prescription medications from patients so I could self-medicate. Before I knew it, I was an addict. Then I found out how easy it was to purchase marijuana and cocaine. I combined these drugs with hard liquor. My nursing supervisor was quick to pick up on my mood changes and she had me tested for drugs. I ended that chapter of my life when I was fired." She was struggling, yet, she was not about to stop until she told her whole story. Once a person gets past that initial barrier that they hide behind, they tend to pour their hearts out.

She took a deep breath and then continued. "I needed money to feed my habit and that meant turning tricks. Hell, I even took my kids with me when I went to a crack house to score drugs. The arguing between me and Carl started to get really ugly and then it spilled over to my parents. The next thing I knew, I was divorced with no place to live and the court barred me from seeing my two children. For a long time, I continued living a life of crime and immorality. I did unspeakable things and after several arrests, I ended up in prison. I did a three year stretch and that was how I got off drugs. Naturally, with my record no one would hire me and I was not about to go back to my criminal lifestyle. My life was a total mess. This is how I ended up being homeless. I have no one to blame but myself. I can't point to any single incident that sent me on this path to nowhere. I built my life on the worse foundation possible."

Frank considered what Gerty had said and knew that there was nothing he could do for her except encourage her. She needed to find a way out and seize the right opportunities and then pursue them tenaciously with confidence. "You know, Gerty, I think you would make a terrific drug and alcohol counselor. You have the experience and training to deliver a meaningful message to others who are headed to the same place you have been. You need to make your experiences, as horrible as they appear, to count for something in both your life and in the lives of others. You would make a great motivational speaker. Can I make a few calls on your behalf?"

"Sure, why not. If things work out I think I would be a lot better off than I am right now. Just remember, I have been trapped here on the bottom for a long time. Don't expect a miracle because I don't know if I can make such a switch overnight."

Frank thought about what she had said and realized a flaw in his assessment that was common to men. Men tended to want immediate results: they see a target and move toward it at lightning speed. Women, on the other hand, were more prone to feeling their way to a goal. For Gerty, the process had to be structured and guided. He hoped that he could deliver her to a good mentor; one with patience and understanding; one who had been down a similar path.

Now, it was time to focus on Jonas. He had been sitting back quietly while Gerty poured her heart out. Frank had the impression that Jonas was like a child in grade school who feared being called on to answer a question. Jonas probably wasn't intending to be timid; he was just taking his time to properly assess what was going on with Gerty. Most people feared being judged when being encouraged to reveal their personal and private demons. At any rate, Jonas was not chomping at the bit to talk.

"Jonas, is there one thing in your life that you would like to do over? There has to be some things you wish you had done differently knowing what you now know. Myself, I have had more than my share of things that I would like to have a second go at. Without a doubt, I chose to live a very dangerous and adventurous lifestyle. I have already shared one trying part of my life with you, and Gerty has just done the same for us. It is only fair that you share some of your most challenging or disappointing things from your life." Frank hoped he was using the right technique on Jonas to get him to open up.

Jonas realized that he was in the proverbial fishbowl with all eyes fixed on him. He was understandingly challenged and his hesitancy reflected his fear and anxiety. It is not always easy to be put on the spot over past failures, poor decisions, and flawed judgments.

Jonas sat there with watery eyes and when he finally began to speak his voice was shaky. "I certainly helped turn my world upside down. I'll never forget that day. It was August 29, 2005, and I knew Hurricane Katrina was out there in the gulf and heading toward Louisiana, Mississippi, and parts of Florida's panhandle. I was stupid. I ignored the warnings and the call to evacuate. Do you know what I did at 3:30 a.m. that morning?"

Frank responded to Jonas' question in the simplest format he could think of so it would only be seen as a cue to continue. "No."

"I told my wife, my sweet loving wife, to keep an eye out for the storm. Hell, it wasn't just a storm; it was a category 4 hurricane. That's what Hurricane Katrina was. It was a killer storm." Jonas couldn't look at either Frank or Gerty. He looked down at the floor as if searching for enough courage to continue.

"So what did you do at 3:30 a.m. that morning?" Frank wanted to keep Jonas on track.

"I went to work. I went to the shipyard and found another worker and a supervisor there. We went around making sure everything was as secure as we could make it. The force of Katrina was nearly on us by 5:30 a.m. so we headed for high ground. I ran like hell. There was no time to get my wife. Katrina was everywhere at 6:10 a.m. and I mean everywhere. It was my fault that I never made it to my wife. Two weeks passed before I learned that she had drowned."

"That must have been devastating for you." Frank read Jonas' face and realized that the story was far from over.

"My son tried to save his mother and they both perished. My son was the man in our family that day and I was a total failure; I was absent. Take a good look at me and you will know how the rest of my story went."

Unlike Gerty, Jonas blamed a single event for ruining his life. However, the interview was far from over because in a cognitive interview the subject is taken back in time. Frank was looking for detail and a depth of understanding. What were the underlying factors that made Jonas the kind of a man that deserted his family during a crisis? Maybe there were other incidents in his life that needed to come out. Frank's instincts told him to keep prying until he knew he had the truth; the whole truth.

"What was your life like when you were in the Navy?" The question sent Jonas adrift like an astronaut severed from his spacecraft; his support system. "Was your time in the Navy full of calm seas and smooth sailing?"

Frank was looking for some kind of a reaction that would mean there was still something worth finding that was hidden in Jonas' past. If it wasn't something from his Navy service, maybe it was something from his youth. The reaction Frank was looking for was short in coming.

Jonas' reaction was defensive as well as defiant. He reached into his backpack and rummaged around until he found a single sheet paper; an official document of some sort. "The Veterans Administration got this for me. It's my DD 214. Here read it. It says I got out of the Navy with an Honorable Discharge. I never got into any trouble in the Navy." Jonas nearly threw the paper at Frank.

Frank knew that Jonas' reaction was over-dramatic and clearly indicated his Navy service included something contentious; something he wanted not to be exposed. Otherwise, why was Jonas so eager to show proof of his honorable service? Whatever happened to him in the Navy was strong enough to leave a lifelong imprint, and it was not something that Jonas wanted to discuss further.

At this point there was no reason to delve any further back in time. Yes, Jonas was haunted by something more than losing his wife and son to Hurricane Katrina. Jonas' state of mind was caused by a compilation of his family loss and something that had occurred in the Navy. Frank would now pry, although carefully, to expose the truth behind one homeless man by the name of Jonas Jackson. He would also have to pry when out of earshot of Gerty so Jonas would not be embarrassed in her presence.

Frank's thoughts were interrupted by a noise; the sound of his cell phone ringing. It was the vet calling about Leo. "Well Doc, what's the good news?" Frank was optimistic because of his confidence in the vet's abilities. The news would soon change Frank's mood.

"I'm sorry Frank. I wish I had good news, but I don't. Leo has an abdominal mass with a low platelet count so I performed an ultra sound on him." The vet's tone was disheartening. "I tested a sampling of the mass. Your kitty has a malignant tumor. I'm afraid this is a fatal condition. I recommend that he be put to sleep.

He's suffering and there's little I can do for him, but give him pain medication."

"Oh no!" This was all Frank could manage to say as his mind absorbed the bad news. "I'll be right there Doc. I want to be there when you do it. What I mean to say is: I want to say goodbye, personally." Frank was fighting back tears. He hung up the phone and sat there staring at the wall, but not really seeing anything.

Gerty was quick to pick up on Frank's mood change. "Is something wrong?"

"That call was from my vet. He has to put my cat, Leo, down. I've had the poor little guy for twelve years. We've been through a lot together." Frank looked out the window at the rain. "I'm going to call a taxi for you guys. Do you have a place to go to ride out the storm?"

Gerty looked at Jonas and read his face. "There are two missions; both called 'Union Gospel Mission.' One place is for men and the other for women. But we don't have any money for a taxi."

"Don't worry about that. I'll prepay the taxi driver. Can we meet up back here tomorrow? According to the weatherman, the storm will move out of here this evening. Oh yes, I almost forgot." Frank reached into his desk drawer and pulled out an envelope. "This is the lottery ticket you wanted, Jonas." Frank offered the envelope to Jonas.

Jonas waved the envelope off. "It's best you keep it here. There's no telling what will happen to it if I take it. By the way, when's the drawing?"

Frank shoved the envelope back into his desk drawer. "It's tonight. When we meet tomorrow, you can open it up and I can check the numbers on my computer."

"I'm sorry about your kitty. It's easy to get attached to a pet, especially when you have had him as long as you have. I had a dog when I was a boy. I hated it when he died." Jonas was doing his best to sympathize.

Once the taxi arrived, Frank and Gerty agreed to leave her shopping cart at Frank's office in the back room. They quickly put her belongings back in the cart because they were now dry. There was nothing in it that she would need at the mission.

Twenty minutes later, Frank was in the back room of the vet's office. The vet quickly administered the shot that would end Leo's suffering, and his life. Frank petted his friend and whispered words of comfort and love to his pet. Leo's eyes glassed over and his breathing slowed, and then he was gone.

Whenever a living creature that is capable of feeling dies, there is always an internal struggle to survive and live. From the time we all take our first breath, we have an innate will to survive, but that will cannot escape the reality that we all have to leave this world at some point in time. Frank wondered if Leo knew and understood the concept of death. Did he know that his life here on earth was over? Surely, dogs and cats all go to heaven, if there is such as place.

Frank thought it was strange how the living can recall profound words when under extreme pressure; especially when it comes to death. He recalled what Oliver Wendell Holmes once wrote: "Most persons have died before they expired—died to all earthly longings, so that the last breath is only, as it were, the locking of the door of the already deserted mansion."

Chapter 6

At the break of dawn, Frank's eyes slowly squinted open, searching the room through an imagined haze while trying to focus. He stared groggily at the ceiling as if he was awaking from a hypnotic trance. Without a doubt he was not fully awake, only trying to escape from some surreal state of unconsciousness. Yesterday's events must have been more trying than he had realized.

In spite of the beams of sunshine that were sifting into the bedroom through the curtains, his thoughts were still not at his command. His thoughts floated somewhere between the despair over losing Leo and a sense of anxiety over facing another meeting with Jonas and Gerty. Anticipation was not always the same as preparation. If he could only manufacture more enthusiasm, he would be able to snap out of his low mood.

Sleepily, and in the aftermath of recent events, he was trying to understand and evaluate the depth and meaning of his own life; a life-long endeavor with no end in sight. He wondered when it would be right to begin thinking about the end of his life. Maybe that was what priests and ministers were for; after all, they had a philosophical understanding of such things and they had comforting words for those who searched for some degree of clarity. Right now, however, he needed to snap out of his inward concerns and struggles if he was to adequately deal with the things waiting his attention. Being half drowsy and in a dark mood were not the best physical and psychological tools for kicking off a new day. First on his agenda was to shower, shave, and dress while in an empty house. A person never knows how important it is to have a pet until the pet is gone.

Frank was aware that Jonas was an altogether different situation. In comparison to him, maybe the only difference between him and Jonas was that one of them had shelter and a means of support. What a sad commentary. Notwithstanding current environments, Frank concluded that he was just as liable to be as lonely as any given homeless person. Frank smiled, realizing that he needed a more traditional life if he was to achieve any degree of happiness. When would that day come, he asked himself?

He swung his feet out of bed and sat up, rubbing his eyes, then with a shudder, he finally shook the cobwebs out of his head. A new day had officially begun. He always prided himself on being able to look beyond his perceived limitations and achieve some semblance of a practical reality that he could call his own. With that thought in mind, he was finally ready to tackle a new day.

Once his shower was finished, he took a minute to study his face in the bathroom mirror. He was suddenly aware of an old lesson he had learned decades before. Moving his face from side to side, he knew that he had to find a way to change the sourpuss reflection staring back at him; change it into a smiley face. He had nearly forgotten the importance of attitude. The last thing he wanted to become was a cynic with a heart of stone.

After fretting away the morning, lost in unproductive thought, he was finally driving along in his little pickup on a beautiful morning filled with sunshine and hope. As usual, there was no telling how the day would play out, but, for those who wanted it to be a fine day, there was optimism in the air.

In the distant sky there was a single dark rain cloud lingering behind from the day before. It lacked any power to influence his day and soon it would be gone.

Up ahead, he recognized Gerty trudging along with other pedestrians that were out walking, enjoying the warmth and sunshine that had replaced the storm. Frank pulled over to the curb to greet her and provide a lift to his office.

Frank was beginning to see Gerty as a hound on the scent of a new and better life. Soon, he would follow through on his promise to her and start making some calls on her behalf.

"Good morning Gerty." Frank called out to her.

"Thank you and I would like to toss a hearty good morning back at you too, sir." Gerty appeared to be in good spirits.

An elderly man raking leaves in a yard behind Gerty paused long enough from his work to smile in recognition of their good natured greeting.

"Would you like to ride along with me to the office?" Frank addressed Gerty like an old friend, a status she was achieving with little effort.

"I graciously accept your offer, sir." She smiled while adding to her response an abbreviated curtsy. The old man raking leaves blurted out an uncontrolled chuckle. All in all, Frank's impression of Gerty was that, among the homeless, she was a rose in a ditch.

Once inside the pickup, Gerty twisted in her seat, leaned her back against the door and looked directly at Frank. "Since we're alone, there's something I'd like to say." She didn't wait for Frank to acknowledge her intention. "I'm not sure why you are pressing Jonas the way you are."

Frank was caught off guard by her change of tone.

She continued. "He's been through a lot and he is doing the best he can to deal with it. What I'm trying to say is that I don't want to see him snap and fall back into that dark hole he's trying to crawl out of. Inside that hole there's no hope for him. Jonas is my friend. Just be careful how you push him. I saw the tension in his face yesterday when you were questioning him."

"I totally agree with you, Gerty. The last thing I want to do is hurt Jonas in any way. I'm only trying to learn from him. We all have lessons we can learn from each other. We get through life by learning and growing. My aim is to help Jonas with his learning process while I learn from his mistakes. I can't help him unless I understand what is driving him. How can I connect and empathize with him if I don't understand him? I have to first understand before I can be understood. Besides, it doesn't hurt any of us to open up once in a while." Frank felt like he was giving a sermon.

"Well, just remember, Jonas is not a lab animal in your personal social experiment. He's a human being and he is fragile at this point in his life. Hell, I'm just as fragile as he is."

Gerty's point was a valid one and Frank vowed not to cross that fine line between caring and exploiting. "I want you to work with me on this, Gerty. I want you to be my check so I stay in balance. I think that when we try to help people we are being normal. We are doing what is expected of us. You have nursing experience and training and that gives you a different insight that I don't have. My strengths are grounded in research, investigation, and analysis. We need to pool our resources. Do we have a deal?" Frank pulled into his parking lot, parked, and waited on Gerty to answer.

Jonas was sitting on the walkway, leaning against Frank's office door. Frank and Gerty both saw him. Gerty said, "Let's play it by ear. I'll let you know what I think as we go along. The important thing here is Jonas's wellbeing."

"I agree." That was all Frank had time to say because Jonas had nearly reached them.

"I see you two found each other. I got here as fast as I could because those people at the mission were all up in my face with scripture. I bet I know the 'word' just as well as any of them do. The 'haves' always think they are smarter than those of us that have nothing. My day will come, you better believe it. I'm sorry. It's too early for me to have a bad attitude. At least the weather is nice." Jonas faked a smile for everyone's benefit.

"Let's all go inside. Maybe we can get Gerty to brew some coffee for us while we figure out something to do." Frank was out of his pickup with his keys in his hands and leading the way to the office door as he spoke.

"Coffee sounds like a great idea. If you want, I can clean the office for you, too. It's the least I can do since you have been feeding us." This was the first morning in months that she was not craving a drink.

While Frank went through his faxes and phone messages, Jonas grabbed a broom, following up on Gerty's offer to help out. They all downed their coffee without much conversation. Out of nowhere Jonas blurted out to Frank, "I'm sorry about your kitty. Just be glad that God let you enjoy it as long as He did."

"Thank you, Jonas. I appreciate the sentiment. I had a rough night last night without the little guy."

The exchange between the two men prompted a smile on Gerty's face. In fact, she wanted to lighten things up and was desperately trying to come up with something cute to say.

"Come on Jonas; let's check your lottery numbers. Who knows, maybe you beat the odds." Gerty motioned Jonas towards Frank and his computer with a wave of her hand.

"Winning would certainly give me a boost." Jonas stood up and followed Frank behind the desk so he could watch Frank fire up the computer. He was only going through the motions of looking at the lottery results because his expectations were realistically low.

Gerty, on the other hand, was disenchanted with the men's attention to such a hopeless game where the odds were stacked against them. Instead, she made a crude attempt at creating some levity. "Hey, did you guys ever hear the one about the two cats watching a tennis match?"

No one looked her way. Frank, with Jonas looking over his shoulder, was tapping away on the computer's keyboard.

Gerty, not wanting to be ignored, continued with her joke. "Those two cats sat there quietly watching the two tennis players swatting the ball back and forth. After a while, one of the cats said to the other one, 'I didn't know you were interested in tennis.' The other cat smiles and says, 'Oh, didn't you know, my dad was once in the racket.'" She laughed hoping to inspire the men to laugh with her. There was no response from either of them after a short pause.

Suddenly, she recoiled in stark amazement as the two men erupted in unrestrained hoots, shouts, and screams. "Come on you two, my joke wasn't that funny. In fact it was kind of corny."

Frank and Jonas started hugging each other and dancing some sort of spastic version of a jig. Then she realized that their sudden outbreak of effervescent merriment had nothing to do with her crude attempt to promote a touch of cheerfulness. She slowly moved behind the desk to see what the ruckus was all about.

Jonas slapped his lottery ticket into her hand and nearly yelling he said, "Look here! Look here, honey! I just won the biggest lottery in history. Me, little old me, I'm a winner!"

This was big; a really big thing if it was true. Wanting to make sure there was no mistake, she took her time to compare the numbers on Jonas' ticket to those on the computer screen. Satisfied that everything was in order, she cried out, "Mother of God, I can't believe this. This is wonderful! This is glorious!" Matching their enthusiasm, her voice rose to a crescendo that could have been heard in heaven.

Soon they were all dancing around Frank's office until their lungs were ready to give out. There was no telling when the adrenalin would wear off and all of them would reach the point of exhaustion. Their minds kept on rushing even though their bodies were wasted. After heaven knows how much time had passed, they all settled down to a point where they all just stared at the computer screen in hypnotic amazement.

Frank was finally able to speak coherently. "Jonas, it says here that there were so many people playing this session of the 'Power Ball Lottery' that the cash option reached a whopping $420 million." Frank fumbled with a hand-held calculator for a minute and then continued. "Take out around 40% for Uncle Sam; that's about $168 million, and you have left roughly $252 million. You have just jumped from being the poorest man I have ever known to the richest man I have ever known. With all this money coming your way, there are some things you need to start thinking about." His tone was changing to one of concern. "First, there is no way you are going back out on the streets. Second, lunch is on me. You can pay me back later." Frank laughed out loud so Jonas would know that he was only cracking a joke.

Frank settled back in his chair and wondered about the direction Jonas' life would take as he embarked on a new journey; one propelled by an enormous amount money. Wealth alone never made anyone smart or wise. Going from rags to riches was quite an adjustment to make for any person. The least Frank could do was to see Jonas get off to a good start. Once the word got out, there would be predators galore trying to empty his pockets. Jonas needed a reputable accountant and a savvy attorney. He would also need a good business manager and personal advisor.

"Look Frank;" Jonas was suddenly wearing a worried look on his face. "Where can I store this ticket until I get things figured out?"

At last, Jonas was showing signs of reason and logic. "I'm glad you're thinking first before rushing off to a world full of sharks. Too many lottery winners failed to plan properly and ended up broke after a fool-hearty ride in extravagant luxury. But, as you just pointed out; securing that ticket is your first concern."

"I haven't survived this long without money to allow myself to squander away everything that God has now blessed me with. You haven't only showed me and Gerty kindness, but you have opened up your heart to us. I want both of you to share this blessing with me. Besides, I will need your skills as a detective. We'll talk about that later. Right now, where can I store this lottery ticket?" Jonas held the ticket cradled in his cupped and trembling hands.

Frank was quick to address Jonas' concerns. "First, we tell no one about this ticket. Second, we lock it in my safe, or if you prefer, we can go to a bank and put it in a safety deposit box. Third, we go to my home and put our heads together and come up with a plan; one that you feel confident with."

"I would prefer to lock it away in your safe. People in banks don't like doing business with street people. They always think we are trying to put something over on them. You seem to be good about business matters, so why don't you draw up an agreement between us. I think it is best to have something in writing. I'll give you a million dollars of my winnings if you agree to work solely for me for one year. Does that sound fair?" Jonas wore a serious expression on his face, but, Frank also read a secondary motive in Jonas' face.

Frank was nearly shocked by the officious and logical approach that Jonas was suggesting. "I totally agree with you. What kind of an agreement do you want for Gerty?"

"I want to discuss Gerty with an attorney. I have something different in mind for her." Jonas smiled at Gerty who looked stunned over how Jonas was taking charge of his new situation; his new fortune.

Frank knew, deep down on a different intuitive level, that Jonas was contemplating some ulterior motive and direction. Winning all that money was only a means to some end that only Jonas could relate to. Frank would find out his new client's secret; he had to, especially if he was now going to be looking after some of Jonas' affairs. Learning other people's secrets was something that kept his life interesting and rewarding; on a multitude of levels. Now, adding to the mystery surrounding Jonas was the question of why did Jonas need a private investigator? Learning the answer to this new question would surely lead to solving the bigger mystery concerning what was driving Jonas. At least with all this mystery and uncertainty there had to be some expectation of an emotional gain that would complete his life. There was something more than simple happiness involved here.

Chapter 7

Frank marveled over Jonas' appearance once he was cleaned up and attired with newly purchased clothing, albeit from a big-box discount store. It was amazing at what a shower, shave and clean clothing could do for a person's image. The redo was topped off by a trip to a local salon for a haircut. The transformation was astonishing and did wonders for Jonas' self-image and esteem. The change made Jonas walk taller and prouder; a metamorphosis that reflected the beginning of a change for the better. Without question, there was a pronounced sense of improvement. It was certainly a huge step up from the stench of the gutter.

Mid-morning of the next day was just as impressive as was the changes in Jonas' appearance and demeanor. The attorney that Frank had chosen for Jonas had been a long-time client of Frank's who had ethical standards that suited Frank's concerns. He was one of the few attorneys that Frank enjoyed working with and for. Frank was not surprised over how the attorney aggressively assisted his new client; a client with monumental impending wealth. Attorneys are adversarial by nature and they can always be expected to be mercenaries, especially when large amounts of money were on the plate. Money always generated more attention; patronizing attention. Oh well, that was the way of the world. If the attorney, or anyone else for that matter, would have seen Jonas a few days earlier, they would have turned up their nose at him and done their best to avoid him. Yes, poverty is a deadly disease and unfortunately a very prevalent disease in our world. The poor economy had pushed many middle-class people over the brink of poverty. Sadly, those who are well-to-do tend to go about avoiding the poor without knowing that they have no guarantee that they won't someday join the ranks of the poverty stricken. The lesson here is obvious; never be too quick to judge because risking one's karma is a foolish undertaking.

Frank sat out in the attorney's foyer with Gerty by his side and watched the receptionist and paralegal as they scurried about each time the attorney called on the intercom. Suddenly, after an excruciating wait of two hours, Frank was summoned to the attorney's office. Just as quickly, the receptionist, who had been sitting and watching Gerty with an annoying look, was now attending Gerty as if she was a princess. The news of impending wealth had somehow penetrated the inner walls of the attorney's office. Until that moment, Frank had regretted not having enough time to put Gerty through the same cosmetic changes as Jonas. At least Gerty was classy enough to understand that Jonas was the priority; the newly appointed bread winner. There would be plenty of time for Gerty to go through the "Pygmalion" change since she was Jonas' "fair lady."

Predicated on a contract that Frank had negotiated with Jonas at the insistence of Jonas, the attorney had prepared a power of attorney so Frank could perform most administrative tasks as if he was Jonas. The attorney commented to Frank as he handed the document to him. "Even though you two have only known each other a relatively short time, my client is placing a great deal of trust in you. I agree with his decision based on the work that I have done with you. You are certainly the best option he has available considering his recent circumstances. Even though I envy your new position, I will always be available to assist with legal issues as they arise. There is no doubt in my mind that you will do a superb job."

Frank looked at Jonas and then back at the attorney, then spoke. "Well, all I can say is thank you. I think being trusted is one of the best complements a person can ever receive. As a matter of honor and integrity, it is my duty to look after Jonas as if I was looking out for myself. All and all, I have to note that I will do my utmost to look out for Jonas' best interest. I have always been loyal to those I serve and this time will be no different." Frank stood and shook hands with both men because a hand shake is the true way to seal a deal; a moral and dignified obligation.

When the attorney dismissed Frank he asked him to send in Gerty. Frank could tell by the looks on their faces that Gerty was an integral part of this arrangement. The idea pleased Frank because friends should always look out for one another.

After sending Gerty into the attorney's office, Frank sat on a chair and stared at his copy of the power of attorney and his copy of the contract he had negotiated with Jonas. His prevailing thought was clear and reminded him of something he had read in college. It was written by E. B. White, the author who wrote such classics as "Charlotte's Web" and "The Trumpet of the Swan." The words summed up a lot about agreements and went like this: "There is nothing more likely to start disagreement among people or countries than an agreement." Yes, agreements are no better than the people that make them and if not properly done they can turn out to be a trap. So, when can, or should, an agreement ever be annulled or ignored? As a side note, politicians tend to be vague when it comes to their word. Frank was glad that he was not a politician in the literal sense.

Frank couldn't help but think about his original motive for befriending Jonas. He had wanted to discover and study the driving force behind a man; not just an average man, but a homeless man. Every man and woman has a story behind them and Frank made it one of his life's ambitions to learn the secrets that made people what and who they were. His goal was only an academic one. At least his motive would not hamper his trust and loyalty to Jonas since it was only something of a personal interest; now a side interest. Understanding is not a tangible goal, but it does help us achieve and grow within ourselves.

Another question that would soon be answered was a totally different matter. How would Jonas go about unfolding his next journey through life? The next year would be different from anything Frank had ever experienced before. He was looking forward to what would surely be a novel adventure.

A man dressed in a dark blue suit and carrying a briefcase walked in and approached the receptionist. Their conversation was hushed and officious. After conversing with the receptionist, the man, a tall bald middle-aged man wearing thick, dark-rimmed glasses walked to the far end of the room and sat alone. For the next few minutes the man continued to nervously fidget and squirm in his chair. The man's actions caused Frank to wonder about what was making the man so nervous. Sometimes stressing over something was a bigger deal than the actual event. Frank figured that life was too short to sweat the small stuff; but, nothing is small when it comes to looking after Jonas because Frank had a commitment to him. Nevertheless, way too many people lose sight of the magic and beauty of life when they don't take some matters in stride.

Frank's eyes jerked back to the attorney's door as Gerty closed it behind her and sauntered over toward him. She was smiling and crying at the same time and Frank saw this as an encouraging sign. She clutched a wad of tissues in her hand and then daubed her eyes with them. Frank stood to greet her and they embraced amidst sobs and guttural sounds of chuckles.

"Frank, Jonas is the kindest, sweetest man in the world and he is the best friend I have ever had. My whole life is about to change for the better because of him. Two days ago I wasn't sure I even had much of a life at all, and now I have the world by the tail. Do you know what is even better?" Her eyes, bloodshot from crying tears of joy, pierced deep into Frank's caring eyes as she spoke.

In the most comforting manner Frank could muster under the circumstances he answered. "Come on, honey, let it out, let me have it."

"You and I and Jonas are all going to be together for the next year, and who knows how long after that. I don't know everything, but, I know enough to be thankful for you. Don't you get it; you were the key to everything. Jonas trusted you and you came through for him and that means everything to him. Our lives were a hopeless mess before you came along. I think that God sent you to save us. Thank you and thank God." Gerty was now hugging Frank with the grip of a bear.

Looking over Gerty's shoulder, Frank saw that the nervous man in the suit was entering the attorney's office clutching his briefcase with both hands. Gerty saw Frank watching the man and explained. "Oh, that's the accountant that the attorney got for Jonas. The attorney is making sure everything is covered. He has to make sure all the "t's" are crossed and the "i's" are dotted."

Frank admired two things about Henry Silverton Esquire: One was that he had a tremendous confidence when it came to his abilities. The other thing came out when Frank once asked him if he ever got nervous in the courtroom. Henry simply answered, "why should I get nervous when I made all A's through law school. Most judges can't say the same thing." Henry was not only dedicated to his clients; he was also dedicated to the truth and the law itself. Anyway, that was Frank's opinion after working several contentious cases for him.

Refocusing on Gerty, Frank continued to address what she had said about him. "Gerty, don't make this about me. We are all equally together in this. The best that we can accomplish will come about because we are doing them together; always looking out for each other. We should never, ever lose our togetherness because once we do; there is nothing more we will be able to do. Remember, the team is more important than any individual." Frank smiled at her.

"I guess we are now the three musketeers! Wow, who would have thought? You must have learned all this wisdom in the military." She was now smiling confidently.

Frank chuckled at her analogy. However, on a deeper level, he realized the truth behind what he had told her concerning working together, as a team. For him, his spoken words had substance; a substance he did not want to lose sight of, especially when grabbing at the shadows that often enter a person's life. Hopefully, his message had sunk in to Gerty's thought process and awakened in her something about life that would never sleep again; the importance of having others in your life. No one can go through life all alone and expect things to work out. In this case, as in every case, time would tell.

Inside the attorney's office, Jonas was experiencing something new, something he had only, days before, thought would never happen again in his life. Yes, he was having an epiphany that he hadn't seen coming his way, never in a lifetime. Now, he could look ahead to a future that was bright and filled with optimism; the depth of which was soothing to his soul.

His newly acquired attorney and accountant looked at him with warm eyes as if they were family members. Jonas was not stupid; he knew their cordial demeanor and warm-heartedness were only products of wealth and status; all bought and paid for by others.

Their day's business was now complete and the meeting was coming to an end. Jonas had played the game as well as he could in the midst of all the excitement. Ceremoniously, they all stood, and one by one, Jonas shook hands with them while smiling goofily. From this point forward, he vowed to have Frank take care of his business matters, as well as other matters that he might be struggling with. The curtain had just fallen on this act in the drama of his life. Besides, as far as he was concerned, the world could think that Frank had all the money. Jonas was wisely experiencing a comforting conclusion; the bliss of anonymity would, by far, outweigh any notion of celebrity status. His thoughts reeled back to something an old Chief Petty Officer kept saying; "It is the KISS Principle: Keep It Simple Stupid."

As Jonas was escorted out of the office he was relieved to see Gerty and Frank shooting smiles at him. Their efforts were not bought; they were genuine. After all, they had been his friends when he had been a penniless and destitute street urchin.

"All of us need to meet back here tomorrow to wrap things up. Is that all right with you?" Jonas directed his question to Frank since he was the one with the transportation and he was the person allowing him and Gerty to stay in his house.

"Of course it's okay. After all, I'm working for you for at least the next year. I'm just as excited about this as you are, Jonas. I have never experienced anything like this in my life, and I have witnessed a lot. This is going to be an adventure that none of us will ever forget as long as we live." Frank was sincere.

"I can't believe I am this rich and still have to impose on you to buy lunch for us. Oh well, I guess you could say that I have a lot of experience at being a leech." Jonas was grinning from ear to ear.

"Don't sweat the small stuff, Jonas. In the future you will have ample opportunities to buy my lunch. Once you claim that prize money, your future will be as bright as anyone else's and it will be paid for." Frank was already turning toward the door leading them out as he spoke.

While walking across the parking lot Jonas commented. "You know Frank, it's funny that you said something about me buying you lunch in the future. Last week I didn't even know I had a future. Over the last few years, I don't know how I got by every day. Now, here I am with the same mind and same skills that I had then, and suddenly I have a future to look forward to. I am the same person I was then, except now I have money. Before, I was always afraid of the future and now I can wrap my arms around it without fear. Why has God chosen me to have a future unless it has something to do with my past?"

Frank put his arm around Jonas' shoulders. "Jonas, don't struggle with the 'why' of life because you will never come to a full understanding. Take it all in stride and enjoy as much of it as you can. Also, remember that money isn't the answer to how we live our lives. Right now, I can't tell you what they will be, but, there will be consequences attached to having all that money. The best piece of advice that I can offer is this: Don't be greedy and don't be wasteful. Most importantly, do some good with some of that wealth. If you do these things, you will sleep better and be able to look at yourself in the mirror each morning without guilt."

"Believe me, Frank, I know something about guilt. You and I will have a talk about that someday soon." Jonas wanted to change the topic of conversation and his tone made that clear.

They all squirmed and wiggled until they were, once again, crammed into Frank's little pickup. Frank figured that it was time to focus some attention on Gerty. It was time to buy her some clothing and get her to a hairdresser.

They all ended up at a mall in Frisco. Since Frank was the only one with money at his disposal, he had to be present for everything that Gerty required. After purchasing clothing, shoes, and some cosmetics they were off to the hairdresser.

The progress of her transformation was realized when Gerty came out of a dressing room wearing a new pant suit with makeup on her face. Jonas was the first to remark. "Look here, Frank. We have found Princess Gerty."

The smile on Jonas' face was equal to the glow that Gerty was projecting. Frank saw more than he had expected. It was not only Gerty's beauty that was shining brightly; there was something else. It came from getting to know Gerty. The amazing thing that Frank realized was that Gerty possessed something that he could only describe as grace. Her grace had been there all the time and it never needed nice clothes to be apparent. Yes, Gerty was not only reclaiming her dignity; she was returning to the nice person she had once been before her drug addiction.

Gerty looked over at Frank and said the obvious. "I'm beginning to dust off over a decade of filth. I hope you guys see that I clean up quite nicely. I appreciate the looks you're giving me."

Frank was forever remembering quotations and applying them to situations he was facing, this occasion was no exception. As he and Jonas faced off with Gerty at this tender moment, his collective impression could only be summed up one way. John Keats, a great English poet during the Romantic Movement once wrote: "The excellence of every art is its intensity, capable of making all things disagreeable to evaporate, from their being in close relationship with beauty and truth." Yes, Gerty's artful grace was helping tremendously to clean her up.

Bored at being in the waiting area at the beauty salon, Frank and Jonas wandered around the mall for over two hours. Upon their return, Gerty once again shocked their senses. If it was not for remembering what Gerty's new clothing looked like, they would not have recognized her when she was finished. Her waist-long grey hair was no longer dangling in stringy strands below her waist. In fact, it was no longer long or grey. She was now a dark brunet with stunningly styled hair; her hair was feathered back on the sides and only slightly covering her neck. The trip to the beauty parlor had taken twenty years off her appearance.

Frank got a glance of his reflection in a mirror and realized that he was now the scraggily looking one among them. Just as quickly as he caught sight of his image, he set it aside. Not wanting to waste the moment, he decided to show his friends off. "I don't know about you two, but, I'm hungry. Let's go grab a bite somewhere. How does Italian sound?" He put an arm around Gerty's shoulders and, as if he could not restrain himself, he remarked. "Damn, you look fabulous."

Chapter 8

The next few weeks were crucial and demanding in spite of their administrative nature. Add to that a sprinkling of adjustment and one could find a smattering of progress being achieved. During this time the three of them made a series of decisions that would improve their health and wellbeing. Gerty, with her nursing background decided that they all, including Frank, needed to have complete physicals. The goal was nothing less than remarkable and was easily achieved. The end result was that none of them had any major physical ailments that needed attention. In spite of a harsh existence on the streets, Jonas and Gerty had weathered and aged well.

Jonas decided that Frank should get rid of his little pickup by trading it in on something that would better accommodate the three of them. Jonas dismissed the idea of purchasing a Cadillac sedan because it was too flashy and extravagant. Wisely, he did not want to draw any extraordinary attention. He had never been a flashy person. On an unconscious level, Jonas did not want his newly acquired wealth to taint his frugality; something he had always prided himself in. When Frank suggested a Ford Explorer, Jonas simply said, "That's what I'm talking about. Don't worry; I'll pick up the tab on it."

When it came to life-altering decisions focused on self-improvement, Frank's mind moved in another direction. Since he wanted to give up his addiction to Pepsi and while Jonas and Gerty wanted to give up their addiction to alcohol for reasons of good health, both mental and physical, Frank proposed that all three of them should start going to the gym to get into better shape.

As sure as the world spins around the sun there will be change and it is a blessed thing if those changes were for the better. With the wealth incurred by Jonas, and by his newly adopted example, the trio sought to make those changes based on both need and virtue. Anyway, that was the immediate plan.

Collectively, they went about getting fit and healthy. As for virtue, charity rang supreme. Jonas made anonymous donations to various orphanages and select shelters. The recipients were not concerned about the source of the donations and no matter when or how often they received the money they always publicly thanked God, and according to Jonas that was the way it should be. In Jonas' heart, he believed that charity was a sacrifice to God based on the blessings that God had given to him in the form of money. As long as he was blessed with the means, he would be charitable for the sake of honoring God; that was his belief, pure and simple.

Jonas' attorney, accountant, and a new financial advisor by the name of Eli Stein, made sure the right investments were made to ensure a healthy return on his money. However, Jonas insisted that the bulk of his money was to remain in limbo because he had a plan for the future; the details of which he was not yet ready to share. In spite of Frank and Gerty pressing for information, Jonas decided to keep them both guessing until such time that he would surprise his cohorts by revealing his more strategic intentions. Hopefully, they would warmly embrace his plans. His goal was a life-long mission that only he understood.

Jonas paid the rent on Frank's office forward for a year. The office was a good place from which to coordinate matters that interested him. Gerty was content to do quite a bit of the cooking for them in Frank's modest kitchen. She was somewhat reluctant to take on a society that had once shunned her. It was not that she was shy for she was not; she just didn't have anything she wanted to prove to others or to herself. The lowness to which she had sunk would take a long time to recover from. Besides, she liked being the rose in the midst of her two pals. For the immediate future, and possibly longer, Jonas and Frank was her family; her entire world.

Frank's house was a modest three bedroom home. He immediately observed that Jonas and Gerty did not share a bedroom. All three of them had their own. Frank always thought that Jonas and Gerty were a couple, an indivisible unit, and not merely best of friends. However, their affection for one another never crossed over the line to anything of an intimate or physical nature, and that surprised Frank. Jonas' and Gerty's relationship was only based on love in a Platonic way. In Frank's mind, there was nothing wrong with that arrangement. In fact, it was admirable. Frank smiled at the idea of Platonic love and the thought reminded him of something he had once read by a writer by the name of Dorothy Parker: "Love is like quicksilver in the hand. Leave the fingers open and it stays. Clutch it and it darts away."

Perhaps, Jonas and Gerty had other reasons for not taking their relationship to the physical level. Jonas still had not gotten over the death of his wife and son and his guilt had not had enough time to heal his heart. Maybe it never would heal because it had left a deep scar across his soul. When it came to Gerty, well, she had destroyed her loving relationship with her husband and children by way of her drug addiction. In spite of being only a little less than middle-aged, she was thinking more like a grandmother who had lost her loved ones in some horrific tragedy; in this case one of her own making. At any rate, these were all assertions on Frank's part; purely subjective. Surely, these puzzles, like most puzzles, would unravel in time.

When it came to love and relationships, Frank had his own share of emotional baggage to tote around. During his life, the warming arms of love had been open to him on several occasions. These times had not been fought for or negotiated for; they had come and gone freely on life's terms and fate. It seemed like every time he had wanted to embrace the love of a woman, he had only ended up holding himself or his cat. The prevailing winds told him that life without love, or the chance of love, was a waste for one's soul, and that was a tough thing to endure. Maybe love doesn't necessarily make the world go round, but, it does make the trip worthwhile.

By nature, Frank was a planner and an executor of plans and at the moment there was no plan for him to execute. For the sum of one million dollars, a year of his life had been bought and paid for. A business arrangement, on the surface, was certainly not a plan. Only a month had passed since Jonas won the lottery and all routine matters that could be settled had been. Everyone had a roof over their head and food in their belly. Basic needs had been obtained in abundance. Still, something was missing, total fulfillment had not been achieved.

Settled as things were, Frank was far from being content. One thing he did not want was idleness. He glanced at the calendar in his office and wished for something to happen that would make better use of his time. Frank was already missing his insurance cases. His fax machine had become as idle and as content as a mouse in a cheese factory and that type of contentment was appalling to him. On this particular day, he was feeling the weight of boredom to the point of melancholy. So he decided to ask Jonas for something to work on.

Jonas was sitting on the couch in obvious deep thought. What was this new millionaire contemplating? There was only one way to find out. "Jonas, I need something to work on. Do you have any ideas?"

"You bet I do. I want to do some traveling and I want to clean up a few loose ends in my life." Jonas snapped back with a renewed tone of enthusiasm that was strong enough to surprise Frank. Jonas' face was stern as he sat up a little straighter, projecting an image of boldness. He looked directly at Frank with piercing eyes. "I want you to find out where my wife and son are buried in Louisiana. I want them moved to a more suitable place. I want them in a nice mausoleum in New Orleans. I don't care what it costs as long as they are honored properly. Do you know what I mean?"

"Yes, I understand. I know that you miss them dearly and moving them to a better resting place is not only a good thing to do, but, it is a great tribute to them."

Frank picked up a notepad and pen. He got up and handed them to Jonas. "Please, write down their names, dates of birth, and anything else you can think of. At this moment, I can't think of anything more worthy of doing than helping you honor your loved ones."

This was a righteous and meaningful undertaking for Frank. Recalling the story that Jonas had told him concerning his family told Frank that Jonas was still grieving, and like Gerty had said, Jonas was a fragile, and in some respects a broken man, and wealth alone was not about to change that. For the next two days, Frank took on bureaucracies, ran leads, and coped with frustrations until he had at last located the remains of Jonas' family. One would have thought that with the passing of time, and the ending of the chaos in the aftermath of Katrina, that the assignment would have been easier. Fortunately, and in spite of all the administrative obstacles that had been in his path, his perseverance finally paid off.

After contacting officials at the famed cemetery, Saint Louis Number 1 on Rampart Street in New Orleans, Frank learned that all the tombs were above ground and the cemetery had avoided the wrath of Hurricane Katrina. The cemetery was well established, having been founded in 1789. Following a substantial bribe, the remains of Jonas' wife and son would be placed in an extravagant tomb at this most famous cemetery in New Orleans.

This was the same cemetery where the remains of Voodoo Queen Marie Laveau rested.

Frank was surprised to learn that the contentious Queen was being considered for canonization for sainthood by the Catholic Church. Apparently, she had been a Catholic and some of her work in the healing of others approached the level of being a miracle. Frank did not know what to make of Marie Laveau and her work. Someday, he would take the time to conduct a more in-depth inquiry into the matter. He enjoyed researching controversial topics and drawing his own conclusions.

Frank knew that one of the places Jonas would want to travel to would be New Orleans. However, he did not know what other destinations Jonas might have in mind. He would do the logical thing and ask. The collective ambiance that was beginning to prevail in the room told Frank that, like him, his two friends were growing antsy and travel was now a good option.

The rewards of travel are many and self-fulfilling on multiple levels. There is a certain freedom or liberty associated with travel. When traveling about, a person can freely think and feel as he or she wants. A traveler can also do as they want, within reason, because when they are among strangers they don't have to put on a special façade to hide who they really are; unless traveling to some middle-east countries. When traveling, there is also the aspect of education through exposure to other cultures; the rewards of which could certainly enhance a person's wellbeing.

After filing his successful report concerning the remains of the Jackson family, Frank diplomatically posed the question of travel to Jonas. "I'm certain that we will visit New Orleans so you can pay your respects to your wife and son. After that, where will we travel?"

Jonas smiled and then delivered the strangest answer. "Yes, yes, we are going to New Orleans, but not as quick as you think. You are my task master, Frank; you know how to get things done. Before we travel to New Orleans, you have to arrange the biggest purchase that I will ever make. You are going to find and select our new home, an ocean-going vessel. I want to move onboard the same day we visit the cemetery. We'll need the best captain and crew you can find. The same day we move aboard, I want to set sail for the Caribbean. I always told my wife and son that, them aside, the ocean is where I want to be. This first trip is much more than an old man's silly dream. This is something I want to bring to life; this is my calling. I don't know how long you two will be part of my life, but, you and Gerty will have to see me through on this one trip. There is no way that I can do this alone. You have no idea what this means to me."

Frank suddenly had an intuitive understanding, an epiphany, of what was really underscoring Jonas' request. Maybe he had been so busy that he began to lose sight of his original reason for wanting to meet Jonas, the homeless man. Frank's hunch was always that the driving force behind Jonas had something to do with his Navy service. This was the beginning of the next phase for unraveling the mystery and learning the source of the driving force behind Jonas. Also, he couldn't help but wonder how much of this Gerty was picking up on.

Suddenly, Frank's life was about to become a whirlwind of thought and activity. An adventure, a great adventure, was about to unfold and he was at the center of it. He had to orchestrate all of it just as a conductor meshed all the instruments of a symphony.

Breaking away from his clandestine thoughts, Frank returned to the conversation. "It seems as though we all have quite an adventure awaiting us. Tell me, Jonas, what size of vessel do you have in mind?" Frank opined that any ship big enough for all of them to live on would have to be huge and that translated into a lot of money.

"A 150 to 250 foot luxury yacht is what I have in mind. I'm sure you will find a good deal for me. Just remember, I am going to live on this ship for the rest of my life and I will be doing a lot of traveling on it. I want a top-notch crew, too. You shop around and show me what you come up with." Jonas was giving Frank a great deal of latitude.

"Well Jonas, I am excited about this and it beats the heck out of all of us sitting around here in my little office and quaint home; squatting on our laurels trying to figure out how to make life interesting. Truthfully, I was beginning to get a little bored." Frank was suddenly beaming with excitement over the prospect of travel, and the possibility of some adventure thrown into the mix.

"There's one more thing, Jonas. We need to fill out applications and get photos taken for passports. I'll go to the post office and pick up the applications this afternoon."

In Frank's mind a sea-going adventure was boldly traveling to exotic places in search of fun and excitement; challenging nature on the high seas, and encountering a variety of cultures.

However, in Jonas's mind, a Caribbean trip was a sojourn in search of answers to a haunting puzzle that constantly wracked his heart and soul. He was uncertain if he would end up seeking revenge or atonement. He wasn't sure if Father Time had erased the answers he sought or if those at the center of his quest were alive or dead. All he knew was that he had to do his best now that he had the means to do so. Jonas also realized that if he was still alive after all these years, then others, others with answers or leads, could still be alive, and just maybe he would learn the truth that had eluded him and tormented him for the biggest part of his life.

He would lean heavily on Frank because he was a worldly private investigator and adventurer.

Frank saw something in Jonas's eyes that told him that this trip was not going to be a jaunt across the sea for fun and enjoyment. He wondered what was behind this plan that Jonas was springing on him and Gerty.

Frank was well aware that no two adventures or stories were the same. Like a man's fingerprints, no two could be duplicated exactly. Each and every individual adds his or her own nuances and flavor to their story, therefore, the depth of one's own past defines their character and structures their destiny. This was why he liked studying people and their motivations. Yes, every human being is a wizard capable of choosing and changing all the things that become his destiny. He was just as anxious and enthusiastic to turn the next page in his life as Jonas was in his life. Only in this instance, Frank would be looking over Jonas's shoulder when he turns his.

Chapter 9

Frank once heard that there were two great days associated with boat ownership. The first great day is the day you purchase it and the second, and the greatest day of all, was the day you sold it. Purchasing Jonas' new home and yacht was certainly going to be a great first day for him in spite of its difficulty. Of course, Frank hoped he would have nothing to do with Jonas' second great day, if it arrived at all. Besides, these days both belong to Jonas because he possesses both the dream and the money. Frank liked being a facilitator for Jonas. He also knew that investing in a dream has the potential of being one of the greatest accomplishments that any human being can undertake. However, human emotion and behavior are well worth keeping an eye on.

A yacht, especially one someone intends to live on for the rest of his or her life, has to be special. Like a house, you don't want it to be of the cookie-cutter variety that looks like all the others around it. Frank's challenge would be to find a yacht that he thought would match Jonas' personality and still be functionally sound for the rest of his life. This turned out to be no small task.

Surely, there were many people living aboard their boat or yacht. However, the process of purchasing one can be daunting and complex. In this instance there was no difficulty locating a functional yacht; there were plenty of them on the market. One of them stood out among the multitude.

Initially, he had narrowed his on-line search to three vessels. One was in Greece; one was in Italy, and the other was at Fort Lauderdale, Florida. The one in Greece was nice, but not exceptional, in spite of having a price tag of over twenty million dollars. The one in Italy was also nice, but, the asking price was over sixty million dollars. Additionally, out of country purchases were more time consuming and awkward so Frank felt good about ruling them out. Thus, he focused squarely on the one in Florida.

Not only did the one in Florida have good eye appeal, it had a substantially smaller price tag; a comfortable eight million dollars. It was a one hundred and eighty foot floating palace. Clicking through the photo arrangement was a breathtaking experience. It had the same speed and range as the two out of country vessels: a 7,000 nautical mile range at a cruising speed of twelve knots. On the surface, the main concern was its age; it was built in 1961 whereas the other two ships were less than ten years old. The one in Florida was built in America by Ziegler Shipyards and there were seven elegant staterooms that accommodated fourteen people. The woodwork was magnificent with rich combinations of mahogany and teak. Still, Frank knew that he lacked yacht experience and was well aware that it wasn't like buying a used car or RV. He had to find out if it was seaworthy and priced right according to its design and quality of construction. Right away, he knew how to get the answers he needed. However, first he had to discuss his selection with Jonas. After all, Jonas had been in the Navy and following that he had worked at a shipyard in New Orleans so he had a basic knowledge of seagoing vessels.

Frank printed out all the information he could find on the Florida yacht and called Jonas and Gerty over to his desk. After spreading everything out on the desktop, Frank stood back and allowed Jonas and Gerty to have a look.

They hovered over the layout and observed with keen eyes. Each of them displayed moments of jaw dropping expressions along with guttural mumblings. Their reactions were signs of their forthcoming approvals. Frank recalled having the same reactions whenever he had skimmed through old copies of a magazine called the Architectural Digest. The beauty and elegance of those homes were truly inspiring. The difference here and now was that Jonas had the means to purchase what he was looking at.

Jonas scooped up the display and, with Gerty by his side, went to the couch where they sat in silence for about ten minutes. Struggling to contain his excitement, Jonas asked; "What's this ship called?"

Proving that he had been thorough, Frank answered, "Sea Venture."

"I like that name. It has a nice ring to it. What is your next move?" Jonas was attempting to sound officious in spite of his apparent enthusiasm.

As for Frank, his enthusiasm was nothing short of joyous since it was obviously coupled with the satisfaction of doing a good job for his new friend and client. He didn't have to be a world leader or a high-ranking military general to feel good about being able to instill a sense of pride and joy in the faces of others. The bottom line was that he was doing something for someone he liked and that was reward enough.

"First, I'm going to contact the broker and announce your interest in Sea Venture, and then I'm going to find a marine surveyor that specializes in mega yachts. His report should tell us if this vessel is sound, insurable, and priced right. With your permission, I will move on this as fast as I can. I take it that you like what I have found?" Frank knew the answer already, judging by the look on Jonas' face.

"I knew I could count on you coming up with something good. I'm lucky to have you in my corner. Actually, if it wasn't for you, I wouldn't even have a corner." Jonas' last comment turned all of their expressions into joyful smiles, with a few extra tingles up and down Frank's spine.

The following two weeks resulted in a great deal of success. Usually, and something that Frank was used to, success only came about after running into way too many obstacles. However, checking out the Sea Venture was like gliding across a smooth pond in a canoe. Yes, failure, rejection, and mistakes were all absent.

First, Frank thought it would be a monumental task to have the Sea Venture surveyed. The coordination was easy once he had permission from the broker and the ship's owner. The marine surveyor took care of the rest and even his job was easier than he had expected. To everyone's delight, a survey had just been completed two months prior by the same company Frank had contacted. After studying the previous report, the surveyor was able to expedite his work. The prospective buyer who had wanted to purchase Sea Venture had failed to acquire the necessary financing. Jonas would not have that problem since he had the cash to buy the ship outright.

Because of a lack-luster economic environment, the surveyor had no other pressing work to do. The surveyor was also a diver so he was able to personally inspect the ship's bottom and photograph it with an underwater movie camera. All surveyors and insurance companies like photo evidence to back up their survey reports.

The report reflected that Sea Venture was seaworthy and was valued at nearly nine million dollars. After consulting with Jonas an offer was made through the broker. The offer was seven million five hundred thousand dollars. The ship's owners, a corporation, bulked at the offer and countered. Frank bluffed and held fast to the offer. The owners accepted and that not only pleased the broker and Jonas, but it also pleased Lloyd's of London Insurance who would insure the vessel. The entire process took less than a month.

Throughout the entire process of purchasing Sea Venture, Frank maintained a heightened sense of enthusiasm and excitement. He began each morning on a happy note and maintained that feeling all day long. Naturally, his success in such a high stakes venture was more gratifying than investigating those old routine insurance cases. Still, there was more work to be done before the purchase could be enjoyed.

Frank had to hire a crew and with that objective in mind, he was committed to getting the right people for Jonas. The right people meant more than being qualified; they had to possess personalities that were compatible to Jonas and Gerty. Above all, they had to be team players. Twice during the past two weeks he had visited Sea Venture; once with the broker and once with the surveyor.

Jonas wanted to sail the Caribbean and that meant he would need, at a minimum, a captain, an engineer, a first officer, a chef, a deck hand, and a maid. Yes, owning and operating a mega yacht was not like owning a RV. Frank could only thank God that Sea Venture was not a "super mega yacht" over three hundred feet in length. There had to be some kind of a limit to what Jonas wanted verses what he needed.

Since the broker was in line to earn a healthy commission, he was glad to run some newspaper ads and consult some of his contacts in the industry to identify some applicants.

Frank allowed two weeks to pass before doing any interviews. In his favor was the fact that the economy was in a slump and that could only mean a robust response for the advertised positions. Florida was especially hard hit by unemployment in the yachting industry.

The broker arranged for a room at the marina where Sea Venture was docked. The room was nicely laid out in a South Seas motif. The furniture was bamboo and the pictures on the walls were of ships and islands with palm trees and white deserted beaches. There was both iced tea and lemonade in crystal pitchers. There was also a waiting room where the broker greeted the applicants. He was also standing by to answer any questions that Frank might have. The setting was more than adequate.

Frank figured that the most important position would undoubtedly be the captain's. For this reason, he would conduct those interviews first. Frank walked to one of the room's bay windows and looked outside. The sight of moored yachts was pleasant and inviting. It was a warm breezy day with puffy white clouds drifting across a bright blue sky. The sunshine gently accented the array of yachts; both sail and motorized vessels. All seemed well with the world on such a beautiful morning.

The door opened and the broker stuck his head in. "Are you ready for the first interviewee?"

"Sure, send him in." Frank slipped behind the desk and waited.

A man entered and behind him Frank could see the broker shrugging his shoulders in disappointment. That was all the warning Frank needed. Watching the man approach told Frank that the interview would be a short one.

He was a heavy set man in his fifties. He was wearing a denim shirt and denim slacks and they both were in dire need of ironing. He announced himself by saying "good morning, I'm

Captain Slim. I'm here for the Captain's job." With an outstretched hand he offered Frank a copy of his resume.

His fingers seemed to quiver a little and they were stained yellow from nicotine. Frank's nose turned up slightly when he caught a whiff of whiskey. Captain Slim was a mess. His eyes were bloodshot and conscious of his appearance he explained, "Excuse my looks sir, but last night I was out on the town with some old chums and we managed to tie one on. They are shipping out this morning so this was the only chance we had to celebrate old times. I'm sure you have done the same thing a couple of times yourself."

Captain Slim collapsed with a thud into the cushioned chair in front of the desk. Frank surmised that being out on the town was a normal routine for this "good captain." He was a drunkard if nothing else. Frank had to restrain himself from laughing as Captain Slim rubbed the stubble on his face. He was certainly a spectacle. There was no telling what companions he might want to bring along if he was hired. Adding to his deplorable appearance, he kept trying to smile with chapped lips and teeth that obviously hadn't seen a toothbrush in some time. He had loser written all over him.

Frank smiled with forced and somewhat false sympathy. "Captain Slim, I'm afraid I need some time to go over your resume. This is only a preliminary screening today. I will be in touch with you later by mail when I have had a chance to review your credentials. Should I not select you for a second interview, I will keep your resume on file for six months. I would like to thank you for coming by and introducing yourself." Frank stood and shook hands with Captain Slim and hoped he would never see him again.

Once Captain Slim had left the building the broker came in shaking his head. "I'm sorry about that. I think that guy was part of a cruel joke being played on me by another broker. On a positive note, the next two candidates should shine a lot brighter."

"It sure wasn't what I expected. How many showed up for the Captain's position?"

"There's only two more. I thought there would be a line of applicants a mile long. If either one of the next two are not to your liking, I will advertise again. You may have to use one of the agencies that specialize in yacht crews."

Frank regretted not having gone that route in the first place. Everything having anything to do with yachts added up to big money. It was a good thing that Jonas had won such a big lottery. "Okay, send in the next applicant."

There was a sharp contrast between Captain Slim and the next applicant. He was a clean shaven man in his prime, possibly thirty years of age. He had a short military styled haircut and was slim, yet muscular. Smiling with perfect white teeth he handed Frank his resume. "Good morning sir, I am Captain Andy at your service." He stood there at a modified position of "parade rest, "waiting to be asked to sit.

It was as if a breath of fresh air had blown into the room. The man's demeanor was contagious and that caused Frank to sit up straighter. "Please be seated while I scan your resume."

Frank's smiles grew wider as he read. "This is very interesting Captain Andy." When Frank read Captain Andy's full name, he instantly realized why he chose to be called Captain Andy. His full name was Andrew Peabody Porter.

Frank's voice betrayed more than a casual interest in this applicant. Although, he did have to admit that Captain Andy's credentials were not perfect. "I see that you only earned your Captain's License five months ago."

"Yes sir, becoming a captain ended a three and a half year process and that makes me the new man on the block in a very rewarding profession. I have admired the sea and ships since I was a little boy. The only thing I ever wanted to do more was to become a Green Beret. Now, I can say that I have done that and enjoyed every minute of it. However, I can't be a Green Beret for fifty years, but, I can be a ship's captain for fifty years if I take care of myself. As you can see from my resume, I have served aboard a variety of yachts. I have met the minimum standards and am ready to build on that experience."

"Well Captain Andy, let's go through some questions. Name a major crisis that you handled and tell me how you handled it?"

"Sir, Special Forces soldiers are always encountering some kind of a crisis. One crisis that I can recall was when I was in Afghanistan while conducting a patrol in a mountainous area. We were on a long range reconnaissance patrol trying to locate enemy strongholds when we came under attack at close range. One member of my team was killed and another one wounded when we came under fire. I couldn't tell how large the opposing force was, but, I had to do something to save the rest of the team who were pinned down by automatic fire. The enemy didn't see me circle around above them. My team did what they were trained to do when under close attack; they went on the offensive. Since I had sniper training, I began taking out two enemy machine guns and then they were no match for the rest of my team. I called for a medical evacuation and extraction. The thing that saved us was our training. When a soldier is trained properly he will soldier properly." Captain Andy lifted up his shirt and revealed a scar across his ribcage. "That took forty stitches and at the time I didn't even know I was hit."

Without any noticeable emotion Frank responded to the story. "I am retired from the Army myself. I have seen my share of dead and wounded soldiers so I know where you are coming from. You are right about reacting to a crisis based on your training. By the way, thank you for your service."

Continuing with the interview Frank asked the next question. "What is the most and the least rewarding aspect of being a yacht captain?"

"The most rewarding thing about sea duty would be that you are connecting with the powers of nature. I guess you could say it's having a reverence for the sea. It's all in the challenge and how you respond to it that's gratifying. When it comes to the least rewarding aspect, I would have to say it has to do with the people you meet. There are good and bad people everywhere you go. I have run across some low-life scum in this business. The sea doesn't pick friends or enemies; it treats them all alike and that's fine with me."

Frank busied himself with writing notes on a legal pad. When he finished, he asked his last question. "Tell me about the worst boss you ever had?"

"That's easy. I was working on a freighter as the first officer and the captain was a real jerk. We were unloading in Australia when a dock worker was killed. The captain remarked that he would rather lose three men than one piece of cargo. I'll never work for that man again as long as I live."

"Captain Andy, I want you to have a seat out in the other room while I conduct another interview."

"Yes sir." Andy stood and did an about face and marched out of the room with his head held high.

The broker came back into the room and faced Frank. "Mr. McLaughlin, I want you to take a good look at the last applicant for captain. This is Captain Jack, one of the most experienced captains in the mega yacht industry. You can be as tough as you want during the interview. In other words, don't hold back, not for a second. I would be hard pressed to come up with a better candidate." When he turned around where Frank couldn't see his face, he smiled confidently because Frank had no idea how interesting the last candidate would be.

Frank was already favoring Captain Andy for the captain's position, in spite of his lack of experience. However, he was a bit biased when it came to ex-military personnel. The doubt that was lingering in the back of his mind was that he knew next to nothing about ocean travel and yachting. To this point, the broker's candidates were drifting between great and stinky bad.

"Okay, send in Captain Jack." Frank shuffled some papers around on his desk and turned to a blank page on his legal pad. He heard the door open and close and looked up with a degree of anticipation of seeing this hulk of a man that resembled John Wayne in one of those old war movies when he played the captain of a WW II Navy warship. When he saw Captain Jack, he did a double take; no, a triple take.

Captain Jack was all of five foot six and probably weighed in at about 115 pounds. Captain Jack had red, shoulder length hair and her skin was tanned with a mixture of freckles. Her muscular tone told Frank that she was used to hard work and spending endless days out on the open sea. Her eyes were bright blue, sparkled, and had a way of penetrating through the armor of any man. Frank almost didn't distinguish her words because of her voice. She had a throaty, but feminine, voice that could be seductive in another setting. All these attributes aside, she had a commanding presence; pleasant, yet, professional and business like.

"Good morning Mister McLaughlin. My name is Jacqueline Murphy, however, I'm better known as Captain Jack." She offered her hand to Frank who was hesitating, perhaps too stunned to react.

After a couple of awkward seconds he managed to shake his head slightly as if he was suddenly being rousted out of a daydream. Standing up, he reached across the desk and shook Captain Jack's hand. Her grip was firm in spite of her hand being small enough to become lost in Frank's hand.

"With a name like Murphy, you must be Irish?" He was trying to recover from a slight moment of embarrassment.

"Yes, I am Irish. The name Murphy means sea-battler. In my case, it couldn't fit any better. Here's my resume." She handed it across the desk and remained standing.

Frank was still trying to recover from being surprised as he started to sit down. He caught himself and stood a little straighter. "Please, have a seat. Allow me to take a minute to scan your resume."

"Please, take your time Mister McLaughlin. My time is all yours."

Frank read through her resume twice before speaking again. "I see you have a Master's Degree in history from the University of Florida. Becoming a ship's captain is quite a vocational and academic jump isn't it?"

"I minored in marine biology and I did my dissertation for history on female pirates of the Caribbean. Even when I was a little girl I dreamed of living in the Caribbean. My father was a tugboat captain so I was exposed to the wonders of ocean going ships at an early age. My dad was my hero."

She had a backpack by her side and reached into it and retrieved a stack of journals. "Here's a record of my experience. Captains have to keep a record of their service aboard ships. There is twenty-one years' worth of my life documented on these pages. Most of it is boring, but all of it is insightful when it comes to knowing me." She slid the stack across the desk to Frank.

He glanced at the stack of journals and then back at her resume. Everything was overwhelming on more than one level. Looking over at her he knew he couldn't ask the question that was bouncing around in the back of his head, the one about age. He guessed that she was somewhere in her mid-forties. She was very attractive in a rugged way. Her fitness portrayed a peasant quality and that was an appealing quality. After thumbing through a few pages, he closed one of the journals because he wasn't sure what to look for.

Frank was looking forward to interviewing Captain Jack and promised himself that he would give her a good hearing, but, he had trouble focusing on a proper line of questions. The unexpected things life throws at a man have a way of taking their toll on a man's concentration. After a little shifting in his chair he finally found his list of interview questions.

Trying to project an official presence was not that easy. His voice faded and became gentle, too much so for a proper interview. However, he managed to recover before his emotional side betrayed a more than casual interest in Captain Jack. Finally, he was able to view her, not as an interesting woman, but as an applicant for a position. All those years in the Army began to filter through. He was able to filter out biased traces of such things as gender and age. Like in the military, he would view Captain Jack as if she was nothing more or less than a soldier wearing a green uniform. At last, he was able to set aside any distracting thoughts and focus on the task of interviewing.

"Tell me about a major crisis you encountered and how you handled it?"

"Well, the trick to handling any crisis is to manage it so that you weather it with the least amount of harm or destruction. Staying calm is not always easy, especially when the crisis is a matter of life and death. However, calmness goes a long way when working through a crisis. You always have to think clearly and objectively.

"I was sailing off the coast of the Dominican Republic on my sailboat; a forty foot Island Packet. I was alone and that meant I was pretty busy. I came across a fishing boat that had capsized. The crew, six in all, was clinging to anything they could get a grip on and it would only be a matter of time before they began clinging to each other in a desperate, last-ditch effort to survive. Their boat was about to go under.

"Panic is never a pretty sight. I wasn't about to dive in to save any of them because I didn't want to be added to the list of casualties. I circled my boat while keeping an eye on their position. I grabbed every spare line I had and secured them to my cleats and tied a loop to each end with a bowline knot. I pulled my main sail down to reduce my speed and when I passed by those poor souls, I tossed all my lines to them. I got them all in one pass while sailing only under my jib. I saved them all." Her tone did not reveal any hint of pride. She simply was not one to brag, even during an interview where she had to sell herself.

Frank simply said, "I bet you made a few friends that day."

"Anytime I have a hankering for a free locker of fresh fish, I know where to go."

Frank decided to add a leading follow-on question to dig a little deeper. "What about some minor crisis where you lost your cool a bit?"

"I guess you're looking for something a bit more personal. Well, I wasn't always calm, cool, and collected. About twenty-five years ago, I had a disagreement with my now ex-husband. I never should have married that jerk. A judge ended up ordering me to take an anger management class."

Frank knew he had hit a raw nerve and his curiosity begged to be satisfied. "It must have been a real bad disagreement."

She knew she was being baited, but, what the hell. "My ex-husband told me to wash his car while he sucked down a beer with one of his pals. The jerk admonished me, in front of his buddy, by telling me that I didn't get the windshield clean enough. He pointed to a couple of smudges on it. I picked up a brick and broke out his precious windshield. Then I asked him if he could still see any smudges on it. The whole thing was not the shiniest moment in my life. Hey, I was only twenty-two; a young gal on 'spring break' from college."

Breaking out in laughter, Frank added his personal commentary. "We all have had times in our life when our star didn't shine very brightly."

Once he had recovered from his laughter, Frank fired off his next question. "Have you ever had any difficulty working for a yacht owner?"

"When I was a new captain, I got off to a rocky start with one yacht owner. In fact, it was my first job as a captain and it was the yacht owner's first yacht. We were both testing the water of our relationship. When I realized that we weren't connecting, I asked for a meeting. He turned out to be a decent guy and now I use him as a reference. It was all a matter of communication."

"Tell me about the worst boss you ever had."

"I don't like lumping bosses into categories of good and bad. I try to learn something from each one and take it with me. I chalk it up to experience and I have had a good many years of it."

Frank commented, "I'm sure you have learned a lot."

She smiled back at him and said, "Learning and understanding are not always the same thing. When I was younger, I learned a lot about the sea. Now that I'm older, I actually understand the sea, and that makes me a great captain."

"I can see that being out at sea is different from being on a road trip." Frank meant to acknowledge her experience.

Captain Jack was not short on responding. "When you are out on the ocean, hundreds of miles from land, you have to be on top of your game. The crew has to be doing their jobs and paying attention. If you fail, people can get hurt, even die. Dead is forever. The bottom line is: failure is not an option. I enjoy what I do because I am a professional."

"You are also a leader and I like that. Things can get pretty ugly during a crisis if a person is not careful and ready to act. I think you set a good example and I am comfortable with that. According to my broker, you have a solid reputation." Frank was sincere.

"I would like to thank you for your confidence in me, Mr. McLaughlin. You seem to be a seasoned person; a veteran of life. Should you select me, I won't let you down."

Frank couldn't end the interview in the midst of complements so he managed to ask one final question. "In one sentence, please tell me why I should hire you for the captain's position?"

"I'm thorough, polite, loyal, and can sail Sea Venture anywhere in the world."

"Captain Jack, welcome aboard, you are now the new captain of the Sea Venture." Instantly, Frank knew he had made the right selection.

"Thank you Mr. McLaughlin. I won't disappoint you. I have one request that I would like to make at this point."

"You can call me Frank. We will be working too closely to be formal. When we are in mixed company we can use titles. Don't worry; you will be in charge of the ship. I may ask a lot of questions because I want to learn about the sea and sailing. I'll always be picking your brain. Now, what's your request?"

"There's a young man sitting in the other room who also applied for the position. We talked at length while waiting to be interviewed. I would like you to offer him the first officer position. He is learning and I can see that he has a great deal of potential. It isn't easy to break into this profession and I would like to see him get off on the right foot. He reminds me of myself when I was getting started."

Frank didn't hesitate. "I think that's a good idea. No, I think hiring Andy Porter is a great idea. While we are on the subject of hiring, I would like you to help me select all the crew." He slid the list of positions across the table so Captain Jack could have a look.

After glancing over the list she made a recommendation. "Speaking from experience, I would like to add another position to the list. I think you should also hire a purser. A purser will make your administrative life a lot easier. When traveling at sea a purser pays all the bills; fuel, docking fees, parts, materials, and even food. During extended stays at home port, you can get by without a purser. However, at sea and jumping from one port-of-call to another, a purser is indispensable. I know of two, both retired accountants that will do the job for very reasonable rates. They like to travel in luxury in the Caribbean and either one of them will be good company for your owner."

Frank didn't hesitate to grant her request. "Go ahead and make your calls, Captain, and see if you can set up interviews for this afternoon, if possible. My plan is to have you get the crew in place and bring Sea Venture to New Orleans as soon as possible."

Captain Jack was ready to take charge. However, there was one question that had not been discussed. "By the way, Frank, how much does this job pay?

"How does room and board and $300 a day sound?" He was holding his breath because he knew that experienced captains can earn much more than he was offering.

"It's a deal." She extended her hand to shake the deal as sealed.

After shaking her hand, Frank sat on the corner of the desk in the most unimposing manner he could manufacture and spoke to her. "May I ask you a personal question?"

She smiled and then said, "You can ask, but that doesn't mean I will answer."

"Don't worry Jack, I'm not going to be intrusively intimate. I only have a casual curiosity that I want to satisfy. Is there some lucky guy out there that's going to miss you while you're out at sea?"

She gave a light-hearted laugh and answered. "I'm not going to give you a simple answer of yes or no. I'm going to give you a simple explanation of where I am in my life. You see, I call all the oceans of the world my home. In my mind that's not just a metaphor, it's a reality for me. Continuing in the same vain, the Caribbean is my back yard. This translates into me not being married to or beholding to any man in the flesh. At the moment, sailing is my only suitor. Now, what lucky woman is there lurking in the shadows of your life?"

Frank had expected her response to be natural and off the cuff so he was ready to answer quickly and directly. "In spite of being a hopeful romantic, I have a rather lackluster resume when it comes to women. Actually, and unfortunately, I have loved and lost more times than I think I deserved. At this point in my life I am too shy; no, too scared to get involved with anyone. I'm not damaged, just somewhat scarred when it comes to relationships. Like you, I'm courting my profession."

She cleared her throat before continuing in this rather impromptu dialog. "Since you are new to the yachting world, I have to ask the obvious question. Exactly what is your profession?"

"I'm a private investigator and currently working for the owner of Sea Venture, Jonas Jackson."

"I don't know if it is relevant or not, but I see a crude correlation here. I too am an investigator. That's what historians do, they investigate the past. I seek facts about events and people that were around centuries ago."

Frank scratched the back of his head and appeared a bit bewildered. "It must be tough for you to find eye-witnesses to interview."

"I tend to find more clues than solutions. When I am able to solve or explain historical acts I get really excited. It really is rewarding on more than one level."

Frank stood up to let Jack know that he was finished with his inquiry. "Perhaps, when we find the time, we can compare notes and strategies."

"I would like that, Frank. Maybe we can learn something from each other."

Chapter 10

Frank reached his home in Dallas at well past midnight. Due to the late hour there was no use in rousting either Jonas or Gerty from their sleep. Besides, he was much too travel-weary to give them a proper briefing on his trip. Contrary to his decision, there was little doubt they would have gladly gotten up to hear about his progress.

At least one of them, anticipating his late arrival, had left the porch light on as well as a table lamp in the hallway. There would be plenty of time to brief them in the morning when everyone's mind was fresh.

In spite of his travel exhaustion, he found himself in a familiar state of mind where old habits were hard to break. His eyes wandered to the now bare spot on the floor at the end of the kitchen counter where he had always placed Leo's food and water bowls. There was no telling how long he would miss and grieve over his old furry pal. On a deeper level, he hoped he would never allow his memory to drift far from those fond remembrances of his late furry friend. Remembrance was a suitable tribute to any friend that had unexpectedly passed from his earthly presence. Losing a pet was certainly the same as losing a family member.

In his weariness, he couldn't help but think of all those sleepless nights he had endured in Vietnam when that much needed sleep finally arrived as a blessing; a well-earned reward. Sleep had a way of taking him to a place where he was truly free and he embraced that moment whenever he had the chance. Once his head hit the pillow he quickly drifted into a deep, dreamless sleep. Tonight, a sound, restful sleep was reward enough for the tasks he had completed.

Following hours of restful slumber, the night finally lost its hold on him. Although, it was earlier than he preferred, the knock that came on his bedroom door cut through the stillness like a muffled explosion, if it was possible to lump the two sounds into one. At any rate, the sound helped him to shake off some of his grogginess. Squinting at his pre-dawn surroundings, he was able to make out the outline of the door. The pale stream of light that beamed through the blinds announced the beginning of a new day. However, it seemed to be arriving much earlier than it should have.

He stiffened his body under the sheet, stretching and yawning at the same time. "Okay, I'm awake. I'll get up; just give me a minute or two." He tried not to sound irritated.

It wasn't long before the fog of sleep began to vanish. Like most men, he wished he could have vividly dreamed of, or even symbolically dreamed of, a sound reason for being left alive to greet yet another day. That's a war weary soldier's dream. Sadly, the details of such a dream could seldom be recalled, unless they had been inspired by God. When this latter instance occurred, a silent prayer of thanks was always in order. It was one of life's ironies. Perhaps it was better not to dream at all if a person couldn't have one filled with details that he or she could fully recall the next day.

"I'm sorry I woke you so early. I'm just antsy to hear how your trip went." Jonas' voice was much too crispy and perky for such an early hour.

"Jonas, have Gerty put on a pot of coffee while I jump in and out of the shower." Frank was stalling for time to gather his thoughts.

Encouraged over knowing that Frank was awake, Jonas announced. "We are already on our third cup of coffee."

Frank groaned. "Yes, I'm back and I have loads of things to brief you on." He tried to speak in a monotone because he didn't want to ruffle any anxious feathers by sounding antagonized over being rushed. At least Gerty was being quiet. "Just give me twenty minutes or so to get myself together. I'll hurry as fast as I can." He promised in spite of knowing that Jonas would probably keep prodding until he came out of his bedroom spitting facts and details.

Sitting up on the edge of the bed, he cast a lazy eye on his briefcase that was resting on a chair across the room and in the corner. He almost stumbled as he stepped over the pile of dirty clothing he had tossed on the floor when he had hastily undressed. After grabbing a bathrobe from the closet he headed into the bathroom where he would make good on his promise to quickly get ready.

The man staring back at him in the mirror was tousled and weary. He was used to traveling, having done so much of it over the years. However, this trip had somehow managed to wear him out. Seeing the proof in the mirror only reminded him that way too many years had slipped away. The stubble on his face was a mixture of brown and grey. His temples were nearly white. In a few more years, to his dismay, he would acquire that stately grandfatherly appearance. The years were catching up to him and that meant he wasn't that far behind Jonas when it came to age. The passing of years was not a state of mind; it was a reality that was going to be hard to deal with. Staying fit and trim had allowed him to live a robust lifestyle and, in short order, age would slow that process down until the highlights of his adventures dwindled away; lost to old journals and forgotten diaries.

With showering and shaving out of the way, he found himself once again sitting on the edge of his bed. This time he was doing his best to pull on a sock that was not cooperating. Adding to his frustration, another anxious knock came to the door. To his own amusement, he smiled teasingly and ignored the noise. Jonas was paying him good money, but this was ridiculous. A few more minutes wasn't going to kill anyone.

When he was fully dressed, he opened the door. Jonas and Gerty were standing there grinning devilishly. Their antagonizing demeanor had been orchestrated in fun. Sometimes they were like kids playing jokes on their friends and Frank did find that somewhat amusing.

"You two are something else," Frank laughed good-heartedly. "You guys almost had me going there, and yes, I am ready to give you a report."

The three of them gravitated to the kitchen table where Frank arranged his notes while Gerty poured coffee before taking a seat. After clearing his throat, Frank smiled warmly at his two friends. There certainly was an immediate surge of restless anticipation among the trio.

Frank's voice was laced with optimism as he began speaking. "Things are moving along faster than anticipated. The entire crew has been hired and at this very moment they are making ready Sea Venture for passage to New Orleans."

Jonas wore a pleased look on his face as he interrupted Frank. "Please, tell us all about the crew you hired. When in the Navy, I sailed with the best and worst of crews. The reason I want to know all about them is that we will all be working in close quarters. You see, a crew is a lot like a family and that family has to get along. All of us have buttons that don't need to be pushed. I think you get my point."

Frank knew the importance of teamwork because of his military background. "I feel confident that you will find my selections satisfactory. As with all groups, there will be some peculiarities." Frank paused for a reaction, but neither Jonas nor Gerty displayed any hint of concern or alarm. Even homeless people out on the streets had to get along in order to make it from day to day. They sat there patiently, willing to wait and see what the peculiarities were and if they presented any problems.

With the ball clearly in his court, Frank continued with his report. "First and foremost, I have to say, without any reservation, that the one I picked to be the captain is first class. Her name is Captain Jack."

Jonas was quick to react. "You mean you hired a woman who calls herself Jack?" Clearly, he put the most emphasis on the word 'woman.'

Frank met Jonas' challenge with equal, if not more, force. "You bet I did and for good cause. Her full name is Jacqueline Murphy. Jack is only an affectionate nickname among her comrades. She has been a yacht captain for over twenty years. She is level-headed, experienced, confident, and comes from an Irish background. A lot of male captains would like to have her credentials."

Gerty cast a steamy glare at Jonas. "Hey, you aren't going to come off like some male chauvinist pig, are you? Who says a woman can't perform in a man's world. Even men do well in a woman's world. There are male flight attendants and male nurses. Times have changed, Jonas."

Jonas was eager to recover from his archaic and chauvinistic stance. Gerty was his long-standing friend and he wasn't about to jeopardize that tried and tested relationship. "No, I know women can do tough jobs, especially in this technical world we now live in. Sometimes, I'm a bit old-fashioned. I just hope this Captain Jack isn't bossy, though."

"Believe me, Jonas, she will fit in nicely. On character alone, I give her an A plus. Look at it this way; she's not only a woman of integrity; she's a captain of integrity. Trust me; I'm a good judge of character." Frank hoped he had put Jonas' concerns to rest.

"Okay, you made your point so you can keep going." Jonas knew he was entering a new world; one he wasn't used to.

"In fact, Captain Jack helped me select the rest of the crew and she was instrumental in weeding out the ones that had the potential for trouble. I knew we were a good team when she helped me select the first officer. The man's name is Andrew Peabody Porter and he is best known as Andy. Andy is younger than Captain Jack and he is an ex-military man. Together, we convinced Andy to take the first officer position so he could build on his experience. Andy is the macho element you were looking for on the crew and he's a strong, clean-cut man." Frank was doing his best to settle the male/female issue.

Unfortunately, Jonas still had a hint of doubt lingering in the back of his mind. Out of a nervous reaction, he scratched the back of his head before speaking. "I guess if this gal doesn't work out, we can switch them around. I like having a backup when it comes to running a ship. In the Navy, we always had the executive officer on board."

Frank was eager to move on to his other selections. Only time and observation would win Jonas over on the issue of having a female captain. In the corporate world, Jonas' out of vogue ideas concerning women would earn him an affirmative action law suit.

There are still isolated incidents of bias in the military and this can ruin a commander's career in spite of his courage and loyalty. Yes, times have changed and will continue to change. Most people like to call this progress.

Frank switched to another page of notes and when he found his place, he pressed on. "Our engineer is a middle-aged man of Italian descent. He once served as an engineer on a destroyer in the British Navy. His name is Mateo Medina. We will call him Matt since that is the English translation of Mateo. Two of his references gave me the same line; if Matt can't fix it, it can't be fixed."

Gerty asked, "How well does he speak English?"

"He speaks English as well as you and me. Although, I have to admit that he does have a slight British accent. Like I said, he served in the British Navy." Frank wondered if Gerty was really listening or just going through the motions.

Actually, she was listening and proved it by adding something to the conversation. "He was in Her Majesty's Service; HMS. I learned that from watching James Bond movies." Since she had no actual experience as a world traveler, she had to rely on movies as a point of reference.

"Alright, keep going Frank." Fearing he would forget some important detail about the crew, Jonas was taking notes. He tried twirling his pen with his fingers and dropped the pen more times than he wanted. Boys, even old ones, liked fiddling around with their hands.

"The next position I filled is equally important to all of us. I'm talking about the chef. Just for you, Jonas, I picked one from Louisiana; New Orleans. Her name is Colette Pinsonault. She's fluent in both French and English. When living in France, she studied food preparation from the best master chefs the country had to offer. However, she was born and raised in Louisiana. You can take the girl out of Cajun country, but you can't take the Cajun out of the girl. I'm throwing in that cliché for the hell of it. As a teenager, she learned to cook soul food and good old-fashioned country food. Additionally, Cajun food is another of her specialties. About five years ago, she tired of cooking in high-end hotels and restaurants. That's when she began cooking on yachts and ocean liners. She not only loves cooking, she also loves interacting in easy-flowing social environments. She is the most peculiar element among the ones I hired." Frank paused to allow his remarks to sink in.

Jonas put his pen down and started rubbing his chin. "I wondered when things would get more peculiar than women in men's jobs."

"Well, I can't explain it in any other terms than this. Colette is a part time Catholic and a full time practitioner of Voodoo. She's a middle-aged black woman with restrained savvy."

Frank's comment did little to excite Jonas. "In New Orleans, Voodoo is not all that peculiar. I don't have a great deal of knowledge and understanding of Voodoo, but, I do know some things. Hell, a couple of times I actually got to attend some Voodoo rituals out in the bayous. They were colorful and very high-energy. What can I say; blacks have rhythm and love a party. The important thing here for me is that she knows how to cook the kinds of food that I like. A bad cook can ruin a trip and put everyone in a bad mood. Yes, I like the idea of having a French cook from my home town; especially when that person is a female. You can bet that I have known a few women just like her."

Frank saw that Gerty was displaying a puzzled look on her face. Perhaps the notion of Voodoo was too overwhelming for her. In any sector of society there are mixed reviews over such odd phenomenon as Voodoo. Surely, Gerty was doing her best to process and accept what she was hearing.

Gerty finally threw in her two cents worth on the selection for chef. "It looks to me like Colette is an intriguing woman with impeccable credentials. I'm glad you picked her. I can't wait to eat all these different kinds of cuisines. Sure sounds like she can come up with some very exotic sauces. As far as Voodoo is concerned, I would like to hear what she has to say about it. That's a topic I always wanted to look into. I guess if this was the 1960's everyone would want to look into it. Those must have been some great times with all the hippies and flower children. All that New Age stuff is fascinating to me."

When Frank heard Gerty's response he was able to discount any problems or objections from her. While putting a checkmark next to Colette's name and shuffling his papers, he added a comment. "I think Voodoo has been around for a lot longer than the 1960's." He didn't give her time to respond.

"Next, I hired a maid just to make life easier for all of us. Her name is Georgia Wallis. She's taking a year off from college and hopes to see some of the Caribbean on someone else's dollar. This will be her third job this year as a maid on a yacht. The others were short trips and she enjoyed them immensely. I called the two yacht owners on her resume and they said she was a bundle of energy with a flair for neatness. She's my definition of what a maid should be."

"I would say you have done your homework and made some good selections. Are there any more?" Jonas started to lay down his pen.

"Yes, there's two more. I hired a deckhand by the name of Roy Kirkpatrick. I figure we can keep him busy swabbing the decks and polishing whatever needs it. He's kind of a Jack of all trades, but mostly he's a merchant marine guy. Roy is a quiet reserved guy and when I checked his references they said he was a good hand and never complained."

Jonas agreed. "There is always something that needs to be done on a ship. I sure did my share of swabbing, polishing, and painting when I was in the Navy. I sure don't want to turn my mega yacht into a bucket of rust."

Eager to wrap up his report, Frank drew in a deep breath like a runner heading for the finish line. "Lastly, I decided to hire a purser. His name is Thomas Ruskin and he is a retired accountant. He likes being called Tommy. His wife passed away five years ago after they retired and moved to Florida. He has no immediate family and he has found that yachting people are the next best thing to being part of an extended family. This is his fourth year of being a purser on mega yachts. His rates are low and he enjoys traveling and hobnobbing with yacht owners and crews. I contacted two of his references and they said he was a meticulous record keeper who kept the bills paid. I did a conference call with him and your accountant and they worked out all the details and set the ground rules for financing your yachting trips."

Jonas was finally able to put his pen down and relax. "Frank, you did a good job. I knew all along that you would handle things right. I can't wait to meet the crew. With all these characters and females, I don't know if I'm going to end up with a circus or a Broadway show. That's the way it was in the Navy, too. This guy Tommy and I have something in common when it comes to losing a family."

Strangely, Jonas' words struck an emotional chord in Frank. Frank's parents had died when he was young, he had lost fellow soldiers in war, he had lost the love of several women due to circumstances he could not control, and he had been as lonely as his two new friends when they were homeless. His thoughts were sending an unexpected surge of longing through his bones. Suddenly, he saw the long-suppressed images from an old nightmare that used to awaken him on countless lonely nights. His loses had always been final; never to return. Like he had done so many times before, he shook his head until all the haunting images evaporated into thin air. His eyes blinked uncontrollably for a few brief seconds, and then he was back to the present. Yes, he too had a need for an extended family of sorts; even if they were odd and unconventional.

Thinking the meeting was over; Gerty collected the coffee cups and headed to the sink to wash them. Jonas, on the other hand, remained in his chair.

Frank shifted his weight and was about to stand when Jonas reached over and placed a hand over Frank's arm. "Please, I have another task for you." He slid a piece of paper across the table to Frank. He was whispering and that could only mean one thing; their conversation was for their ears only.

Reluctantly, and with a suspicious eye, Frank studied the slip of paper. He also sensed an atypical intensity in Jonas' tone. This task was going to be significant; a far cry from something trivial or mundane like some of the other tasks Jonas had given him.

"There's a name on this paper that I want checked out. This man may be living in New York City and he is about my age. I met him briefly a long time ago when I was in the Navy. It means a lot to me to be able to talk to him so I will need a phone number.

"I'll see what I can do." Frank decided not to press for any additional information, especially with Gerty milling about barely outside of hearing range. On a gut level something was sounding an alarm. Frank's mind was ratcheting toward the probability that the name on the piece of paper was a key to the past and to whatever was haunting Jonas.

Acknowledging the importance of the task, Frank did not add the slip of paper to his other paperwork. Instead, he tucked it neatly away in his wallet. "How soon do you want this taken care of?"

"If you could do this in the next day or so, I would be grateful."

"I'll start on it today unless you have something else planned."

"Thank you, Frank. I really do appreciate your patience with me. I know I'm a troubling old man and I'm leaning hard on you. Once my life levels out, I'll make it up to you. I'm telling you this as a friend and not as someone paying you to do a job."

Frank smiled without further comment. Some things just don't need to be spoken out loud to be understood. When it comes to learning and understanding no one can exclude the passing of time. He thought about the time that had passed from when he first noticed Jonas and Gerty, a homeless couple, walking along the street trying to figure out where their next meal would come from, not to mention that they didn't have a clue about their future. Weeks had glided by since then without any revealing of factual evidence pointing to what was driving Jonas. However, in time, the depth and meaning behind Jonas' intent would surface. That was Frank's prediction after observing Jonas closely. Frank knew how to recognize old demons and he knew that some were tugging at Jonas' soul. In the meantime, Frank would continue to make mental notes and assess his findings.

Fortunately, Frank was staying busy and that allowed time to pass quickly. Not having to watch the clock was liberating.

Chapter 11

Frank did his best to plan, according to everyone's concerns, the trip from Dallas to New Orleans. He had rented a non-descript van since no one felt comfortable with traveling by commercial airline. Owing to the impending Caribbean cruise, the van was on a one-way trip to New Orleans. Once the van was unloaded at the dock where Sea Venture had been birthed since yesterday afternoon, it would be picked up by the rental agency. Frank wondered if there were any statistics on how many millionaires preferred cross country travel via a rental van. Escaping the faster pace and congestion of urban crowds and public transportation was comforting, especially for Jonas and Gerty.

Since Frank was the only one among them with a driver's license there was no chance of him napping or getting much of a break during the trip. Things could have been worse, though. As long as the journey was from Dallas to New Orleans, it wasn't as bad as driving from San Antonio to El Paso. The main difference was that East Texas and Louisiana had trees and green foliage to look at as opposed to the monotony of open desert and hypnotic long stretches of seemingly endless highway. He was also thankful for the shaded places to stop and stretch and grab a cup of java.

Still, the scenery passed by in a blur most of the time. They detoured frequently, doing their best to stay on major roads and interstate highways while appreciating diversity of scenery. It was a welcome sight for Frank as they approached Lafayette after leaving Alexandria on I-49. Shortly, they would pick up I-10 to Baton Rouge, the Louisiana state capital. The sky was growing dark and they could feel the humidity climbing in the air. A mist was beginning to dampen the windshield to a point where Frank had to turn the wipers on slow in order to see.

Their blank faces stared out at the taller buildings as they breezed along into the city limits of the capital. Frank put the radio on a local station in time to pick up a weather report. The dreary damp weather that was entering the area had made its way along the gulf coast from Houston. That was the usual pattern for Southern Louisiana this time of the year. The announcer gave the forecast for the rest of the day and it called for scattered and often severe thunderstorms.

The first thought that entered Frank's mind was that the weather would make the visit to the cemetery a very disheartening and dismal affair. Even if the weather had been clear and bright, he knew that the cemetery visit would be extremely stressful for Jonas.

Jonas was a poor soul who was still in morning for the loss of his family, and by his own word, he was guilt-ridden. At a minimum, Jonas would have to render a few heart-felt and apologetic words to give a proper sendoff to his wife and son. He would also have to search his heart for some semblance of closure. Tasks like this were never easy for anyone. Total closure was never truly possible when it came to the loss of a loved one; not even when the loss was a pet.

As predicted, the mist graduated to a steady rain as darker, heavier clouds began to move in. Frank was glad he had purchased raincoats and umbrellas for each of them. Adjusting to the quickly changing weather, Frank turned the wipers to a faster setting and switched on the defroster to attack the milky film that was forming across the windshield. Such was their experience of the trip, thus far.

Like all his duties, Frank was taking the trip seriously. He dropped his speed by ten miles per hour because of the changing road conditions. There was no use risking an accident because prolonging the trip was no big deal. Aiming high in steering was a trick he had learned as a young man when he started venturing into big city driving. He took a deep breath and focused on keeping his mind clear, his body poised and alert. His mind was always assessing all activity in the distance to anticipate traffic changes that could impact his driving.

The road surface glistened when the van's headlight beams struck the rain drenched pavement. The resulting glare was a constant reminder of possible danger. He slowed in time to avoid a pickup that was beginning to fishtail to his front. The stone-grey clouds continued to unload their burden. The darkening sky to the south and southeast warned that the thunderstorms could suddenly become severe. Veins of lightning were flashing across an ominous sky.

When Frank finally wheeled into the entrance of Saint Louis Cemetery #1, he braked to a stop. It was an eerie feeling that overtook the three of them. The forty-two cemeteries of New Orleans were known as "The Cities of the Dead" because the tombs, crypts, and vaults created street-like patterns. The rusty gate at the entrance gave the place a mysterious and gloomy appearance; more like a warning than a welcome. He also recalled how he had to pay a bribe because a local ordinance only allowed multiple family members to be buried after waiting two years between burials of each member. He also remembered the stern warnings from cemetery officials that there were frequent muggings of tourists at the cemeteries. The thunderstorms would hopefully keep criminals away on this particular day.

He turned on the inside dome light to study his hand written directions. Once he got his bearings, he was ready to probe the cemetery's confines. Grey puddles of water were everywhere and the maze of above ground graves added to the bleakness.

There was nothing but silence in the van as Frank eased it over to one side. The rain began to come down in sheets and that caused their nervous skin to crawl with cold shivers. Frank imagined that the hair of his entire body was standing up. They were certainly receiving an eerie welcome to this particular city of the dead. No one seemed to know what to say so they all said nothing. Surely, Jonas was struggling with more difficulty to maintain his composure.

As they began wiggling into their raincoats, Jonas finally broke the silence. "You guys don't have to get out. Really, there isn't anything you can do here. This is a moment that I have to deal with."

"I'm sorry, Jonas. But friends don't step aside that easily." Gerty was not about to let her friend walk out alone in a cemetery on a dark stormy afternoon. The strength of her loyalty was unshaken by the gloomy surroundings and circumstances.

"That goes for me, too." Frank added his support. "Remember, we are a team. Also, there could be a mugger or two out there and there is strength in numbers."

Thus, it was settled. Friends don't abandon their friends, not even in the midst of a grim moment in the middle of a gloomy storm. Off they went, sloshing their way along into the maze of tombs. Frank led the way, umbrella in hand. Gerty held tight to Jonas' arm as they followed along, umbrellas overlapping overhead.

When they entered the darkness of the crypt, Frank removed a flashlight from the pocket of his raincoat. He quickly searched the room until the beam of light rested on the names of Jonas' wife and son.

Shocked and numbed by the sight, Jonas felt his legs go weak. Frank and Gerty held their friend upright until he could recover well enough to stand on his own. They both instinctively put their arms around Jonas to lend him some degree of comfort, rather than support.

Shadows from the flashlight crept across Jonas' face. He reached over and shoved the instrument away. "Please, take the light and wait for me at the door. I have some private things to say to my family. I have to do this alone. I've been waiting a long time for this. Trust me; my faith in God has prepared me for this moment."

"We understand, Jonas. Some words are only for the ears of loved ones and God; no one else. You can take all the time you need." Frank sensed the tears that he knew were streaming down Jonas' face. It was a powerful moment for many reasons. Gerty didn't say a word as she turned and accompanied Frank to the dim outside light at the door.

Frank knew that the time that had passed since Hurricane Katrina was of little consequence to the grief that Jonas was experiencing. There was no way to soften the moment. That's right, there just wasn't any way to lessen or soften the pain attached to such monumental mistakes; mistakes that were irreversibly entrenched in time. Even ministers of religion can't counsel away grief; they can only console and lend support. Some things are just what they are, plain and simple. This was a time where praying to a merciful God was appropriate and Frank was confident that Jonas would do just that.

Frank and Gerty stood there cuddling to stay warm out of the reach of the rain and wind. The rain thrashed, without mercy, the marble and granite crypts and tombs. The noise of the rain was all that could be heard. Their senses were nearly useless as they stood there. Thirty minutes must have passed before Jonas appeared. The redness in his eyes told Frank and Gerty that there was no use in asking Jonas how he felt. Emotional pain was difficult to disguise.

Hopefully, the impact of the cemetery visit had not dampened Jonas spirits to such an extent that he couldn't continue on with some capacity to enjoy his new ship and home; Sea Venture. He would soon be tested again, albeit to a lesser degree, when he met the crew. Even Jonas had to know the cemetery visit had to be set aside in order to move forward. Naturally, some of life's chapters are difficult to close out without a degree of reflection.

There was also his out of vogue ideals about females in key roles that were traditionally given to men. Could he face having a female run his most-prized possession; Sea Venture? His life was just one highly charged emotion after another.

The storm's intensity was coming in waves and it would be several hours before it moved on. Frank pressed on through the foul weather, dodging potholes with care. As they closed in on the Port of New Orleans, Jonas began rummaging through his luggage. Alerted by looking through the rear view mirror, Frank became curious about what Jonas was searching for. More often than not, Jonas had a way of astonishing him. One case in point was when Jonas insisted on having a book on astrology. Frank had little doubt that Jonas had done some shopping in his absence. Jonas was full of surprises and Frank knew Jonas was about to show off like a kid who had been saving his allowance for something special.

Frank pulled the van to a stop in front of the loading ramp for Sea Venture. Jonas spoke with heightened excitement, "You two go on up. I have something to do before I come aboard."

The rain slowed to a temporary drizzle. Gerty and Frank seized the opportunity to take care of a small chore. A stiff breeze blew Gerty's hair into a tangled mess as she stacked her luggage under the ramp out of the rain. Frank did likewise while Jonas remained inside the van with a large box on the seat next to him. Frank's curiosity got the best of him as he stopped and stared at Jonas. A kindly smile crept across Frank's face as he realized what Jonas was up to. Not worrying about getting wet in the rain, Jonas was changing clothes before going aboard and meeting the crew.

When he finally exited the van, Jonas stopped, looked about, and then sniffed the air as if to test it. His actions were not all that revealing; it was what he was wearing that made a statement. He was decked out in a white uniform, no doubt of Navy origin. Placed squarely on his head was a white, black-billed dress hat adorned with gold trim and markings. Yes, without question, Jonas was dressed much like a Navy admiral. Frank concluded that Jonas was making a visual statement that he was of a higher status than any female ship captain.

Jonas strutted up the gangway with Gerty in tow. When they reached the top, he stepped boldly in front of Gerty, and speaking with proper protocol and tone, he addressed the person he assumed was Captain Jack. "May I have permission to come aboard, Captain?" He even rendered a somewhat lackluster salute.

Coming up behind Gerty was Frank, grinning ear to ear. He would also play the game in spite of knowing that Jonas, being the ship's owner, did not have to be so formal. No one was more aware than Frank that tradition was important in the military. It was even important among strangers and civilians when wanting to board another's ship. Sailors at yacht clubs often hold fast to old customs and traditions and that was truly a nice thing in this day of common rudeness and disrespect. With customs and traditions as they were, Frank hoped that Jonas was not going to insist on everyone speaking and acting with all the pomp and ceremony attributed to flag-grade officers.

Jack did not hesitate when she gave the proper response and greeting. "Please, welcome aboard Sea Venture. I am Captain Jack at your service, sir." She was glad that Frank had warned her that the ship's owner, Jonas Jackson, had been in the Navy. She was also aware that military officers, who met formally for the first time, did so with the highest degree of respect and correctness. A formal greeting was a great way to begin a proper relationship. She gave a snappy salute and then shook Jonas' hand.

Jack continued, "Sir, I will assemble the crew in the galley in ten minutes so you can meet them. After we meet, I will be glad to give you a tour of your ship."

Jonas welled with an inward sense of pride. However, he knew the formality would be temporary. On another level, he was impressed with his captain's adherence to protocol and tradition.

Jonas glanced over at Gerty who was wearing a puzzled expression on her face. Soon, he would have to put her at ease, just not quite yet.

Jack wasted no time ensuring the luggage was safely aboard before assembling the crew in the galley. One of her most admirable traits was that she was extremely efficient and the ship's flawless operations would reflect her efforts. The trip from Miami to New Orleans gave her ample time to work out the kinks of a new ship and crew.

She momentarily recalled hearing some negative comments from some dock workers after arriving at New Orleans. The crew had followed her down the gangway to the dock where they gathered around her before catching a taxi to the French Quarter to play tourist. Colette was there guide. Everyone liked Jack and they were all addressing her as Captain Jack. Their discussions and appearance drew some odd looks from a group of dock workers.

Jack had to admit that, collectively, the dock workers looked like a motley crew at best. One bearded man even sneered and made a disrespectful comment about Sea Venture being cursed by having a female captain. The words were not new to Jack because she had sailed those waters before. A voice in the back of her mind asked how the dock worker's credentials would stack up to hers.

She made sure that the chair at the head of the galley table was vacant for Jonas as she seated everyone. A yacht owner had the same status as the chairman of the board of a major corporation; that went without saying. Besides, Jonas had made it clear that he favored proper protocol. However, Jack's intuition told her that after some time at sea under close quarters, some of the protocol would begin to fade to a more cordial atmosphere.

Everyone was seated when Jonas, Frank, and Gerty made their appearance. Jonas was still in his fancy uniform. Naturally, he wanted to make a favorable impression on his crew. Jonas had a lot of faults that he wished to hide and there was no better mask to hide them behind than one of pride.

Jack kicked off the meeting by introducing herself. As the ship's captain, it was her duty to take the lead. Right from the start, her red hair and blue eyes captured Jonas' attention. However, it was her demeanor and tone that established her as a leader; a ship's captain. She was confident in a pleasant, yet, commanding way. Speaking boldly, she made it clear that Sea Venture was in capable hands and that meant it could sail anywhere in the world as a first class vessel.

"Mister Jackson, you have a fine ship here. It has all the elegance and comfort that a king would desire. The electronics are state-of-the-art and the accommodations are magnificent. At this point, I have only one thing to add, and that is my thanks and appreciation to you for allowing me to be your captain." This was as close as she was going to get to patronize a prideful man.

Jonas liked the way Jack addressed him. Still, he wanted to see how she ran the ship for himself. In the meantime, he would be polite to her. "Captain Jack, Frank speaks highly of you and I look forward to having you aboard as my skipper."

"Thank you, sir. I will do my best not to disappoint you. Next, I would like to introduce you to my first officer, Andy Porter." She intentionally omitted Andy's middle name, Peabody. The poor man probably had enough ribbing over it during his youth.

Andy sat up a little straighter, bracing himself for his turn to speak. He had placed a small notebook and pen on the table to his front. Unconsciously, he fingered the pen while clearing his throat. His prior military training was shining through, a clear indication that he was a man of strength and firmness even though he was a bit nervous at this point.

"Sir, as your fist officer, I will deliver the same professional skill and service as your captain. Like her, I have previously served as a ship's captain, although not for as many years as she. What you see assembled around this table is a team of professionals. We not only will get you to where you want to go, but, we will take you there safely and in style." First Officer Andy did not smile because he didn't want to make light of his commitments.

Jonas was pleased with Andy. Also, he couldn't help notice how trim and muscular Andy was. Andy's closely cropped hair reminded Jonas of his own military days. All military, and in most instances ex-military, personnel knew the importance of fitness and grooming. A little voice in Jonas' head told him that someday he would regain some of his old fitness that he had lost while being homeless; he had already been working out in a gym, although sporadically. Concerning Andy, Jonas was convinced that he would be loyal to the bone and diligent in his duties.

Mateo Medina was the next in line for an introduction. "Sir, I am your engineer. Please call me Matt. I want you to know that I have gone over the mechanical aspects of Sea Venture with a fine toothed comb; a critical eye, if you will. Your ship is in excellent shape and we have ample spare parts for emergencies. God forbid if we should have an emergency, but, if we do, we are ready." Matt rendered the sign of the crucifix across his chest.

Jonas smiled warmly and gave the same sign of the crucifix across his chest. From the moment Jonas sat down at the table, his eyes continuously zeroed in on one person in particular and now it was her turn to speak. She was colorfully attired in a red blouse with gold and silver embroidered fringe. Her eyes were dark as coal and her skin was nearly as black as his. Resting in her cleavage was a large ornate silver crucifix, which only accented her shapely breasts. In his eyes, she was breathtakingly beautiful. Jonas couldn't wait to hear her speak.

His heart was beginning to race and he unconsciously shoved his precious admiral's hat back on his head until he appeared like a sailor that had drank one too many cups of rum. The image he had expected for the cook was that of an overweight and older woman. A thought rushed through his mind; oh how those Cajun Voodoo queens could fool a man every time.

Recognizing that Jonas was taking a more than casual interest in her, she hesitated to speak long enough to allow his anticipation to build. Most women have an innate ability built into their genes for recognizing such things.

She spoke in English with a mixture of French and Cajun accents. "Mister Jonas Jackson, I am Colette Pinsonault, the ship's chef. Captain Jack has told me about you, so I know that you are from New Orleans. My understanding is that you have been away for some time, so I wanted to give you and your friends a proper welcome. I have prepared a Cajun gumbo for tonight's meal."

Fearing that he might stutter, Jonas paused before responding to Colette. He wanted to make a good impression on her, one that would equal her ability to impress him.

"I am pleased to make your acquaintance, Colette. You are right; I haven't had the pleasure of eating a good Cajun gumbo for several years now; not since Katrina. Your gesture is a nice touch, a very sweet thing indeed. I'm certain that it will be the very best gumbo that I have ever eaten." He hoped he wasn't being too over-appreciative or over exaggerating the value of a meal he had not yet eaten.

Gerty and Frank exchanged sheepish looks. They were amazed at how suddenly Jonas' flair for formality had melted away. Was this an indication that Jonas' inner circle was about to open up and allow another to enter? Gerty and Frank silently vowed to keep an eye on this developing situation. Yes, there was a growing potential for a relationship. Frank thought about something he had heard as a kid concerning potential. "Anyone can count the seeds of an apple. Few people can count the apples in a seed."

First impressions can be powerful. Frank's eyes kept shifting to Jack while Gerty focused on Matt. The impending cruise was beginning to show additional signs of promise; more potential. Since they all would be together for an extended length of time, there would be ample time for them all to get to know one another. All relationships had to have a starting point; some end quickly and others never end at all.

Obviously, some of them were already ensnared in a spell of sorts, however, there were other introductions still pending.

"I guess I'm next," a voice interrupted. "I'm Thomas Ruskin, your purser. I have been doing this for about five years now. I have been conversing with your accountant back in Dallas and we have come to an agreement on how to manage the ship's accounts. Please, you can either call me Tom or Tommy."

Tom was a portly, bald man; a man vastly divergent from the others who were fit and trim. His voice was louder than the others and he acted with more familiarity toward Jonas. He was surely an extravert by nature. However, he was not the least bit disrespectful; he was just more flamboyant.

Everyone could not help but notice how Tom's double chin seemed to quiver when he spoke. His stomach hung over his waist line and his khaki trousers were so huge and baggy that he looked like a walking tent. He wore a polo shirt, but, he would have looked better wearing a flowery Hawaiian shirt. All in all, he was a working tourist with a likeable personality.

Jonas was handling all the attention with poise and dignity. His gentle nature was an asset which helped him to assimilate and interact with others. He was still in the process of emerging from an emotional cocoon as a result of being homeless. However, being able to take charge of his affairs was an aspect of his persona that still needed nurturing. His sudden wealth was something that he had to get used to. Going slow was his best course for achieving his goals. There was only one thing that needed his immediate attention, the true purpose of the cruise, and that was waiting for him on an island in the Caribbean.

Most homeless people live and survive by being as isolated as possible. Isolation was one of their coping mechanisms. Jonas figured that the best way of making a transformation from isolation to properly interacting with the rest of the world was to remain alert and cautious. He also knew that he would need help when it came to tackling his past. Leaning hard on Frank was something he had to do because he didn't have any investigating experience. Frank had a background in digging up facts and establishing truths and he was an honorable man; one that could be trusted. Gerty was trustworthy, but lacking in worldly experience. In time, everyone would have to know what the new millionaire wanted to accomplish. Looking around the table, he wondered who would bail on him and who would stay the course.

The deckhand was up next. "Mister Jackson, as your deckhand, I'm your laborer and chief assistant to whoever needs something done. While making your rounds, you are likely to see me scurrying about at the most unexpected places. My name is Roy Kirkpatrick and I have been a sailor for most of my adult life. I've served Great Britain in Her Majesty's Service in the Royal Navy and I have done my share of sea time in the Merchant Marines. Now that I am older, I prefer to work aboard private yachts, especially in the Caribbean." Roy reached across the table and shook Jonas' hand; he was the only one at the table to do so.

At once, Jonas knew that Roy was no stranger to hard work. When their hands clasped, Jonas could feel the hard leathery calluses and the power of Roy's grip. In the U.S. Navy, as in any Navy, it was the lower enlisted deckhands and seamen that kept everything aboard in ship-shape. Jonas had no difficulty identifying with Roy.

At last it was the maid's turn. Throughout the meeting she had sat quietly listening to and studying everyone. Her patience was the mark of a good student. "Good afternoon Mister Jackson. My name is Georgia Wallis and I am the ship's maid. My credentials are not as colorful as the others around this table.

Naturally, I will do my best to be an asset; that's a promise. You can see from my youthful appearance that I'm not as seasoned and experienced as the others. I'm a college student and I have taken a couple years off from school to see some of the world, especially the Caribbean. The most economical way of traveling is to work as I go. While some of my pals from school are backpacking around Europe, I prefer palm trees and golden beaches to towering mountains and stately buildings. I have already ventured out on a few yachts for short excursions and now I am ready for a long voyage. I believe I have enough maid-time under my belt to keep the staterooms clean and tidy while earning my keep. Should you need anything else, please feel free to call on me. Oh yes, I've always been a team player. I learned the value of teamwork playing college sports such as soccer and volleyball."

Georgia had an athletic build, good muscular tone, and an engaging smile. She also had a beautiful golden tan.

The meeting adjourned quickly so everyone could get back to their duties. Captain Jack escorted Jonas, Gerty, and Frank to familiarize them with Sea Venture. Everywhere they went the wood and brass was highly polished. Jonas was forever running a finger over something. He had to admit to himself that his ship was more elegant than anything he had ever seen aboard a U.S. Navy vessel. One thing that made it more impressionable was that it all belonged to him. For him, the entire experience was next to spiritual; even though he was not prone to materiality. The extravagance that often accompanied wealth was something that required a good deal of adjusting to.

Jonas was glad that Sea Venture had a fitness room. It was small by comparison to the fitness center that Frank had enrolled them in. Crowded into the room were free weights, a treadmill, and a combination elliptical machine. Everything was present that would meet their fitness needs.

The bridge was the heart and soul of the ship. There were radar and sonar scopes, a weather center, a communications center, and there was the wheel. It was so magnificent that it was overwhelming. Captain Jack explained the purpose and intricacies of each piece of equipment. Her knowledge and expertise established Jack as a valuable asset; without a doubt the most valuable asset aboard. Jonas had spent little time on the bridge of a ship when he served in the Navy. The orientation that Jack was providing was a real education for him. His acceptance of having a female captain was growing by the minute.

Everything was equally impressive when they all arrived in the engine room. Matt prided himself in keeping the room spotless; it was clean enough to eat off the deck. Gauges and lines were highly polished and wires of various colors appeared new. There were maintenance and safety charts posted and manuals stowed in bins. Matt spouted specifications, procedures, and performance data like a college professor in a classroom.

Following the orientation, Jonas announced that he did not want an immediate departure. He wanted to leave the port under daylight conditions so he could see the outline of New Orleans under a bright sky. After all, he had been gone a long time.

Andy showed them all to their quarters so they could unpack, and get settled. It had been a long day of travel in a van followed by an emotional stop at the cemetery. They all looked forward to a great meal and a good night's sleep.

Chapter 12

The eastern sky gave birth to fresh sunbeams intent on gripping a new day with warmth and seemingly endless visibility. However, there was still a slight chill lingering in the air from a long night. Fresh coffee was perking in the galley and Collette was busy making biscuits, gravy with chips of beef, and eggs. The aroma stirred everyone's senses. Soon swirls of steam were escaping from coffee mugs as people collected on the port side to watch the sun claim its dominance over a new day. Jonas was absent from the gathering.

Instead, Jonas was on his ship's stern galvanized by the sight of New Orleans's outline as it grew smaller in the fading distance. Sea Venture's bow was slicing its way through calm water toward the open sea. He watched in earnest as his blessed home town disappeared over his ship's churning wake. Leaning against the rail, he took another sip of coffee and wondered how long it would be until he was fortunate enough to return. He also wondered if he would be the same person when he returned. Throughout his entire life he had always been adapting and changing to something and this trip would be no exception.

Jonas was certainly homesick, but the act of returning home was not his strongest emotion; not now and not in his immediate future. A sense of melancholy floated about in his head and then it evaporated with the disappearance of the city's outline. It was not New Orleans that he was longing for; otherwise, he simply would not leave. He was being called back in time to a highlighted spot in his past. Recently, the strength of that call was growing stronger by the day, and now it was overwhelming him. Hopefully, it would not consume him or condemn his soul to the depths of some murky blackness.

Before he knew it, there was nothing but water in every direction. His senses shifted as sight gave way to sound; the monotonous prattle of Sea Venture's huge engines was generating a hypnotic resonance in his mind. It was like listening to a Gregorian chant in the halls of an ancient cathedral. The sea swells deepened and Sea Venture pressed on, unchallenged, inching its way across the Gulf of Mexico.

Jonas found a lounge chair and reclined. Relaxing was out of the question as he placed his now empty coffee cup in a holder. He was no longer cognizant of time and space as he gazed lucidly at the sky. Large billowy white clouds were beginning to crowd the sky. It was as though his body was lifeless lying there, all alone. After a few minutes, his mind began to drift off to another time and place, far back in his past. In his youth, he had been vibrant and daring; an adventurous soul.

There was a metaphysical aspect to what he was experiencing. In this dream-state, he was free and content. He was feeling the same way an old farmer felt when recalling youthful leisure in a meadow of wild flowers. All people surely experience such fond recollections. Unfortunately, most people are not blessed enough to be able to return to those old times and places. For the moment, Jonas was content to reflect on his memories while hoping to recreate them to some degree. Hopefully, he was closing in on that goal.

Following a hearty breakfast, Frank strolled about on the upper deck until he ran into Jack on the starboard side. Like Jonas, Frank also had experienced the disappearance of New Orleans and the fading of the shoreline. He remarked to Jack; "I guess this is the point where we lose track of distance by sight."

"That's an interesting concept, Frank." She smiled because she was ready to attach some reason and explanation to his comment. "This is where we have to question the validity of perception. For instance, as we sail along, we will encounter other vessels out here on the open sea. As we try to judge or estimate how far away they are we have to take into account what size they are. Look over there." She pointed to a speck on the horizon.

"Does that sail belong to a large sailing vessel like a schooner or does it belong to a little sailboat? Likewise, when looking at a shoreline, we have to ask ourselves if it is a continent or a small speck of an island. Is whatever we are looking at a large far-off mass or a small and very close one? Thank God for radars, maps, and GPS. I would hate to be forced into digging through an old locker and dragging out an old weathered sextant and point it at the sky. Technology has certainly changed the way we perceive the world around us while at sea. Technology has certainly changed our culture and the way we experience the world."

"You are a most remarkable and interesting woman, Jack. I have a lot to learn from you. I expect that sea captains, like yourself, are used to a life where you are constantly experiencing and assessing your environment. You are truly an exceptional person." Frank began to sense that there were a few threads of attraction being weaved by unseen forces between him and Jack. There was certainly a bond forming between them.

They stared at one another, speechless. Suddenly, they were aware of someone approaching.

Jonas greeted them by blasting a hearty "good morning" to them as he touched the bill of his admiral's hat with his index finger. His melancholy had subsided and he had reassumed his role of a proud yacht owner.

Frank concluded that Jonas was somehow beginning to reacquire an old fun-loving nature that he had temporarily misplaced. It was usually the intangible things that were the most telling aspects of a person. In Jonas' case, the highs and lows had been a bit extreme.

"Good morning, Jonas," Frank returned his greeting, as did Jack. "I was just about to engage our captain in a conversation about time while at sea. Would you like to join us?" Frank was not exactly honest about his intentions. Fortunately, this was only the beginning of their journey and there would be plenty of time to get to know Jack.

Jonas enjoyed hearing intellectual conversations that were initiated by Frank. Life on the streets was never as interesting as some of the simple, yet meaningful, topics that Frank could come up with. "If you two don't mind, I would love to listen in."

Frank and Jack both nodded their approval. At once, Jack was eager to take the lead. "Unless some crisis is at hand, time at sea is usually swallowed up by a good deal of leisure-taking. I think we all long for the rest and quiet that are associated with sea travel. Also, all of us probably agree that a tranquil sense of laziness can be extremely invigorating to a tired soul. Over the years, I have learned to appreciate times like this, where the ship's clock is useless as an instrument of measurement. The only exception is that the ship's clock does let someone know that it is time to go on watch.

"Additionally, you can't talk about time without mentioning the ship's bell. In a strange way, the clanging of the bell has its pros and cons. On one hand, it is an annoyance because it interrupts rest or play. On the other hand, it can come as a blessing because it relieves us from too much leisure; in other words, boredom. As a captain, I see the importance of a crewmember assuming the watch with a clear head and a well-rested body."

Before anyone could respond to Jack's comments, a shout could be heard from the forward port side. It was Matt's voice. Everyone scurried to his location where they found him pointing at the water. He was yelling, "Look over there. It's a group of porpoise swimming alongside of us."

Everyone took notice at once. After half an hour, the magnificent animals were gone and the excitement and wonderment subsided. Collectively, no one could find any reason not to be delighted by the event. Even experienced sailors appreciated Mother Nature when she exhibited some aspect of her beauty or magnificence.

Frank couldn't help notice that Gerty had an arm around Matt's waist, even though the porpoise were no longer visible. Perhaps Gerty was attracted to Matt. Yes, there was an advantage to living in close quarters with others. Maybe living aboard Sea Venture was a way of indicating or facilitating other ventures into uncharted realms of friendships and relationships.

Moved by the moment, Frank nodded at Matt and Gerty so Jack could see. "Jack, I have a good feeling about being on a ship called Sea Venture. I hope she continues to work her magic for all of us."

"Yes, Sea Venture is a fine ship. However, this is not the first ship to be called Sea Venture. Let me tell you a little story that is a historical fact." Jack paused long enough to allow Frank time to acknowledge his approval for hearing what she had to say.

"Please go on; I'm all ears." Frank liked the prospect of spending time with Jack and a good story was just icing on the cake.

"Listen closely, because this story is proof that I was a history major in college. I'm going to take you back to the early 1600s. English settlers in Jamestown, Virginia were having a tough time. They were desperately in need of supplies from England. England recognized their dire situation and its urgency so the Crown put together an emergency plan that included building a new ship named Sea Venture. In fact, they dispatched an entire fleet of eight ships to Jamestown.

"The fleet encountered a monstrous hurricane and the ships were scattered far and wide. No ship had any idea as to the demise of any other ship. Suddenly, each ship was out to save its self. Admiral Somers was aboard Sea Venture. Because Sea Venture was newly constructed, the caulking and joints had not had time to properly seal. She began to take on water and was in danger of sinking. Admiral Somers saw land and ordered Sea Venture to run ashore or as close to shore as possible."

Frank interrupted Jack. "Where in the world were they?"

"I'll get to that in just a minute." Jack continued her story. "Sea Venture made it close to shore before wrecking. About 150 crewmembers survived. They lost most of the twenty cannons on board, but managed to salvage much of the cargo.

"Now, back to your question about Sea Venture's location. The land had not yet been discovered so Admiral Somers claimed it for England; calling it Somers Isle. Later, it was renamed Bermuda."

Smiling ear to ear, Frank added a complementary comment. "That is an amazing story, Jack. I have often said that truth is usually more exciting than fiction."

Now Jack was smiling. "I'm glad you liked the story. However, it is not quite over. You see, after several months passed, the survivors were able to salvage enough material from Sea Venture's wreckage to build two smaller ships; 'Deliverance' and 'Patience.' Most noteworthy was that one of the survivors who boarded one of the ships was a man named James Rolfe. James made it to Virginia and courted an Indian maiden by the name of Pocahontas. As you might well know, that relationship became another well-known story for our historians and authors to capitalize on.

"There is one more little bit of information that is worthy of mention. The wreck of Sea Venture launched one of the biggest mysteries of all time. I can't think of any person who has not mentioned this mystery at some time during their life. Naturally, that mystery is known as the 'Bermuda Triangle.'"

Frank scratched the back of his head, astonished, as he thought about Jack's story. Finally, he expressed his thoughts. "I think I was a little premature when it came to seeing Sea Venture as being an omen of sorts for something good and positive. Maybe I had better take a wait-and-see approach until this trip is over."

"One never knows what the future holds for us until we begin to live it." Jack turned to look out at the open sea. She had simply and neatly placed one of life's realities into a quaint little nutshell.

Frank yearned to open up to Jack about his feelings for her. However, for now, he would not express his feelings for fear of appearing foolish; it was just too soon. Instead, he would wait on some sign from Jack; a sign that reflected her interest in him. He was sure she had encountered other men who had fancied her attention and he did not want to spend the rest of the trip looking like any of the other village idiots who had pursued her. Besides, at the moment, Jonas was still standing idly by anticipating more intellectual stimulation.

Frank was still standing shoulder to shoulder with Jack, leaning against the railing. For a moment, Jack's thoughts were elsewhere. Perhaps she was only studying the sea or maybe she was attacking some other issue.

Jonas, not wanting to be ignored, said, "You know, Jack, a man could lose track of time out here. It's hard to judge time, don't you think?"

Jonas' question pulled her back from whatever she had been dwelling on. "You have a point there, Jonas." Jack was quickly prepared to discuss the issue of losing track of time. Sometimes the best way to discuss something was with an example. "I read an article once about a group of miners that had been trapped after a cave-in. They had been shut off from the world without any light so they couldn't tell day from night. Once they were rescued, they told their rescuers that they thought they had been trapped for three days. They were surprised to learn that they had actually been trapped for ten days."

Jonas looked at Frank for a reaction. After all, Frank was truly the greatest analyzer he had ever known. Jonas also knew that most people had some knack for assessing things, albeit in a variety of ways. However, Jonas liked the way Frank expressed his views and assessments. Yes, he could easily relate to Frank's explanations.

Without hesitation Frank began to relay his opinion. "Well Jonas, Jack's story from the article she read certainly confirms what you just said about losing track of time." After a short pause, Frank continued. "In my mind, I would have thought that the opposite would have been true. Maybe the miners had been too scared to accurately assess time. Obviously, they had been experiencing a great deal of fear and that would have added quite a bit of suspense to their situation. I'm really surprised that they didn't think they had been trapped for a longer length of time. I would have thought they would have thought they had been trapped for two weeks or a month. I am convinced that stress does alter our perception of time."

Jack laughed loud enough to acquire their attention. "Just when you think you have human nature figured out; it throws you a curve ball."

Wanting to add a bit of levity to what Jack had said, Jonas quipped, "The only time I want to lose track of is my age."

"And exactly what is that length of time, Jonas?" Frank teased.

"Oh, I forget. I guess I just lost track of the years." Jonas answered with a grin.

At this point, Jack casually dropped out of the conversation. "I'm going to bid you gentlemen a good day and make my rounds. Our discussion has been stimulating and I certainly look forward to more of the same." She headed off toward the deck below.

For a few minutes, Frank assumed the same activity that Jack had been occupied with a few minutes prior; he began watching the sea under some unrevealed spell. Soon a gentle spray of sea caught him in the face detaching him from his thoughts. This was a good time to visit the bridge and see how the ship's operations were going. Besides, without a parting word, Jonas began to wander off in the opposite direction. The whole discussion about time had somehow run its course.

At the bridge, Frank found Andy alone at the helm. He was certainly a happy man; a motivated sea artist with a passion that seemed to always be driving him to excellence. He was perfect for the job. The door was open and that gave Frank an opportunity to observe Andy without him being aware. By all reason, Andy seemed to be enjoying a communion between him and Sea Venture.

Truthfully and inwardly, Andy knew that Sea Venture was the finest vessel he had ever had the opportunity to pilot. The other vessels he had been steward over had been of less quality and cosmetically lacking. Sea Venture seemed to have a soul of its own and Andy couldn't be happier or more content with her as he maneuvered across the sea in eloquence. Soldiers and sailors, young and old, all possessed some romantic sense; one not so much of intellect as it was one of feeling.

Jonas made his way to the galley where he squinted through the port at Colette. She was sitting alone at the long mahogany galley table; either lost in thought or perhaps meditating. In the back of his mind, Jonas knew he was restricted to watching her through the glass pain. Sea Venture was his and everyone aboard, save Gerty, was on his payroll. Yet, he liked studying Collette without her being aware. The expression on her face, especially the look in her eyes was captivating, if not hypnotic. Jonas couldn't give himself a clear reason for why he was drawn to Colette. He only knew that he liked the vibe her countenance was projecting.

Jonas was also unsure of himself; afraid that he would say the wrong thing and drive her away. Nonetheless, Colette had a certain magnetism about her that was driving him crazy. Oh well, he thought; nothing ventured meant nothing gained. He entered the galley.

He did his best to act as if he was just strolling in for another cup of java. However, in the back of his mind, Jonas knew that he wanted to establish himself as a friend and that meant he would have to test his ability to present himself in a favorable light. Hopefully, he would appear to her as being nonchalant and just someone that wanted a cup of coffee.

"Excuse me, Colette; can I trouble you for a cup of coffee?" There, nothing could go wrong with that simple, yet direct, approach.

"Sure, come on in and make yourself comfortable while I pour you a cup. I was only sitting here thinking about what to fix for lunch. Do you have anything special in mind?" Her smile was friendly and engaging.

"Can you whip up some cold cuts; sandwiches with cheese maybe." He was not about to ask for anything that would require a lot of time to prepare because that would mean cutting into their time to visit.

"Would you like cream or sugar, Mr. Jackson?" She spoke softly while trying to be polite. After all, Jonas was her employer as well as being a man of wealth. Money had surely given him prominence.

"Please, Colette, call me Jonas. I don't want to come across as being more than I actually am. A few years ago, I worked in a shipyard at New Orleans. I'm sure you are a lot more cultured and educated than I ever was or ever will be." Jonas was trying to put Colette at ease by showing her that he was nothing less than a commoner who had acquired wealth through pure luck. "By the way, I will take my coffee black."

He cleared his throat and then continued. "You can ask Gerty about me. A few weeks ago we were two lost, down-and-out homeless people milling about the streets of Dallas, Texas, dressed in rags. You can also ask Frank who I consider a friend even though he is on my payroll."

Colette responded pointedly. "I see where you are coming from, Jonas. We are not always the person we appear to be. A man can acquire or earn money, but, money alone does not make a man the person he is. If we are genuine, we present ourselves as the person we are on the inside." She tapped her breast with a thump. She then spun around to pick up a napkin for his cup of coffee. When out on the open sea one never knows when a rogue wave will make the ship pitch.

Jonas watched her with a thoughtful eye. He truly wanted to create a positive awareness between them. No clear reason popped into his mind that would reveal why he wanted to generate a more personal awareness with her. Still, he wanted to plant a seed that would tell Colette that he was a good man with good intentions.

Jonas did have a firm understanding of what a façade was. The last thing he wanted to do was alter the true person that he was and that meant the person he was on the inside. On the other hand, he wanted to put his best foot forward with a clear goal of being favorably portrayed and noticed. Shaking his head, he wondered why relationships had to be so complicated.

The odd attraction he was developing for Colette did not, in any way, diminish the love he carried for his deceased wife. He was not out shopping for a replacement for her because that was not possible. Yet, there was a loneliness or void in his heart that needed to be filled. Oh well, maybe Colette did not even have the correct light in her soul that would brighten the darkness in his soul. Adapting and changing does take time.

Jonas watched Colette's long slender fingers uncurl from the steaming cup's handle. His eyes shifted to hers. There was no doubt in his mind about her being a strong, passionate woman with warmth in her heart.

Sipping from the hot cup, he couldn't help but realize that there were too many unsettled things in his life and those things would not permit him to pursue any kind of meaningful relationship with anyone. Perhaps that could change once this trip had ended. There, he had thought the matter through and came to his own conclusion.

"Thank you for the coffee, Colette. I'll let you get back to fixing lunch. I hope we can have a more in-depth visit later. You seem to be a very nice and interesting lady." He took his cup of coffee with him as he left the galley.

Presently, Tommy's purser duties were not taking up much of his time so he went prowling about the ship. The same held true for Georgia since she had already cleaned all the staterooms and made the beds.

Tommy ran into Georgia on the ship's bow where a light occasional spay of seawater settled on the deck. "Georgia, what did you think of all those fish we saw this morning?"

"You mean the porpoise? They were beautiful."

"They certainly were. I hope we can spot some more later on." Tommy spoke with optimism in his voice. There was nothing more dreadful for him than being alone.

“Tommy, let’s go to the galley and play some cards. I bet I can kick your butt in a game of gin rummy.” Her face was filled with enthusiasm.

Tommy jumped at the opportunity because he was bored. Georgia eagerly led the way. The important thing about playing cards with someone was that no human being could play cards without conversation and if the conversation soured you could always blame it on the cards.

Chapter 13

The noontime meal did not carry the same significance or sense of purpose as the prior evening meal. At this time passengers wanted only to share their morning's experiences with others. At any rate, this was how the schedule fell into place on this particular day.

The sun was directly overhead and everyone aboard seemed to drop in for lunch whenever they pleased and that made cold cuts a wise decision. Actually, they were only prompted to show up at the galley when they felt a hunger pang. It was not until dinner was served that they all gathered as a group, except for Andy who still couldn't be pried away from the helm. Jack made it clear that she would relieve Andy, whether he wanted to be relieved or not, as soon as she finished her meal.

No one was surprised when Jonas took his time eating and then volunteered to stay behind to help Colette with the dishes. His desire to perform a common task with the help certainly was not typical of the average millionaire. By now, everyone knew that Jonas was not the typical millionaire.

Of course, Jonas' newly inspired attention to the galley came as no surprise to anyone. The afternoon's gossip already revolved around the way Jonas was acting toward Colette. Naturally, no one disapproved of Jonas' interest in Colette. Besides, Jonas' fascination over her was none of anyone's business but his own. Basically, it was only drawing the amount of interest that all budding relationships generated; a focal point for mundane conversation.

Gerty hardly touched anything on her plate and she certainly paid little attention to any of the conversations taking place around the galley table. In fact, she seemed to have tunnel vision when it came to socializing. She did not attempt to disguise her sole interest which was directed toward Matt. She whispered a lot in Matt's ear between giggles and occasional outbursts of laughter. The whole idea of seeing Gerty flirt with Matt was something that tended to please everyone.

Tommy did his best to interact with everyone at the table, even when they didn't respond. At least all of his conversations reflected a lighthearted tone. To everyone's amusement, every time he laughed, his belly seemed to bounce while his double chin quivered with every word or gesture. One and all seemed to be having a great time, a festive time.

Even the deckhand, Roy, got in on the fun. At first he was reluctant to interact, but that approach quickly faded. Mostly, Roy laughed along with Georgia at Tommy.

Frank sat and ate next to Jack until she excused herself to go relieve Andy. Frank wondered how long it would take until he and Jack were the central theme of the ship's gossip. After all, he couldn't keep his eyes off of her. Frank didn't mind the idea of being closely associated with Jack and he had no objection to others viewing him and Jack as a couple, of sorts. At least, for now, they were a modest couple exhibiting little or no intensity. For all everyone aboard knew, their relationship was of a professional nature.

Frank had little doubt that there was a spark between him and Jack, and hopefully that spark would flare up a little brighter and steadier as time passed. As for everyone else, things were going well in spite of only being at sea for less than a full twenty-four hours.

Frank did the polite thing and waited for Andy to arrive. He would sit with him as he ate and find out what he liked about Sea Venture.

Gerty and Matt abruptly finished eating and announced that they were going to stroll around on the upper deck to check out the sunset. Tommy, Roy, and Georgia announced that they were going to play more gin rummy in Georgia's cabin. All over the ship, everyone seemed to be bonding in some way or another and that was as expected. After all, they were all living the good life.

Frank was glad that there was no one among the crew and passengers that was quarrelsome in any way. Peace and tranquility was always a blessing. There was a pleasant dynamic to the way everyone was coming together. They had all been thrown together either by necessity or circumstance and those situations could easily have arrived with challenge and growing pains. Silently, Frank thanked the powers above for the way things were turning out.

The ambiance aboard Sea Venture reminded Frank of his military service days where men and women from diverse backgrounds were forced to adjust and form teams. Obviously, their success with adjustment ranged in intensity from extreme to nonexistent.

Luckily, Frank had a knack for studying and understanding human behavior. Based on his experience, he decided to keep an eye on how all the various relationships aboard Sea Venture were playing out. He was especially concerned about Gerty because of her history of alcohol and drug addiction. She was pursuing a relationship with Matt that was reaching an unexpected fervor. Frank's understanding of Gerty was based on only a few weeks of observation and he had virtually no understanding about Matt other than he was a gifted seamen.

When it came to Jonas, all Frank was sure of was that Jonas was on some secret quest derived from his distant past and that it somehow involved his Navy service and the Caribbean. Frank felt an unquestionable and heightened sense of responsibility when it came to Gerty and Jonas. The immediate question for Frank was how long he would have to wait until Jonas tipped his hand. Jonas was certainly playing his cards close to his chest.

Also lost to the immediate future, was how the group, as a whole, would react when they learned the trip's true purpose. Moreover, there was the question of the amount of risk involved, if any? Frank and Jonas, each in their own way, were the only ones aboard who were realizing some degree of intrigue.

All these thoughts and concerns had a troubling aspect to them. They were also keeping Frank awake, late into the night. At last, the pitch and roll of Sea Venture making her way across the gulf rocked him to sleep, a sound sleep.

Frank woke fully rested. He glanced out his room's window and saw that the sun had not yet shown its glowing morning face. He picked up his wristwatch and saw that it was only 4:20 a.m. so he decided that he had plenty of time to have a quiet workout in the ship's little fitness room. The odds had to be in his favor that he would have the place all to himself. He decided to go bare-chested, wearing only exercise shorts and sneakers.

Outside, the air felt balmy so the humidity was probably high. He would probably sweat a good deal as he worked out so he pulled a towel around his neck and made his way to the fitness room.

Much to his surprise Jack was already there running on the treadmill. Her hair, face, and neck were glistening with sweat. She was every bit as muscular and toned as he had expected. She spoke first. "Are you going to stand there in the hatchway gawking or are you going to come in and work out?" She puffed her words and smiled through lips dripping with perspiration.

Frank knew that Jack had strength of character and was as good a captain as there was. Now, he was also convinced that she possessed true physical strength. He also realized that he had spent way too many hours sitting on his duff in his office. Looking at his reflection in the room's wall mirror told him that his recent trips to the gym had been inadequate. Jack was the one who sported the best athletic appearance. Frank silently vowed to get on a more rigorist training program. He was inspired by Jack's fitness.

Frank smiled at Jack. "I take it you keep yourself fit. I think I have some catching up to do."

"Having a fitness room aboard is one of the perks that I like about this voyage. In this business you never know when you will be physically tested. Whenever I get the chance I like to go swimming, too. I'm especially fond of SCUBA diving." She pushed the stop button on the treadmill and jumped off as it ground to a halt. "Now that I'm warmed up, I think I will hit the free weights."

"Okay, don't be such a showoff. By the time we get to the end of this trip, we'll see who is the fittest. I'm no stranger to working out. Mark my word, I'm not so out of shape that I can't handle myself in a clinch. Besides, muscles tend to have good memories and that means they will get back on par fairly fast." Frank's vanity was kicking into high gear.

"Take it easy, big boy. You don't look all that bad. All you need to do is shed about ten pounds. I'm sure you don't have to worry about the pretty girls giving you a second look." She hoped her slightly off center complement would be accepted.

"Hey, maybe I might even get a second look from you. I think you have more going for you than most women." He hoped he wasn't being too forward with her. They were beginning to share a mutual admiration for one another and that had to be a good thing.

"This is a long trip. Anything could happen before it's over." She knew that she was being coy and that she could have taken this opportunity to close the door for any future intimacy between them. She didn't because she was interested in getting to know him better. She also knew that they were both playing a cat and mouse game with each other and sometimes there could be a fine line between flirting and courting.

Frank grabbed two forty pound dumbbells from the rack and started doing alternating curls. He kept an eye on Jack as she picked up two thirty pound dumbbells and started doing the same exercise. They were both aware that the other one was watching them in the mirror. They continued to pump iron, smile, and sweat while being aware of each other.

They eagerly worked out on various pieces of equipment for the next hour without speaking a word. Sometimes silence can be a form of communication. Jack finally broke the silence between them. "I think I have had enough. I'm going to clean up and head over to the galley for some breakfast before getting some shuteye. Do you want to join me for breakfast?"

"I would love to." He followed Jack out of the fitness room where they felt the growing strength of the morning sun.

Jack turned away from the sun's brightness as she began to speak to Frank. They ran into each other and the collision could not have been better. He put his arm around her waist and leaned in slightly. Their lips touched and Jack put her arms around Frank's waist. The passion of their embrace and subsequent kiss was mutually received.

However, the encounter was short-lived. Roy ran up on them puffing with excitement. "Captain, Captain! You had better come with me on the double. I think Miss Gerty needs some attending to. Please follow me to the upper deck to the lounging area. She needs some looking after, she really does."

Roy's tone and excited demeanor was over-trumping the thrill of Captain Jack and Frank kissing. Roy had something more important on his mind than their open display of affection.

The three of them were taking two steps at a time up the stairs that led to the upper deck. Roy spoke as they went. "I found her this way when I went out for a cigarette. I have no idea how long she has been out there like this."

Roy slowed his pace as he approached Gerty's location. He stepped aside and then stopped to allow Jack and Frank to look at Gerty. They knelt down to examine her. Frank felt for a pulse while Jack looked at her eyes and then listened to her breathing. Frank looked at Jack and said. "At least she's alive."

For Gerty, yesterday's radiance was now nothing but a dark shadow. Nearby there was a clanking of glass as the ship pitched. Frank picked up the empty bottle of Jim Bean whiskey. It sparkled under the sun's light. Frank tonelessly declared. "This is one of the curses of addiction. In this case it's alcoholism."

Gerty reeked of alcohol as she leaned back in the deckchair. Her eyes were half closed as if under a spell. Her hands were lying open in her lap, empty now because the bottle had been emptied. She could have passed for a corpse had her breast not rose slightly with each shallow breath. At least her breathing was profound and rhythmical. Had not Frank known that she was a live human being, she could have passed for a wax figure at some theme park.

Jonas and Matt walked up to see what everyone was looking at. Jonas squeezed in between Jack and Frank. When the reality of the scene sank in, Jonas spoke with a sigh and a heavy heart. "Oh God, have mercy. My poor Gerty has fallen off the wagon."

Frank was saddened by the whole scene. He had hoped that Gerty had been undergoing some remarkable recovery from her alcoholism. In her present condition she was nothing but a spectacle for everyone to watch and speculate about. Deep down, he realized that it was not easy for anyone to just walk away, unscathed, from an addiction.

Gerty had been Jonas' friend for a long time and he had seen her in her present condition many times. In fact, he had been in the same condition more times than he wanted to admit. A tear trickled down his cheek as he looked at her. He looked at Frank and whispered his feelings. "Frank, this is like being asleep and having a bad dream. You know, one of those where you do your best to wake up and can't. I have to do something for her."

Matt stepped forward and addressed both Frank and Jonas. "Can I have a word, in private, with you guys? I think I am partially to blame for Gerty being like this."

"Sure, let's move away." Frank led the way toward the aft portion of the deck so the three of them would be out of earshot of the others.

Matt hung his head and then cleared his throat before speaking. "I'm sure you have noticed that Gerty and I have been hanging out together. I thought we were clicking pretty well. I like her a lot and I think she likes me, too. She is smart, witty, and fun to be with."

Frank interrupted. "We get the point Matt. Just tell us why you feel some blame for Gerty being drunk."

"Okay, okay, let me explain what happened last night." Matt conceded that he was getting carried away with laying the groundwork for what he was trying to say. "Last night when Gerty and I were walking around the ship, she started coming on to me. I'm just a man, and sometimes I'm just as weak as any man. I am a lonely man and I have urges. Anyway, last night Gerty said she would like for us to go to her cabin, but she thought it would be nice if we could have a drink, a nightcap. She thought that would be nice and would help us loosen up a bit. Well, I told her that there were a few bottles of bourbon stowed in the storeroom. We agreed to meet in her cabin."

"Go on, you are painting a pretty clear picture." Frank encouraged Matt.

"I hope you guys aren't going to be mad at me. I really feel bad about this." Matt's guilt and shame were showing through. "Anyway, we had a couple of drinks and then we made love. Afterwards, Gerty said she was tired and wanted to get some rest. She shoved the bottle under her bed for safekeeping until we were together again. I had no idea that she would drink the whole bottle. I had no idea that she had a drinking problem. I swear it. You have to believe me."

Jonas addressed the obvious in simple terms that rendered some emotional relief for Matt. "Relax Matt. You didn't take advantage of Gerty. It was the other way around. She must have known that if there was any liquor on board, you would know where it was and have the best chance of getting to it. She used you. Gerty has been struggling with addiction for a long time. I had hoped this trip would somehow become part of a cure for her. Please, don't fault her. She is not a bad person. The evil here is not Gerty. The evil is her curse of addiction, nothing more and nothing less. I have had similar struggles in my life, and still, I am a slave to my addictions. I'm just doing a good job of keeping them at a safe distance. My point here is that you should not judge Gerty based on her weakness."

"Thank you Mr. Jackson. Both of my parents were alcoholics and I still loved them until the day they died in an automobile accident. My father was drunk at the wheel. If I have your permission, I will throw all the liquor overboard." Matt was eager to make a positive contribution.

Jonas was decisive with his response. "Please see to it at once."

"There is one more thing, Mr. Jackson. Can I still be friends with Gerty? I really am very fond of her."

Jonas placed a hand on Matt's shoulder and smiled. "Yes, you can see her. I think she needs as many friends as she can get. Just promise me that you will never consciously enable her with her addiction."

"Thank you, Mr. Jackson and now that I know about her addiction, I will do what is right for her."

"Matt, don't call me Mr. Jackson. It makes me feel like an old man. Call me Jonas." His words were in stark contrast to his recent façade of pride; that swagger where he strutted about as an authority figure. However, he still had that admiral's hat on his head. Surely, he would eventually unleash his actual persona.

Jonas and Frank watched Matt head off to the storeroom so he could complete his assignment. Suddenly, they were aware that Jack was standing behind them.

"Jonas, you handled Matt tactfully and thoughtfully. I don't know if you are exhibiting old Navy training or you are just a decent man. I bet it's a little of both. You are a good man and I admire you." Jack meant every word.

Wearing a sheepish grin, Jonas responded to her kind words. "Captain Jack, you've turned out to be a rather decent captain. I'm glad you're running my ship."

She ignored Jonas' complement. "I think we should let Gerty sleep it off right where she is. I think the fresh air out here will do her more good than a stuffy cabin. I have alerted everyone to keep an eye on her. Roy said he will do some touch-up painting where he can watch over her and he will erect a canvass over her so she won't get a sunburn."

Jonas agreed with Jack. "That sounds like a good plan to me. You look tired. What time did you get off watch?"

"I got off at 0400 hours and then I worked out in the fitness room." She was speaking to Jonas, but her eyes were smiling at Frank. Their earlier embrace and kiss were still lingering in the back of her mind.

Frank hoped he wasn't blushing as he addressed everyone. "Why don't we all head to the galley for breakfast?"

Jonas was quick to agree to the idea of visiting the galley. Everyone knew that Jonas didn't really need much of an excuse when it came to seeing Colette. Any pretense would probably have worked.

"Yep, that sounds like a good idea to me." Jonas tapped his stomach as he spoke.

Chapter 14

No one knew exactly what time Gerty had finished drinking let alone when she had conked out. At this point the timing of her excursion with booze had little relevance. Roy decided to forego eating breakfast so he could immediately begin his task of watching over Gerty. Placing his mission first, he only allowed Matt to relieve him for a quick lunch. The sun's rays on his face were softened by a southerly breeze. The combination of fresh air and the passing of time was working because Roy saw that she was beginning to stir in her chair. He dashed off to fetch Matt.

When Gerty finally opened her eyes, Matt was there, favoring her with a concerned look. After rubbing her eyes with the palms of her hands she managed to focus on him. "How long have I been out?"

"The best I can figure, you have been out all morning and half the day." He looked at his wristwatch. "It's a little past three in the afternoon. I'd say you tied on a good one last night." He forced a half-hearted smile. That was as nice as he was going to get with her.

She tried to stand up, but her legs were a bit wobbly. He had to put an arm around her waist to stabilize her. She turned as if to face him. Instead, she put her arms around him and placed her head on his chest. She was seeking reassurance and not judgment.

"By now I guess you realize that I have a little problem when it comes to booze." She spoke with an apologetic tone.

"I have been down that road a couple of times myself. At least you admit it and that's a good start." He held her a little tighter. "If it wasn't for AA, I probably wouldn't be here now."

They both lapsed into a sullen silence for a few excruciating minutes. It was her voice that broke their silence. “How many of the others know what I did?”

“Well, I have to say that everyone knows.” He had to be honest with her.

“How many of them are pissed off at me for being a hopeless drunk? I wouldn’t blame any of them for not speaking to me again.” Her guilt and shame was beginning to surface.

“I don’t think anyone is mad at you. They are only concerned about your health and state of mind. In my opinion, you are physically sick and spiritually weak. In an odd way, you are your own patient. I heard that you were once a nurse so you know how to treat illnesses. It is up to you.” He was diplomatically leveling with her.

“I know you’re right. When I was on the streets I attended a lecture on drinking at a homeless shelter. The speaker told us that first you take a drink, then the drink takes a drink, then the drink takes you. So I know it’s wrong to take that first drink. If I only had the strength to say no to that damn first drink I could turn my life around for the better.” A tear rolling down her cheek confirmed that her problem with alcohol was a serious one.

Matt hoped that he could somehow get through to her. He decided to throw a few personal examples her way. “There were plenty of alcoholics in my family and you would think that I would have known better than to pick up the habit. I guess I was following the only examples I had to go by. Listen to me Gerty. I care about you, but I’m not about to become an enabler. Seeing you like this is the final straw for me. As far as I’m concerned, from this time on, I quit; no more alcohol for this sailor. That’s right, I quit. I swear on my parent’s grave that I will never pick up another drink. I have to save what's left of my life and you should do the same." Matt was taking a bold stance. He had taken this step before and could only hope that this time would be the one where he succeeded. Naturally, he knew that he would always be an alcoholic; that's the reality of the disease.

"You mean we aren't going to have one final drink before we stop." Gerty was trying to make light of a serious moment.

"We have to quit. We don't have a choice since Jonas had me throw all the ship's booze overboard. I say; out of sight, out of mind. I think Jonas is a lot wiser than we give him credit for." Matt stared up at the sky hoping to find some divine sign from God.

"I guess it's for the best. I know Jonas cares. He's always trying to do the right thing. Until last night, I thought I had this thing licked. I'm sorry I used you, Matt. I had no idea that you were trying to quit, too. I guess we were using each other. At least the sex was good. I like you a lot." Gerty was now looking Matt in the eye in search of inspiration.

A breeze was blowing Gerty's hair in her face and Matt brushed it away. "Yes, we're two peas in a pod. I don't know about you, but I hate alcohol." Matt's tone was one of firmness.

Gerty tried to force a smile. "I hate it like Satan hates holy water. Let's hate it together. What do you say, partner?" Gerty kissed him and they walked off, hand in hand, to her cabin. Reflecting on their situation, she realized that there were no perfect people in the world, only perfect intentions.

Frank saw Gerty and Matt entering her cabin. Surely, Gerty was now in good hands. Matt seemed to have his head screwed on right and he had already demonstrated, through his own words, that he cared for Gerty. Hopefully, they had a future together.

Frank wandered about until he was in front of Jack's cabin. He had missed her at lunch and hoped she was getting the rest that she deserved. He leaned against the railing and thought about their early morning kiss and warm embrace. Maybe he would run into her again at the ship's fitness room in the morning.

His eyes scanned the empty sea until they settled on the horizon with a metaphysical gaze. At times like this, he thought of the sea as being infinite; no beginning and no end. Nevertheless, he concluded that time always strides on and that meant things would change.

The grinding prattle of the engines with the pitch and sway of the bow told Frank that Sea Venture was inching her way across the sea. With nothing in sight, as far as the naked eye could see, told Frank that distance at sea could only be measured by time, and not by miles. Boredom must be settling in, he concluded. Why else would he be thinking about time and distance again?

The vast swells between the waves served up a monotonous and endless scene. At times like this, he had ample time to ponder anything he wished. His restless body seemed to follow suit with his equally restless mind. In fact, his now idle mind could easily turn into a breeding ground for cultivating new thoughts and themes. He could feel it in his bones that he was about to enter a deep mental and emotional state. There was so much to consider, especially when it came to Jonas and Jack. The hidden purpose of this trip was clearly not yet ready to materialize. That ball was still in Jonas' court. However, it would not be long before Jonas revealed his guarded secret.

Soon he began thinking about Jack and the chemistry that was at work between them. Frank was attracted to her and she, on some level, was obviously reciprocating with equal energy.

Perhaps, by the grace of God, nature would be allowed to take its course. Everyone knew that God controlled nature.

Suddenly, Frank was aware that music was being piped through all the speakers on the ship. The sound was not what he had expected for a ship sailing to the Caribbean. Music without words had a tendency to express emotions that could not otherwise be put into words.

Music always had a way of playing some vital role in a person's life; that he was sure of. He could find no way to question the ability of music to link one's physical life to his or her spiritual life. This had to be why music, especially chants, was so prominent in Church life.

All these things considered; Frank was moved by the sound of classical music being piped throughout Sea Venture. He couldn't help but wonder how this kind of music was being accepted by others on board. As sure as there was a sun in the sky, he was about to learn how some of the others felt.

Georgia, Tommy, and Roy were approaching from one side while Gerty and Matt approached from the opposite direction. Jack's cabin door creaked open and she joined Frank at his side. Jonas was not there and neither was Colette. They were no doubt spending time together elsewhere on the ship. Andy was at his favorite place; the helm. Whenever anything happened that was outside of the norm, everyone tended to know where they were when it took place.

The moment was not calculated. It was spontaneous with Tommy cutting to the chase. "That music is not exactly party music for a social cruise to the sunny beaches of the Caribbean. Whose idea was it to put a damper on our spirits?"

Frank instantly wondered if Jonas was the culprit behind the music. "Okay, don't get worked up over the choice of music. I'm sure Jonas is behind it. He has developed a newborn flame for culture. He can be eccentric at times. Trust me; he is only trying to project an image of someone possessing a proper sense of culture. I have to say that he is not an elitist. He is simply a man working on his internal issues. This has to be tied in with why he wears that admiral's hat. Think of the music as another phase he is going through."

Jack took a different slant on the classical music. "I'm a Catholic and I'm also a history major. This was my life before becoming a maritime captain. Classical music got its biggest boost from religion during the '*Middle Ages*' and the '*Renaissance*.' Music for the old masses was nothing short of sacred. If Jonas wants to find some religious connection and value through classical music or if he just wants to experience the meditative and relaxing attributes of it, then let him have his day. Just enjoy it while it lasts."

Gerty was also quick in coming to Jonas' defense. "I have two points on this music issue. First, listening to this music won't hurt any of us. Second, this ship belongs to Jonas and he is paying the bills. None of you have a right to judge Jonas or his selection of music. He is my best friend and I will stand by him until my dying breath."

Tommy retreated. "I'm sorry. I didn't mean any harm. I just thought that classical music can be depressing. It launches me into a melancholy state of mind."

No one else made any attempt to jump into such a trivial fray. Nonchalantly, the impromptu meeting began to disperse. This was one battle Jonas won without even showing up. He had no idea that he had generated the slightest bit of discomfort among his crew and guests.

Up on the bridge Jonas was oblivious to all the commotion his music selection had generated. His fingers fumbled with a different CD until he was able to get it going in the player. Andy laughed at Jonas as Colette looked on with approval. Unlike the others, they were all getting into a more festive mood.

From the ballrooms of Vienna to the grand theaters of Western Europe, millions have enjoyed Johann Strauss' Blue Danube Waltz. The elegance and vivacity of the waltz was just as much in fashion in the confines of Sea Venture's bridge as it ever had been anywhere else on earth. Jonas and Colette, their eyes locked on each other, swayed and strutted about the bridge to the time-tested rhythm. In spite of his youth and generation gap, Andy envied them. He also eyed the stack of CDs that was an assortment of different tastes in music. There was jazz, country-western, rock & roll, and even opera. It was too bad the others on board did not know what Andy knew. Variety was truly the spice of life.

Frank placed his hands on the railing and turned his attention back to the sea. Jack placed a hand over one of Frank's and studied them for a moment. Decisively, she looked up at Frank and then pulled his hand away from the railing. She led him to her cabin door and opened it without even a hint of hesitation; especially in her eyes. She was bold and confident and knew that when she wanted something, she would have it.

Her cabin was dimly lit and in a split second the cabin door was locked. Frank was stunned and at a loss for words. He was like putty in Jack's hands and he was well aware of what was happening. He didn't care because he wanted the same thing.

He called her name in a whisper as she pulled him into her embrace. "Jack. Oh Jack. You are so full of surprises."

In the sanctuary of her cabin he was free to kiss her as passionately as he wanted, and he did.

There was no reluctance in her voice as she spoke. "I'm not going to apologize for wanting you." She began unbuttoning his shirt and he did likewise to her blouse.

She moved away from him and stretched out on her bed. His heart was pounding with excitement. The only light in her cabin was a glow from the curtain covering the cabin's window. The soft light seemed to caress her naked body and that enhanced her sensuality. He knelt down next to her and she pulled him down. Neither one of them now wore a stitch of clothing.

Her body was soft, smooth, and warm to his touch. Everything within his being was screaming for her love. Every movement of her body was an invitation to his passion. She rolled over on top of him, blanketing him with her body. Leaning over, her breasts pressed against his chest while her thighs cupped his.

He ran his fingers gently through her hair and she cradled his head with her hands. Their kisses were passionate beyond any semblance of control. Her lips broke away from his only to kiss his cheeks, his neck, and his chest. He called her name in an adoring and grateful whisper. She put a finger to his mouth. "Shush! No noise." Her tone was commanding and left no room for refusal. He was far beyond having any second thoughts; let alone having any capacity for understanding the right or wrong of what was happening.

She sat up and arched her back, straddling him and looked deeply into his eyes which were now wildly aglow like a wild beast. Her eyes flashed brightly like the sun in the clear blue sky that was outside. She moved ever so slightly until he was deep inside her; a place warmer and more welcoming than any he thought possible. Their lovemaking was more powerful than any he had ever known, or would ever know. It was magical beyond thought and reason.

Even though she had condemned him to silence, he managed to whisper an age old phrase. "I love you."

When the lovemaking was over, and they were lying next to each other, she addressed him with a firm voice, dropping an unexpected bombshell. "You had better love me. I'm Catholic you know, and we have just sinned. The first chance I get, I will have to find a priest and confess. Right now, I'm praying that this is the beginning of a life-long journey. You better not turn out to be one of those guys that jumps in bed with someone every time they get the chance."

A good memory can be a curse at times. Frank began to recall some of the times he had looked at a woman with lust in his heart. Now, he wondered if those times had also been sinful. They probably had been. Then there were the few times that he had sex with women that he had loved, but, was not married to them. Surely, these were also sins according to God's word.

He had never been married and he knew little about Church doctrine. Jack had certainly put a damper on the lovemaking they had just indulged in. On the other side of the coin, he wondered why she had initiated the sex that they just had. Life, faith, and God were such complex phenomenon. Instantly, he realized that he should have said no to her, turning her down flatly without hesitation. He hadn't because he had feelings for her. If she had first brought up the subject of sex and its relation to sin and the Church, he would have certainly declined her invitation. The whole situation had everything to do with instinct and free will; that he was sure of.

After contemplating on the subject of sex for the whole of a minute of two, he had to ask the question that was foremost on his mind. "Why did we just make love if it was wrong in the eyes of God?"

She stared up at the ceiling instead of looking at him as she spoke. "Anytime we sin we damage our relationship with God. However, all sin is not equal. That is why God's punishment for our sins ranges in severity. Don't get me wrong, no sin is a good thing. My belief is that sex outside of marriage is not a deadly sin if it was done out of love for the other person. The reason I wanted to make love to you is simply because I knew it would make me feel good and it may very well lead to the sacrament of marriage. Outwardly, you probably can't see that I am a lonely woman. Right now, I think we are well on our way to falling in love and I don't think God sees our act as a deadly sin. I believe, right or wrong according to Church doctrine, in God's eyes, it all boils down to intent. I hope that I have not misplaced your intentions. If I have, I won't hold it against you, but God might. I hope my reasoning is not faulty. God, I hope I have not made a big mistake here."

Frank was ready to discover a better understanding of his feelings for Jack so he willed his state of mind away from his primal urges; lust being the most apparent. "Jack, I think I am no longer falling in love with you; I am in love with you. I also think it is about time for me to reach down inside myself and find my true faith. I'm beginning to think that maybe I should establish my spiritual and religious path. This is a monumental and dramatic change in attitude for me. It is up to me to make it a divinely inspired beginning. I'm just not sure where to begin. There seems to be a church in every neighborhood in America, yet there is so much evil in each of those neighborhoods. Maybe God is everywhere, but not seen and felt by everyone. I need to clear this up on more levels than you can imagine."

She looked over at him, and with tears streaming down her cheeks she continued to establish a solid foundation from which to build. "I think there is a good reason behind the Song of Songs in scripture. The exact author is unknown. However, it was introduced in the Old Testament by Solomon. Without any doubt, it is poetry celebrating the love of a husband and wife. It says: 'My lover belongs to me; and I to him.' Don't ask me to explain further. There must be a good reason Saint Paul referred to marriage as a 'mystery.' Marriage is a sacrament and I believe in it." Hopefully, a sacramental seed had just been planted in each of them.

For years she had done her best to erect an insulating wall of protection around her, albeit a little late in this instance. Now there was a crack in her spiritual curtain and through that crack she had sinned. Yes, she was human.

Frank still felt guilt and he attributed that feeling to being humanly weak; a common man lacking in faith. He knew he had a long way to go and he also knew that he did love Jack. "Jack, I think Christians are never off the hook when it comes to sin."

"The way to getting off the hook is through Christ. Since we are all sinners, we all need the Church to help us find our way to God's mercy. That is why the Church is full of sinners; as it should be. They are all searching for their own salvation. The ones that are not in the Church are in even more spiritual danger. The first chance I get, I'm going to confession. Even the Pope goes to confession because he is human. We can talk more about this later. Right now, I need to get some sleep." She kissed him and held him tightly before turning away. Her parting comment was: "Don't forget, the Catholic Church is one of those neighborhood churches you spoke of and her roots go all the way back to Christ and Peter. I'm not pressuring you; just give it some thought."

Closing Jack's cabin door behind him, Frank squinted at the bright sunlight. A revelation occurred to him: If Christianity was a true thing; then it was infinitely important to all people. Surely, he had finally found his path to faith and it had been delivered by the most marvelous woman.

Chapter 15

At some time in our lives every man and woman will experience periods of loneliness. Tommy had his share of such experiences. Considering the depth of his loneliness, he had to wonder if any of his new friends had ever encountered the same naked terror that he had.

When his wife passed away he had thought his life was over. He had desperately tried to avoid his emotional pain by maintaining a festive mood. That's why he wanted to laugh and joke so much with Georgia and Roy. Currently, they were filling his void of loneliness by playing gin rummy with him and laughing at his corny jokes.

Some people clung to solitude as some sort of glorious reward while others saw it as a death sentence. He was keenly aware that love was missing from his life; replaced by fear, and that made him a bit desperate at times. If he had given up completely he would have already died. But, that was not the case; not yet anyway. Tommy remembered something the famed Sociologist Eric Fromm had written: "Immature love says 'I love you because I need you' and mature love says 'I need you because I love you.'" Unfortunately, he had no one in his life to love. All he had were casual friendships and they were temporary.

Georgia and Roy were only stand-ins for what was missing in his life; his wife. They were good company and their friendship was growing. However, they would never fill the black hole of emptiness that was in his heart. Sadly, his loss was permanent and his new friends were only weak substitutes. The last thing he wanted was to become a cold-mannered man without any close friends or immediate family. So, in the meantime, there was no pressure to win at the silly card game they were playing. The real goal was to pass time with a light-hearted interaction; a cursory bonding of pals. It didn't even matter if one of them repeated some joke about a traveling salesman and a farmer's daughter. What mattered was that their spirits were higher than if they had been sitting alone in their respective cabins. They were living the journey and not the destination and that was good enough for now.

Tommy excused himself and stepped outside for a smoke. He knew smoking was not good for his health, but in the culture of contemporary life, there was little that was good for anyone's health. He drew forcefully on the stub of his cheap rum-soaked crook cigar. He had lately grown fond of its sweet taste and moderate aroma.

A few minutes later, Georgia and Roy came outside and joined him. Respectfully, they had all avoided talking about the drama he had brought on concerning classical music. Georgia and Roy both knew that it would be a touchy subject with Tommy. However, a sufficient length of time had passed for the subject to be brought up. Roy and Georgia only wanted the issue to be put to rest.

Georgia opened the dialog. "You were a real tiger when it came to the music. Like you, I wasn't crazy about the music when I first heard it. At least it was different. In fact, it was totally new to me. What's your take on it now, Tommy?" She was focusing on the music and not his staunch objection to it.

"Oh, I guess I was being a jerk. I hope they didn't take me too seriously. I only thought that classical music was too much like meditating and reflecting on things that are best left alone. Classical music reminds me of some of that New Age psycho-babul stuff. You know, some of that touchy-feely stuff that was so popular in the 1960's. During the last five years, I have had my fill of reflecting on things I can't change. Maybe I should have continued my grief counseling when my wife passed away. The irony here is that my wife and I had actually liked classical music and we often sat and listened to it as we gathered around our fireplace before bedtime."

Roy and Georgia were listening to Tommy in silence and with unconscious concentration. Not wanting Tommy to struggle on with his apologetic tone, Roy rendered a decisive wave of the hand to signal the whole affair was settled. Besides, he knew that neither he nor Georgia was mentally equipped to address Tommy's emotional short-comings.

Tommy attempted to blow a smoke ring, but a strong southerly breeze did not cooperate. They all laughed at his wasted effort.

After Jonas and Colette wrapped up their dancing audition they parted ways; her with an eloquent curtsy and him with a stately and complementary bow. She headed to the galley to review some recipes and he strolled around until he settled down on a lounge chair on the foredeck near the ship's bow.

Sea Venture's bow was pointed south by southeast and its progress cut slowly through a prevailing breeze and current from the south. The combination left the impression that the ship was traveling faster than it actually was. Jonas figured that the Florida Keys were somewhere just out of sight to the east. He really wasn't sure about his ship's location and on another level he didn't care. All he knew for sure was the temperature felt warmer and Sea Venture was moving in the right direction.

He closed his eyes hoping to relax. Pale memories of his past slowly crept into his unconscious, disturbing his rest. Before long, the hush and silence of echoing thoughts from his Navy exploits in the Caribbean reminded him of the real purpose of this cruise.

Until he found acceptable answers to questions that had tormented him for decades, he would never be able to find the rest he desired. He forced his eyes open to deflect the confusing daydreams that so often grappled with his heart and soul.

The day was nearing the point when the answers he sought would come like shinning knights ending their quest for the Holy Grail. Just a mere two weeks, a fortnight, and he would be in the thick of his inquiry. Yes, he was on the final stretch and no one knew exactly what he was in search of. The others, especially Gerty and Frank, were aware that he had some secret objective in mind. They were not stupid so they knew something was up. Frank knew the most because he had already helped with some of the preliminary details.

Jonas had gone too far to turn back now, so it was no wonder that he was seething with impatience. The weight of his emotional baggage was taking its toll on him, though. His advanced age was chipping away at his body, but thankfully not his resolve. Still, at the passing of all these years, he knew that he was challenging the laws of probability. Notwithstanding all that stood between him and his goal, he stood reassured and glad that he still possessed enough vigor and strength to continue.

The thing that he needed at the moment was laughter and cheerful conversation so he stood and looked around for someone, anyone; no one was around. He decided to go to the galley and spend some quality time with Colette. There was no way to dismiss the fondness he was feeling for her. She projected a real aura of feminine confidence and in his eyes that was an admirable quality. Once his quest was over, he would surely seek out more of her loveliness and eloquence. Just being in her company was a feast that he was quickly becoming addictive to.

Andy was busy at the helm; a place he couldn't seem to get enough of. He checked the global positioning system (GPS) and saw that he was on course and Sea Venture was about to leave the Gulf of Mexico and enter the Caribbean Sea. He was careful to steer clear of Cuba because the Cubans did not favor vessels sailing under the flag of the United States. He would not let his guard down until he reached Jamaican waters.

Matt entered the bridge and greeted Andy with a smile. "How are we doing Andy?"

"We are on course and making fairly good time. Our pace would be better if we weren't bucking such a strong current and headwind." Andy was eager to convey anything that reflected his ability to maneuver Sea Venture.

Matt was inquisitive about every condition or force that could either hinder or enhance the ship's performance. He went about sorting through charts, checking the radar, and noting the barometer. Suddenly, his large dark eyes became fixed and his expression turned stern as he assessed the situation.

"Andy, have you taken a look at the weather reports and instruments lately?"

"Not really. The sky is clear and blue. It looks like a normal day in paradise to me." The tone in Matt's voice was beginning to make Andy's stomach a bit queasy. Did he find something wrong in the paperwork?

"Andy, I'm going to fetch the Captain and then I'm going to check out the ship. The barometric pressure is dropping and the weather report indicates a large storm is building between the Dominican Republic and Columbia. It is directly in our path." Matt was out the door before Andy could respond. Andy sat the auto pilot and began sifting through the data in the weather reports. It didn't take him long to conclude that he had dropped the ball.

For centuries sailors have stared at a bare horizon for weeks on end in anticipation of seeing anything other than calm seas. The greatest joy had to be when they sighted land and the worst fear they ever encountered was when they saw a massive storm approaching.

Jack wasted no time in getting to the bridge because she trusted Matt's judgment. He had been around the sea for a long time and had survived many a storm. Even though he was not a licensed captain, he did have a great deal of experience and that sat him apart from Andy. He also had the ability to recognize a real safety issue.

Andy had been caught up in that boyish element where it was fun to drive huge things with powerful engines. All boys who were too young to drive cars and trucks often wanted to drive farm tractors. That boyish obsession probably had something to do with him not seeing the full picture. There was even a theory that it was incorporated into a boy's genes.

The look on Jack's face as she walked in conveyed at least a civil interest. She was not one to panic. Jonas and Frank came in on her heels to see how serious the problem was. Matt was not in attendance because he was already running around trying to ensure that Sea Venture was operating to his high standards.

Jack looked at Andy and fired a declaration of fact at him. "Andy, sometimes it is not enough to trust your five senses. That's why we have instruments on board ships like Sea Venture." She spared him a robust admonishment because she could tell by the look on his face that he knew he had not done his job as well as expected.

Jack stood tall and faced the group with an expression of confidence painted on her face. "Let me lay it out for you, ladies and gentlemen. We are in for a rough ride. The wind will pick up a little at first and then it will calm down. Then we will likely face a few intermittent squaws mixed in with an otherwise clear blue sky. The squaws will constitute the outer bands of the main storm and the occasional clear sky will be the calm before the storm. At times, the squaws will come with a few hateful downpours that really won't amount to much. Then the southern sky will turn black as coal. When we finally reach the storm's outer edge the sun will disappear and Sea Venture will be wrapped in a thick mist and then our visibility will be reduced to feet instead of miles or yards. Our instruments will be our only guide." She was preparing them for what she knew was coming. She was also not going to be an alarmist, only a realist.

Gerty asked the lingering question that all the others were holding back. "Are we going to die?"

Jack was quick to answer Gerty's dreaded question. "Of course not, we will be okay if we keep our nerves in check and pay attention to what the ship is doing while watching for any surprises the storm may have for us. The hurricane season is over and this storm does not have the potential to become one. It is only a big bad storm with sixty mile an hour winds with gusts up to seventy-five miles an hour. We will have to contend with it for two, maybe three hours at the most. Hopefully, it won't blow us off course."

Frank asked the other important question that was in the back of everyone's mind. "How long will it be until we hit this big bad storm?"

She glanced down at some plotting sheets she had consulted. "I would say we will be in the thick of it about the time when it would normally get dark. It will be sometime after dinner.

The weather reports show several models for this storm. This has been a crazy year for meteorologists. There has been drought where there is normally rain this time of year. Snow has come later to the northern states and there have been tornados all over the country. We can't blame the weathermen for everything being out of sync."

Georgia, who is normally silent, had her say. "Why can't we just back up and hide somewhere from the storm?"

Jack shot a stern glance at Andy before answering. "If I had known about the storm three hours ago, we could have steered north of Cuba. However, there was one model that indicated that the storm could go that way, too. Truthfully, even two hours ago, no one could really predict where this damn storm would go." That was as far as Jack would go to let Andy off the hook.

Frank fired the next question at Jack. "What do we need to do to prepare for the storm?"

"The storm is big enough to toss us around quite a bit. So we need to button down everything that isn't already secured. We also need to, as a safety precaution, and as routine operating procedure, have a quick class on survival and life boats and jackets. Everyone needs to be familiar with these things in case everything suddenly goes to hell. Murphy's law is still alive and out there somewhere." Without sounding rude, she dismissed any further questions.

"Roy, go round everyone up and bring them up here on the bridge for a briefing. We have to play this by the rule book. I wish we could outrun this thing but we can't. Please, I don't want any of you to worry because you are all going to come through this just fine." Her professionalism and confidence were once again shining through.

Jonas was glad Jack was running his ship. In a Freudian slip of the tongue he quipped in a half whisper. "When this is over, I'm going to promote her to admiral."

Jonas impatiently stepped outside and began searching the southern sky for hints of the storm. All he found was a cloudless blue sky with a few patches of white floating harmlessly along the horizon. The view was oddly picturesque considering what was headed his way. The thought of the storm somehow damaging his precious Sea Venture began to absorb his mind. He was also taking stock of what he would do if the storm kept him from staying on schedule. Not reaching Isla de Vieques by a certain date was going to be problematic for him. Jonas realized the difficulty of planning against the uncertainty of Mother Nature; he had been down that road before.

During the next few hours, the wind sped up a few knots causing the huge swells to be highlighted by the arrival of crisp whitecaps. Yes, the sea was truly magnificent; breathless. Throughout the afternoon Sea Venture ploughed on through the endless waves; bold and free. The ship and crew were poised and ready for the storm to arrive.

Just as Jack had predicted, a deathly stillness reigned just before the storm struck. If it wasn't for the hum-drum of the huge diesels below deck, the silence would have been absolute. Everyone was tense and keenly aware of the purely primeval silence that was overtaking them. The faces of each person showed no signs of being at rest in such unfamiliar surroundings.

The approaching black wall was the only warning of change. A storm like this one could become a menace, impersonally dangerous if one was not careful. Jack was the skipper and she could not ask for a more attentive group of followers.

Everyone but Jack and Andy gathered on the bow to have a quick final look at the impending monster that was inching its way toward them. Matt had given them a pair of binoculars and they passed it around so everyone could have a look. Dusk was already setting in so they couldn't see as much as they wanted to. Everyone gasped when a streak of lightning shot from the black mass, licking the water like it was the tongue of a savage dragon. Seconds later, thunder boomed and they all began to fear what was before them. Sea Venture's bow pitched sharply as the ship sliced its way forward toward the storm. As pre-arranged, they all headed to the galley and slipped into their life jackets. Without being asked they doubled checked each other's equipment.

Up on the bridge, Jack respectfully watched the approaching mass of blackness. Soon it would enwrap Sea Venture, blocking out what little moonlight was left. All the electronic maps and reports on the table clearly indicated that the storm was dangerous, but manageable. How comforting, Jack thought sarcastically. Intuitively, she knew that nature had a way of fooling experts and instruments. Nothing was ever pure and absolute in either nature or life. Still, she had ridden out a couple of other storms of this size and magnitude and that was a notably reassuring feeling; her confidence was unshakable.

"Andy, I want you to be steady on the helm and aim for the center of the storm. We don't want any broadside action." She picked up the intercom and gave another order. "Matt, give me all you can safely get out of those engines. However, don't redline those babies. We don't want to lose whatever they have in reserve."

Sheets of driving rain whipped across the bow and thrashed the bridge windows with so much force that Jack couldn't see anything outside but a black wall. The windshield wipers were doing their best, but they were unable to make much of a difference. Between the rain and wind the sound was deafening.

Something came untied and slammed into the windshield and then it was gone; condemned to a shadowy grave in the sea. She had no idea what it had been, but was confident that it was not something essential. A fierce storm like this one always came with some degree of chaos.

After all her years of sailing Jack never really got comfortable with storms; especially ones of this intensity. She thanked God that she wasn't out in her sailboat, struggling to survive this storm. There was a sense of enhanced safety and comfort associated with a vessel the size of Sea Venture. With the grace of God and some luck, Sea Venture could probably survive a hurricane. At least this vessel would do better than the first ship named Sea Venture. Materials and technology had come a long way since the 1600's.

Jack smiled with reassurance as the ship's bow rose and fell with grace as it took on the storm. She was able to get glimpses of the ship's lighting from time to time. At times Sea Venture seemed to shudder as she shook off gusts of gale force wind. She was a fine lady.

Andy had never experienced a storm of this magnitude. His knuckles had turned white as he clutched the wheel. He wasn't about to let the storm defeat his stamina or break his will. This would be one he would brag about some day over a couple of beers at some neighborhood bar.

"Andy, you have been at the helm all day and need a break. I want you nearby, but I want you to rest awhile. Get a blanket from the locker and take a nap for an hour or two. I'll wake you if you're needed. I think this is as bad as it is going to get. I want you to know that you are a real trooper. By the way, did you learn anything today?" She wanted to get a feeling for how he was developing as a captain. Experience always delivered the best lessons.

"I learned not to take the weather for granted. Hell, when you are in charge you shouldn't take anything for granted." He was sincere.

On this stormy night the galley was full of people and it was certainly full of many different points of view when it came to life.

Frank sat alone, wedged in a corner of the galley. He was lost in thought, making an earnest endeavor to figure out what to do next when it came to Jack. The whole ordeal of making love to her was setting him off balance. The tension in his heart was mostly focused on guilt. He wanted to blame her, but couldn't. After all, they both had been willing souls.

He just couldn't stop agonizing over what had occurred between them. No matter how he tried to rationalize it, that sinful sword known as guilt always ended up drawing some spiritual blood. Maybe his faith, or lack of it, was his real problem. He always considered himself to be a decent man. Yet he was always making mistakes that ended up hurting someone. He wondered if Jack was having the same discussion with her conscience.

Gerty sat at the main galley table along with Georgia, Roy, and Tommy. She was doing her best to follow the conversation about the storm. However, her mind was on Matt and his safety. He was all alone down in the engine room, doing his best to maintain the ship. Matt possessed an inner strength that she admired.

She hoped his stated concern and affection for her was genuine. She liked the way Matt was able to grasp the reality of her addiction to alcohol. Somehow, she just had to get past it. Sure, she knew that the closest thing for a cure to alcoholism was abstinence. Much to her disappointment, all she could come up with was: what could not be cured, must be endured." The first step toward happiness for her would be to never again allow her lips to touch booze. The likelihood of that happening was unlikely, but not impossible. Her addiction was every bit as intimidating as the storm outside.

Tommy was not his usual self. All of his good jokes failed to come to mind and he had no desire to play cards.

"Can I light up a cigar? I promise not blow any smoke in your face. I hope I'm not coming down with seasickness. I'm not used to this much motion under my feet." Tommy was on the verge of pleading for permission to smoke.

Thankful for the distraction form her thoughts, Gerty slid a lighter across the table to Tommy. "You can light up if I can have one of those nasty looking things, too."

Tommy pulled one out of his shirt pocket and handed it to her. After lighting up his cigar, his mind drifted off to a place in his past that he was trying to avoid. Then he made a strange pronouncement to everyone. "Here is a thought for everyone to think about. When you pit life against death, the odds are in favor of the latter. I think the best we can do is make the best of the former. What do you guys think?"

Georgia was bored more than the others so she decided to tackle Tommy's pronouncement. "I don't think anyone can argue that point of view. How could anyone possibly argue in favor of death over life? Once you die you are out of the equation."

Roy jumped into the conversation as best he could. "The only reference I can come up with is what we are facing right now. Storms scare the hell out of me. I love the sea, but I have to give it its due and respect its power over life and death. I don't want to die at sea. I want to die in a rocking chair on my back porch while admiring my flower garden. So there is no way I am going to die out here in this storm, not today. I have another life waiting for me beyond the sea."

Georgia came back within the same scope she had complemented Tommy's point with. "I'm right with you, Roy. We are all too young for a final exit from life. I think Captain Jack is going to get us through this in fine shape."

Gerty lit up the cigar and excused herself from the trio. Her steps were a bit unsteady because of the way the storm tossed Sea Venture about. However, her determination won out as she made her way over to Jonas and Colette. "Pardon the intrusion, guys. Is there any way I can have your ear for a few minutes, Colette?"

Colette knew that she had been monopolizing Jonas' time. Besides, she wanted a little break from all his flirtation. "Sure, honey, I'm available. I take it you want to speak in private?"

"Thank you. You're right; I want to talk woman to woman."

They made their way to the back of the kitchen and sat on the floor with their backs against some cabinets. Colette smiled warmly at Gerty while hoping the conversation had nothing to do with Jonas and all the attention he was giving to her. "Go ahead, girl; I'm all ears."

"I know that you have heard about my drinking episode. Hell, everyone on the ship knows about my drinking."

"I have seen that sort of thing many times in my life, Gerty. Every time I am honestly asked my opinion, I do my best to help. The consumption of alcohol as an addiction has never been a part of my life. I have to admit to you that, in my younger days, I was known to tie on a good drunk from time to time. I even experimented with drugs, but never acquired a habit. My good fortune was that I was able to walk away from drugs and alcohol, unscathed." Colette was opening up just enough to encourage Gerty to talk about her addiction.

"I here tell that you are a Voodoo Priestess. Can you use your powers to help me out of my addiction? I want to make a new life for myself. I also hope that Matt will become a part of my new life." Gerty knew what was at risk and she wasn't afraid to tap any sources, no matter how far out they might be, for help. She only wanted to begin some sort of recovery process.

"Yes, I am a Voodoo Priestess. For several hundred years, the Voodoo religion has consistently intermingled Roman Catholic practices to enhance its goals. I am also a practicing Catholic so I do blend Voodoo and Catholicism and sometimes that tends to taint my image. Yes, life is sometimes odd and hard to figure out. As a Voodoo Priestess, I often ask the same Saints and Angels that Catholics admire to intercede for me and I believe their prayers do help. They do forward my prayers to God in Heaven. All Voodoo practitioners know that Jesus is the chief shepherd of His flock, and as such, He has God's authority to assign lesser shepherds to help Him in His ministry. That's why I have no problem asking Saints and Angels to help any way they can. Where I come from, in Louisiana, there are many like me who practice aspects Catholicism to further their Voodoo pursuits. Our aim is to keep the devil out of our lives. Saints and Angels are heroes of the Voodoo faith. Oh, I know you can't mix apples with oranges and come up with an apple, so purity is at stake. I can only hope that the bleeding of paths will somehow get me to the right place.

"Following the chosen tenants of two faiths gives me no guarantee that I will end up in heaven. But, I do believe in God and I do honor His Saints and Angels. The duality of my faith is certainly an eclectic approach to worshiping. I'm sure many Christians turn up their noses at Voodoo with an understanding that we will surely go to hell. At any rate, I do believe in God."

"How do you see my addiction to alcohol?" This was the area where Gerty really wanted to focus her energy. She was seeking help and not a lecture on religion. At this point in her life she was desperate for a solution.

Colette placed her hands on top of Gerty's and spoke pointedly. "You may never eliminate your addiction. The best you can hope for is to dominate it. Remember, you can never tackle an addiction without faith. As for Voodoo, it has more to do with African custom. In my opinion, you don't fit the right profile. It's simply not the answer for you. Spells are easily broken and they can be temporary. Oh, I have seen some strange things when it comes to Voodoo, but the effect is more pronounced for believers. My advice to you is to go to a Catholic Church and speak to a priest and then go to an Alcoholics Anonymous meeting. Also, remember this and take it to heart: not having any alcohol on this ship does not mean your addiction is on the mend."

"Thank you for being candid with me, Colette. I think you are an honest and straightforward lady." She should have known that there would be no quick fix or gimmick that would halt or curb her addiction.

"Colette, can I talk to you again sometime?" Gerty was reaching out because she knew the importance of having friends, especially a female friend, for support.

"You can bend my ear anytime you want, honey. My understanding is that the road to recovery is a long one and it can sometimes be a lonely one. Temptation can strike with amazing speed and it can come at the most inopportune times. I'll also keep you in my prayers." Colette smiled at Gerty and then leaned over and hugged her.

Chapter 16

Jack was glad to see that the wheel was no longer pulling against her efforts to maintain a steady course and she was now able to clearly see Sea Venture's bow; an indication that the storm's strength had significantly waned. Fortunately, the storm never got strong enough to form an eye and that was in line with the weather reports and predictions. At its highest point, the storm still had a lot going for it, though; torrential rain and whipping gusts of wind, and that had made for some rough sailing. Thankfully, the heart of the storm was now moving north of Sea Venture and that meant the worst had past.

The confines of the bridge were beginning to smell a little stale so she opened a small vent to allow some fresh air in. The damp air that blew in was no longer chilling as it had been half an hour ago; another encouraging sign. "Andy," she yelled. "Get your butt up and take the wheel. We're home free."

Andy bolted upright from his blanket. Jack's news came as a comforting relief, in more ways than one. He stuck his head out the door before taking the wheel. "I'm glad that one is over." His eyelids blinked uncontrollably while he squinted for focus. "It shouldn't be long until we are back to normal. In the meantime, I could use a cup of coffee."

"I think you're right, Andy. I too would love to wrap my fingers around a hot cup of coffee. I'll make sure a cup comes your way." Any hint of stress in her voice had vanished. "Yes indeed, it is a good feeling when you weather a big storm without as much as a scratch."

Jack picked up the intercom and called down below. "Matt, you can come up for air once you check the engines out. I want a status report as soon as you can. We now have smooth waters and a full moon."

Sea Venture's engines no longer labored as she left the storm's grasp. Moonlight was beginning to glisten as it peppered the sea through breaking clouds. The rain stopped completely so Jack stepped outside. She looked at the black sky that was now beginning to show a few bright stars. Moonlight was reflecting across Sea Venture's wake marking her trail. "Thank God for our return to safe seas and another tranquil Caribbean night" Jack thankfully mumbled.

Patches of steam rose from the ship's decks as the temperature climbed in search of its Caribbean norm. Jack noted a couple patches of isolated fog in the distance. There was no need to worry about them because they would soon dissipate. Echoing in the distance was the last mutter of thunder that signaled the storm's final farewell salute.

Jack entered the galley in high spirits. "All right, you guys, that storm is now history. Everyone is clear to do whatever you want. Be careful as you walk around outside because the deck is still slippery in spots. We don't need any skinned knees or sore rumps. Georgia, would you do me a favor and take Andy a cup of coffee. He's at the helm and he's trying to shake the cobwebs out of his head."

Roy, Gerty, and Tommy filed out of the galley to see if they could get a glimpse of the departing storm. Colette busied herself in the kitchen and put a fresh pot of coffee on to brew. In a few more hours it would be breakfast time and she intended to whip up something nice.

Jack poured a cup of freshly brewed hot coffee and Georgia headed to the bridge with a cup for Andy. Jack hoped her cup wouldn't keep her awake because she was beginning to feel a tad bit tired. She was looking forward to hitting the sack for some well-deserved slumber. In the meantime, she was content to sit for a while at the galley table and relax while she chatted with Frank who had just entered the galley.

Frank immediately zeroed in on Jack and sat down next to her. Colette shoved a cup of coffee in front of him and before retreating back to the kitchen she spoke coyly to the couple. "I'll leave you two lovebirds alone. I'm sure you have things to discuss."

That discussion did not have time to take place. The door flew open with a bang and Gerty rushed in out of breath and full of so much excitement that she could barely speak coherently. "You had better follow me, pronto! We have an emergency out here. There's a man bobbing around in the water and he needs our help."

Gerty's loud and breathless voice penetrated Colette's thoughts and sent a shiver down her spine. Suddenly the galley was completely empty. There were two spilled cups of coffee and two overturned chairs left behind as proof that an emergency did exist and it had to be dealt with quickly. Everyone was aware that seconds counted when there was a life and death crisis unfolding on a ship at sea.

Roy looked like a cowboy about to lasso a steer on the starboard side. Andy was already bringing Sea Venture about with the engines on slow. Georgia and Tommy were not about to take their eyes off the man in the water. Jack had instructed them well on the man overboard drill. In this case it was a man adrift.

During life and death situations, and this was one of those situations, time tended to stand still, suspended in heart-pounding suspense. In an emergency like this, time could only be used wisely or disastrously lost. At this moment, time and timing meant everything. This is when every fraction of a second had more value than the rarest jewel on earth.

Frank dashed to Roy's side and stood ready to help him pluck the man from the water. Everyone wanted the rescue to take place during the first pass; and thank God it did.

Once the man was aboard, he was officially characterized as a survivor. Everyone gathered around him feeling as much relief as he was probably experiencing. His dark skin glistened under Sea Venture's deck lights. Jonas spoke first, "Welcome aboard my ship, Sea Venture. Today, son, the Lord has extended His merciful hand to you. If you are a praying man, then this is a good time to say a prayer of thanks."

The man looked scared and confused as hands touched him from every direction. After a few brief seconds, he began to speak in broken English with a French accent. "My poor *pere*! My poor *pere*! He gave his life for me."

Colette squeezed between Roy and Frank and spoke gently to him in French. Everyone waited patiently while Colette conversed with him. They were all anxious to hear her translation even though they suspected what had happened.

"Oh my God," Colette finally said. "This young man and his father had been out fishing in their boat when they were caught in the storm. Their boat capsized and then it started to sink." Colette could only shake her head back and forth in shocking disbelief.

Jonas interrupted, "Then we have to search for his father."

Colette looked up at Jonas. "No, no, Jonas; that is not possible. You see, they only had one life jacket between them and the boy's father made the boy put it on. His father went down with the boat. I have to say that what his father did is an act of true love; a love that only a parent can have. Sacrifice of one's life is always the greatest love."

Jack looked at Colette. "My best guess is this young man is from Haiti. Considering how poor that country is, I'm surprised they even had a life jacket."

"Yes, you have guessed correctly." Colette confirmed.

Jack looked at Roy. "Please go to the bridge and tell Andy that I said to change course. Tell him to make for Port-au-Prince. We are going to deliver this young man to whatever is left of his family."

Jack looked at Jonas, not for confirmation, but for understanding. Jonas didn't take his eyes off of the soaked young man. He simply said "Yes, that's what must be done. I know what it's like to lose someone you love to a storm. Let's get him inside and into some dry clothing. Colette, tell him what we are doing and then fix him something to eat."

Dawn arrived slowly, first in a veil of grey, and then sharply and brightly. It came as only it could in the Caribbean; full of promise and full of challenge. On this particular morning, however, the sun's brightness would shine down on a ship carrying people with heavy hearts. That was not a new occurrence in and around Haiti. The news of yet one more death would not be news at all; it was a way of life to Haitians since that January day in 2010, when the great quake struck without warning.

Misery and despair just never seems to end in Haiti, the poorest country of the hemisphere. Charities, churches, governments and people of good will had extended their hands to help the Haitian people. They gave millions of dollars and even came to work alongside people who were emotionally and physically devastated. Pain, suffering, dead bodies, filthy sanitary conditions were the things that outside volunteers had to contend with when they arrived.

In spite of the monumental efforts of a world community, medical supplies, food, clothing, and building materials remain stored in warehouses because of bureaucratic entanglements and a multitude of other factors and barriers that defy logic and conscience. All the good intentions of people and institutions are useless without actual delivery and follow-through. Charity should be an integral part of what defines us as human beings and organizations.

Once Sea Venture was tied off at the pier, Jack and Colette took the young man ashore. Jack went because she was Sea Venture's captain and Colette because she spoke French. However, Jack also had a hidden agenda; one predicated on something that was nagging at her on a personal and spiritual level. The latter purpose had nothing to do with the rescued fisherman.

Once ashore, the young fisherman they were accompanying used his local talents of persuasion to arrange a ride for all of them on the bed of a truck. The trip from the port to the city of Port-au-Prince covered ten miles on a bumpy, but serviceable road. The trip gave the trio ample time to talk and share life experiences.

Colette was horrified to learn that out of the 320 Catholic Missions and Churches in Haiti, 150 had been destroyed during the quake. One of the two Archdioceses in Haiti had been destroyed and Archbishop Joseph Serge Miot had been killed. Even with all the turmoil in the country, the news of his death had spread fast to the 2.5 million Catholics that lived there.

It took the Pope a year to appoint a new Archbishop and the rescued boy's father, a fisherman, personally knew the newly appointed priest. His name was Archbishop Guire Poulard. Since the Archbishop was acquainted with his family, the devastated young fisherman wanted Colette and Jack to be with him when he informed the Archbishop of his father's fate; and sacrifice.

The whole idea appealed to Colette and it also opened a spiritual door for Jack. Through her religious upbringing, she knew that sin was a reality of daily life for everyone. She also knew that God expected His followers to avoid sin because sin was offensive to God. Fornicating with Frank outside of marriage was a sin. She had to find a priest and take part in the Sacrament of Penance; in other words confession. How else could she demonstrate that she was sorry for her sin? She would gladly do penance and make amends for this sin and any other ones she might think of during confession. Only God, through His mercy, can set a sinner free. She had to free herself of that early morning with Frank in her cabin. Her sin had been the product of poor impulse control and it had been more her fault than Frank's. She had been the instigator of her sin and Frank probably would not have participated without being enticed.

The meeting with the Archbishop went well and as expected. His daily tasks were demanding and often equally important so it came as no surprise that he had to summon another priest to take Jack's confession while he dealt with the fisherman and his family's loss.

Colette stood by quietly, somberly, and in reserve for any needed support. Sometimes a bystander only has to be seen in order to be effectively appreciated. Right from the beginning, she had admired Jack as a sea captain and now she could add her as a friend. The things people do will always draw a person's attention, especially if they are going out of their way to take the moral high road as now was the case with Jack. Friendship had to be the best desert a chef could serve up for a person.

Jack's ordeal was dispensed with quickly and efficiently. In her mind and heart her act of contrition had been fulfilled. Now, she and Colette laughed and joked with each other all the way back to Sea Venture. Laughter was always the soul's sunshine. Jack had done her penance. She had said enough Hail Mary's and Our Father's to make her throat sore, and in her mind, it had been worth every word. She knew in her heart that God had heard her loudly and clearly. God's compassionate grace had lifted a great weight off her shoulders.

All those aboard anxiously wanted to hear the details of the trip. However, they also knew that some things were best left unruffled. There had been enough stress for this day.

Sea Venture sailed out of the harbor with Jack fast asleep in her cabin. Andy had the ship back on course and he was forever checking the barometer and weather charts. Roy was cleaning and polishing everything from top to bottom. Tommy and Georgia were lost in a rousing game of gin rummy on the upper deck. Colette was holding Jonas' hand across the galley table, connecting now on a deeper level than they had two days earlier. Matt and Frank were sitting in deck chairs sipping ice tea and exchanging old tales of military service. Gerty was watching the seascape with optimism while trying to come to terms with her alcohol addiction. Once again, life was stable and calm on Sea Venture. Everyone seemed to be doing something they wanted to do with people they cared about, and they all had something to look forward to; a good cruise. Happiness and contentment are always wonderful blessings.

Chapter 17

Jack's reddish-blond hair glistened with perspiration in the early morning sun as she stepped out of the fitness room. After standing her early morning watch on the bridge, her well-deserved rest from the vigor's of the storm, and subsequent rescue of the fisherman, and the stress of her confession, she had pretty much been out of sight to most everyone aboard Sea Venture. Right now, however, all she wanted to do was sit down with Frank and have an earnest conversation.

Unlike Jack, Frank had slept in on this morning because he had stayed up late the night before, wrestling with himself on an emotional level; trying to make sense out of what had happened between him and Jack. He was almost to the fitness room door when it suddenly opened. At first sight neither he nor Jack spoke. A smile crossed his lips and she smiled back at him with warm searching eyes.

All he wanted was some form of redemption for his part in what had taken place between them. Immediately after they had made love, she had let him know that what they had done was a sin according to her faith and church. Her unexpected pronouncement had certainly put a damper on their act of intimacy, placing it in a realm that was unfamiliar to him. He hoped it wouldn't drive a wedge between them. More than anything else, he wanted to build on what had happened and turn it into a solid relationship with a high probability for a lifetime commitment; marriage. His feelings for her were genuine, that he was sure of.

"Frank, we need to talk." She alerted him.

"To say otherwise would be an understatement." He was concerned that their talk might not go well. Concern aside, they had to have a frank and open conversation so they stepped into the fitness room for privacy.

"Frank, I don't know any other way to express why I decided to make love to you the other morning than to speak plainly about it. When I pulled you into my cabin, I was distracted by a sweet seductive desire for intimacy; I had hoped the pleasure of the moment would somehow speed us toward an everlasting love. Oh, I did mean to make love to you. In fact, at the time, I meant it wholeheartedly. Unfortunately, in the process, I had wandered from my church and the tenants of my faith. I apologize to you for pulling you into my sin. I also think I have fallen in love with you and the last thing I want to happen is to lose you. I hope you will forgive me and not think I am some easy tramp. If you still have feelings for me, real feelings, then I want you to take your time and make sure I am the right one for you. I should not have moved our relationship along as fast as I did. So this is your chance, should you decide that I am not that one special person deserving of your love, then I will understand and respect your decision?" She silently hoped that she had judged Frank correctly and that he was truly an honorable man.

"No, it is I who should apologize to you, Jack. For the most part, I have lived a life of moral confusion, plagued with one disappointment after another. You see, I have always lived life on the edge. I have been an adventure junkie, always searching for truth and meaning while plowing through death and destruction. I have now come to a point in my life where it is time for me to step up to the plate and hit a home run for something bigger than myself." Frank was taking a giant step toward defining himself.

Her response was right there on the tip of her tongue. "Frank, I think that you do have depth of character. Perhaps we both had thought, at the time, that having sex would somehow make us happy and bring us closer together. We had taken a giant leap when a cautious step would have been more prudent. Additionally, and wrongly, I was acting out of desire while thinking I was taking a shortcut to true love. In the end, all we accomplished was making ourselves miserable.

"We have been chasing our own shadows instead of trying to become the best version of ourselves that is possible. Had we kept it up, the sun would have quickly gone down on our lives and those temporary shadowy figures of who we thought we were would certainly have been lost in the darkness. Oh, in one form or another, our lives would have once again temporarily appeared with the next sunrise. However, there is no permanency to that. We really need a clear understanding of who we are at all times. Real love has an around-the-clock schedule with no intermission." Like Frank, she was learning something about herself as she spoke from the depth of her heart.

"I have an idea, Jack. Let's make a fresh start. This time we will do it right."

She was overcome with relief as she heard his words. "I'm for that. By the way, I think you are a terrific guy and I do care for you. I just want it to last. Our relationship has to be built on a solid foundation. In the process, I also want to eliminate as much sin as possible from my life. I want to give you a woman that is as clean as I can make myself."

They embraced and kissed each other with the same passion as when they had kissed for the first time. However, this time it seemed to mean much more.

She went on to clean up for breakfast while he stayed behind for a vigorous workout. Both of them were at peace with the world. She was mending her relationship with God and they were both working on improving themselves. He needed to define himself spiritually and become the best version of himself as he could attain. He also was aware that he had his share of emotional baggage that had to be dealt with. All rugged old soldiers had excessive emotional baggage; it is a byproduct of battles won and battles lost for causes that were often not clear, let alone worthy of the effort.

On this morning, Jonas was experiencing his own realizations which were far different from those of others aboard Sea Venture. The distance to his obsessive goal was shortening; the island of Viegues was calling to him with an ever-increasing intensity. In the midst of that calling, the past was inviting him, not with open arms, but with challenge.

He didn't know how many tests were ahead. All he knew for sure was he would take those tests on with a sincere heart. Although he wished it was possible, he was aware that he could not do this alone. At the center of his struggle was the harsh reality that his faith was at odds with his failings, thus, there were inherent flaws. Presently, his only glimmer of non-spiritual hope was with his new friend, Frank. He would have to rely on Frank to guide and coach him through his investigative experience and expertise. Jonas had to thank God for Frank coming along when he did. This was a good time for prayer. "God, give me strength to get through this. And thank You for all the friends You have delivered into my life. Amen!"

Jonas' spirit was troubled by a combination of both pale and vivid memories from his past. Somehow, Frank would help him figure things out to a point where he could resolve all these nagging issues. Without resolution there would be no peace for him.

He was amazed at how Frank was able to philosophize about life. Perhaps, this was a good time to try that technique for himself. For thousands of years people had looked up at the heavens for answers and explanations about their lives. Since that was something people were accustomed to doing for thousands of years, then it couldn't just amount to a bunch of hocus-pocus. Don't all people of faith, especially religious scholars, look up to heaven when they speak to God? It couldn't just be a matter of astrology. Yes, God is up there somewhere and He has all the answers for what ills us; that Jonas was sure of. He just didn't know if he had the capacity to do his part. He had heard many times and had read it in the Bible that God gave everyone a free will. How to use this gift was what he had doubts about.

Jonas thought about life in other terms, also. Everything in life seemed to be cyclic, even the seasons. So was it possible that the occurrences in his life could be linked to some long-repeating cycle that could be figured out?

"My goodness," he said out loud to his self, "if I'm cycling like the seasons, then, at my age, I'm entering the winter of my life." Throughout his life he had cycled in and out of so many things that he couldn't begin to count them; except the obvious ones. He was getting old and that meant time was running out. Why wasn't Sea Venture going fast enough? Soon, very soon, he would have to have a conversation with those around him.

When he finally revealed his mission to his friends, Jonas hoped they would not perceive him as a madman. He was aware that he had drifted from some safe, sheltered place in reality to a dark abyss deep in his soul. This was not a matter of life and death, but rather a matter of the results of life and death. This was a place where a person was held in darkness by the chains of fear and a lack of understanding.

All these thoughts were beginning to give him a headache. Surely, Colette would have a remedy. At least she could serve up a nice breakfast and some stimulating conversation. She was a warm and caring person who happened to be living an odd and eclectic life. Maybe it was her oddness that attracted him to her. At any rate, she had penetrated his inner circle and that pleased him immensely. Naturally, she could never replace his wife, but, she could possibly follow her. She was unique, warm, and projected an animal magnetism that was more than intriguing to him. He could learn to love such a woman. Everyone deserved a bright spot in their otherwise deplorable lives.

Once he was finished with Viegues, he would have to pursue his options with Colette. She was slowly becoming the goal behind his big goal.

Chapter 18

Sea Venture was clear of the Dominican Republic, and Puerto Rico was just beyond the horizon. Soon the schedule would take on a new life and that meant change and perhaps some juggling. In the short run, Jonas was doing his best not to measure the time he was spending at sea, in spite of his mounting impatience. He had his eye on a fixed point; Vieques. Vieques was part of Puerto Rico proper and he had only seen it briefly a long time ago. There was no way he could bring himself to enjoy the scenery; not at this point when he had so many other things on his mind. Yes, his thoughts were squarely on the past; during his brief history on the island.

Jonas' didn't have much quiet time left and that was good since solitude prompted too much reflection. He had had his fill of reflecting. What he needed now was action. Fear was eating away at his heart and soul, yet, he knew that he could never turn away from his quest, not when he was this close.

More than anything, at this very moment, he wanted his world to be arranged in such a way that it was conducive to his wants and desires. He knew that this was pure selfishness on his part; but too much was at stake for him to be distracted.

He kept asking himself if his feelings of guilt were justified or if they were a figment of an over-active imagination? That question would probably keep nagging at him until he left Vieques. In the final analysis, this trip was the only shot he had at closure. He had struggled and suffered for over forty years with an eye on a goal that was, at best, immersed in brackish water. There was no telling what he might learn during the next few days.

On this day, while he was still out here on the open sea, there were no distractions or obstacles; all around him order and harmony were constant, and ruled by Mother Nature under the will of God. The open sea was one of his favorite places, even though he would soon have to set it aside until his mission was complete. He filled his lungs with fresh air and smiled at the billowing white clouds that floated across a beautiful blue sky. Where was a rainbow when a person needed it?

Jonas walked forward as far as he could go on Sea Venture's bow. Like a beacon in the night following a storm, there it was, right there before his eyes. Vieques was stretched out in a sunny freshness of tropical blend. The water faded from a deep blue to a clear green and on to a breathtaking clarity that met a white sandy beach. The cove ahead was nothing less than a great splendor; a place that everyone should experience sometime in their life.

Suddenly, Jonas's was having gut-wrenching feelings that were emotionally charged on a grand scale. When everything in a man's mind was suddenly about to collide with an unpredictable force, it was not unlikely that he would end up feeling queasy and uneasy. Over the years his life had become flat, stale and useless in many ways. During the last four decades there had been several times when he had considered suicide as a way of escaping his demons. Now, he was thankful that he had toughed it out. Somehow, he would have to pull himself together.

There must be clues there on Vieques and Jonas would do his best to find them. There was a mystery there on this tiny little island; maybe even more than one mystery. He was not about to leave any stone unturned. Like the Holy Grail, humanity and reality was a mystery; one worthy of trying to solve. He didn't know why, but, mysteries had a way of driving even strong men crazy.

Jonas felt like a knight in search of something magnificent and cleverly hidden. In his case it certainly was not the highly coveted Holy Grail. Strangely, at this moment, he seemed to share something other searchers had surely experienced. Like others who had pursued similar ventures, he guessed he would find and follow leads; some false and others on target, that he was convinced of. He also knew that small puzzles, like great mysteries, would not be worthy of challenge if they were simple and easy to solve. He didn't care if one lead led to another as long as he was able to continue his search. He was living an obsession.

The whole world knew about honorable and spiritual men who understood the importance of being committed to a quest. For many of these select men and women, their greatest reward was in the journey itself. The pursuit of such things as the proverbial "Light" or the great "Redemption" had become the essence of their lives. All said and done, for these men, it beat the heck out of any other undertaking. However, Jonas was not chasing some mystical concept. He was trying to solve something that had actually occurred in his life. The reason he was searching was very personal.

Sea Venture came to a stop and within minutes Andy was dropping the anchor. Goosebumps were racing across Jonas' skin while he drank in the island's features. The palm trees and dense foliage appeared deeply green and bright. He could smell the rich tropical fragrance that was drifting across Sea Venture; it was the island's welcoming tribute. It was a pure and delightful symphony of scents. The island was just as alluring now as it had been the first time he had laid eyes on it.

By this time everyone aboard was out on deck gawking and admiring the scene. Everything was so pristine and inviting. There was not a soul in sight on the island's pure white sandy beach. The foliage was spotted with colorful flowers of all sorts of size and heights. At first sight, it was nothing short of a lush paradise. There just wasn't any way to separate God from Nature; they had to be one and the same.

Throughout the years, Jonas had struggled to recall details of Vieques. Regretfully, he had only spent two days there, yet, that exposure made a lasting impression on him. Mesmerized, he stood there looking at the island in an attempt to recall, to the best of his ability, the events and impressions that formed the nucleus of his internal conflict.

His memories were many and varied, hard to classify because they were all so interwoven and muddled in an odd way. His only chance for clarity was to investigate and that would mean he would have to confront the man who most likely held the answers.

Tommy spoke loud enough for everyone to hear. "Yes, I have to admit that this is a beautiful island. But there are hundreds more just like it. I don't know why we have to pick this one when the others have so much more to offer in the way of facilities and entertainment. Oh well, I guess we will just have to make the best of it?"

Georgia countered Tommy's remarks. "Tommy, quit sulking and whining like a spoiled brat. I'm ready to grab my bathing suit and hit the beach. I'm sure this beach can produce the same tan as any other beach in the Caribbean."

Jonas ignored Tommy's opinion and made an announcement. I want to see everyone in the galley in ten minutes. I have some things to tell all of you. Viegues is not a destination for pleasure; it goes much deeper than that, especially for me."

Everyone did their best to speculate about why they were here at Viegues. Generally, they all thought Tommy had a point about coming to an island that was so lacking in popularity. The

Caribbean was full of beautiful islands that catered to the appetites of tourists. Their thoughts were running wild as they headed to the galley to hear some special announcement from Jonas. Perhaps he was finally going to let the cat out of the bag when it came to the purpose of this cruise.

Jonas sat quietly, stone faced, at the head of the galley table. Not a single word crossed his lips until they were all seated with their eyes fixed on him.

He nervously cleared his throat a couple of times before speaking. "Believe me when I say that I am ashamed of myself for deceiving you. The weight of my shame today is only added to the guilt that I have been carrying around for the biggest part of my life. I wish I had had the courage to tell you about this island and what it means to me. You see, this is not the first time that I have been here." Beads of sweat were breaking out all over his face and neck. "Damn, this is a hard thing to talk about. In fact, I don't think I have ever talked about it to anyone before."

Jonas tried to scan their faces for some reaction, but was unable to discern what they were thinking. Besides, second guessing what was on their minds was only a waste of time. Catching a glimpse of Vieques through a porthole prompted him to get back to the salient points of his impromptu meeting.

"I have to be fair and tell you what happened here and how it has haunted me for most of my adult life." He stood up and walked to the open door and studied the island for a few seconds in search of inspiration and remembrance. "After all these years, I am finally back here to face my past. A few minutes ago, I prayed to God for enough strength to get me through this. I also prayed that I am not somehow putting any of you in any danger." There was a hint of fear in his trembling tone and he knew that he would have to over-trump that fear with sheer determination.

Everyone's attention was now riveted on Jonas as they unconsciously leaned forward to make sure they caught every word he was saying.

"I believe that God has punished me long and hard. There's no telling the extent or degree of anger He might have towards me for how I acted so long ago. In fact, I'm not sure He was ever truly angry at me at all. I only know that I gave Him good reason to be angry with me. You see, my relationship with God has been somewhat lacking at times. I do think that God has been disappointed in me for failing to look out for someone that was the best friend I ever had. I should have been my brother's keeper; that's according to scripture. You see, my best friend was a man of great faith who dedicated his life to God. I have no doubt in my heart and soul that God had great plans for my friend."

Jonas was now speaking between sobs as his eyes welled with tears. The outside tropical light that poured in through the opened door and windows made his sweaty and tear-covered face glisten.

"My belief back then is the same as it is today. What happened on this little speck of an island sat in motion everything in my life that turned out wrong. I think that you all know that everything that happens in life is all connected in some way. Our past always has something to do with our future. As you can see, I'm not very good at explaining things; especially life." He glanced over at Gerty.

She smiled back with encouragement. "Go on, Jonas, you are doing just fine." A voice in the back of her head was telling her that Jonas was about to reveal some deeply guarded thoughts about his life; things she wanted to know about.

Her smile calmed him sufficiently to continue. “I was in the Navy back then and I was assigned to the U.S.S. York County. My best friend served on the same ship. Like me, he was black. His name was Cornelius West. Everyone aboard the York County affectionately called him ‘Corn Dog.’ He was the chaplain’s assistant. Corn Dog was going to become a minister when his enlistment was up. Our plan was to live together in New Orleans when my enlistment was up. We knelt down and prayed together every night. If it wasn’t for him, I don’t think I would have ever known anything about God.”

Jonas continued to struggle emotionally as he forged on with his story. His long-harbored torment was a compilation of many symptoms that he had managed to hide from those around him. He was suffering from an emotional and spiritual illness that was constantly ripping and gouging his soul. All along, he suspected that the cure for his spiritual ailment was locked up inside his heart and mind. The key was close by, now that he had arrived at Vieques.

When he sat back down, he twisted about in his chair in search of a more comfortable position; there was none. He closed his eyes hoping to see a clear way forward in his explanation. For a few brief seconds he was psychologically blind. Like so many other times in his life, he was once again all alone with others watching; earnestly searching for clues to what was driving him crazy. Hopefully, he would not become trapped by his own state of mind. That agonizing thought was frightening to him.

He grabbed a napkin and wiped his face. Then he did the unexpected, he removed his admiral’s hat and wrung it like a wet washcloth. With it clutched in his hands he found the where-for-all to resume speaking.

Jonas had saved his biggest bomb to drop on them when it came to his friend Corn Dog, and drop it he did. "My friendship with Corn Dog ran deeper than any of you could realize. You see, as we got to know one another we discovered that we were kin. We had the same father. That concept is not unheard of around New Orleans, and the rest of the world for that matter. Yes, we were both products of the same man's misadventure. No matter how we got there, we were blood. I also believe that it was God's doing that we ended up on the same ship at the same time. From the moment I learned that I had a brother, I became my brother's keeper until the day I failed him." He waited for them to digest what he had just divulged.

Their wide eyes and dropped jaws revealed their surprise. That verbal bomb left some of them emotionally shell-shocked.

"After being at sea for more than a month we were ready for some liberty. It was my idea that we should go ashore while we were docked at the Naval Station in San Juan, Puerto Rico. At my urging, we got a three day pass. We pampered ourselves with a classy meal at the Normandy Hotel. After dinner, we went to the basement bar that was called the 'Voodoo Lounge.'

"We sat at the bar and downed a couple of beers over Corn Dog's objections. You see, he was a bit uneasy when it came to drinking because alcohol had a tendency to invite sinful behavior. I told him not to worry because I would look out for him.

"Right when we were ready to leave, this dude joins us at the bar. We could tell by his haircut that he was, like us, in the military. He insisted that we have a round on him so we graciously sat back down. He said he was a Navy Corpsman from New York City and he was stationed there at the San Juan Navy Reservation. His name was Bernardo Calici and he was pure Italian. Right from the jump-start we called him Bennie. Bennie was one of those typical in-you-face Italians from New York. Personally, I didn't like the guy; he was too pushy for me. Every time I tried to say something, he interrupted by talking over me. Corn Dog was impressed by him, though."

Jonas stopped to catch his breath. This was the longest he had talked to anyone in a good many years. He wished someone else would say something to give him a break and allow him to collect his thoughts. No such luck, so he kept the stage to himself.

"Bennie started talking about life in the Caribbean and after a few more drinks they were on the topic of pirates." That raised an eyebrow of Jack's. She liked the topic of pirates and possessed considerable knowledge of the subject.

Jonas sipped some ice tea from a tall glass Colette had placed in front of him. "Corn Dog got real excited when Bennie began talking about Vieques and some story about pirates stashing treasure and loot on the island. Bennie said there was a secret hiding place there and smugglers were still using it. It was a bunch of hogwash, like you might see in an old movie. In my opinion and using a Navy term, it was pure scuttlebutt." All eyes shifted away from Jonas to look out the door at the island. Their curiosity was building.

When Jonas started speaking again their eyes abandoned the island and the prospect of seeing proof of pirates and treasure. "Right before my eyes, and against my better judgment, Bennie and Corn Dog put together a plan to search for the alleged pirate hideout. The plan was undoubtedly fueled by all the beers they were tossing back; too many of them. Nevertheless, the plan was agreed to. The three of us would meet at seven the next morning to take the ferry to Vieques. The decision was made far too hastily for me, and it was way too big of an adventure to be taking with a stranger."

Frank had more to consider as he sat there among the others. His interest in Jonas' motivation and wellbeing had been present from the first day they had met. Finally, on this day and during this meeting, Jonas had effectively established a pivotal point in their friendship. The last thing that Frank had expected was that Jonas would begin to unravel his mystery in a single sitting and reveal his demons to so many people. Perhaps, Jonas was attempting to recruit as much help for his journey as he could muster.

Jonas had to be under a great deal of pressure for him to lay all his cards out on the table while exposing elements of his soul. Frank also wondered if any or all of those in attendance would desert his ship and walk away from him during his critical time of need. The meeting was not yet over, far from it. Everyone present was listening and hanging on to every word Jonas was throwing out. That was a positive sign.

Jonas was not about to waver at this point. He would continue until he had said all there was to say. "We all met at seven the next morning. Corn Dog was pumped with excitement. Even after a good night's sleep, I was just as distrustful of Bennie as I had been the night before. Every time I offered some form of objection, it was shoved aside by this wild Italian, Bennie. He played the whole adventure off as some mild form of entertainment. Now that I think back on it, I should have taken a stand and put a stop to the whole thing, even if Corn Dog got mad at me. I was weak. Somehow, I abandoned my instincts when I saw how Corn Dog was enjoying himself. At least I was bound and determined to keep an eye on Bennie for any sign of real danger. I was also hoping I wasn't becoming jealous and envious over how Corn Dog was taking to Bennie.

"Anyway, and to my dismay, Corn Dog was bonding with Bennie like a dog to his master. Bennie talked over and around me whenever I objected to any part of the plan. Although three of us were standing there, only Corn Dog and Bennie were interacting. By this time, I was getting really disgusted with both of them." Jonas took a long drink of ice tea and held up the empty glass for Colette to refill it.

"When we arrived on the island, we caught a taxi to the town. We got out at the town square and walked around for half an hour or so. The town was quaint and probably hadn't changed much in more than a hundred years or longer. The streets around the square were paved with cobblestone. The side streets were a mixture of dirt and sand with patches of asphalt. There were ruts and holes everywhere. The other thing I noticed was that no one seemed to be in a hurry. That was a far cry from the activity on the streets of New Orleans.

Colette placed a fresh glass of ice tea in front of Jonas and re-took her place at the table. She was seeing a side of Jonas she had not expected to see.

"We ended up at a little cantina on the town square. It was owned and operated by a retired Marine who was actually born there. Even though I was sitting at the bar with my brother and Bennie, I just as well have been sitting alone. You would have thought that Corn Dog and Bennie had been life-long buddies.

"After a while, you could say that I had had enough since I had no way to change things. Hanging on the wall was an advertisement for rum that was a hundred and fifty-one proof. The bartender saw me looking at it and told me that it was a real man's drink. At my age back then, that was all that had to be said; the challenge was on. I ordered a double and when I saw the bartender mixing it with Coca Cola, I showed my pride and ignorance. Over the sounds of a jukebox and Bennie and Corn Dog yakking away, I yelled at the bartender. I demanded that he give me the drink straight. I told him that I wasn't a kid and that I was in the U.S. Navy. This proved to be a bad choice.

"I downed my double with a single gulp and then I ordered a triple shot, straight up. All the fuss I was making with my drinking didn't faze Corn Dog or Bennie. I don't know how many drinks I had before falling off the barstool. At first, I felt like I was spinning around in outer space. Then I didn't feel anything. Yes, I was out cold.

"I woke up the next morning on a cot in the back room of the cantina. Some men were sitting around a table playing dominoes. My head hurt like hell."

Jonas' last comment encouraged a few smirks and laughs around the table; with the exception of Gerty who was regretting some of her own drinking escapades. At some time in their lives, each one of those sitting at the galley table had experienced a rough drunk and the horrendous hangover that had followed it.

Jonas shot a quick grin at everyone. At least he wasn't boring his audience. After waving a hand to dismiss his sheepish grin, he was ready to continue. For the first time during his meeting, he didn't need any throat-clearing before speaking.

"I asked the bartender about the two men I had been with. All I could get out of him was that they paid a local man to take them across the island to a spot near where a U.S. Marine Corps unit was camped for training. They had left me behind because a passed-out drunk would only have slowed them up. I let my brother, Corn Dog, down. But worst of all, I left him with a crazy stranger. I failed my best friend.

The eyes of all those around the table accurately read the guilt that was expressed on Jonas' face. To this point, the story was a remarkable one and it underscored the lesson of disloyalty; the failure of friendship between one man and another. All sailors know that whether they are out on the sea or on land, everything depended on teamwork and the buddy system. The reality of not caring enough to act correctly for others will always result in fear, mistrust and guilt. All men act or fail to act through their own God-given free will. When these natural rules fail to take root properly in our minds, then we cannot be relied upon to be our brother's keeper. At this point everyone had a clear understanding of Jonas' guilt and shame. They braced themselves because they knew that the rest of Jonas' story was not going to end on a good note.

"Let me get to the bottom line, here." Jonas broke their hasty intent to assess his story. "I caught the last ferry back to San Juan, and I made that ride alone. Aboard the U.S.S. York County, Corn Dog was listed as Away-Without-Leave (AWOL). From that time to this day, he has never been heard of. After interviewing me, the York County's Captain notified the authorities at the San Juan Navy Reservation. They in turn were able to interview Bennie. All they gleaned from the interview was that Corn Dog had wandered off on his own while visiting Vieques. Now, here I am with the means and determination to conduct my own inquiry. You see, I have to do something about Corn Dog or my life is a total waste."

Jonas sat there with watery eyes, but, it was clear to everyone that he was not a defeated man; he was a driven man. Collectively, everyone whole-heartedly empathized with him. He was a crushed man, but he was not a helpless dying man.

Admittedly, some of those present saw Jonas' determined effort as a waste of time. After all, the trail to finding Corn Dog was not just cold; it was frozen and obliterated by time.

"Okay, you all think this is an impossible mission. Don't think for a minute that I am some old fool that only needs some comforting and sympathy. That man over there is the best in the business and he has opened up a door for me." He pointed directly at Frank.

"You see, Frank has located Bernardo Calici for me. The day we sat sail, I talked to that crazy Italian and told him that I was going to take Vieques apart, stone by stone, and tree by tree, in order to find Corn Dog. At first Bennie wouldn't say much. Then after he gave it some thought something told him that he needed to be on top of whatever it was I was about to do. Tomorrow, Bennie is going to meet me on Vieques. All I need to know from you guys is: are you with me?"

Jonas leaned forward toward his captive onlookers and spoke boldly and honestly. "Look at me, my body grows old, but my faith and spirit has never been stronger. I am a man who has made some really awful decisions in life, but I'm not a bad person; I am only a sinner like everyone else. A truly evil man would not go through life feeling ashamed and guilty seven days a week and twenty-four hours a day. Please, I don't want you to see me as some kind of a monster. So right now I'm going to give you an opportunity, an option, to walk away if you don't agree with me. I won't hold it against you. In fact, I'll buy anyone who wants it a ticket to anywhere they want to go. Give me a show of hands of anyone who wants out!"

They all looked at each other to see who would raise their hand and walk away. No one said a word and no one raised a hand. For whatever reason that motivated each of them, they were all in.

Jonas was not pursuing pleasure or possessions. He was pursuing redemption for his own failings and that message was resonating clearly with him. As far as everyone else, Jonas' story was easy to listen to because they were positioned comfortably at a cold distance as casual observers. But, they also were willing to allow Jonas' story to penetrate their lives and move them to help and participate in some undefined way. They were accepting the challenge to get involved. Even Tommy, the often disagreeable one, was not so hard-hearted that he would not get involved. They were, one and all, now officially coming together as a team.

All eyes were now squarely planted on Frank, whose mind was racing as fast as anyone's. He speculated that there may be some who would take some middle course and not be totally committed to the cause. Naturally, there was a strong incentive, even if it was nothing short of mercenary, for being supportive of the initiative. At any rate, Frank did not expect any wholesale desertion at this juncture. It would end up being the degree of enthusiasm each of them would display that would tell how much of their heart was in it.

The meeting ended in a flood of enthusiastic 'high fives.'

Chapter 19

Jack was giving Jonas' presentation a great deal of thought as she followed Frank into his cabin. Closing the door behind her provided the freedom and privacy to speak candidly. "That was quite a confession, don't you think?"

Frank zeroed in on the word 'confession.' "Yes, that's one way to look at it. Jonas certainly blames himself for the disappearance of his brother. I think his guilt has been hacking away at his heart for way too long. You would think that the passage of time would have had more of a healing effect than it has. By the way, I had no idea why Jonas had me locate Bernardo Calici."

Jack began analyzing Jonas' distressful situation by applying some of her home-grown logic. "Well, his brother was a grown man, an adult. Adults have to accept a lot of responsibility for what they do in life; even children do as they mature. All of us own our mistakes and decisions. So, in Jonas' case, who owns the most blame; Corn Dog, who went off alone with a stranger or Jonas, who failed to look out for him?"

Frank took a more neutral position. "I think they both contributed to an unfortunate situation. I have trouble seeing it in terms of good and bad."

Jack was not ready to give up her rationale. "I guess the answer to my question is that they betrayed each other. All this leads us back to the same question; the important one: who should own the guilt? We probably will never know. After all, it happened a long time ago and the only details we have are coming from the one that survived; our friend Jonas. Winners of wars and survivors of ordeals tend to write their own histories and they rarely match the versions of the ones who lost. For Jonas' sake, I hope the truth is not lost."

Frank sat on the edge of his bunk and invited Jack to sit next to him. He knew they both had more to say. "The confession Jonas just gave was obviously heart-felt. I can't imagine anyone suffering emotionally for that many years over something cloaked in such a fog of uncertainty. Personally, I can understand why he wants to clear it up. Unfortunately, the odds of uncovering the truth are rather remote. One way or another, we have to help him arrive at some closure so he can enjoy what's left of his life.

"As you know, Jonas lost his wife and son during Hurricane Katrina. Right now, he owns quite a bit of emotional pain and guilt. Guilt in any form or degree can put a strain on any relationship, especially marriage. So often, we take our frustration out on the ones we love the most, and that only compounds our problems. I wonder how much of his inner anger and guilt he projected on his wife and son before he lost them." Frank was doing his best to work through his discussion with Jack.

Jack was able to come up with an example from her own life. "Once I worked for a yacht owner that would scream at his wife for the smallest of reasons. It wasn't that he didn't love her because I'm convinced that he did. You could tell by the way he looked at her and showed affection to her when he was not angry. Months after I stopped working for him, I learned that several years before I went to work for him, he had accidentally killed his brother in a hunting accident. One of his coping mechanisms was to vent his guilt-ridden anger onto his wife. There is probably a psychological term for that, but I don't know what it is. Maybe it's something like 'transference.'"

"Well Jack, man's ability to reason and feel can sometimes be a curse to him."

"Thank God man is also capable of love. We all need love in order to cope with life; especially when it comes to bitter memories and heart-felt mistakes. Adding a good dose of God's love helps me through my tough times." The serious look on Jack's face was a further testament of her Catholic faith.

Frank, on the other hand, still had a ways to go when it came to faith. Oh, he had love in his heart. However, he had difficulty balancing it with what was in his mind. He consciously knew and understood that most people were delighted, to no end, with their ability to love and to be loved and that had to be a comfortable place. Still, there was a small place in the back of Frank's brain that sometimes doubted God's love for him. Each time he had loved a woman, God had taken her away. No less than a thousand times, he had asked himself why God would deny him his earthly loves? Somehow, he had to come to grips with how he perceived and understood reality and spirituality. How could love be both simple and complex at the same time?

He knew that men were greatly challenged as they attempted to find their way through the mist and fog that often held them captive to earthly wants and desires. Just where was that thin line that a man had to cross in order to discover the blessing of unconditional love; God's love? Was that line in a man's heart or was it in a church? That is if there was such a thing as unconditional love. The concept of love sounded like something a poet or philosopher would come up with to explain life to the novice or uniformed. Oh well, Frank was sure that God, and only God, had the authority to apply conditions to love. Maybe this did have something to do with things like: worship, prayer, the Church, sin, reconciliation, and absolution. Frank had a long way to go in this area. He often wondered how he could know so much about human behavior and so little about faith.

One look at Jack told him that he would not give up on his search for the brightness of a proper relationship with her. Hopefully, the veil of God's mystery would be lifted soon and he would be blessed with the enduring love of a mate; one Jacqueline Murphy, AKA Captain Jack.

Sensing that Frank was struggling with some perplexing investigational theory or some great dilemma, Jack wrapped her arms around him and placed her face on his chest. She could not reject what was in her heart; she was in love with him. Silently, she thanked God for delivering a good man to her. Oh she knew he was a troubled man, but most men were when it came to women and relationships. Yes, he was not perfect, but neither was she. It was a given reality that she had often strayed from her faith. Suddenly a warm feeling came over her and she realized that she was truly returning to her faith and that was filling her head with optimism. She was on God's side and He was on hers.

Jack and Frank had so much that they needed to convey to each other. Communication from one heart to another is no easy task. They were like a lot of people, they had to open up to their own feelings and expose them to the one's they trusted most. Love travels closely behind trust.

Now that Andy had set Sea Venture's anchor, he could relax. There were no predictions of foul weather so this was a good time to venture outside for some fresh air and sunshine. The cove was deserted and its tranquility was a sight to behold. Strolling to the port side he joined Georgia for some casual conversation. Her eyes were bright with interest and enthusiasm. She wasted no time in filling him in on all the details of Jonas' meeting. Andy had been stuck on the bridge during the meeting and no one had briefed him. He studied Georgia's face with earnest as she presented all the salient points of the meeting.

Among Andy's attributes were physical strength, endurance and a hardy appetite for challenge and adventure. Deep inside, he thought of himself as a younger version of Frank. Military people tended to have a lot in common with each other; a camaraderie that approached kinship and brotherhood. He felt fortunate to be in Frank's company and working for a great captain like Jack. She would have done well in the military. Andy knew that he certainly could have done a lot worse when it came to working under a captain.

While Andy's mind was evaluating the details and drama of Jonas' meeting, he was becoming encouraged over the prospect of some adventure heading his way. Suddenly, Georgia interrupted his thoughts. "I'll be darn, it looks like we are about to have company."

Andy looked to where she was pointing. There was excitement in her voice as she spoke. "That yacht is as big as Sea Venture and it looks like it is going to share the cove with us. Excuse me; I'm going to go fetch Captain Jack. That ship could have something to do with why we are here." Georgia charged off in search of Jack while Andy did an about face and walked back to the bridge in case there was any radio communication coming in from the arriving vessel.

Within a couple of minutes everyone aboard Sea Venture was lined up on the top deck of the ship's port side as they watched the newly arrived vessel drop anchor less than a hundred yards away.

Captain Jack presented the first observation. "I see she flies the same ensign as us; she's from the United States. I guess we're not the only ones with an interest in Vieques."

Jonas spoke to no one in particular. "I see Bennie has arrived right on schedule. It won't be long until things begin to get interesting."

Andy returned from the bridge. "The skipper of "Dark Shadow" radioed." He pointed to the other vessel. "He says Mr. Calici wants to meet Mr. Jackson on the beach at noon tomorrow."

Jonas looked at Frank like a nervous mouse looks at cheese on a mousetrap. Frank smiled encouragingly to demonstrate his support for Jonas. "Radio the skipper that Mr. Jackson will see him on the beach at noon tomorrow."

Frank was eager to meet this New York physician that was wealthy enough to sail about the Caribbean on a mega yacht. However, the big question was why this doctor was motivated to meet with a former acquaintance who had been a lower enlisted navy man who was looking into some obscure event that occurred more than forty years ago. Frank hoped that the good Doctor Bernardo Calici would somehow tip his hand during the meeting on the beach.

There was an embryo of a theory taking root in the back of Frank's mind. All the loose talk of pirate stashes and centuries of smuggling in the Caribbean smacked of organized crime in today's lingo. Just maybe, somewhere in the mix of what Jonas was probing, there was an intermingling of codes of silence; lines of authority; strange behavior patterns; and a sense of loyalty to something larger than any individual involved. Frank's job was to look out for those aboard Sea Venture, especially when it came to Jonas. For everyone's sake and for Frank's peace of mind, his embryonic theory was probably just a product of an overactive imagination.

The investigator in Frank spoke clearly; he needed to acquire enough additional information to satisfy his curiosity or lay the groundwork for further action. He needed to cultivate, mostly through elicitation, some background knowledge from local sources. Perhaps, there was some information to be gleaned from local law enforcement, bartenders, taxi drivers or even officials that oversee the operation of the island. If he had to, he would not be opposed to paying for some information.

Frank spotted Jack entering the bridge. He didn't waste any time catching up to her. "Jack, how would you like to tag along with me for a few hours? I want to go ashore and nose around a bit."

She seized the opportunity. "Sure, I would love to hang out with you." She refocused on Andy and continued. "Tell Jonas that Frank and I are going ashore for a while. We just want to check the place out."

"Eye, eye Captain, I'll take care of it right away." Andy liked the idea of being in charge of Sea Venture, even if it wasn't out on the open sea.

Matt and Roy were tasked with readying one of two rigid hall inflatable boats (RHIB) that were aboard Sea Venture. They were both Zodiac DB 600's; the best that money could buy and when not in use they didn't take up much storage room. Matt piloted and Roy went along for the ride as they took Frank and Jack to the beach.

Jack gave Matt notice on what to expect for her and Frank's return. "I'll call you on your cell phone when we're ready to be picked up. Keep an eye on everything until we find out what's up with those aboard the new yacht in the cove. Don't take anything for granted." It was in her nature to be overly cautious.

Once they were ashore, Frank and Jack used fold-up bicycles for ground transportation. She wore khaki shorts and a light blue halter top while Frank stayed with his faded blue jeans and polo shirt. All islands in the Caribbean were casual.

Before riding off, Jack walked over to Frank and put her arms around him. "This is our first official date, even though we are on a fact-finding mission. How about we start it off with a nice kiss?" They kissed warmly.

Back on Sea Venture, Jonas was watching Frank and Jack through a pair of binoculars. He smiled approvingly as he saw them kiss. He had no doubt about them being a good match. He also hoped that they would always be part of his extended family.

"You took me by surprise." Frank held her in his arms for an extended embrace. "Thanks for reassuring me that we are still boyfriend and girlfriend. Sometimes my mind gives me tunnel vision. I like the idea of experiencing a pleasurable afternoon while gathering information that might come in handy in the near future. Yes, I love surprises like this where we can capitalize on opportunity. In fact, let's make this a habit." He hoped dating, under any circumstances, would last a lifetime with Jack.

Peddling the bikes proved difficult along the beach since the road was sandy instead of being paved. Luckily, that changed once they got closer to Isabel Segunda; the only town on the island. The terrain was also challenging with the road winding around in tight turns and jutting up and down hills. The reward, for Frank, was watching Jacks muscular lags as she pumped the pedals on her bike with less effort as opposed to how he was handling the trip. He still needed more time in the fitness room; that went without question.

Isabel Segunda was on the north side at the center of Isla de Vieques. The whole island had less than 10,000 residents and nearly all of them were in town. Once they reached the town plaza, Jack announced her first observation. "This town, the whole island for that matter, seems to be caught between two worlds and cultures, past and present. I can't believe all the horses we saw roaming around freely. Seeing what we just saw, you would think the place hadn't changed much since the late 1700's and early 1800's. The noticeable change, though, is all the people walking around talking on their cell phones."

Frank added to Jack's observation. "It looks like the only vehicular traffic is here around the town square. Some of these young guys driving flashy cars look out of place. The rest of the population must be stuck in a time warp like in one of those science fiction movies. I just don't know which ones are in the right place. Places like this make me glad I'm able to travel abroad. Travel is a good form of education."

Jack revealed what little she knew about the town. "In college, I read about this town, but I never had the chance to visit it. Isabel Sequnda is named after the Queen of Spain and the local inhabitants call the town El Pueblo. On each end of the island there is a Nature Reserve, and there are literally hundreds of little beaches to explore. If it wasn't for the Nature Reserves there would probably be fancy hotels everywhere." She picked up a brochure from a stand outside of the Post Office that was located just off the main plaza.

"Those are good observations, Jack. I bet this place was somewhat contested during the British Colonial times. I mean Spain and the new colonies in America probably both coveted beautiful places like this." Frank had an academic curiosity about all places.

Jack had some trivia on the tip of her tongue. "Yes, the British had a different name for this island. They called it Crab

Island. But, the United States ended up with ownership. Sadly, my perspective is that the U.S. did not take advantage of the place's beauty and charm. They turned it into a bombing range and testing ground for the U.S. Navy. Every time I wanted to sail around this island, it was off limits. Thankfully, the U.S. Navy left here in 2003. All the former Navy property is now a wildlife refuge. When I looked at the maps aboard Sea Venture this morning, I saw that the old Navy names for some of the beaches are still the same. The primary ones are called; Red Beach, Blue Beach, and Green Beach. These beaches, I'm told, are spectacular and are listed as some of the top beaches in the Caribbean because of their azure-colored waters and white sands."

"Jack, you should have been a tour guide. How do you keep all this stuff in your head?" Frank was duly impressed with Jack's reservoir of information.

Frank scratched his head as he thought about the island and its history. "I wonder if this place did attract any pirates."

Jack smiled confidently as she responded. "Funny you should mention pirates. At one time, Taino Indians lived here. As I recall from my studies, they rebelled against the Spanish in the 16th century. The ones the Spanish didn't kill were imprisoned or enslaved. For the next 100 years or more, the island was nothing less than a lawless outpost, frequented by pirates and outlaws."

"That's sad. I mean, you would have thought this place could have produced something worthwhile besides piracy." Frank was editorializing.

"Oh contraire, my dear friend, allow me to elaborate! Like most Caribbean islands, Vieques had some sugarcane plantations. For a time, many black laborers came from St. Thomas, Nevis, St. Kitts, St. Croix, and many other Caribbean islands to work on the plantations. During the 1920's and 30's, the bottom fell out of sugar prices and most people left the island. However, the big change for Vieques came during World War II when the United States purchased most of the island as an extension to the Roosevelt Roads Naval Station which was on the Puerto Rican mainland. The U.S. intended to use the island as a safe haven for the British fleet should Britain fall to Nazi Germany. Of course, that never happened. At any rate, you now have the Reader's Digest version, according to me, of what this place went through. I'm sure there is a lot more good information I could did up if I wanted to hit the books a little. You have to remember, I was a history major who concentrated on the Caribbean and piracy." Obviously, Jack was pleased with her summary.

Frank put his arm around Jack's waist and kissed her on the cheek. "Let's go dig up some more recent information on this place." He figured that the most impressive and pertinent information they could collect would come from the local inhabitants. Frank headed to the nearest bar while Jack slipped into the local Catholic Church.

An hour later they met out on the plaza and sat on a bench under a tree. Frank made his report first. "I picked up some good gossip. It appears that Bennie's ship, Dark Shadow, is a frequent visitor to the island. It usually anchors on the western end of the island in a cove not far from where it is now located next to Sea Venture. It seems that Bennie is well known here on the island. He is a bit of a nature buff and spends a great deal of time rummaging along the coastline, especially in the dense foliage. A few times he has ventured over to the old Live Impact Area (LIA) on the eastern end of the island. Get this, sometimes he meets up with another ship from Columbia. No one really knows who is on this ship and it usually doesn't stay long. Bennie, on the other hand, often stays for several days at a time. What did you come up with Jack?"

"Bennie, the good doctor that he is, sometimes volunteers his time and talents and tends to the medical needs of some of the less fortunate on the island. He also has a Captain from the local Police Department as a guest on Dark Shadow each time he visits; which sometimes is monthly. That doesn't give him a lot of time to be a doctor back in New York." She just came up with some good background to complement what Frank picked up.

Frank placed his index finger on his temple as he thought about what they had come up with. "I guess you could say that Bennie is plugged in pretty good around here. He's nearly a local fixture. His familiarity gives him plenty of cover for action. I wonder if he has ever stepped on any toes around here."

Jack bounced back with more news. "Back to what you said about Bennie spending time on both ends of the island; I have another note for you. As you said, the eastern end is the old LIA, but the western end is where Marines and Navy forces used to camp when they were using the eastern end for firing missions. Based on what Jonas said during his meeting with us, I would have to say Bennie and Corn Dog probably were rooting around near the camp area when they went off looking for pirate hideouts and treasure. I bet the LIA was most likely off limits in those days. With all this smoke we are seeing, there must be a fire somewhere. We are back to having more questions than answers."

"That's the way inquiries and investigations usually play out in the beginning. Sometimes they even end up that way." Frank was making mental notes and hoping they would all come in handy. "Jack, we have to be extremely careful when we're nosing around. A word or question to the wrong person could place us in an awkward position; even put us in real danger."

Jack smiled and added another comment that she thought was interesting. "Did you know that the highest point on the island is called Monte Pirata? That translates into Pirate Mount. This could be an omen of things to come. On your point about being careful, I agree. Being adventurous is one thing, but the possibility of getting hurt takes it to another dimension."

"Your point is well taken, honey. All this is looking like something sinister, or at least criminal in nature. We need to look into this other ship from Columbia. That ship and its purpose here is a critical link to what is going on here. Even if we don't find out what happened to Corn Dog, we may be on to something just as important." Frank's mind was already racing toward his next step.

Jack was a thorough historical researcher and Frank was a career investigator and both pursuits had a lot in common. There was no way to demystify either of their pursuits. There was no disagreement, research and investigation came with an inherent need to understand the past in order to make sense out of the present and prepare for the future.

"We don't have a lot of time for a great deal of patience, Frank. We need to learn more before Jonas meets with Bennie. That means we have until noon tomorrow." Jack was doing her best to be a realist.

Frank had to admit that Jack's assessment was correct. However, he could smell the scent of something just out of his reach. Like a hound, he had to keep his nose to the ground, pressing on for details and clarity. At the moment, his curiosity was his keenest emotion. Sometimes, a man has to take risks if he is to succeed. No, at this point, he didn't care if he stirred the pot a little too much. If adversity raised its ugly head, then he would just have to match its challenge with ingenuity and courage.

Frank took hold of Jack's hand. "Let's go see what we can find out about this mystery ship."

Chapter 20

Jack knew the best way to find out about a ship was to ask someone who worked around them or lived by the sea. "Come on hero, let's peddle our bikes to the western side of the island and talk to someone that fishes the area and lives there."

Frank grimaced over the thought of peddling ten miles along a sandy road with the off chance that they might gain a critical loose end to their mystery. "Okay, my tough little warrior princess, lead the way! I think you just want to show off that you're in better shape than I am."

She fired back. "When the going gets tough; the tough get going. Isn't that what all you macho guys say?"

"Jack, if I get cramps in my legs tonight, will you massage them?"

"Don't be such a whinny little boy. Who massaged your cramped legs when you were out fighting with your soldier buddies?" She couldn't resist being a bit of a wiseass.

After two and a half grueling hours and five rest stops, they were on the beach at the west end of the island. They both had been tempted to stop at Sea Venture when they had passed the cove where it was anchored. The sight of the other ship, Dark Shadow, motivated them to keep going. At least there was a nice breeze coming off the ocean and that was refreshing to both of them.

There was a man and a boy leisurely riding horses along the beach. A yapping little dog pranced along behind them. Their clothing and the man's unshaven face made them out to be locals out for a jaunt.

When Jack began speaking Spanish to the older man, he interrupted her explaining that he spoke English. Thus, the communications issue was set aside.

The man spoke to the boy and he responded by digging into a sack tied to his saddle. The boy produced three lukewarm bottles of beer. Apparently, they rarely had the opportunity to entertain guests. While the boy hobbled the horses, the three adults congregated under a huge palm tree.

The man lit a cigarette with an old-fashion Zippo lighter, and after a long puff, he began looking at something on the ground a few feet away. To the unknowing eye, it appeared to be just a whole in the ground. The man acquired a mischievous smile and removed a small can of lighter fluid from his pocket. He squirted some fluid around the whole and then puffed smoke into it. Shortly, a huge tarantula crawled out and started moving toward them. The man then lit the ring of lighter fluid and they all watched as the giant spider burned up trying to cross the fire.

Jack was horrified at the sight. Frank, on the other hand, figured what they had just witnessed was probably a favorite pastime for island residents who resided in spider-infested areas. Frank and Jack did their best not to show any unfavorable emotion to the disgusting event. They were in search of information and that meant tolerating something they disliked.

The man extended an open hand and introduced himself. "My name is Jose and this is my son Ramon. As you can see, we don't get many visitors on this part of the island; especially friendly ones."

Frank gripped Jose's extended hand. "My name is Frank and this is my friend Jack. We are just out trying to admire some of your beautiful island. You are truly fortunate to live in such a beautiful and peaceful place. I'm sure you have a lot of visitors here."

The man smiled widely in obvious appreciation of Frank's remarks. "No, not many people come here since the military left. Some people here on Vieques did not like the military being here because they thought the military interfered too much. That caused many strangers and political agitators to come from the main island of Puerto Rico and demonstrate against the military. Myself, I liked the military very much and I made a good living working for them when they were here. Now, I have to fish the coves and try to grow some cows and chickens. I think it was better for my family when the military was here. Yes, I miss them."

Jose unknowingly had thrown the door wide open for conversation and that produced an opportunity for elicitation. Frank was quick to take advantage. "I think troublemakers are everywhere in the world and they are always making it difficult for everyone who happen to be around them. It's hard to believe that troublemakers would want to disrupt such a beautiful place like Vieques. Now that the military is gone, I guess the troublemakers are also gone." Frank's words were more of an invitation to continue talking about the island than it was a simple acknowledgement of the local environment.

Jose seemed glad and eager to continue the conversation. "No, those troublemakers are gone. But, others have come to replace them. I call them troublemakers that are mean if you have to deal with them. They only talk to a man like me to say move out of the way or to stop being nosy. They only want me and many of my friends out of the way so they can play around on the island. One time, two men knocked me down and then threw a wad of money at me and told me to go home while I still had a home."

Jack prompted Jose with another question. "Did you report them to the police?"

"You have to be making a big joke, lady." He quickly responded. "Our police captain was with them. He told me to think of my family and be thankful for the money."

Frank prodded a little more with a follow-on question to what Jack had asked. "Well, maybe these mean men won't come back here again."

"Oh, they come here once or twice a month. They have been coming for years. Even now, as we talk, they are here." Jose shook his head in disgust.

Frank and Jack both immediately thought about Bennie's ship; Dark Shadow. Jack asked as nonchalantly as possible the overriding question that she and Frank had on their minds. "We came here on a ship that is in a cove near here." She pointed in the direction where Sea Venture was anchored. Another ship arrived near ours. Does that belong to the mean guys you told us about?"

"No, I know about your ship and about the one next to it. The one next to yours belongs to Doctor Calici. He is not a bad man, but, he is friends with those who are and he is friends with the police captain. No, the really bad men have pulled into the next cove over." Jose pointed to the west and opposite direction. "I won't go near them. A friend has told me that the crewmen on that ship are from Saint Croix and Jamaica. The ship flies the flag of the Republic of Panama sometimes and at other times it flies the Columbian flag. No one knows the owner's name. None of us want to know any of those men."

Frank fired another quick question to Jose. "How long has that ship been here?"

"It pulled in about two hours ago. That's why I put my fishing boat away and decided we would go ride our horses. It is not wise to be anywhere near that boat." Jose was making his position and concerns clear.

Frank knew that the first order of business had to focus on getting a look at the new mysterious vessel that seemed to be associated with a lot of meanness. The second order of business would be figuring out how to watch two suspect vessels at the same time. And the third order of business was to figure out if this new vessel was here because of Jonas. Frank was getting a very uneasy feeling about what was developing.

"I don't feel very comfortable having that strange ship of bad guys so close to our ship. Jack here, is our captain and I'm sure she doesn't feel good about this either." Frank pulled out his wallet and retrieved some twenty dollar bills. "Here is some money, Jose. I'll give you some more before we leave Vieques. If you see any movement on or near that ship, I want you to get in your boat and come tell one of us. We don't like surprises and we don't want to see anyone get hurt. Do we have a deal?"

Jose took the money. "This is more profitable than fishing. I like the idea of sitting in the shade, drinking beer, and relaxing while making some money. How long will you be staying around here?"

"I don't know. I will meet you back here every morning and afternoon. There's one more thing I would like to say, Jose. Don't take any chances with these guys. I don't want you or your son to get hurt. Please be careful." Frank was always sincerely concerned about the safety of those around him.

"Don't worry about us. On this island, I know where everything is and that means I can hide from all these strangers." Jose couldn't resist bragging a little.

Another thought suddenly occurred to Frank. "Since you know the island so well, where do these people go on the island when they are here?

Jose turned and pointed inland. "They always go into the trees over there. There's not much of a trail since it grows over very quickly. Half a mile in, there is a small hill that is overgrown. There is some kind of a bunker there and it has a big door on it. Years ago, I tried to get into it and couldn't get the door open. There must be a trick to it. I told the military about it once and they were not interested. They were always under orders not to bother anything that might have any historical value. I lost interest in it a long time ago."

The idea of something having some historical value immediately piqued Jack's interest. She also wondered why strangers were drawn to it. She also wondered if this cave had anything to do with the disappearance of Jonas' brother, Corn Dog. The whole idea was already bolstering her natural tendency for having a curious nature.

Their chance encounter with a local inhabitant proved to be immensely rewarding. Sometimes luck plays a crucial role in figuring out a mystery. However, for the moment, their eagerness to explore the clandestine structure would have to be put on hold. So they shook hands with Jose and his son and parted ways.

Frank's legs were about to cramp from riding the bike in the sand so he persuaded Jack to walk back along the beach. When they arrived back at the place where they had been dropped off, Jack pulled her cell phone out of her front pocket and placed a call to Matt. Now, the question was: How would Jonas respond to what they had learned from their outing on the island?

Once Matt and Roy arrived, they wasted no time shaking the sand from between their toes and getting aboard the Zodiac so they could get under way. Matt spoke cordially. "Jonas is anxious to hear about your trip. He has called for another meeting in the galley as soon as you are aboard."

The calling of a meeting by Jonas came as no surprise. In fact, it was expected. Frank was keenly aware that Jonas would have liked to have accompanied them, but, he was probably also aware that his presence would have been a hindrance since he was not in good enough shape for the rigorous demands of covering the distance that was needed.

Frank was the last to enter the galley and was greeted by a blanket of chatter and whispers. Colette was in a frenzy as she quickly put away culinary utensils that she had just finished washing and drying. In her hurried state of mind, she was generating more clatter than usual. She had been present when Jonas informed Matt about the meeting so she had already placed a pitcher of ice tea on the table. She had also placed a glass in front of each person and a dish of ice in the center of the table. She was the last one to take a seat at the table, and as she was accustomed to, she sat next to Jonas.

There was a pot of stew simmering on the stove. The aroma reminded everyone that it was already dinner time, and the aroma had no difficulty reminding Frank and Jack that they had worked up a hearty appetite.

Jonas scanned all the faces to make sure everyone was present. His position at the head of the table was as close to a throne as he would ever have; after all, he owned Sea Venture and everything aboard and everyone present was in his employ or a personal friend. Those thoughts aside, he considered everyone at the table a friend.

On this occasion, he was attired in a white shirt with matching white slacks. His admiral's hat was conspicuously absent. His poise, dress, and mannerisms, made him appear as a gentleman, bordering on being a stately man of means, like an old English Squire or Duke. Otherwise, he was a wealthy man on a Caribbean cruise. Thus, the stage was set.

Once Frank began his report, the details were received with great interest. All around the table there was an assortment of facial expressions that reflected individual concerns and interests. While Frank spoke, Jack interjected her antidotes and opinions which tended to enhance and clarify various aspects of what was learned.

Around the table, responses were as predictable as the weather; some came as expected while others came as troubling glimpses of questionable motives.

Tommy took the lead in responding, speaking his mind, as usual. "Jonas, I can't, for the life of me, get over how much concern you have for finding out what happened to your brother, especially when you hardly knew him. I don't know what is in your heart since I never had a brother. I just can't wrap my mind around what you are going through. As for all these other people who are here because you are looking into your brother's disappearance, well, I personally don't think they even give a damn about your brother. I think they are only interested in what you might find out about what they are up to on this island. My advice to you and to everyone here is to keep your eyes peeled for anything out of the ordinary."

Tommy's position was more self-serving than it was a matter of devotion to Jonas. He obviously felt ill at ease over how the trip was turning out. Being a purser usually did not involve all the drama that he was now experiencing.

Next, Andy brought up an important issue; security. "I don't know about the rest of you, but, I think it is time for us to figure out how we are going to protect ourselves should our situation start to take a nasty turn."

Since Matt knew Sea Venture better than anyone else, he was in the best position to assess their ability to protect themselves. "In the forward hole there is a locker in a small storage room and the contents might help us out should we get into any real trouble with any bad guys. It looks like one of the previous owners had some outdoor hobbies that required having some shooting skills. I found two 12 gauge shotguns there. They are double barreled guns that were used to shoot skeet or trap with. There are a couple boxes of rather old ammo with them. I also found two spear guns with three sets of SCUBA gear. Outside of these items, there are only three flare guns aboard. After our meeting is finished, I'll check these items out for serviceability."

The ambiance around the table was taking on a sincere defensive nature. There was a general agreement among all that the best course of action, at this stage, was to be adequately prepared.

More noteworthy to Frank, and especially to Jonas, was that there was no outward inclination from anyone to opt out of the situation. Their prior commitment was still firm. They truly were in for the long haul; regardless of the potential for danger. Maybe they had all watched too many action movies on late night TV and had become desensitized to real risk and danger.

Frank decided not to mention having his 9 millimeter Taurus pistol stowed away in his cabin. Frank opined that if anyone else aboard would likely have a firearm, it would be Andy. Andy had worked special operations in the Army and that meant he was probably harboring some innate fancy for guns and firepower. Frank figured it was in the DNA of most military and ex-military personnel.

Jonas had sat quietly assessing what was occurring until he could no longer maintain his silence. "I feel really bad about dragging all of you into my mess. I don't know what worries me more; Bennie and his associates or you guys, my only friends, wanting to arm yourselves? Maybe my brother met with an accident and I'm wasting a lot of time and resources for nothing. I just don't know. If Bennie did have something to do with Corn Dog's disappearance then he has to be held accountable. I saw a movie once where a detective spent most of his life trying to find out who killed someone just so he could bring closure to his case. Sure, I want justice, but I want closure more than anything. Now that I know all of you, I would want the same thing if something bad ever happened to any of you. It's all about caring and doing the right thing."

Jack took a deep breath and then expressed a view of the situation that was deepening in her mind. "I don't know about anyone else, but, there's more going on here than your brother's disappearance. I want to get into this old bunker and find out what's inside that is so important that someone put this big door on it centuries ago. If there's something inside of historical significance, then I want to record it for the sake of history. Without a doubt, the Caribbean is still full of secrets and relics waiting to be discovered and there will always be people trying to set history right so others can appreciate it."

Matt supplemented Jacks view. “As long as I have been a seaman, I have heard a thousand stories about pirates, sunken ships, and treasure. There have been maps galore; most were probably not legitimate, and the genuine ones were probably flawed in some way. Personally, I have never seen a good result. Right now, I have this gut feeling that we are on the brink of a legitimate discovery; one that all sailors would love to be in on. For me, it doesn’t matter if there is only one Spanish coin in this bunker or a whole chest of pirate treasure. It is the thrill of finding something; anything, that is driving me to take the risk. I’m not about to miss out on a single minute of this adventure.”

“Well stated, Matt,” Frank agreed. “The quest is every bit as important as the prize. There is no secret about me being an adventure addict for most of my life. There are a lot of things surfacing here that have my interest. On some level, I bet everyone here has some kind of a dog in this hunt.”

Gerty, who had been notably quiet for the past couple of days chimed in. “This whole thing sure as hell beats sitting around craving a drink of booze.” She looked directly at Matt. “I want to check out all the medical supplies on Sea Venture. I was once a nurse, a damn good one I might add. As we prepare for the worse, we have to pool all of our talents. As we pull together, we all should be praying for the best outcome possible.”

Colette’s turn was next. Her eyes were warm, yet intense. Like everyone else, she was focused on coming together as a team. Soon, they would encounter Bennie; one of several unknown elements. “I agree with everyone’s attitude and I am exceedingly pleased with each of your motives and enthusiasm. I’m equally excited over what is playing out and I want you to all count on me as a team player. Just remember, the main issue here is Jonas and what he is going through. This is his journey that we have joined. Anything else is just added excitement. I’ll make sure the kitchen is ready and that everyone is nourished. I would also like to help Gerty with the medical and first aid part of this."

Roy and Georgia exchanged looks. Roy spoke and Georgia nodded in agreement. "Like Matt, I'm a long-time sailor with more stories than you can imagine. Whatever you need in the way of help, I'm here for you. All this talk has my adrenalin flowing. Like always, I'll be your soldier and your workhorse."

The meeting broke up with a flurry of energized activity. Tomorrow's morning sun would arrive as normal and with it there would be the beginning of a new phase to this unfolding story.

Chapter 21

A new day had already begun before there was any hint of the sun rising in the east. Wanting to get things underway, Frank and Jack hurried through their workout in the fitness room. Their thoughts were not on the exercises as much as they were on Jonas and the big noontime meeting that was scheduled to take place on the beach. There was a cloud of caution floating in the air that warned of some kind of a confrontation between Jonas and a character from his past and that combination had the potential to become ugly. Presently, no one knew if Bennie would even turn out to be of the same character that Jonas had described. After all, some people do change over time.

When they came out of the fitness room, the glitter of twilight had arrived. Hand in hand, Frank and Jack walked around enjoying the freshness of a new Caribbean day. The morning breeze was always refreshing, but it was even more so after a rigorous workout. Chirping birds on the island caught their attention so they stopped for a long contemplating look at the beach. A cool breeze ruffled Jack's hair while it soothed her sweaty skin.

A clump of palm trees on the island protruded out over the water's edge. The trees were noticeably tucked neatly within a miniature cove that rested within the larger cove where Sea Venture and Dark Shadow were anchored.

In the early dawn, the trees looked quaintly somber and peaceful along the white sandy beachfront. The shade from the massive and mature palm leaves fell heavily upon the clear water below. The shadows seemed to bury themselves, impregnating the water's depth with an eerie darkness. Was it a prelude to what would occur during the day? Sometimes nature has a way of warning us through subtle expressions.

Frank pulled Jack close to his side as he pointed to the trees. "Is that a message or an omen?" He asked. "I have had this feeling before. How can something look that beautiful and yet transmit such a spooky sensation?"

Jack kept her eyes on the trees while she responded to Frank's comment. "That's the way nature operates. It is up to us to interpret its message. Maybe it is because we are so on edge over our pending meeting with Bennie." Her eyes remained fixed on the trees and their watery shadows.

"I think you have a good point, honey. Hopefully, Bennie's intent will be made clear; not like the dark shadows we are looking at." Frank tried to smile, but failed in his effort.

"We'll just have to do our best to measure Bennie and his words. I wonder how much he will reveal about his past and his character. Some people can be extremely crafty and deceitful. I've seen all kinds of nastiness as I traveled about these waters." She wasn't mixing words when it came to doubting a new and mysterious character like Bennie.

This wasn't the first time during the trip that Frank saw Jack's clarity and wisdom shine through. He knew that he had been truly blessed the day he had met her. She was certainly worth cherishing. At this moment, he would gladly take any path in life that resulted in journeying it with her.

There was certainly a restless beauty in her eyes that held his interest. Fortunately, or unfortunately as the case might be, he also knew that he would have to distance himself enough to secure a clear and objective outlook until Jonas' mystery was resolved and everyone was out of danger. Being emotionally involved can sometimes be a distraction that clouded one's judgment.

Jose's mission was not without its own problems. Anticipating and fearing that he might be spotted, Jose decided to disguise his presence. He hoped that if spotted he would appear to only be a lazy peasant wasting the morning away. He set up a hammock between two palm trees. Nestled next to him in the sand was a cooler of beer. Hopefully, the setting was what any visitor would interpret as a peaceful scene and acceptable considering the island's economy and culture. After all, he was a part time farmer and part time fisherman trying to etch out a meager living.

Jose was barefoot and attired in tattered shorts and a soiled sleeveless T-shirt. He reclined in the hammock and pulled a wide-brimmed straw hat part way over his face. He was careful enough to leave just enough room for a clear view of the ship. Surely, he was not the first islander to take on a new day like this.

Unfortunately, someone on the bridge of the mysterious ship was intrusively, with the aid of binoculars, taking note of Jose's presence. The onlooker's face was black as coal and his teeth were white as pearls; except for the ones that were shiny gold. He was wearing a white shirt that was starched. The smile he wore was a confident one.

Without lowering the binoculars, he issued an order with all the authority of a military commander. "Something is not right here. That man is always out fishing or working his shitty little farm. This isn't like him; not here and not at this time of day. I want him gone, permanently. We have too much at stake to risk a meddlesome intrusion."

Back on the beach, Jose was mentally reviewing his instructions from Frank and Jack. He was to report any activity on or around this ship and now he was witnessing a high speed skiff suddenly departing the ship and racing in his direction. Instinctively, he grabbed the cooler of beer and vacated his post.

The three heavily muscled black men in the skiff were certainly not packing fishing poles; they were wielding machine pistols.

Once Jose entered the dense foliage, he immediately changed direction. That was a good move on his part as he heard bullets ripping through the leaves and overhead branches. There was no question about it; these men were out to kill him. He would move his family out of any possible danger and then he would make his report to his new employers. At this moment, Vieques was no longer a tranquil paradise in the Caribbean. It was being transformed into a battlefield for guerrilla warfare.

Another unforeseen situation was also developing in the next cove over. Georgia leaned stiffly against Sea Venture's life rail on the lower deck. She was in an apparent quandary, perplexed about something. Her face and demeanor was normally exquisite and warmly composed. In other circumstances, her slender form and calm disposition would earn her many admirable looks from the opposite sex. However, this was not one of those occasions. Her normally bright and irresistible eyes now were heavily troubled.

She now watched in earnest at one of Sea Venture's Zodiac boats as it sped toward the beach. She was both angry and disappointed as she looked on with a scowl on her face. Her frustration needed no interpretation or translation; she was only exhibiting the language of her soul.

No definitive outcome came to mind as she watched Matt at the controls with Roy assisting at his side. Tommy took up most of the second row seat. What rational or irrational ploy had Tommy used on Matt and Roy to convince them to take him ashore without anyone's permission? The worst part was that she did know Tommy's true purpose for the trip. He was on his own private treasure hunt and he was way out of his league. Tommy was determined, no obsessed, to locate this secret pirate hiding place.

He was not a team player after all; he wanted his own treasure hunt and its rewards. There was no bigger fool on Sea Venture than Tommy. There was no telling how the others would react once they found out.

Too stupefied to render Tommy and his venture any more of her time and curiosity, Georgia decided to turn away from the unfortunate scene. She considered Tommy to be a friend, however, he was simply acting wrongly and he was betraying an implied sacred trust to the others. Tommy was a grown man and would have to face his own consequences.

She headed to the galley for breakfast and to see what else was going on. Hopefully, she was not too ill at ease with Tommy's treachery that she would not be able to eat a hearty breakfast. She had gotten out of bed with hunger pangs and now that did not seem as important as it was earlier. She thought it was strange how her emotions could override an empty stomach.

Andy was up early because he was too nervous to sleep. His nervousness hinged on the importance of the big meeting that was only a few short hours off. He tried reading manuals and examining navigation charts to no avail. Several times he caught himself feeling over-anxious as he unconsciously prepared himself for the possibility of action. He was too nervous to gain any good from reading any of the manuals so he decided to sharpen a knife he had sheathed at his side.

He finally surrendered and placed his feet up on the consul and leaned back in the captain's chair. Consciously, he allowed his senses to succumb to a much needed catnap. For the next twenty minutes he was completely unaware of his surroundings. When his eyes finally popped open, he was glad that he had taken the nap. His dozing had given him new life. A shot of caffeine would help even more. He knew that even stale coffee had caffeine so he grabbed the coffee thermos, but, it was empty.

Stepping outside, he stretched and enjoyed a fresh cool breeze. The next order of business had to be a light breakfast and a cup of fresh coffee.

He was about to head to the galley when he was momentarily distracted by the sound of a Zodiac racing toward Sea Venture. After rubbing a bit of lingering sleep from his eyes, he saw that the skiff was being operated by Matt and Roy. He wondered why on earth they were out there at this time of the morning. Had they been to the beach? Certainly if something had happened, he would have been told. The next obvious move was to meet them and find out what was going on. Naturally, he was not comfortable about being left out of the loop if something was amiss.

Andy watched closely from above while Matt and Roy rushed to secure the skiff and hustle up the ladder.

When Matt and Roy saw Andy poised before them as they reached the deck, they acquired the look of condemned criminals coming before a judge.

"Why were you two out in the Zodiac?" Andy's tone was a mixture of alarm, challenge, and disbelief.

The senior of the two, Matt, was quick to explain. "I thought you knew. Tommy said he was told to check out the area behind the beach where the meeting was to take place."

Andy did not doubt for a minute that Matt and Roy thought they were acting correctly. However, Tommy always projected an image conducive to causing trouble. Andy also knew that no one in their right mind would have given such an assignment to

Tommy. Andy knew that such an assignment, as conducting a reconnaissance, would have been detailed to him. After all, he had the tactical military experience to perform a recon mission. One thing special operations personnel knew was counter-surveillance and counter-ambush techniques.

"You two need to come with me to brief Captain Jack and Frank. I think you guys have been conned by Tommy. Hopefully, we can find out what Tommy is up to. It seems like there is always someone in every group that doesn't want to play by the rules." Andy was plainly agitated by this unexpected development.

Andy shortly arrived at the galley with Matt and Roy in tow. With the exception of Tommy, everyone was present in the galley. Andy wasted no time explaining what was happening.

As the details were revealed, the common reaction seemed to be one of annoyance. Without exception, everyone tended to cast a questioning eye toward Georgia. She must know something because she spent more time with Tommy than anyone else. All those card games had to lead to some sort of bonding between the two.

For Georgia, the whole mess was becoming a nightmare. She was caught in the cumbersome position of betraying a friend and betraying an entire team. Questioning one's own loyalty is not always easy. She did not want to be a snitch, yet, she did not want the others to see her as some kind of co-conspirator. Sometimes life is not easy.

The cumulative effect was taking its toll on her conscience. "Okay, I know what is going on with Tommy. You see, he wants to be a key player while scoring a lot of points at the same time." She realized that there was some element of a lie in her statement. "I don't know everything that's going on in his head, but, maybe there is some greed mixed in with his motives. He told me that he wants to find the pirates treasure if it exists. And if it doesn't exist, he wants us all to move on to better places than this disgusting island. I'm sorry; I should have said something earlier so you could have stopped him." Her emotions sent tears streaming down her face as she confessed her knowledge of the situation.

Frank spoke with composure. "Tommy will have to fend for himself out there. The last thing we are going to do is split our ranks any more than we have to. We are a small group and we may very well be outnumbered. In fact, I will guarantee that we are. Bennie and his friends would like to see us split up into small groups so they can do a better job of taking us down; if that's their intention. I want you to remember that old saying: 'divide and conquer.' Can anyone tell me if Tommy has a weapon with him?"

Matt did not hesitate to report on weapons. "He doesn't have any of our weapons; they are all stowed and ready to issue whenever the order is given."

Georgia attempted to edit Matt's report. "Tommy carries a little pocket knife. I don't know if that counts. I know that's not much of a weapon."

Andy interrupted. "In Tommy's hands, a pocket knife adds up to nothing."

In reply to Andy's comment, Frank twisted one corner of his mouth into a half smile and decided against any additional sarcasm. "There is no use dwelling on Tommy and his dumb scheme. Right now, we have to get down to business and prepare for the worse. Matt, take Roy and bring all the weapons to the galley so we can issue them. Then we need to come up with some contingency plans. Now, you all have the next forty minutes to do whatever you need to do." They all understood that they were now entering yet another phase; a notch up on the danger scale. Everyone was aware that they had to keep pace as new situations came about.

On the island, Jose was dealing with his own situation. He had cleverly concealed a small motorboat at the beaches' edge along the cove's western shoreline. Sea Venture and Dark Shadow were resting peacefully at anchor. Nearly fifteen minutes had passed when he barely missed making contact with two of Sea Venture's crew as they dropped off a rather plump appearing man. There had been no point in trying to intercept the man since he appeared to be on a mission of his own. Besides, the man had wasted no time in disappearing into the island's thick foliage.

The intense horror of coming under attack from the men in the high speed skiff had rendered Jose extremely cautious. There was no way to dismiss that close encounter in any matter-of-fact way; he may have to fight for his very life. All he knew for sure was he had to reach Frank and Captain Jack and warn them about the violent nature of these unknown men. His new friends and employers needed sufficient time in order to prepare a proper defense or affect an escape, even though he did not read any inclination toward Sea Venture's crew running from a possible fight. This was serious business and he was now a part of it.

Sea Venture was anchored at least three hundred yards from where he was hidden with his little motorboat. The perspiration that covered his face was heavy with salt and it burned his eyes. His irritated eyes were constantly scanning the water and beach for any sign of his attackers. His mind was doused with fear because he knew his pursuers would not be inclined to give up the chase. This had to be the same feeling soldiers felt during a lull in battle.

Although his T-shirt was soaked with sweat, it was all he had to wipe the irritating solution from his eyes. The wiping effort from his soiled shirt only gave him temporary and partial relief. At least his breathing was slowing somewhat and that gave him a moment to think and gain a little bit of composure. It all came down to this: Deep in his heart, he knew that it was time to man-up and do what was needed to be done. If he waited another minute, he would surely run away and that would eat at his conscience for the rest of his life. A man was no better than his word.

He shoved his little boat into the water with a burst of energy that he didn't know he had left in him. It was pure adrenalin at work. The little outboard motor did not hesitate, as was normal, when it started with the first tug of the rope. He was quickly off, his boat plowing through the water.

Halfway to Sea Venture, his eyes picked out the dreaded skiff of gun-toting thugs. It was well beyond Sea Venture's port side and appeared to be idling along in a searching mode. But that would not be for long.

Aboard Sea Venture, Andy was on lookout for anything unusual and that was exactly what he found. He recalled from Frank and Jack's briefing that Jose would come to Sea Venture with any news concerning the mysterious ship anchored in the next cove.

Andy quickly discerned the risk to Jose when he saw the initial burst of spray from the skiff's powerful engines as it revved up and made a wild dash to intercept Jose in his little motorboat. Without a doubt, it was a race of life and death. Along with their determined shouts, they waived their weapons about with increasing determination.

Andy frantically yelled out an alarm to his shipmates as he picked up the double barreled shotgun that he had been issued only minutes before. Everything was turning into a race; a real competition between the good guys and the bad guys.

At the top of his lungs, Andy continued to yell. "Everyone, I need all hands on deck! This is an emergency!" He continued repeating the alarm until he saw the others running toward him.

They were all packing their assigned weapons as they lined up along the life rail near Andy. No one needed an explanation when they saw what was happening.

Jose reached Sea Venture just in time and tossed a line to Roy who had climbed down the ladder to assist him.

At a distance of slightly less than seventy-five yards, the dreaded skiff of gunmen veered off and headed back out of the cove. For them, this was not the time for a full scale assault. They would have to wait for the appropriate order from their leader.

Although relieved, Jose still climbed the ladder like frenzied prey in a hunt; he wanted to put as much distance as he could between him and his pursuers. All the way up the ladder he muttered unintelligible words in Spanish. The safety he reached was comforting even though he did not know how long that margin of avoidance would last. Moreover, this was not one of those times when a guest had to request permission to come aboard a ship. This was a rescue at sea situation and that meant protocol was set aside.

Colette shoved a glass of ice tea into Jose's hands. "Can I get you anything to eat? You're in safe hands now."

Jose ignored Colette's question. He was in a more gracious and spiritual mood. "Thank you God. That was too close for it not to be a miracle. The saints have smiled on me today."

While Georgia dabbed perspiration from his head with a clean dry cloth, Jose drank the cold tea like a man drank water in the desert heat. Sea Venture was his oasis.

This initial greeting did not last long. Frank and Jonas ushered Jose off to the galley for a thorough debriefing. Assessments and plans had to be made and made quickly. As they headed to the galley, Andy took charge of the rest. He assigned guard positions and reassured them that all would be okay if they all did their part.

Twice in less than an hour, Jose had escaped death at the hands of armed triggermen. He was clearly shaken half out of his wits even though he was safe and unharmed.

Unexpectedly, Jack was moved by what Jose did next. He recited the Jesus Prayer. "Lord Jesus Christ, Son of God, Have mercy on me, a sinner."

Realizing with heart-felt inspiration that Jose was a Catholic, she followed up by reciting the Hail Mary. "Hail Mary, full of grace, the Lord is with you. Blessed are you among women, and blessed is the fruit of your womb, Jesus. Holy Mary, Mother of God, pray for us sinners, now and at the hour of our death. Amen."

Colette also was inspired and thusly recalled an aspect of her mixed Catholic and Voodoo roots. She had joined in with Jack when she was reciting the Hail Mary.

Frank was duly impressed by the way these three people were following their faith. Even though he could not chime in with the recitations, he felt compelled to thank God in his own way without a formal prayer. He lacked the formality, but not the spiritual force of faith. He admittedly had a lot to learn and a ways to go in defining his relationship with the Almighty.

Chapter 22

Considering all that was going on, Jonas was maintaining an unexpected façade of calmness; he was projecting an image of passivity not unlike that of a 1960's flower child who was one with his environment. He seemed indifferent to the world around him as he sat quietly in the galley.

Overall, the world he was facing had come about by many factors that had been out of his sphere of influence; although he had to admit that he had contributed to some small degree. Hurricane Katrina had been an act of nature and no man had much control over that, but, prior to that deadly storm he should have done things differently.

It was already midmorning and he nonchalantly sipped ice tea in a listless manner, which was his norm as of late. He was not bored, just a man in need of direction. Between sips his fingers fumbled unconsciously with his admiral's hat and he didn't seem aware that it had now lost its value as a symbol of his authority; a statement of his vanity. Thus, in this withdrawn state of solitude he was struggling with low spirits and a lack of optimism.

One option that rested heavily on his mind was that he should strike his colors and make a hasty retreat away from Vieques. No, there was no way he could do that without first learning Tommy's fate. Jonas was stressed and he was aware that all people under stress experience some degree of depression when they are unable to see a favorable end. So it went without saying that he was feeling the claws of low morale wrapping around his heart and that could be a costly phenomenon when it arrived just ahead of a confrontation. He saw himself as a leader on a mission while, at the same time, he was pursuing circumstances which he was partially the blame for. The last thing he wanted was to make a mess of things. He had to ask himself why his life had to be so convoluted.

A strong contributing factor, a positive incentive, was that he had developed a deep affection for Colette. Her importance and wellbeing had become increasingly important to him. She was an intelligent and caring soul; there was no question of that. In a short length of time, she had established herself as an invaluable friend.

At this point in his life, Colette was the most romantically desirable partner he could have hoped for. Naturally, he thought the world of Gerty as a friend and confidant. However, as a female companion, he only harbored a platonic attraction to her. Colette, on the other hand, was a romantic prospect worthy of pursuing. Naturally, the last thing he wanted was for any harm to come to either woman. These were not foolish thoughts of an old man that could easily be dismissed. Both women were valuable gems in his otherwise dark and disjointed world. For the moment, he was stuck in this confused state; weighing relationships while trying to be unselfish. It seemed like everything in his life was demanding special attention so he wasn‘t sure where to focus.

Up on the bridge, Andy had the foresight to bring a weather warning to Jack's attention. A storm was about to move in on their position from the east. It was not a great storm like the one that had eluded his attention near Haiti. Nevertheless, it was packing a substantial wind and a significant amount of rainfall. This one would strike relentlessly and then be gone within an hour's time.

Correctly, as the ship's captain, Jack made the call to alert the others. "Andy, this thing will most likely hit around one this afternoon. I want everyone to button down everything on the ship as quickly as possible. I want Matt and Roy to throw out the storm anchor as a safety precaution. I think the cove will provide adequate protection. The last thing we want is to have Sea Venture beached like the first Sea Venture did in Bermuda. The storm anchor should do the trick." Jack was aware of all the advancement of sea going technology that had been developed during the centuries since the first Sea Venture disaster. However, she also knew that old-fashioned seamanship was still the most viable approach.

While Andy, Jack and the others attended to the storm preparations, Frank had a different challenge on his mind; it was the upcoming meeting with Bennie. Whenever there was a crisis looming, decisions had to be made. More often than not, the true nature and severity of a challenge was not always apparent and it could easily be compounded by unexpected developments. So how does one anticipate and prepare for challenges that are not apparent or fully defined?

When individual perspective was coupled with reality, it had a lot of influence on the way a challenge was to be dealt with. On this day, Jonas had one perspective linked to his motive while Frank had another. Frank would have to use tact and diplomacy to advance his objective approach. Sadly, Jonas was clueless when it came to focusing on his position.

There was no question about both of their perspectives coming to light in the midst of potential violence. Their initial contact with Bennie, and possibility of a confrontation, was only a few short hours away and already anxiety was riding on the wings of uncertainty.

Similar and related thoughts were creeping into Jonas' reasoning. He had already reached the bottom of a downward spiral in his life. Winning the lottery had only allowed him to inch up a smidgen from his lowest level. Desperately, he wanted to begin crawling up to a more emotionally stable place in his life. But first, he had to make a truce with himself or die trying. There was no way he could face this challenge without Frank at his side. Jonas' optimism tended to bud and blossom when Frank had the reins, and for that Jonas was appreciative.

Jonas closed his eyes tightly and prayed for closure; that was the result he was hoping to gain from his meeting with Bennie. Even if Bennie had no direct hand in Corn Dog's disappearance, maybe Bennie would point him to someone else who had the answers he was seeking. Maybe there was no use continuing if he was on the wrong trail. Jonas hated this wait and see routine.

Jonas felt bad about pulling so many innocent people into his problem. Hopefully, his zeal and tenacity would not make victims of those who were supporting his quest.

Frank's challenge, on the other hand, was just as demanding as Jonas'. While Jonas struggled with his interests in one way, Frank leaned forward in another manner based on his experience. Frank was not worrying over blame and guilt; he was attacking his challenge with a different view. His objective was to get everyone through the whole ordeal without any injury or loss of life. He had his share of this type of challenge when he had served in the military and he had taken on a few intense cases as a private investigator, thus, he was more prepared than the others.

This was Frank's type of game; this was what he lived for. Now was the time for him to keep himself as emotionally detached as possible. He had his eye on the ball and that ball begged for clarity and operational security. There was a hidden core-reality to this mess and he was determined to find it. Once he knew the why of it, he would be able to find and exploit weaknesses. Naturally, everything was based on need.

He expected Bennie to be a hardened and callused man with thick emotional armor. Another thing that would come about, in due course, would be Bennie's connection to that mysterious ship in the next cove. As facts became evident, they would be recorded in a time-event chart and then a clear link analysis would unravel the whole mess. This was basic intelligence analysis. Hopefully, this would also answer Jonas' questions about his brother's disappearance. Information was power in anyone's hands.

Frank would not allow himself and the others to be sequestered into the realm of being victims. There was no room for a defeatist attitude. Everyone from Sea Venture was an asset and he would do his best to use them wisely. Order and calmness, coupled with good contingency planning were going to be crucial to his strategy. He would keep his eye on success and not calamity. Frank also wondered about the extent of planning and motivation that was taking place on the other two ships. Where was that proverbial crystal ball when a guy needed it?

Frank had the prospect of a loving relationship with Jack and that was certainly a bright star in his future. However, he had too much at stake not to maintain a clear and analytical mind. Most often than not when emotions alone drive tactics for an organization, its losses will be substantially higher.

All his life, Frank always found it more to his advantage to invite and embrace all challenges because he knew the experience would make him stronger and smarter. So many times challenges had pushed hard against his will and each time he had found a way to adapt. In his mind, the thrill of competition was always worth the effort; it was an education.

At this point, he was comfortable with the drive and physical attributes of Andy, Matt, Roy, and Jack. They were all physically fit and seasoned professionals. Jonas was a different case. He was too emotionally involved to make sound tactical decisions. However, in spite of his emotional involvement, Jonas had the heart of a lion and that meant he could be counted on to fight hard in a clinch.

Gerty, Colette, and Georgia were going to be good in support and logistical roles. In a pinch, they could also be counted on to fight, although less effectively as their male counterparts. Admittedly, when it came to men verses women, women were increasingly distinguishing themselves on the battlefield. Joan of Arc was a noted commander and warrior in her time and she certainly defied men's stereotyping of women. As a young woman, she had a spiritual calling and her faith allowed her to press on to martyrdom. She led a nation in war before she was twenty-one years old. In today's world, women are effectively demonstrating their value in combat roles.

Even military truck drivers, cooks, and office personnel were capable of fighting a good battle; many were even cited for bravery during major military campaigns. When you are on the team, well, you are on the team. The bottom line for this venture was that no matter how daunting things become, no one would give up without giving their all. Too often, Frank had seen many veterans with broken and dismembered bodies who were still alive because they had not given up.

Tommy, of course, was out of the picture and even if he hadn't been, there was a lingering doubt about his value and loyalty.

Hopefully, there would be no fighting or skirmishes. The one thing that any soldier hated was war. The irony in this belief was that soldiers are always training for war and rarely for peace.

The conversation aboard Sea Venture was less than cheerful. The spoken word tended more toward utility than cordiality. Everyone learned how to handle and operate assigned weapons and then placed them strategically for quick access. The ship was also made ready for the approaching storm. It was a morning of hard work and not leisure.

Georgia found Jack lashing down some canvass over some deck equipment. "Jack, do you have a couple minutes for something personal?"

"Sure, fire away. I need a break." Jack grinned warmly.

"Thank you. What do you know about Andy and his past? I'm sort of interested in him." Georgia spoke in a low voice because Andy was working on something on the aft lower deck and she didn't want him to overhear what she was asking.

"Not much, I'm sorry to say. Based on what he has said in casual conversation, I think the Army did a great job of cleaning him up. In fact, I would say it put a pretty good shine on him."

While speaking, Georgia continued to watch Andy with a noticeable degree of admiration in her eye. "Looking at him now, I would imagine that he came from a good family."

Jack decided to take the opportunity to make a point to Georgia. "A pedigree doesn't make a man good. His character and actions do. The best dog I ever had was a mutt. A mutt can provide just as much love and loyalty as any registered dog. Don't worry about where Andy came from; just be glad he is going somewhere worthwhile." Jack did her best to impart good advice. "I would say that Andy carries himself as a solid man with strong integrity, don't you think?"

"Thanks, Jack. Your points are well taken and that means a lot to me. You are as good a person as you are a ship's captain." The conversation ended with mutual smiles.

Colette and Gerty wandered up to Sea Venture's bow where they found Matt, Roy, and Jose gathered. They were having a conversation about Tommy. The general consensus was that Tommy was a deserter.

At once, Colette interjected her opinion into their discussion. "I know all of you are disappointed in Tommy. There is no surprise among any of us that his likeability has waned to some extent. We should not be too quick to judge him, though. We don't have enough facts to put the man on trial. And, if the verdict turns out to be that Tommy has deserted us, and he is wicked to the bone; we are not the ones to punish him. It is for God to punish wicked men. Our duty is to do our best to forgive. We contribute to life more effectively when we try to be the best person we can be. Our goal should be to emulate Christ."

Roy was seemingly more prone to anger than the others. His anger was predicated on being friends with Tommy until he pulled his stunt of running off to look for pirate loot instead of standing with the team. "I'm afraid I would like the satisfaction of being the one to tell Tommy what I think of him. I guess I will never be a saint or a holy man. I'm just a sailor with a sailor's attitude." Losing a disloyal friend is one thing; letting that betrayal go is another thing.

Colette made a parting comment. "I think we all need to control our impulses toward anger and disappointment. The world isn't as simple as we would like it to be."

Gerty was eager to put an end to discussing Tommy. She looked at her wristwatch as a reminder. "Shouldn't we all be double-checking things before the big meeting?"

It was ten forty in the morning and the weather pointed to another fine Caribbean day because the storm was not yet in sight. The sun was bright and the sky clear. The thermometer on the bridge rested on eighty-five degrees; a great temperature for a pleasant day. There was also a light breeze making its way across the cove. Had the beach been on a California or Florida coast, there would have been sunbathers galore. Instead, this Vieques beach was sadly devoid of human life. For anyone wanting to escape the faster life of tourist locations or the claws of big city life, then this place was the answer. The scene gave no notice of the predicted storm.

Even Frank had a momentary vision of himself resting in the sun on a beach blanket with Jack by his side. Sometime in the future, if he had his way, that scene would come to fruition. Love always arrived with the prospect of beautiful scenes and joyous thoughts. Unfortunately, this was not the time or the place for dwelling on such hopeful fantasies.

Jonas and Frank, putting all other thoughts aside, as best they could, made their way down the ladder to the Zodiac. Roy was already there waiting on their arrival. He made sure that Frank and Jonas were familiar with the skiff's controls and operations. As expected, Jonas had no objection to having Frank at the controls.

Jonas' concentration was interrupted as he noticed the launching of a similar skiff from Dark Shadow. Two men were standing and a third sat behind them. "It looks as though Bennie is coming with two men. Do we need a third man with us?" Jonas did not like the idea of having a difference in odds.

Before answering Jonas, Frank reached behind to the small of his back. He only wanted to touch his 9 mm Taurus; his equalizer and insurance for the meeting. "I don't know what they are up to; they know the rules for the meeting. Let's stick to our part of the plan and be ready for any indication that they are going to jump us."

Jonas nodded in agreement and then sat down and opened a small hatch door. Inside was the skiff's flare gun. That was his assigned weapon for the meeting.

"Jonas, let's wait a few minutes to see what they do when they get to the beach. There's no use rushing in when we still have fifty minutes until the meeting. Just because they are there early doesn't mean we have to rush in." Frank knew that a wait and see approach had its merits.

Roy, seeing that Bennie was jumping the gun on the meeting decided not to untie the Zodiac. He then yelled up to the first deck to get Andy's attention. Andy acknowledged by a nod that he saw what was taking place. He also started scanning the cove with binoculars for any other activity.

Once Bennie and his men landed on the beach, Jonas' crew was able to set aside some of their concerns. Bennie's two men unfolded a table and four chairs and then set up an umbrella over the table. The additional odd man on Bennie's team went back to their skiff and sat down. He lit a cigarette and seemed to relax.

Frank signaled Roy to untie the Zodiac as soon as he had both engines idling. Once the Zodiac was clear, Frank revved up the engines and they were off to meet Bennie.

The trip and subsequent landing took less than ten minutes. Bennie and one of his men stood next to the table and waited for Frank and Jonas to approach.

Frank observed that Bennie had a round face with dark eyes recessed under thick black brows. There were a few grey hairs mixed in his brows. Bennie projected an arrogant image with shoulders back and chest thrust out. He would have had a sturdy look if his stomach had not protruded farther than his chest. Also distracting was the annoyed frown on his face.

Early on, Frank had a physical expectation of Bennie etched into his mind. What he was looking at was not the image he had in the back of his mind. Oh, he knew that Bennie was at least the same age as Jonas, perhaps even older, but, age was not what distinguished him. Because Bennie was a medical doctor, Frank had expected him to be better preserved. Instead, Bennie was too portly for his own good; way overweight. His hair, what was left of it, was peppered with enough grey for it to be classified as white. At least it was nicely cropped.

Bennie's voice and tone gave the impression that he garnered a peevish displeasure over having to attend this meeting. Although, there was an off chance that he was normally a man with a sour disposition and that, under most circumstances, he was not very conducive to a good bedside manner. So how was he able to acquire a reputation of being a good doctor who charitably tended the locals? If first impressions meant anything, Bennie was not matching his reputation.

Bennie tended to growl like an agitated beast when he greeted them. "Jonas, you have no idea how your visit to this island has become an irritation to me and my friends here. I have been frequenting this little spot of tranquility for a good many years. So it should come as no surprise that I am well established here. Whenever anyone tries to associate my name with this place the manner tends to concern me." He uttered his words with clinched teeth and a threatening dare in his eyes. He was not out to win any awards for pleasantness.

Frank diverted Bennie's attention from Jonas to him. "Exactly why do you think we are here, Doctor Calici?"

"You and your little bitch of a captain have been all over the island poking around. You tell me why you are here." Bennie launched the first challenge.

"Your displeasure is duly noted, Bennie." Frank decided not to give any additional honor to the doctor who was acting like a common ruffian. Never again would Frank call him by his title; he was simply a thug called Bennie. "Bennie, I have to say that you are setting a bad tone for first impressions and you have done so without allowing us to discuss our intentions."

Jonas did not flinch in the slightest over Bennie's rudeness and tone. Bennie was acting like the man he remembered. In fact, Jonas countered with his own icy stare, followed immediately by his own words of bravado. "You are as much of an asshole today as you were when I first met you. You didn't scare me then and you don't scare me now. This time, if you push me, I'll push back twice as hard."

Bennie was not one to cower in the face of challenge. He mumbled something to himself that sounded like "we'll see." Bennie's message was clear; he was going to be hostile.

Jonas leaned across the table and looked Bennie in the eye. "Look, all I want to know is what happened to Corn Dog. You see, Corn Dog and I have the same father and that makes us brothers. Yes, we are blood. You were the last person I saw with Corn Dog and all I want from you are some answers about what happened to him. If you don't tell me, then I will stay here on the island until I find out some other way. I'll poke around all I want and you can't stop me. This island, and all of Puerto Rico, belongs to the good old U.S.A. and that means I have as much right to be here as you. Now put that in your pipe and smoke it for a while. By the way, I have one more question for you. Why do you always act like some kind of a gangster?"

Bennie clenched both of his fists on the tabletop and the veins in his neck and forehead looked like they could explode at any second. His posturing intimated that there was a risk when one interfered where they were not invited.

"Jonas, I would think that you would possess enough decorum in your ignorance to at least respect what I have done for this island. I treat the poor, eat dinner with the police chief and mayor, and I go to church when I'm here. What have you done for this island? I'll answer that question for you. You haven't done squat for these people. As for your brother, he either deserted from the Navy or something happened to him. I really don't care what you think as long as you stay out of my way. By the way, the Navy closed the case a long time ago, and that's the end of it. As for me and my ruthless ways and hardness, well I learned them from a master and I intend to serve him to the best of my ability. We think the world of this island for our own reasons. We don't take kindly to strangers sticking their noses into our business. The best thing you can do is to move on and enjoy what's left of your pitiful little lives."

Frank watched the two men as they bantered harshly with each other. He accepted the concept that it was sometimes difficult to distinguish between stupidity and cleverness. Most likely, Bennie was trying to play Jonas by dismissing any notion of finding his brother. The mask on Bennie's face was not one of stupidity; it was a disguise intended to deflect Jonas from his mission. Bennie was all about drama and theatrics. If nothing else, Bennie was dispensing a heavy dose of gamesmanship in an attempt to discourage Jonas. If Jonas refused to walk away things would most likely take a bad turn. Frank also could smell the foul scent of a trap being set. Intuition always has a place in life's drama.

"I can see that my power to persuade you to leave has failed, Jonas. My orders, should this happen, are simple. My boss, the master if you will, will meet with you. He is nearby so the meeting can be easily arranged." For the first time during the meeting, Bennie showed a hint of regret.

Poor Jonas only wanted simple answers to decades of troubling questions so he was willing to do anything to fulfill his goals. He was not sure if this new meeting was a sign of progress or danger. Yes, the seed of uneasiness was growing in the pit of his stomach. The thoughts in his mind were growing heavier while his heart began to tremble. Had he pushed too hard? Only time would tell. Jonas' time on the streets taught him that when there was a combination of good and bad competing with each other, things rarely worked out for the best. He just didn't know whether to laugh or cry.

Lightning veined across the eastern sky and thunder trumpeted the storm's arrival. There was something scary about a black sky at any time of day, but when it came on a day full of sunshine at one in the afternoon, it made the hair stand up on a person's skin. Huge splats of raindrops could be heard striking the umbrella overhead. The wind began to whisk through the broad palm leaves along the beach.

The advancing storm telegraphed the end of the meeting. At least the heated exchange would not get any uglier for the time being.

Bennie stood and nodded approvingly to his man in the boat who already had its engines started. The other man had struck the umbrella and was folding the table and chairs. "We'll meet back here at the same time tomorrow. I only have one boss and he is a hard man. Don't expect the meeting to be a picnic. This is your last warning; you need to get your butts out of here, and do it quickly.

Oh yes, as a side note; there is no pirate loot or pirate hideout. I've walked this island from end to end on more than one occasion and came up empty. The only treasure here is the island's beauty."

As they cast off from the beach, Frank and Jonas looked back through the rain and wind that ferociously whirled across the island's plant life. To their front they could see Sea Venture tugging against the anchor lines. Storm or no storm, there was a lot that needed to be done before tomorrow's meeting.

In brief, the weight of the meeting's tone suggested that Bennie was operating on behalf of some evil or criminal enterprise, and that was cause enough for alarm.

Chapter 23

The storm was gone by two thirty in the afternoon. There was not even a single lingering patch of black cloud to remind anyone that it had even struck. The sky was once again clear and the accompanying wind didn't even have enough gusto to make the U.S. Ensign on Sea Venture's stern to flutter.

Frank thought back to Bennie's parting words about a pirate hideout and treasure. Why did Bennie bring up the topic unless it was an issue? Besides, Jose said he knew where the place was located and that made it a point worth pursuing. Surely, the others would be up to the task of having a look. Pirate lore was part of the lure of Caribbean life.

Jose helped Matt load the skiff with flashlights, a couple of machetes, some rope, insect repellant, and a makeshift tool box complete with a hacksaw and a cordless driver. Colette packed enough food and water to sustain them for the afternoon. Jose and Matt climbed in after Frank, Jack, Georgia and Jonas. The Zodiac was now equipped for the miniature expedition. Fifteen minutes later they were all on the beach and ready for most any contingency that they might encounter. Frank had his pistol and Matt carried one of the shotguns slung over his shoulder.

Within a few minutes they had penetrated the thick foliage far enough to extinguish the soft sea breeze that caressed the open beach. Their dry faces and bear arms now had rivulets of perspiration and the salty moisture burned their eyes. Heat and humidity were aspects of tropical island life that was not pleasant.

Frank was glad to see that Jonas had lost his vague distant look of disappointment that he had acquired immediately following his meeting with Bennie. Jonas now joined the others in their adventurous distraction. Not one of them was too old or too young to enjoy a good pirate treasure hunt.

Only a half hour passed when Jose announced their progress. “We are getting very close now. The place you are looking for is just ahead of us.” They were all silently appreciative of Jose’s time, patience, and effort. He was equally appreciative of the additional eighty dollars he had pocketed for being their guide. They most likely would not have been able to stumble onto the structure without his help.

It was hard for them to believe that they had left a picturesque white sandy beach only two hundred yards behind. The going had not been easy, though. The dense jungle-like foliage turned their progress into a physical challenge. Even the sunlight was now reduced to a few patches of shadowy existence.

Even though they were making their way along what appeared to be some kind of a game trail, the machetes still came in handy. Jose stopped long enough to point something out to them. “Look there, those are footprints. They are different from ours and I would say that there were a least four people making their way through here. It could have been yesterday or this morning; I’m not sure exactly. They knew where they were going because they didn’t cut their way through with machetes like we are doing.”

Jose’s announcement caused everyone to scan their surroundings with more focus. No one gained any sense of comfort about the situation. More alert now, they pressed on, albeit cautiously. In their now nervous state of mind, their conversation, little of it as there was, now amounted only to short muffled utterances. Their progress was now more curtailed and cumbersome. Also crossing everyone’s mind was the thought that Tommy might be out there somewhere, lost and scared.

Jose's voice interrupted their focus. "Well, my good friends, we have arrived."

Like a slinky toy, they all bunched up to the front. A rusty metal door shadowed by mossy grey-green stone was tucked deeply in the dark underbrush. It was imbedded in the side of a small knoll. The structure was cleverly concealed by nature. There was a cluster of ancient tree trunks near the entrance and that was where everyone began to stage their equipment. Georgia sat on one trunk and began drinking cold water from a thermos.

The small clearing in front of the door was only large enough for them all to crowd into, shoulder to shoulder. The ground was covered with wide flat stones with grass and weeds creeping out of the seams. Jose conveyed his opinion of the place.

"Should I take a guess, I would say that behind that door there is most likely a cave that runs into volcanic rock. I have no idea how deep it will go or what might be in it. All I know is that the U.S. Navy declared it a point of historical interest and put it "off limits" to all military personnel. I have lived on this island all my life and I know of no person that ever went inside. None of my friends or neighbors has ever paid any attention to it. To us, it has been no different than an old tree."

Frank advanced his opinion. "I don't know how old this place is, but, I do know that the lock on that door is rather new. In other words, someone is using this place for something. Matt, let's get that lock off. This is public land and there is no warning sign here. We'll make our own assessment of the contents, if there is any."

They had all come too far and endured too much to disagree with anything Frank was saying. Matt sped the process up by putting a carbon disc on the cordless driver. The lock was of good quality, but, it was no match for the disc.

Everyone stood around with a flashlight in their hand. Light beams made the area appear like an amusement park; a spectacle of sorts. Their hearts were racing with excitement. The only one harboring a fearful thought was Jonas. He was fearful that Corn Dog's remains might be somewhere behind that ancient-looking door. He was well aware that the last time he spoke to Corn Dog, his brother was looking for this very place. The big question was: did Corn Dog find someone like Jose to guide him to this spot?

The next thing that Frank noticed was that the hinges on the thick metal doors were well-oiled; dripping to the ground. Before Frank could get a grip on the door, everyone had a hand on it. "Okay! Will all of you please step back? Everyone will get to look inside once we open it up." He tried not to yell because he didn't want to be too pushy. No one seemed to notice the harsher inflection of his voice. They only wanted to have a look inside.

Jack landed a big concern that tended to halt all their efforts. "I want to remind all of you that if this is really a pirate hideout of some kind, there might be booby traps here that can hurt a fellow."

They had all seen enough adventure movies to know that Jack's warning may have merit. Whether this was the reality or not, the possibility did exist. Frank knew that even in modern times, men often planted improvised explosive devices to deter strangers.

Everyone took a step back while Frank eased the door open enough to get the beam of his flashlight through. There was something there alright, but, it was not any kind of an explosive device or trap. There was some type of a keypad that had to be battery-powered. He conveyed his assessment to the others:

"I'm afraid that there is an alarm system installed here. Since we don't know the combination, I'm afraid we will have to set off the alarm. It probably sends out a radio signal like the emergency devices they have on life rafts. There is no telling how far away the response force will be. They could be a few yards away or they could be hundreds of miles away. Once we trip this thing, we will have to look around quickly and then get the hell out of here. Is everyone clear on that point?" Everyone nodded in agreement. "Also, I need someone to stay out here and keep watch for us. Do I have any volunteers?"

Georgia answered the call for a rear watchman. "I'm your guy, Frank. I don't like confined quarters very well. I would rather walk up ten flights of stairs than ride an elevator. When I was a kid, my cousin accidentally locked me in a closet one afternoon and my mother had to take me to a shrink for six months." She was not joking even though she did want to have a look at what was behind the door.

Jonas grinned ruefully while shaking his head. He did pity all of them because they were in this predicament because of him. This was that awkward point where a man must either run away or go deeper into his trouble. Just as fast as he felt pity for them, he was able to dismiss the feeling with manly sobriety.

They filed in with Frank taking the lead. Jonas stayed next to Jack because he did not want to interfere with anything Frank did. They all found themselves in what appeared to be some kind of a foyer. There were three passages leading out of the room and they all went deeper into the depths of the facility. There was only a single table in the foyer and Frank surmised that it was used for sorting whatever was to be deposited for safekeeping.

"Let's split up here. We need to search quickly before someone comes in and ruins our day. Jonas, you come with me;

Matt and Roy, you take the center passage; Jack, you and Jose take the passage on the right. Okay, move out and be careful." Frank did not want to waste one precious minute.

Each team found things that excited them to the point of making loud exclamations. Matt and Roy sounded off first. "We found guns, lots of guns and ammo. There are machineguns here; enough to start a small war. The guys using this place must be gunrunners." Matt was already checking out a gun while Roy began loading a magazine. They were quick to capitalize on their discovery in case they had to fight their way out.

Frank yelled out. "Over here we have about fifty kilos of what might be cocaine. These people are also dealing in drugs."

Jonas concentrated on searching for any sign of his brother. "If any of you see any clothing or personal belongings, please give a shout out to me." Jonas' primary purpose for being in the hideout was steadfast; to find something that would lead him to finding out what happened to his brother.

Jack and Jose came across another form of contraband. Jose shouted out what he saw. "We have art over here. There are old paintings and some jars in here. These guys must be into everything."

Jack's search did not end with the room she and Jose were in. She found a narrow opening that only she was small enough to squeeze through. She only made it through by letting out all the air in her lungs. The small room she entered was so musty that she had trouble breathing.

The wall was full of crevices and looked like a collage of shadowy nooks and crannies. Eventually, her eyes fell on something that was in a dark corner. She could barely see into the small opening with the help of her flashlight. Then she saw an object that made her heart race. There was some kind of leather pouch stuffed inside. She withdrew a knife from a sheath on her side and began to pry and scrape the opening until she was able to retrieve the pouch.

Gently, she pulled three pieces of old parchment out of the pouch. She arranged them on the floor and with the aid of her flashlight, she began to read and decipher the writing. It was old English handwriting and it was also dated at the top of the first page. For Jack, this letter was worth more than the total of all the other loot.

The letter was dated 15 September, 1720. Jack read the letter with a tingle of excitement running through her entire nervous system. The letter read as follows:

Dear Jack, you son of a devil,

You are a worthless drunkard and a scoundrel and for that I love you. Since you have allowed me to stay for a short time on this beautiful island I am now regretful of you doing so. I can't wait for you to return from Jamaica. If any other vessel happens by this desolate place, I will seek passage and search the islands for your brutish soul.

Meanwhile, I will leave this letter in the usual hiding place so you can put your cursed hands on it. I also pray that you keep your word and keep your scurvy hands off my friend, Mary. Should your desire run out of control, then I beg that you will return Mary to New Providence until I am once again with you. I know not about Mary, but, as for me, I am quick with your child. Every time the cursed thing kicks inside me, I beg you feel twice the pain as I.

I fear that the gallows will someday take us all, but not without a valiant fight with pistols and cutlass.

Should you come across me elsewhere, then I will someday likely return here to collect this letter.

With all my love, as much as is left of it,

Ann Bonny

Jack knew that what she held in her hand was an important historical document concerning pirate characters of the Caribbean. She was well acquainted with the stories of Ann Bonny and Mary Reade who were both female pirates of great notoriety. The letter was without question from Ann Bonny to Jack Rackham (Calico Jack). This letter belonged in a museum and not hidden away in a cave on some obscure island. The letter also demonstrated that, especially in this case; a pirate's soul was made of love, gold, adventure, and crude manners. Without a doubt, piracy was nothing short of glorified crime; still, it was part of the give-and-take, the ebb-and-flow of humanity on our planet.

The other historical irony advanced by this letter was that Ann Bonny and Mary Reade were eventually captured, tried, convicted and sentenced to death. As crude as the justice system was when it came to piracy back then, they were both spared the gallows because they had been pregnant.

A voice in Jack's head was telling her to guard this letter at all cost, including a risk to her life. She would write a paper on this and then turn it and the letter over to some museum.

She looked around and saw nothing else in the room except one of those old rum bottles with a square top that were popular in the 1700's. However, its historical value paled in comparison to the letter. Fearing for the letters safety, Jack immediately started to squirm her way back out of the room. She did not want to become associated with pirate lore through her death while in possession of such a letter.

Outside, Georgia paced about nervously. She studied the area and noticed that there were two other trails leading to the site besides the one they had used. Thinking that she needed to do something more constructive than sitting and listening, she decided to venture a few yards down one of the other trails.

She took her time, stopping frequently to listen, and continued on for about ten yards. Even in the dense foliage, she was able to make out something just a couple of feet off the trail. The closer she came to the object the more it appeared to be some sort of an effigy; perhaps even a scarecrow.

She cautiously took two more short steps and then stopped suddenly; frozen with shock. She winced, feeling as though her heart was being snatched from her chest by an icy hand. The object hanging from a tree limb was no scarecrow; it was her friend Tommy. The scene projected a solemn image of savage, yet, austere appearance. His eyes were wide open with obvious fright and that only meant he had seen his death coming. The ground beneath him was stained, probably from the blood that had drained from his dying body. The sight was all she could stand; she had seen enough.

Leaves and branches tore at her face and bear arms as she ran back to the pirate hideout. She was screaming well before she reached the entrance.

Frank heard Georgia's frantic yells and was first to react. "Okay, I want everyone out of here this minute. Matt, I want you and Roy to grab as many of those guns as you can. If we have to fight our way out, then let's show the bad guys what we are made of." He was unaware that Georgia was sounding the alarm for a different reason than an attack.

Brandishing his 9 mm Taurus, Frank was the first to come through the door. Georgia had one hand resting on one of the huge tree roots.

She panted heavily and her attempts to speak bordered on hysteria. Frank shook her to her senses and then put an arm around her shoulders to reassure her.

Georgia trembled and sobbed like a frightened child. Consoling her would take time and patience and Frank could not afford either. At last, she collected her emotions and began speaking coherently. She described the scene that had frightened her and pointed out the trail where she had discovered Tommy's remains.

While the others trotted off to see what was left of Tommy, she sat down on a tree root with her elbows on her knees, and held her face in cupped, shaking hands. Jack stopped long enough to see that she was not injured in any way. Georgia's thoughts seemed to be wrapped in a hypnotic state of fear and Jack was considerate enough to leave her in that state for a few minutes.

Frank did not cut Tommy down since that would only alter what would eventually become a crime scene for authorities. Hopefully, the rest of them would not fall into a similar condition as Tommy. Frank made a mental note that Tommy's body was not only riddled with bullet holes; he also had what appeared to be stab wounds. The attack must have been brutal and was intended to be a message to whoever found it.

Tommy's savage murder caused them all to share a fearful gloom and that, in turn, was distracting them from their immediate objective; safely getting back to Sea Venture. Frank was not about to allow their despair to cloud their thinking. It was time to get them out of their emotional rut and moving toward the beach.

"Everyone listen up; there's nothing we can do for Tommy at this time. We have to stay united and focused on our situation. We all need to rely on each other and remain a team." Frank was stern, but his tone was confident.

Jose, because this part of the island was familiar to him, took the point position and everyone else followed him. He understood the seriousness of their situation and the importance of getting back to Sea Venture and the others. The pace he set garnered no complaints as he sprinted short distances and took pauses long enough to listen to their surroundings.

Jack held tight to the leather pouch she had retrieved. She had plans for the contents and a hope that the letter inside the pouch would earn a proper place in the recorded history of the Caribbean.

Georgia did her best to dismiss from her mind the image of Tommy's mutilated body swinging from a tree limb. It was one thing to see death; it was another thing to see the death of a friend; especially when that friend had been tortured to death. Even with the hideous vision of Tommy's corpse occupying her subconscious, she was able to carry all the flashlights which had been entrusted to her care.

Matt carried three machineguns and all the tools he had brought with him. He also knew that the machineguns were useless without ammo, so he kept an eye on Roy who was weighted down with 9 mm ammo.

Frank kept his pistol tucked neatly in his belt at the small of his back. He also carried one of the machineguns. His biggest challenge was Jonas who was so physically challenged by age and lack of fitness that he had difficulty keeping up with the group. Frank would never leave Jonas behind as long as he was alive and breathing. Poor Jonas was gasping to fill every cubic inch of his lungs.

When they finally reached the beach Frank remained in the thick brush with Jonas while the others went on to the Zodiac. While Jonas leaned against a palm tree doing his best to catch his breath, Frank searched the beach for any sign of their unknown aggressors. Sure enough, he spotted an unmanned skiff pulled up on the beach near a clump of trees. It was only a matter of time before they discovered the hideout's breach. Frank figured that the killers were not far behind so he pulled Jonas to his feet.

"Come on, Jonas, we have to get the hell out of here and do it fast unless you want to end up like Tommy." Frank's message had no trouble getting through to Jonas. Jonas was on his feet and running as fast as his heart and lungs would allow.

By the time the Zodiac was loaded and all were aboard, Matt had it turned around and speeding toward Sea Venture. In this instance, timing was everything because four men burst onto the beach waiving and firing their machineguns. Luckily, Matt had cleared enough distance to put the aggressor's weapons out of range.

Frank grabbed a pair of binoculars and took a close look at the men on the beach. They had stopped firing their weapons and one man was speaking on either a handheld radio or a cell phone. Tommy was dead, murdered, and men were angry and egos had taken a hit. The war was officially on and more hostile contact was inevitable.

Once they had safely returned to Sea Venture, Frank decided that they would not meet in the galley this time. The bridge was better suited for them to keep watch for their enemies, whoever they were. During the meeting, they would first reflect on what they found on the island, and second, they would strategize until they came up with a safe plan for a quick departure. Tomorrow's meeting with Bennie's boss was no longer a route to learning about Corn Dog; it was about learning the terms their adversaries would offer.

Once everyone was up to speed on what had occurred, Georgia was inclined to make a few comments concerning Tommy. She did her best to collect her emotions, improving only to the point of acquiring a frown. "I think Tommy was just a proud man; too proud for his own good. Now I see why pride is a liability and a sin."

Jonas interjected his hint of an excuse for Tommy. "You have a point Georgia. A man's pride has a tendency to bring him more sorrow than what a humble man would receive. Don't get me wrong, I don't think Tommy was a bad person. He was just somewhat misdirected when it came to his friends and his ambitions.

Frank thought it was pointless to waste a lot of time discussing Tommy. "Unfortunately, Tommy was not given enough time to amass any shame for his behavior. Once a person departs this world it is a little late to morally convert him. We can debate the pros and cons of his motivations when we are out of this mess."

Chapter 24

All eyes were on Frank to come up with an adequate response. He was keenly aware that the pirate cache was physical evidence of a sea-going smuggling enterprise and that meant the U. S. Coast Guard would have the greatest interest in pursuing a criminal case. Presently, the most important thing that needed to be done was to file a report with the Coast Guard. Any interaction with the local authorities was out of the question because of Bennie's known association with the local police captain.

Jack, Andy, and Frank began putting their heads together to prepare an accurate and detailed initial report. Additionally, the arrival of a Coast Guard vessel would send Dark Shadow and the mystery ship out to sea; no matter how well- prepared these thugs were, they were no match for the Coast Guard. Naturally, the arrival of the Coast Guard would ensure the safety of those aboard Sea Venture.

In short order, the report was officially filed via radio fax. Distressingly, as luck would have it, the U.S. Coast Guard contingent that serviced this area had all its assets committed to other sea rescues. There was no chance of a response for at least twenty-four hours. The Coast Guard's unavailability coupled with the prospect that Bennie had island authorities in his hip pocket meant that Sea Venture was on its own.

While their new situation was being considered another unforeseen occurrence was about to throw an additional torpedo their way. All eyes turned to Dark Shadow as it suddenly hauled its anchor. At first, Sea Venture's crew was encouraged by the prospect of Dark Shadow's departure. However, the scene quickly deteriorated when the mystery ship pulled up behind Dark Shadow, blocking its departure. By repositioning, they had successfully blockaded the entire cove, thus, also blocking Sea Venture from escaping. The good guys aboard Sea Venture were essentially caged by their enemy.

Frank quickly speculated on the development. "They must have monitored some of our calls to the Coast Guard as well as the Coast Guard's response. They know the cavalry is not quite on its way. Time wise, they are pressured to do something to us before help arrives. If they don't launch an attack right away then we should at least be hearing from them in short order. They will want to bring all the pressure on us that they can. They know the Coast Guard will arrive at some point so they are also under the gun to do something with their contraband in the pirate hideout."

Andy called for a quick training session. With Matt's help they began test firing the newly acquired machineguns until everyone aboard was familiar with them. They all knew the importance of self-defense as their situation was taking a bad turn. Even Gerty and Colette seemed to master their assigned weapons. Jonas did not care for the machineguns and chose to fire a couple rounds with one the shotguns. The importance of them doing something constructive could not be overemphasized.

Their attention returned to monitoring the two ships that were restricting and intimidating them. All observed activity was quickly shared with the others. Additionally, tension was building among everyone.

With an eye on Sea Venture's pulse, Frank called for a meeting to discuss contingency plans. "I think we have two options to consider at this point. We can fight off an attack here on Sea Venture or we can make a break for the island. Should we make it to the island, we can hide out until our adversaries run out of time and are pressured to leave. No matter where we go or what we do, things are going to get tough for us. We don't know how many men they have, but we do know they mean business and they are willing to kill."

Colette offered a questioning thought for consideration. "What are the odds of reasoning with them or even cutting some sort of a deal with them?"

Georgia's face was strained with two competing emotions: fear and anger. Neither emotion was strong enough to keep her from responding to Colette's notions. "They murdered Tommy and God knows he was no threat to them or their smuggling operations. No matter what we do, I think we will have to fight them. The real question is: Where do we have the best fighting advantage?"

"You should have been in the military, Georgia." Andy exclaimed admiringly. You are right; those guys are up to something. Even as we sit here debating, they are up to something." He pointed at the other ships. "Look there, men are climbing into two skiffs and they are all armed to the teeth."

"Thanks Andy. They almost caught us off guard. Everyone, get off your ass and grab a weapon and find some cover. I don't want anyone to shoot unless I give the order. Our weapons are only good at close range. Let's see what they are up to."

All eyes were on the two skiffs, but they were not launching an attack. They throttled their way to the beach. Their wakes were wide and their powerful engines sprayed sea water in the hot air. Frank speculated on what the men were up to. "They are either going to retrieve their loot or they are going ashore to block us from escaping by land."

The worst case scenario was expressed by Andy. "I think they are doing both. They want their loot and they don't want to leave any witnesses behind that might link them to Tommy's murder or their smuggling activities."

Jonas, like the others, was looking for guidance. "Frank, what do you want us to do?"

We are going to sit tight and stay ready for action. They are probably waiting to see what we are going to do. By now, they must know that we are armed, but, they don't know what kind of a fight we can put up. Our best option is to wait until the sun goes down. Darkness tends to even the odds a little."

Jack took her position on the bridge because that was the nerve center of all ships. She leaned over the rail and called out to Frank. "You and Jonas need to come up here. Bennie is on the radio and he wants to speak to both of you."

Frank was afraid that Jonas had his cognitive abilities clouded by too much emotion. "Jonas, please stay cool. If you don't mind, I will do the talking. Bennie might be fishing for weaknesses in our armor and resolve. We need to come across as clever and as bold as they are. I don't want to piss Bennie off, but, I do want to push a few of his buttons and make him sweat a little." They continued talking as they made their way to the bridge.

"You are the man, Frank. This is what I pay you for and today you are going to earn every cent. Besides, anything you do can't make our situation any worse." Jonas was comfortable leaning on Frank and he had all the confidence in the world that Frank would do well.

Frank and Jonas arrived at the bridge. Before picking up the radio microphone, Frank managed to cast a sheepish grin at Jack. Yes, he knew Jack was the right woman for him and was the right captain for Sea Venture.

Frank's tone was all business. "Bennie, this is Frank and Jonas is here with me. What's on your mind?"

The radio speaker crackled as Bennie's voice filled Sea Venture's bridge. "I think by now you know that we mean business. We have you outnumbered two to one. I believe you know that it's time for you to throw in the towel. I want your weapons, your ship's log, and everything you took from our storage facility. That's the only way I'm going to let you out of this cove alive. There is a time to fight and there is a time not to be foolish. I'm giving you a chance to leave this place in one piece and go on to enjoy the finer things that the Caribbean has to offer. You need to decide quickly before I change my mind. I'm giving you ten minutes to talk it over with Jonas and your pals. I'm confident that you will do the right thing." Bennie signed off thinking he was ahead in the standoff.

By this time everyone had relocated to be within earshot of the bridge. The idea that a bunch of murdering smugglers would take pity on those aboard Sea Venture and allow them to sail off into the sunset to meet with the U.S. Coast Guard was ludicrous. No one was about to buy into that concept. All Frank could see was heads shaking "no" to Bennie's deceptive offer. They had no choice but to fight Bennie and his henchmen.

Frank wanted to buy enough time for darkness to fall. There was the glimmer of an idea beginning to glow in the back of his mind. Yes, every minute was a treasure worth counting. He sat back in a chair and watched the ship's clock tick off precious minutes. Bennie's set limit went past without any movement by Frank. Then fifteen minutes had slipped away. Bennie had to be sweating over the time and over what Frank was up to.

Frank allowed twenty-five minutes to elapse before calling Bennie regarding his proposal and demands. "Bennie, this is Frank. Are you there?"

"Yes Frank, I'm here. I hope you have conferred with Jonas and your shipmates and that you all agree that my offer is in your best interest." Bennie tried to sound optimistic.

"Bennie, by your own words, you are nothing but an underling for your boss. You are only a foot soldier without a lot of authority to make major decisions. Your word is not enough for us. We want to meet with your boss because his word is what really counts. You see, Jonas brought us all here to find out what happened to his brother. We have to see that mission through. Your boss might have that one thread of evidence that will give closure to Jonas. I propose that you and your boss meet with Jonas and me. We will meet you and him one hundred yards off our bow one hour from now. We would be glad to discuss the terms of our departure with your boss. You have ten minutes to give us an answer. If you don't like our offer, then we can all stay put and meet with the Coast Guard when they arrive. They tend to move a little quicker when the ante goes up. I think you and your boss would be a good catch for them."

Frank knew that Bennie would not like the ultimatum that was just presented to him. No one aboard Sea Venture was about to give an inch to a thug, even if he was a doctor. Negotiation was an art and Frank was no stranger to the process. The clock was ticking and Frank negotiated with his eye on the ball; the one that he hoped would get them out this mess without any losses.

Bennie was steaming through the pregnant pause that followed Frank's bluntness. Following a couple of minutes of dead silence the speaker once again came to life. This time, Bennie's tone was not filled with optimism. He spoke reluctantly. "My boss has agreed to meet with you and Jonas. Should you not come to an agreement with him, then we will be in an all-out war. I hope you know what you are doing, buster. We checked up on you and I think you are nothing but a cheap P.I. You are out of your league when it comes to this kind of an environment. You are gambling with a lot of lives. We will see you in an hour."

Frank ignored the blustery comment concerning his credentials; Bennie was obviously not aware that he was dealing with a seasoned military man. Thugs always tend to beat their chests and talk trash when the heat is on. The important thing was that by the time the meeting was over, it would be dark. The moon was nearly gone and with it visibility would also go.

Andy had Sea Venture's bow pointed east and that meant its starboard side would be out of sight to anyone on Dark Shadow or its unidentified companion ship. Another important development was that the hostile skiffs were no longer ferrying back and forth to the island; they were tied to their mother ships. The smugglers loot was most likely now aboard their ships.

Jonas asked Frank a thoughtful question. "What do you think will happen to Tommy's body?"

Frank answered as honestly as he could. "I would bet that it is either shark bait somewhere beyond the cove with a heavy weight tied to it or it's buried somewhere a long way from the hideout. They wouldn't leave it hanging from the tree where the Coast Guard could find it."

"That's my guess, too." Jonas shook his head regretfully. "What do you think they will do with the guns and drugs?" All Jonas could do at this point was to ask questions out of curiosity. He really didn't care about the answers to his questions; he just felt like he had to be involved somehow.

Andy decided to address Jonas' last question. "I'm sure if the Coast Guard shows up while they are still here; both ships will make a run for it. Should the Coast Guard get too close, they will dump everything they have into the ocean."

Jack asked the big pressing question. "Do you think we will have to fight them to the death?"

Frank provided his best rational response. "We already know that they are all a bunch of killers involved in serious criminal activity. They have nothing to lose by killing us and everything to gain if they are not caught. You can only hang a killer once. They know that we will spill our guts to the Coast Guard if we are left alive. The bottom line is that people are going to die tonight. The point of a battle is to make the other guy die for his cause, and not you for your cause. I have a plan in my head if you're ready."

Frank's conscience told him that it was his absolute duty to protect the others at any cost. For him, the thought of flinching from this duty was not tolerable.

Frank knew from experience that when a guy knows he has to fight, then it is crucial for him to get the first lick in. He had to keep Bennie and his boss off balance while pulling them out in the open where they were vulnerable. The outcome depended on Sea Venture and its crew using the element of surprise. Hopefully, Frank's plan would deliver a shock that would demoralize and scatter his adversaries. When he looked around at the others, he knew he had to turn sheep into wolves in order to walk away from this fight.

Chapter 25

One of the most stimulating and encouraging devices a person can produce is a simplistic plan for preserving the lives of friends while dealing a crippling blow to an evil adversary; a tall order, indeed. In his approach, Frank was enjoying a sense of satisfaction drawn from common sense and simple materials as he pulled his plan together.

Moreover, a decisive advantage begins when secrecy reigns. With that in mind, the last thing Frank wanted to do was telegraph his intentions and strategy. Additionally, the more complex a plan was, the greater danger there was for it to go wrong so he intended to keep his strategy streamlined.

Addressing Matt, Frank began to lay out a portion of his plan. “How many boarding ladders do we have on hand?”

“We have four and they are all serviceable.” Matt prided himself in keeping equipment in good order.

“That’s great, Matt. Now, how much lubricating grease do you have on hand?”

“I have a full ten gallon container that has never been opened and I have another container that is half full.”

“My good friend, you have just made my day. As soon as it begins to get dark, I want you to lower three of those ladders over the starboard side to within three feet of the water. From the bottom up to a height of about ten feet, I want those ladders to be dry as powder. From that point on to the top, I want them to be heavily greased. When the boarders reach those greased rungs, we should be hearing weapons and bodies hitting the water or thumping down into their skiffs.”

Roy started a chain reaction of laughter when he exclaimed: "They will think they are trying to hang on to a greased pig at the county fair."

Gerty didn't join in the amusement. Instead, she wore a puzzled look on her face. "What if they don't go to those ladders? They might have their own grappling hooks and ladders like in those old pirate movies. They might go to the port side because it is facing their ships."

"You brought up an interesting point, Gerty. I thought about that, too. That leads me into the next point of my plan." Frank shifted his head and eyes to Roy. "Roy, I know all ships have extra lighting. I want you to set up some lights overlooking the portside. Our attackers will want to surprise us so they won't want to make themselves vulnerable by trying to board us in all that light. The lights will encourage them to circle wide and come in on our starboard side where it will be darkest. When they see our ladders, they will think we put them there so we could escape and make a run for it to the island."

"You're right, that's what I would do if I was them." Gerty gave voice to the obvious conclusion after hearing Frank's logic.

Georgia hesitated to agree. There was always someone in every group with a preponderance of doubt. "What if they are able to climb the ladders in spite of the grease? What if they don't see our ladders and just go aft where it's dark and use their own grappling hooks?" As with all plans, there are always a few "what if" questions.

"You have two separate concerns. Here is my solution for your first concern. This is war, honey. We don't want to miss an opportunity to strike them effectively. Our lives depend on it. Should the grease not stop them, it will cause them a lot of trouble and slow them down. I'm betting some of them are going to hit the water or fall back into their skiffs. Before they have a chance to regroup, I want you guys to throw everything you have at them. I want your bullets to rain down on them like a thunderstorm. The bullets that don't draw blood should be sinking their skiffs. As for your second concern over them boarding at the aft stern, two of you should be positioned back there to handle that situation. We have the high ground and the element of surprise; all we have to do is use it."

Georgia's voice quivered with an afterthought. "I don't want to go to prison for killing anyone."

Jack jumped at the chance to set aside her fear. "Under Maritime Law, we are empowered to defend our ship. I'm Sea Venture's Captain and it is my duty to defend the ship and crew from an unlawful attack. This is my responsibility and I am authorizing the use of deadly force against these murdering pirates. This kind of response has been supported by governments and courts for hundreds of years and its use today is routinely applied effectively in the waters off Somalia."

Since so many concerns were being aired, Andy decided to throw his hat into the ring. "What if they attack while you and Jonas are meeting with Bennie and his boss?"

"That's what the extra ladder is for Andy. I want that ladder tossed over the port side when you see us approaching. I want you all to see, in clear bright light, that it is me and Jonas coming aboard on that ladder and make sure there is no grease on it. I don't want to be killed by friendly fire. In the event that Jonas and I are killed or captured, then you and Jack will be calling all the shots and you can pull that ladder up. It's just like in the military, when a commander is killed or incapacitated; the next in the chain of command takes over.

"Yes sir!" Andy saluted casually with two fingers.

After playfully returning Andy's salute, Frank turned his attention back to Roy. "After you do the lighting on the port side, will you have any lights left over?"

"We have plenty of extra lights in storage. We always keep extra lights in case we have an emergency. Light is at a premium when we are out to sea so I made sure we have plenty."

Smiling at the way things were coming together, Frank continued. "Since the bridge is our nerve center, I don't want to draw any more attention to it than is absolutely necessary. As much as possible, we need to keep the enemy from knowing where we are on the ship. We can use the red lights of the console for whatever we have to do on the bridge. I want the extra portable lights turned off and pointing at all avenues of approach to the bridge. I want these to be the most powerful lights we have. Should any attacker make it that far, I want them blinded with those lights at the last second. If they don't put down their weapons and surrender, then shoot them. That's the way it is done in a life and death encounter. Trust me, they wouldn't give you the same choice; they would just gun you down. The smart ones, if there are any, will give up. We are dealing them one surprise after another and we want to keep them guessing about our ability to fight."

There were no more concerns left to be addressed. Everyone was on the same sheet of music so the meeting adjourned. Now was the time for all to pitch in and make things ready. Taking a cue from Jack, they all moved about the ship casually, as if they didn't have a care in the world. Anyway, that was the way they wanted to appear to the prying eyes aboard the two hostile vessels. To the outside world, those aboard Sea Venture projected a late afternoon of leisure activity on a typical Caribbean day. No visiting tourist ever appeared to have a worry in their temporary world away from the hustle and bustle of their world back home.

The sun began to drop in the western sky and shadows were beginning to pop up all over Sea Venture. The temperature dropped a few degrees and the easterly breeze it brought felt good to all of them.

Frank and Jonas began climbing down to their waiting skiff that was tied up alongside. Roy hoisted the ladder back up once they were in the skiff. Frank continued to monitor the sun's position and its brightness. He would milk the clock for every minute of time in order to reach darkness.

At the cove's entrance two men could be seen climbing down a ladder over Dark Shadow's side. They were making their way to a skiff. Like Frank and Jonas, they were in no hurry.

Across the board, no one seemed to be excited, either grimly or joyously, in what they were doing. Everything looked routine. In fact, everyone on all three ships was doing their creative best to avoid the slightest appearance of being anxious.

Frank's thoughts switched focus for a moment. He felt as though he was temporarily giving himself over to a spiritual force. This was a break that he had earned. Whatever souls were made of, his and Jack's had to be of the same essence. If only God could confirm this for him, he might be able to define his spiritual purpose in life. As much as he wanted God to respond, he still didn't know how to pray for it. A platoon sergeant once told him that all soldiers have spiritual thoughts when they are facing the prospect of dying. No sooner had these thoughts occupied his mind, they faded.

Jonas pointed at Dark Shadow. "They just shoved off. Are we going to let them sit out there a few minutes before joining them?"

"Sure, we can let them sit out there and stew for a while. I'm sure they see us, so they know we're coming." Frank's focus was now on the impending rendezvous.

A small splash of water midway between Sea Venture and Dark Shadow told Frank that they had tossed out their small anchor to keep their skiff from drifting away from the meeting site. Frank fired up their skiff's two outboard engines. Jonas untied the line and they began idling over to the meeting.

The closer they got to Bennie's skiff, the more Jonas strained his eyes to see their facial features in the waiting skiff. Jonas wanted to see what Bennie's boss looked like. After all, Bennie was only the other man's puppet.

The scene was now clouded by darkness. Jonas was so curious that his eyes became riveted on the unidentified man. The more Jonas focused, the more he was becoming aware of his buried emotions. These strange feelings were creeping up on him and overwhelming his mind. The more Jonas stared, the more surreal the scene became.

When the two skiffs were only about five feet apart, Frank killed the engines and threw out an anchor. The man with Bennie bent over and reached out with large black hands and pulled the two skiffs together. The man looked up and spoke softly to Jonas. "Hello Jonas, it has been a long time since we saw each other."

The man's voice was ghost-like to Jonas' ears; it was a voice that had risen from a dark grave.

Following an eerie pause that reflected decades of nightmares and guilt, Jonas at last knew where his missing brother was. Jonas sat there speechless, ready to faint from shock. He could do nothing in this paralyzed state, but stare into Corn Dog's face.

Life was cruel enough, but, this unexpected recognition shocked the very marrow in Jonas' bones.

With stammering lips, Jonas attempted to speak. He struggled and still he was unable to control his feelings. His head shook as if he was about to have a seizure and then his long-harbored grief began to teeter on the edge of anger. However, Corn Dog did not permit Jonas to get his words out.

"I'm sorry Jonas. You were way too righteous and honest for me. I was more of a sinner than you could have ever accepted. There was no way I was going to return to New Orleans with you and waste away in the poverty that I grew up in."

With tears flowing in rivulets from his eyes, Jonas managed to ask a pointed question. "What happened that day when you disappeared on the island?"

"There's no point in me giving you all the details so I will summarize. Let me just say that I left Vieques with a bag of diamonds and a new business partner." Corn Dog could not have been blunter.

"Corn Dog, you left behind the most important thing you ever had when you left Vieques." Jonas intended to deliver a message.

"What's that?"

"You left your soul!"

"I see it differently, Jonas. I had what I wanted when I left. I wanted to be left alone. I didn't want the Navy and I sure as hell didn't want you poking around in my life. I was sick and tired of you always henpecking me about God and a holy life waiting on us in New Orleans." Corn Dog was essentially spitting his venomous words at Jonas.

"My dear brother, Corn Dog, you have fallen a long way from Christ's teachings." Jonas had to say this even though it was not likely Corn Dog cared about such things.

"I didn't fall very far, Jonas. In New Orleans, I was a bastard with no real family. My own father, our father, disowned me. I was a thief, ripping off tourists. All the Navy gave me were three squares and a ship to work my ass off on. You were okay to talk to, but, you could never set me up to get what I have now. I have a villa in Jamaica and another one on St. Croix. That mega yacht sitting over there is mine. I live and eat like a king and not a two-bit bastard on the streets of New Orleans. So don't try to preach your sanctimonious words to me."

Frank touched Jonas on the shoulder to calm him back to reality and the dire situation they were in. "I'm so sorry my friend. Corn Dog, it seems, deceived you or you misread him. Either way, he was never the good brother you thought he was. Life has pulled a cruel trick on you, Jonas."

The emotional pain inside Jonas was beginning to subside; first replaced by disappointment, and then by savage anger. There was even room for a taste of revenge, should the opportunity present itself.

Jonas managed to squeeze his eyes shut in an attempt to block out the sinful evil of the moment. His effort worked only slightly, though. As a God fearing Christian, he had to bring himself to forgive Corn Dog as if he was an ordinary stranger who had trespassed against him. Sadly, the effort was not working as well as he wanted.

Frank knew the time for talk and reflection had passed. At any time, one side or the other would have to take that proverbial leap from the frying pan into the fire. He studied Bennie and Corn Dog for only a few brief seconds before speaking.

"This whole ordeal would try the temperament of a saint if there was one here. At this moment, I doubt if any of us has much patience left."

Corn Dog did not respond to Frank's declaration. Bennie, on the other hand, responded not by words, but by action. He reached around to the small of his back to claim something. Frank read Bennie's action clearly and beat him to the draw. Fortunately, Frank's reflexes were much quicker. With lightning speed, Frank's 9 mm Taurus was pointed squarely at Bennie's forehead.

"Don't be stupid, Bennie! Before you get that pistol out, your brains will be all over the skiff and your buddy, Corn Dog." There was no question about Frank having the drop on them both. "Jonas, would you be kind enough to relieve them of their firearms?"

Jonas climbed into the skiff with them. He felt safe and he felt confident that Frank would not hesitate to shoot either man, or both, right between their eyes.

"What do I do with their guns?" Jonas held both of their pistols in his hands.

"Throw them into the water. Where these two are going, guests are not allowed to have guns."

No sooner than Frank spoke, there was the sound of two distinct splashes. Corn Dog and Bennie were now officially prisoners under the eyes of the law and by all that was right with regard to human conduct.

"What do we do with these two criminals?" Jonas was seeking additional guidance.

Frank answered Jonas' question by firing his pistol five times; once into each of the engines of their enemies' skiff and three additional rounds into the bottom of their skiff. He was well aware that the shots would be heard by everyone in the cove.

"Unless you two degenerates want to go down with your skiff, you should climb aboard with us." Frank never lowered his pistol after delivering his ultimatum.

Suddenly, the starboard side of Sea Venture lit up like the Fourth of July. Frank was convinced that their adversaries had fallen for his deception. The gunfire was intense, and hopefully decisively in favor of Sea Venture's crew

There was an awkward exchange of looks between Corn Dog and Bennie. Corn Dog attempted to project an authoritative demeanor. "My men are as tough as they come and they are armed to the teeth. Your best bet right now would be to turn your guns over to me and begin begging for my mercy."

"That's really funny. Maybe you should have tried being a comedian. At any rate, I'm not about to surrender. In fact, I'll go a step beyond that. If you so much as blink at me or if any of Sea Venture's crew receive so much as a scratch from your men, I'll blow both of you to smithereens." Frank sat down facing his two captives and Jonas stepped up to the skiff's controls.

Frank was not about to allow them to relax, not even for a minute. "Let's go have a look at what's happening at Sea Venture, shall we?" He could see fear and uncertainty beginning to creep across their faces, and that was a reward in itself.

Bennie was determined to overcome his deteriorating situation. In the back of his mind there was an inkling of hope that Corn Dog's men would prevail in their attempts to take Sea Venture. Should that occur, then Frank would be forced to renegotiate from a weaker position. All Bennie wanted at this juncture was to be able to sail off on Dark Shadow and return home.

A state of fear was equally encroaching on Corn Dog's state of mind. In spite of being afraid, he was still bold enough to take a risk. He had to let his men know that he was a prisoner in need of rescuing. If he could only reach his cell phone in his right front pocket and somehow send a text message to his men, he would have a chance. Surely, his men could set up an ambush alongside of Sea Venture. Time was running out too quickly for Corn Dog, even with Jonas idling the skiff's engines back.

Corn Dog leaned over as if looking over the side at the water. His cell phone was quickly in his hand and he was typing a text message.

Frank caught a glimpse of the illuminated face of the phone. Before Corn Dog could send his text, Frank snatched the device from his hands. With a flick of the wrist, he sent it into Davy Jones' locker for fish to gaze at.

Frank leveled his pistol at Corn Dog's forehead. Like a frightened child, he shut his eyes and waited for Frank to shoot. After all, that was Frank's warning if he even so much as blinked.

"That was a nice try Corn Dog. You just used up your only warning. The next time you make a stupid move like that, you will be shark bait. Am I making myself clear?"

"You are a dead man, Frank. It is only a matter of time until I have the upper hand. I'm personally going to off both of you myself, that's a promise."

Corn Dog leaned back in his seat and relaxed with a sinister frown on his face.

Chapter 26

If experience is the best teacher, then this night would become the arch upon which the crew would build. They were all working as a team to defend themselves or be killed doing their best. Their needs were individual, yet common to all. Moreover, they were at war and that justified any violence they undertook.

As bad as they wanted to have a quick victory, they were content to win in increments as long as it ended decisively in their favor. As for Frank, he knew that every battle or skirmish had its own face. The worse face of all was wearing the face of death. The last ones standing would be the winners and that meant they would be wearing the face of life and that was the biggest prize of all.

Jack and Colette were constantly walking between the two entrances to the bridge. The radio volume was turned down so they could both hear the steps of anyone approaching. With machineguns at the ready, they were ready to switch on the powerful lights to blind any intruder advancing to the bridge.

Matt proudly had the portside lit up like it was under a noontime sun. Gerty kept a nervous eye on the stern with her gun leveled on the darkness below the aft end.

Andy, Roy, and Georgia were each positioned at one of the greased ladders on the starboard side. One and all knew that the first blow would be half the battle; possibly the deciding half. They would deliver their fight with all the force and resolve they could find within themselves.

All their work and preparation was for defense and survival. It had little to do with revenge for Tommy's murder. At this point, Tommy's death was collateral damage. Most likely, revenge would be left to the courts.

Sadly, the strong lance of courtroom justice had more to do with law and procedure than it did with justice. The history of recorded trials often was filled with stories of injustice because our system preferred ten guilty go free to keep one innocent from being convicted. In spite of the flaws of our justice system, the rule of law does exact some degree of fairness and that alone makes it the best one in the civilized world.

Matt saw the first evidence of someone being out in the cove, just out of range of the lighting. Until now, the water in the cove had been smooth as glass. Waves were now slapping at Sea Venture's portside waterline. Skiffs were out there somewhere, circling in search of the right place and best opportunity to launch a decisive attack. Bent over so he would not be easily spotted, Matt dashed around the ship and whispered the alert. It would not be long now.

Andy switched the safety switch to the off position on his gun when he heard the muffled gurgling sound of outboard engines. Georgia and Roy followed his example.

Suddenly, two skiffs could be seen sifting out of the darkness and then idling by. It took them only one pass to see the hanging ladders. As predicted, they assumed everyone was on the portside watching the illuminated water that faced the hostile ships.

The two skiffs idled off out of view to finalize their boarding tactics. They decided to idle and drift slowly and quietly from opposite directions along the starboard side and then each skiff would let two men off at each of the end ladders. The two skiffs with the four remaining men would meet at the center ladder and then they would all begin their climbing assault.

Andy couldn't believe his eyes when he saw that the attackers tied both of their skiffs, the total of their transportation, in one place, at the center ladder. This ladder was his responsibility. He figured the attackers at the two end ladders would be nervous about having nothing but water under them; the attackers had acted foolishly. Georgia and Roy had those end ladders covered. In less than a minute, all hell would break loose. Andy's inner voice cried out, "Come on boys, bring it on!"

Shots rang out and disturbed the quiet night air, but they didn't come from Sea Venture. They came from the two skiffs where Frank and Jonas were meeting with Bennie and his boss. The sound of weapons being discharged sent surges of adrenalin through everyone's body.

The attackers read the shots as the signal to begin their attack while those aboard Sea Venture read them as a signal to begin their defense. The irony was unknown to the participants. On the two end ladders, the attackers had already reached the greased areas. It was like slapstick comedy. When each lead man fell, they fell on the trailing man.

Georgia and Roy unleashed a volley of fire that left all four men on the end ladders dead in the water. The four men at the center ladder began firing wildly skyward when they saw their fellow attackers shot off the end ladders. It was a frightening revelation that they had not expected

Georgia and Roy immediately joined Andy at the center ladder. One attacker kept up enough covering fire for the other three to escape on one of the two skiffs. The one left behind ended up in a watery grave, riddled with bullet holes. Their attempt, so far, to assault Sea Venture had failed, but they were not out of the fight yet as they disappeared, blending with the darkness.

Matt heard the sound of an approaching skiff and figured it was Frank and Jonas returning. He lowered the good ladder over the side when he recognized them. He was puzzled when he saw that they were not alone. Who was in charge of who was the big question? The last thing he wanted to do was miscalculate. Nothing could have prepared him for what happened next.

Bennie and some large black man moved like a bolt of lightning and shoved Frank out of the skiff. Matt did not have a clear shot as the skiff spun about with Bennie using Jonas as a shield. The skiff melted into a mist of spraying water until it was out of sight. It was last seen heading toward Dark Shadow.

Frank, soaked to the bone, was able to grab the ladder and make his way safely aboard Sea Venture.

Roy and Georgia kept watch over the starboard side so Andy could go check on Gerty at the stern. Everything was unfolding so quickly that they were all caught up in a state of temporary confusion. By the time Frank had reached Matt, he was rattled by more gunfire at the stern. Gerty appeared and made a quick report.

"Andy has a man pinned down at the stern. Two men got past me and split up and are heading to the bridge. Where's Jonas?"

Frank blurted out a hasty response. "Bennie and Corn Dog took Jonas prisoner. Has anyone been killed or injured?" Frank knew that he had just delivered unwelcome and bewildering news without any chance to explain. "Gerty, how are the others?"

I don't know about Jack and Colette, but, the others are holding up okay. How do we get Jonas back? I don't know what I would do if anything happened to him."

Frank didn't answer her. "Matt, I want you to come with me. Gerty, I want you to stay here and yell out if you see anyone coming our way. I'll fill you in on everything else when I get the chance. Right now, we have to secure this ship." Frank had to be curt with Gerty because he was short on time.

Andy was on the starboard side of the stern and he had a lone attacker pinned down behind a storage locker. Frank yelled out to Andy. "Heads up, Andy; help is here."

Frank and Matt came at the outnumbered man from the portside of the stern. Andy was able to rush the man while Frank and Matt had him pinned down. Andy pulled the man's gun away and saw that the man had been wounded in the shoulder. Finally, they had a prisoner.

Frank took advantage of the situation and began asking questions of the wounded prisoner. "If you want to live, you had better answer my questions. What were your orders for attacking us?"

The man was reeling from his wound and feeling a great deal of pain. "Our orders were to kill all of you and take your ship. We never let prisoners live; we torture them and then kill them when we learn what they had been up to."

The man was young; probably in his early twenties. He was not yet a seasoned professional. His shirt was covered with blood and his black skin was covered with perspiration. He wasn't far from going into shock.

Frank played on the man's inexperience. "You know, your buddies left you here because they couldn't depend on you in an all-out firefight. That's right, you were expendable. If you cooperate with me, you have a chance to make it through this alive. Do you understand what I'm trying to tell you, son?"

Frank was prepared to press as hard as was necessary to get answers that mattered. "How many men are left on your two ships?"

"Besides the owners, there are only two men left on each ship. I think you have already killed most of us. The others thought you would be easy to take. I just want this to be over." Both emotionally and physically, the young man had surrendered. The whites of his eyes shined with fear and the sight of seeing his own blood was taking its toll.

"What's your name, son?" Frank asked as he thought about the man and the situation he had fallen into. His question was also as close as he was going to come to establishing rapport with the man.

"My name is Charles and I'm form St. Croix. Am I going to die?"

"Not if we can help it. We have the upper hand here and your team has all but lost." Frank decided it was time to show the man a little mercy. He folded a piece of cloth into a square and placed it over the wound. "Keep pressure on this and it will slow the bleeding until I can have you treated properly. Right now, I have to take care of your two pals."

"Be careful, mister; they are mean as hell." He offered the warning because he was being treated fairly.

Frank stood the man up on legs that were wobbly at best. "Matt, take Charles over to Gerty and tell her to shoot him if he tries anything funny. Otherwise, she can tend to his wound. After you have taken care of that, I want you to join me and Andy on the bridge. Make it snappy because Jack and Colette might be in trouble with Charles' pals."

Andy asked a question that should have been on everyone's mind. "Where is Jose?"

Matt had the answer. "Since this isn't really his fight, I told him to stay in the galley and we would call on him if he was needed."

At the portside entrance to the bridge, Colette was facing her own challenges on her own terms. She was wearing a faded red, white and blue housedress with black laced shoes. Her hair was pulled back in a bun at the nape of her neck. Around her waist was a yellow sash with a cluster of silver dimes on the front. The silver dimes were a Voodoo sign of protection. To avoid physical harm or injury she wore an unusual talisman around her neck on a silver chain. Allegedly, it was especially potent when traveling. The design included a dot in the center of a circle within a triangle and represented the Voodoo Loa Gran Siligbo, a protective spirit force. The other symbols on the talisman were simply present to keep this power close to the wearer. Should anyone have had the opportunity to look closer at her hair they would have seen a few stray grey hairs mixed in with the coal black ones. These were signs of a long association with her talents and that lent her a degree of majesty. There was no smile on her face as she placed her machinegun on the chart table; this was serious business.

Soon an attacker would come for her and that meant danger so she began placing select articles on the table; things that would work to her advantage. She would protect herself and the others around her; with the nearest one being Jack. She was certainly not opposed to using Voodoo as a psychic and deadly weapon. After all, she was in the Caribbean where Voodoo was commonly practiced among indigenous people. Even though her roots in Voodoo were of a primitive origin, they were still an integral part of her heritage. People facing fear tended to cling to and use what they know best and she inherited her knowledge through a long family succession that had its origin on the African continent. Thusly, Colette was a product of her cultural influence.

She neatly arranged the following articles on the chart table: a Polaroid camera with flash; a vial of graveyard dust; a miniature black coffin; a black doll inside the coffin; a dagger; a red candle with a book of matches; a vial of powdered chicken blood from a black chicken; and a vial of Devil Powder. Lastly, she shoved a small wooden crate under the table and then grinned approvingly at her work.

Jack was poised at the starboard side entrance to the bridge. She had been watching Colette with keen interest. Contemporary logic and reasoning told her that in the modern world of civilized man, most people were separate and above such archaic practices as Voodoo. She could not understand how such practices could persist in the midst of current technology where man could make a desert bloom; make it rain by seeding clouds; move mountains to make room for highways; make a tropical rain forest in the middle of a city and on and on…. At least Colette was ready to fight with a machinegun in addition to her psychic forces.

"Colette, I'm not going to ask you what all that stuff is for. I just don't want you to let some thug shoot me in the back."

Colette waved a hand across the table. "What I can do with these things is out of your realm. Here in the Caribbean, I am defined in terms of the people I am most likely to encounter. In my world, there is both religion and magic and I know how to use the latter as a weapon. Sometimes, I use magic to appeal for help and at other times I use religion when my soul is under attack by evil. Sometimes, there is a thin blurry line separating the two. You know I am a practicing Catholic and I attend mass whenever I can. You see, God doesn't help anyone unless you give Him his due. With God's power, I can do this work. Without it, I can do nothing. In other words, I need it all."

Colette's points were not likely to convince Jack of their legitimacy. However, people will do what they are comfortable doing; especially during a life and death fight.

Their nerves were on edge as they anticipated being attacked. Shots were being fired at the stern and that meant attackers would be on their way to the bridge. Jack and Colette would never yield to the same savagery that had taken Tommy's life. The best way to view the attackers was to see them as faceless creatures with cruel instincts. Jack vowed to take on the attackers with the same cruelty and determination that they were using; with some discretion, as much as decency allowed, she would fight fire with fire.

Jack heard her attacker's approach as his weapon brushed the lifeline. She knew right where he was and without any delay she switched on the powerful light that was aimed at the right spot. The attacker had no warning and did not anticipate the surprise. No man knew how to react to sudden blindness. He was vulnerable and unaware, but he knew he had to strike back quickly. Firing his gun wildly without a clear target was all he could do. During the seconds of quiet that followed, he attempted to change his magazine. Then he heard a female voice ordering him to lay down his weapon. This was something his male ego would not accept.

Jack issued one final challenge. "Drop your weapon or prepare to meet your maker."

"No bitch will tell me what to do." This was his only reply.

Out of ammunition, he pulled out a long knife and charged toward her voice. Her gun barked fiercely riddling his chest with bullet holes. He fell dead a few feet from where she was standing. The death of each attacker tended to even the odds in favor of the good guys.

Jack leaned against the wall, frozen with sadness at having to kill another human being. Sometimes it was difficult to love your enemy like the good book says. But, this man gave her no choice. It was him or her and surely God would understand. At any rate, she would confess this to a priest.

Jack had escaped death and that was a marvelous thing. As for her attacker, she would pray for his soul even though it was on its way to the fiery windows of hell. There was no telling how long that man had been on that path. A simple thought flashed through Jack's mind: In this world, death is the last experience of physical life. Only the soul travels on.

On the portside at the bridge entrance, Colette was facing her own challenges. A young black man slipped into the bridge as Colette was distracted by Jack shooting. She was at least four feet away from the chart table when their eyes met. He smiled at her as if he was winning a prize. He stepped closer and then lowered his weapon. "Beautiful lady, I think you would look better without that dress on. Let's have a look." He reached for her and then froze.

She stepped confidently over to the chart table and retrieved the Polaroid camera and snapped a photo of the man. As expected, he was surprised, even startled by the flash. He rubbed his eyes so he could see with some degree of clarity. Obtaining a full view of her seemed to stun his senses. He had seen clusters of dimes like this many times in his life and he knew that most Voodoo priestesses wore them. The talisman was the defining distinction for him. He was facing more than an ordinary woman.

His eyes wandered over to the chart table. Many times in his life he had seen the same articles that were now before him. In the right hands, they could be instruments of torment and death. He stood there too scared and shocked to speak. In his heart, he admonished himself for falling into her trap; the blackest magic he knew of.

Reading the fear in the man's face, Colette used her foot to open the crate under the table. Her albino boa slithered out of the crate and onto the deck. The huge snake made its way to the man. Stumbling back he dropped his gun on the floor. The serpent crawled over his machinegun and stopped. The snake's piercing eyes stunned him further.

Colette began unleashing a curse (conjure), that penetrated the man's soul. She lit the red candle while his photo developed. The man watched the paper until he clearly recognized his image on the paper. She rotated the photo around so he could see it better. With great swiftness and accuracy, she plunged the dagger into the center of the photo. "Here and now, I curse you to death with this instrument."

She rocked the dagger to and fro until it was free of the photo. With dramatic formality, she placed the photo in the little black coffin on top of the black doll. Next, she held the red candle over the coffin and poured hot, melted wax into it. First there was black smoke and then the photo crumpled, bursting into flame. "With this red wax, I seal your death with certainty and speed. Like your photo, you will soon be dead."

The man recoiled slightly as he watched helplessly.

Colette was not finished. Some men, strong men, were not afraid to die. She picked up the vial of graveyard dust and sprinkled it on the effigy in the coffin. "With this graveyard dust I bury and seal your fate beyond redemption."

Picking up another vial she continued to torment the man. "With this Devil Dust, I command all the devils and demons at my call to enter your mind and punish your heart and soul with more pain than any mortal man can bear. Shortly you will feel the horror of madness and insanity. Looking into your eyes, I can already see the demons taking possession of your body. No amount of water or salt can cleanse you now. Snakes and spiders are already crawling out of the demons to destroy your mind and soul."

The final touch came next as she picked up the last vial. "With this blood of a black chicken, I close all escape routes for the demons. You can only stop the horror and pain with your death."

To anyone's senses and decency, this "kill conjure" was morbid and evil. It was also effective when used on a believer.

The man was a believer. She had set a curse on him and he had to get her to release it before he could shoot her. Yes, he was yielding to her and to his own fear, ignorance, and confusion. He would rather commit suicide than lose his soul to the Devil's magic.

He was a smuggler and a hired killer and he was a follower. If only he was a Voodoo priest he might be able undo what was now set in stone. The only one at hand who could break the curse was the one who delivered it. Outside of convincing her to release it, the nearest possibility was in Haiti. There was no time for that. He could already feel the demons at work in his body, he was doomed. In a last-ditch effort, he appealed to her mercy. He began pleading with his eyes to this 120 pound Voodoo priestess even though he knew his begging was useless.

Colette had the upper hand in this psychic battle and she was not about to relent; not one bit. If she did, he would kill her. Her stare was cold and unfathomable in resolve.

The snake suddenly slithered across one of his feet and that was the last straw. Screaming like a banshee, he turned about and ran out of the bridge and dove into the warm water of the cove. Colette ran outside and watched the water, but the man never surfaced. He found solace in a watery grave through his own choice.

Colette drew a long breath as if to speak, then instead of a sentence escaping, she simply let out a sigh. She had accomplished her goal without firing a shot.

Jack walked up behind her. "Colette, I have never seen anything like that before. You killed him with Voodoo."

Colette turned and faced Jack. "I didn't kill him. He died from self-induced shock brought on by intense emotion."

Jack scratched the back of her head. "That's a very clinical analysis, but it works for me. That's the way it will read in the ship's log. Maybe that man will make some progress in eternity."

Colette saw her boa making its way out the door. She picked it up and then responded to Jack's comment concerning eternity. "You know, there is no progress in eternity. Progress can only be made during specific spans of time by people who are alive and in this world; physically present. The only thing beyond the grave is a spiritual existence that does not end."

"I see your point, Colette. We all have to make our decisions about eternity while we are here because after we pass on to the afterlife, it is too late." Jack understood the concepts of death and afterlife. Most Catholics have given this matter considerable thought.

Jack looked at the chart table and the articles on it that had converted it to a Voodoo altar. "I feel sorry for the priest that hears our confessions from this trip. Hopefully, this is all covered somewhere in the Catholic Catechism."

Colette added another concern. "I wonder what kind of a penance I will have to do."

Frank didn't know why one of the attackers jumped overboard and he really didn't care. He had bigger fish to fry. Somehow, he had to rescue Jonas and that meant taking more risks.

Jose couldn't stand by in the galley any longer. There was too much shooting and excitement for him to lay low. He joined Roy, and together they took the body of the man Jack had killed and placed it in a storage room. Ten minutes later everyone met on the bridge.

"Does anyone have an idea on how Andy and I can board the ship next to Dark Shadow?" Frank did not have all the answers, but he knew how to ask.

"I thought Jonas was being held on Dark Shadow." Gerty was trying to understand why Frank did not want to go after Dark Shadow where Jonas was being held. All this strategy stuff was confusing to her.

"Let me explain my theory this way. They won't expect us to go after the other ship so it might be easier to take. Besides, I bet the loot is on that other ship and having it will give us a powerful bargaining chip for getting Jonas released. And if that doesn't work, it's better to ram Dark Shadow with the other ship than to ram it with Sea Venture." Frank hoped they would agree with his logic.

Matt liked Frank's reasoning and added to it. "We have the means to pull this off. We have two of their skiffs and there are only two men on the other ship. That's if our prisoner is telling us the truth. We also have their grappling lines from their boarding at our stern. All we need is a diversion to keep them looking at Sea Venture."

"What if I start repositioning Sea Venture like I was going to ram them while you guys come in behind them on the skiffs?" Jack and Matt had just handed Frank a workable plan.

"If we wait too long it won't work. They know the Coast Guard will be here in the morning so this is the last place they want to be. Let's have at it." Frank's enthusiasm was re-energized. Jose continued to make rounds to check on the others and assist wherever he was needed. A ship of Sea Venture's size required a great deal of attention.

Jack checked her watch and saw that her time to act had arrived. With the right touch, she skillfully engaged one of the bow thrusters to maneuver the bow around to the left and used the rudder to assist. Additionally, she put the ship into a gentle reverse.

With Jose's assistance, all of Sea Venture's lights were turned on. Jack sounded the fog horn to make sure she had the other ship's attention. Within minutes, she had Sea Venture's bow pointed directly at Dark Shadow.

Jack picked up the radio microphone and made her challenging call. "Dark Shadow, this is Sea Venture. You have five minutes to turn Jonas over to me or I will ram you and do my best to sink you. The clock is ticking."

She saw Dark Shadow's anchor being raised when a voice blurted a response to her challenge over the speakers. "Sea Venture, this is Dark Shadow, I'm telling you to stand down. You could damage both of us and we would not be seaworthy." The tone was one of panic.

Jack was not about to back down as she responded. "Then we will both be here when the Coast Guard arrives." Something in her gut told Jack that, if necessary, she was prepared to cease bluffing and actually ram Dark Shadow if it meant saving Jonas. This was a decision that no captain would like to make.

She spotted three men scrambling down to a skiff that was tied up to Dark Shadow. At the same time, gunfire erupted on the other ship and that stopped the men from leaving Dark Shadow. Dark Shadow's anchor remained in the water.

Once again, Sea Venture's radio speakers jumped to life. This time it was Frank's voice that she recognized. "We have two wounded prisoners here. The other ship is ours. I want to speak to Corn Dog."

"This is Corn Dog. I have a gun to Jonas' head. Leave my ship or I will blow a hole in his head. I mean it. I have nothing to lose." Corn Dog's tone was approaching a desperate point.

Jack interceded before Frank could respond. "You had your chance, Corn Dog. You are going down one way or the other. You are nothing but a bloody pirate and you know what happens to pirates." She revved Sea Venture's engines and with ear-splitting determination the cove's air reverberated from a succession of blasts from the fog horn. However, something she saw kept her from doing more.

She saw a man climbing out of the water and into the skiff that the three men had intended to use only a minute ago. It was Andy.

Moreover, Frank had left Matt and Roy aboard the captured ship and made his way over to Dark Shadow. He knew the crew would be preoccupied with what Jack was doing so he made his move. He tossed a grappling line over Dark Shadow's stern and boarded un-noticed. Hopefully, Andy was having a similar success. He and Andy had feared that Corn Dog would actually kill Jonas anyway so they had decided to go for broke.

Bennie had ordered a crewmember to hoist Dark Shadow's anchor so they might have a chance to make a run for it. The man had not seen Andy approach from behind until it was too late. The man pulled a knife from a sheath and lunged at Andy. Andy sidestepped the man's effort and took him from behind. He snapped his neck like a dry twig. His Special Forces training was paying off.

No one on Dark Shadow knew they had been boarded. Corn Dog cast a disparaging look at Jonas who was standing witness over two very agitated men.

"Corn Dog, don't you think this might be the right time to take the safe road between two extremes? It's not too late to do the right thing. You let me walk and you will have one less crime to answer for." Jonas doubted that his appeal would alter Corn Dog's desperate resolve.

Corn Dog's face faded to a poignant and ignoble expression. His whole world was close to collapsing around him. His eyes began to glisten and his forehead wrinkled with disgust. Bennie's face equaled Corn Dog's.

Andy met Frank near Dark Shadow's bridge. They were each relieved to see the other had arrived unscathed. This was a do-or-die moment that had to be played by ear. There was a single crewmember, Corn Dog, and Bennie left to deal with. The odds had gotten better; much better.

Andy whispered a cryptic report. "I took out a crewman at the anchor. I'm sure the other one will be coming to see what happened to him. The anchor is still in the water so this ship isn't ready to leave."

Before Frank could say anything there were footsteps coming up behind them. They ducked into the shadows and waited. The man nearly passed them by when he was surprised. He started to reach for his pistol and quickly realized that any attempt to fight would be suicide. He raised his hands and surrendered.

"Where are the others?" Frank's voice was quick and demanded a truthful answer.

"One man is at the anchor. I was on my way to see what was taking him so long. The others are all on the bridge." There was no use lying to his captors. For him, the fight was over.

"Are they ready to give up?" Andy asked hopefully.

"You will have to ask them. I just maintain the ship for Dr. Calici."

Andy spotted a large deck locker and opened it. Frank had taken possession of the man's pistol and Andy motioned for their captive to climb into the locker. As Andy closed the door he gave him a stern warning. "Be quiet and I'll come back and let you out. Otherwise, I'll shove this thing overboard with you in it."

Frank and Andy headed to the bridge to confront what was left of the bad guys; Corn Dog and Bennie.

They were not sure where anyone would be situated in the room so they decided to enter from opposite directions; one from the starboard side and one from portside. As sure as the sun was rising somewhere on the planet, at least one more person would die on Dark Shadow before this was over.

It was warm and humid so both doors of the bridge were left open for ventilation. The lighting inside was dim, but still brighter than what was outside. Frank and Andy burst in while crouching slightly. They knew they would have the element of surprise on their side. Even though they carried their guns at the ready, they would not fire unless they had a clear target. They were not about to chance shooting Jonas.

Corn Dog was looking out the window with an eye on Sea Venture. He was in deep thought trying to figure out the best way to get out of his predicament. Bennie stood behind him with a pistol pointed at Jonas. They were both still in the fight as far as they understood the fight.

When Jonas recognized Frank and Andy, he knew it was time for him to shine. He snatched the pistol from Bennie's hand and shoved him aside. Corn Dog snatched his pistol from the console where he had placed it while talking on the radio.

Andy tackled Bennie just as he was trying to reach for a machinegun on the chart table.

Frank pointed his Taurus at Corn Dog while yelling. "Freeze or I'll shoot."

Three shots rang out in quick succession. Jonas was holding a gun, the one he had stripped from Bennie's hand. Corn Dog fell back onto the console and then slid down to a sitting position on the deck. Blood was oozing from his chest.

Frank gently took the pistol form Jonas' hand and watched as Jonas reacted to what he had done.

"Oh, Corn Dog, my dear brother. Don't you see, you were never a bastard; not to me. You were my brother and I loved you. All I ever wanted was for us to live out our lives together while laughing and singing and praising God, together. I grieved for you all these years and now that I have found you, I had to kill you. Please, say something before you go. Tell me that you did care about me. Damn you for being cruel and damn me for not seeing the man that you really was."

Corn Dog did not answer. His eyes glazed over into submission to another place; his eternal home. He had departed this world without airing a single regret or offering any penance. Death always follows life. The thing that was now bothering Jonas was the way Corn Dog had chosen to live; a life bound together without any spiritual thread. What kind of a life had his wayward brother lived? Did he ever love anyone or anything? Now, there was no way of knowing. The legacy he left was one of mystery and deceit.

Frank saw that it was time to take Jonas back to Sea Venture where he would be among those who did care about him. It was a time for him to mend and put his life into a proper context. He was hurt and emotionally damaged, but he was not beyond repair.

"Let's go Jonas. No matter how long you stare at Corn Dog, you will never find the answers you are looking for. Besides, we have a lot to do before the Coast Guard gets here. I'm sure they will separate us and press hard to find any inconsistencies. In other words, they will conduct a criminal investigation involving deaths, murder, smuggling, drugs, and even piracy. In the time being, your friends are concerned about you and they will want to see you." Frank worded his invitation with the utmost of care.

Andy made sure Bennie and the crewmember that was locked away in the deck locker had no doubts about being prisoners. Until the Coast Guard arrived, they were all prime suspects under citizen arrest. Matt and Roy also had wounded prisoners that needed medical attention. Yes, this would be a long night.

Chapter 27

Upon their return to Sea Venture, everyone assembled in the galley. By the time Frank brought Jonas in and watched him take his place at the galley table, he knew the day's trauma and excitement had dwindled to a more tolerable place. Matt, Andy, and Roy secured the prisoners in an empty storage room. Frank worried about what sort of story they were fabricating among themselves. But, not separating them couldn't be helped because of the limited facilities on the ship.

Colette took the lead with respect to Jonas. What she felt for him was more than a simple fondness and friendship. "Sweetheart, I am deeply sorry for all the guilt and torment that has haunted you all these years. I know that you see it as some sort of punishment. That couldn't be farther from the truth. In reality, your emotional and spiritual pain is baseless. Your new challenge is to restrain your anger and disappointment by leaning on your spiritual faith. That is where you will find guidance and a renewed life. What you went through pales in comparison to what Christ suffered during the Passion and His Crucifixion. So, there is no need for you to wallow in self-pity. Look at it this way; this is the first day of your new life."

Jonas listened to every word and knew Colette was right. "All I ever wanted was the truth. Now I have it and I'm still not sure I'm free. There is still that little kernel of pain in my heart and I'm not sure what to do with it."

Jack saw that Colette was on the right track so she joined in. "The cure you seek has three parts: The Father; The Son; and The Holy Spirit."

"I don't know if I know how to reach God. So many times in my life I thought He was out of my reach." Jonas' tone was a clear indication that he wanted to open up.

"You have to pray to Him for healing. That's how you reach out to God." Jack thought all Christians knew about prayer even though they sometimes had difficulty in applying them.

"I have prayed before and it didn't seem to work." Jonas was having the same difficulty that so many other people had experienced when trying to speak to God.

Jack felt compelled to lecture, albeit with care and courtesy. "Did you ask the saints and the Mother of God, Mary, to intercede? Have you asked others to pray for you? Look, here is the bottom line: Either God will stand up and shield you against your suffering or He will give you the strength you need to endure it. But, if you are not willing to ask Him for it, through prayer, you may very well continue to suffer. Your relationship with God is a two-way street. If you never give up on God; He will never give up on you. All of us have our faith tested; some more than others. Right here in this room you have a circle of friends who will pray for you. The Church is full of more people just like us. You have a lot going for you and your life is far from over; it is just beginning." Jack meant every word.

If thoughts had a physical voice, there would have been unparalleled chatter taking place in the galley. Each one of them was eager to contribute something. However, they respectfully bided their time and held their tongues and listened. All of them would have offered the same message: inspiration and encouragement.

Gerty, the one who had known Jonas the longest as a dear friend took the stage next. "Jonas, I, like you, have troubling challenges haunting me from my past. These are things that I must face. Matt and I have been discussing a lot of my issues and I admit that the road to my recovery will not be simple or easy. Neither you nor I have the luxury of facing life as if it is a simple household task. We are also faced with having to figure out what our purpose in life is and we can't take that challenge lightly. The process we must use is a journey, and as we travel down that road, we have to constantly look inside of ourselves for many of the answers that have been eluding us. Our journey, and all those things that have influenced us, tell me that I have to make some very dramatic adjustments. Look at me and listen carefully, now is the time for us to become poised and grounded if we are to be ready to face ourselves and all the emotions associated with our past. We have to recognize and understand how and why these things have impacted our lives. The important thing for you and I is that we begin this new journey of change now; this very minute. For the first time, in a long time, we have friends around us to comfort and encourage us." Gerty was demonstrating that she was finally seeing life with the clear light of reason, and she was using her God-given free will wisely.

The look on Jonas' face sent a distinct message to those around him. Through some unconscious conviction, he was embracing the moment with an eye on a brighter future; a spiritual resurgence. The words he was hearing were not a bunch of lofty and empty platitudes; they came from people in his life who cared. Jonas' mind and thoughts were telling him that it was truly time for him to rebound from his dark emotional depths.

Without speaking, he stood and walked to the door. He gazed up at a star-studded sky. God was up there; that he was sure of. Silently, he prayed to Him. One thing he knew was that since man took his place on earth, he had always looked up at the heavens for some divine sign that would move and inspire him.

When he finished praying, he looked back at his friends. What he saw in their faces was that God finally was answering his prayers. Yes, his internal conflictions were obstacles that he could now overcome. He now understood that he could make peace with himself through the Holy of Holies, the inner light of his own soul; God. With God's intervention, through his friends, his heart and mind would no longer be the torture chamber for his soul. God was by his side.

Frank approached Jonas and placed a hand on his shoulder. "You have been tortured enough, Jonas. God tends to send us messages through some of the most unexpected venues. By watching you, I have received such a message and learned something. Self-torture is an example of poor reasoning taking the place of God's grace. I too, see that it is time for me to make some changes in my life. I now realize that we don't have second-hand souls that were purchased at some two-bit thrift store. God did not only give us a free will; He gave us our souls."

Chapter 28

As expected, the Coast Guard conducted a thorough investigation. They sealed off the cove and forbid everyone to leave until they were all either interviewed or interrogated; a distinction that was made by the investigating officials.

Fortunately for all concerned, Jack had possessed the foresight to make detailed entries in Sea Venture's log. Naturally, and to some extent disappointingly, the Coast Guard visited the pirate hideout and searched the area around it for Tommy's body. His corpse was not found. Based on the alleged friendship between Bennie and a local police captain, the FBI was notified.

The defining details that went against Bennie and Corn Dog's men were that the drugs and contraband were found aboard the mystery ship and Dark Shadow. In fact, Bennie and Corn Dog had already been subjects in other Coast Guard and DEA investigations. Two of the prisoners went out of their way in search of leniency by spilling their guts. They heaped all the blame on the backs of Bennie, Corn Dog, and the others who had been killed. Bennie clammed up; demanding a lawyer.

The Vieques part of the investigation took a week to complete and resulted in drawing a lot of attention from the San Juan's offices of the FBI and DEA. Moreover, the investigation was expanded to include Jamaica, St. Croix (a U.S. territory), and New York City. The work would go on for months, if not longer, as leads were developed and followed. At last, among much relief and some quiet celebration, Sea Venture and its crew were allowed to leave.

Jack was left with a variety of things to work on. She had a ship to run; an old letter of historic significance that demanded attention; and of great importance, she had a budding relationship with Frank to pursue. Considering all that was on her plate, she was elated over Jonas instructing her to sail Sea Venture to Ft. Lauderdale, Florida so everyone could unwind and emotionally recompose. She also had to find an acceptable replacement for Tommy.

When they finally pulled out of the cove, everyone gathered on deck to wave their farewells to Jose. Vieques was his home and he would never leave. His son stood next to him aboard their fishing boat and waved back at their new, and now departing, friends. This part of the adventure had come to a close.

At mid-day on the first day at sea, Jack sat quietly in her cabin looking at her highly coveted prize; the old love letter from one infamous female pirate to another. She was attempting to relate to her little treasure by giving it a great deal of honor and academic recognition. It had historic value. For years, she had been at sea as a pathless wanderer and now she had an opportunity to make a small historical contribution to others like herself. She would devote a good deal of her time and energy to make sure the letter found its proper resting place.

This was a time in her life when she found herself facing two different paths and that meant she would have to make a choice between Frank and her old seafaring life; unless she could somehow combine the two. The prospect of change was always a challenge. When she finally chose, she wanted to do so with such confidence that no power on earth could tear her from her commitment. Presently and admittedly, she was surprised at herself over her willingness to adjust her temperament toward some new path that was not yet defined.

Her thoughts were in a flux; bouncing from one to another and back again. Refocusing on the letter and its antiquity made her aware of an internal struggle over values. The struggle was between heart and head. Two sets of concerns were warring against each other; heart and intellect. They were like two governing territories in disagreement over purpose and importance of something that was probably mundane according to nature.

She knew that history reflects facts along timelines; this was educational intellect. On the other hand, there were many deeply imbedded emotions associated with historic events; matters of the heart, political agendas. It was not enough that she had recovered a centuries-old article that attested to the private lives of some infamous characters; both male and female characters. The characters had been real and they had lived passionate and robust lifestyles that were out of vogue for their time. The letter was revealing; the two women had lived during a fascinating time when crudeness on the high seas delivered mixed messages to the civilized world. At times, various monarchies had embraced the savage services of pirates and referred to them as privateers, a more politically acceptable term. Once these privateers were no longer useful, they were reduced to being public and political liabilities, thusly, the same monarchs that had exploited them and held them in high esteem had them chased down and hanged as common criminals. This was an example of greed being a sin that corrupted at all levels of society. For Jack, literary compromise was the answer. The letter would be preserved as a historical article based on fact. However, in her write-up, she would show the emotional side of reality. What good is history if we don't learn from it? For Jack, that was the letter's true value and importance.

The letter was important, but so was Frank. In her mind, Frank was a man with rare intellectual gifts, courage, resourcefulness, and a drive for adventure. He also had a knack for leadership. He had come into her life seemingly from nowhere and swept her off her feet. Right from the start, their hearts and minds had jelled into a romance. In some mystical way, she thought of him as her first true love; aside from Christ and the Catholic Church.

She knew Frank possessed strong ethical standards and that she had breached those standards when she had lulled him into a sexual encounter; a violation of her own religious dictates. All men and women have their times of weakness and that makes them prone to sin. By the grace of God, she was able to acknowledge her fault and find a priest. When her sin was absolved through confession, she was relieved and grateful for knowing a merciful God. For her, a free will was both a curse and a blessing; that meant she was fully human.

At least her regard for Frank was of the highest sort; one based on love. She just didn't know how to proceed from this point. One thing they shared was their keen interest in, and inclination toward, adventure. However, she would have liked it better if Frank's pursuit of adventure was more prone to some semblance of holiness. Something like a pilgrimage to the holy-land or missionary work would be more to her liking. Oh well, pursuing just causes in the midst of danger and fighting evil were also good undertakings. The world was full of people needing justice and charity. When it came to Frank being a man of religious faith, he was symbolically like a ship without a compass.

Frank was doing the same as Jack, he was sitting alone in his cabin, reflecting. Likewise, his thoughts were bouncing around in search of solutions. In the true sense of leadership and a concern for others, he was worried about everyone aboard Sea Venture. Leaders, as they should be, were always thoughtful of others, but great leaders put those in their charge above self-interest. Real or perceived, there are always matters that need to be addressed and resolved.

As time had passed at sea, his love for Jack had continued to evolve with increased intensity. Each time he thought of her it was in the highest of terms. He was always on some kind of a mission and a new one was now taking seed; making Jack happy.

If it was possible to write one great testament on the tablet of his heart, he would pen the following: "I shall do my best, if she allows it, to be to her a true friend; that is, to be to her all that the needs of her nature require." This vow he would carry out to the best of his ability.

In the meantime, he would adjust to her whole nature in any way he could. Somehow he would have to attune himself to her spiritual life until his heart was in harmony with hers. Maybe God would somehow allow their spiritual halves to combine and become a "single and complete being;" a marriage in every sense of the definition.

Frank also worried about Jonas. One question he was agonizing over was whether or not Jonas and Colette were truly compatible enough to fall in love? They seemed to be quickly moving into a romance; a relationship that was deepening daily. Jonas needed someone in his life who was stable, and most importantly one that possessed a loving nature. Unless something intervened, their relationship would have to run its course. After all, people have to live their own lives on their own terms. Frank vowed to watch and be reluctant to interfere. He was a confidant and an advisor and those positions only gave him a license to do so much. At least Colette had demonstrated a strong, yet eclectic, spirituality.

Everyone aboard had acquired steadfast routines that addressed their individual and collective wants and needs. None of their desired adjustments came as any great surprise.

Georgia had been spending all of her spare time on the bridge with Andy. They were forever sharing personal stories and warm embraces. Anyone chancing to walk in on them would have seen their conversation fade like they were two teenagers wanting to avoid the prying eyes and ears of adults. When this occurred, their facial expressions would turn into sheepish grins.

When it came to Gerty and Matt, well it looked as though she was his new apprentice. They tended to spend most of their time down below making sure the engines were functioning properly. The more she hung out with Matt, the less inclined she was to dwell on her craving for alcohol. This was not the cure, but it was a step in the right direction.

Roy was the odd man out. With Tommy gone and Georgia devoting her time and energy to Andy, Roy was reduced to being a loner. Fortunately, the others took notice of Roy's isolation and drew him into their activities. On several occasions, they all attempted to play cards with him at the galley table. He never felt slighted or left out and he was happy that he did share a relationship of friendship with all aboard.

Frank and Jack renewed their old routine of meeting and exercising together in the fitness room. They often kissed and held each other while making sure they didn't let their encounters slip into a potentially sinful arousal. They often discussed faith and spiritual topics in a profound and yet realistic manner. Their closeness and relationship was safely staying on a Platonic course. Their thoughts and hearts were quickly becoming aligned.

Finally, Sea Venture arrived at Ft. Lauderdale and did so without incident. The ship took on a madhouse ambiance as everyone seemed to have some private goal that needed to be achieved in the quickest manner possible.

Jonas called an urgent meeting. He announced that everyone could come and go as they pleased as long as they were back for a seven o'clock dinner. During the meal, he promised to let everyone know what his future plans were.

As each of them left the ship, they were checked by U.S. Customs and immigration officials. Oddly, Frank and Jack did not depart the ship together. The others commented among themselves with concluding thoughts that amounted to Jack and Frank having to attend to some official duties that forced them to separate.

At last, all had returned on time and were seated around the galley table. In spite of being tired, they were, one and all, in high spirits.

When Jonas sat down at his customary place, Colette was at his side. She would not serve dinner until Jonas finished the meeting. Thankfully, he did not waste time bringing his meeting to order.

"Friends, I have some refreshing news for you. We have all been through a lot and I know the worst is past." Jonas was beaming like a sixth grader who just won a spelling bee. "Both Colette and me are going to catch a plane back to New Orleans. We will be gone for at least two weeks. One reason for our trip is to allow Colette to pack up more of her personal affects. You see, we are officially going steady." Jonas' eyes searched the table for a reaction.

Gerty was the first to react. "I think you two go together like bees and honey. Colette, I hope this means you are a permanent fixture around here and especially in Jonas' life. As for myself, I have a lot to learn from you; especially when it comes to cooking. You see, Matt and I are getting together as well. A month ago, I would not have thought there was a man like Matt out there for me. Today, he took me to my first meeting at Alcoholics Anonymous. I couldn't be happier or more optimistic." Everyone applauded and wished them success and happiness.

Andy and Georgia were equally ready to state their future plans. Andy was their spokesperson. "Gerty, that is a tough act to follow, as was Jonas' announcement, but, I will do my best. After a lot of soul-searching, I have decided to go back to college on the G.I. Bill. Georgia and I are going to get part time jobs to make ends meet. She is going back to school, too. My major will be engineering and Georgia's will be education. Even though we won't be here with you, we will stay in touch. Friends like you are hard to come by."

No one wanted to see Andy and Georgia leave Sea Venture. They were as much a part of the ship as any of its components or crew. People were what gave a ship its soul.

Jonas did not see Andy's news coming and he immediately realized that it would have an impact on his life and the others aboard Sea Venture. "I think I can help out with some of your college expenses if you promise to return a couple of times a year. You could say it's my way of giving you a bonus. I don't want you to become a faded memory, you know, like that old saying; 'out of sight; out of mind.' You guys are family." Jonas put a warm smile on everyone's face.

Roy didn't really have any news to report. "Okay, all I want to know is; do I have a job here on Sea Venture?"

Jonas grinned widely. "As far as I'm concerned you can stay here until you retire. Oh yes, you have to teach me how to play cards if you don't mind."

"My time is yours, boss." Through Jonas's words, Roy had all the reassurances he needed.

The whole group moved in unison and rested their eyes on Frank and Jack. Jack looked at Frank with a questioning concern on her face because she had no idea of what he might say.

"I do have some news for you. I have been doing a lot of inward looking concerning my faith. I have struggled with this topic for most of my life. From time to time, I tested the waters of different paths and each time I came up short.

"There are literally tens of thousands of churches out there that make a claim that attests to their denomination's right to being dubbed the one true Christian Church.

"Early yesterday morning, my whole world unexpectedly changed. I usually work out in the fitness room right before daybreak. I like to see the sun beginning to rise before I start exercising. There was a slight glow on the eastern horizon and I knew the sun would soon show itself. At first, it was a dull ball of yellowish orange. All at once, a ray of flaming light filled the sky. I guess I had never watched the sun rise with such intensity before. It was spectacular and brilliant beyond simple explanation as it lit and warmed my face. It seemed to reach right down inside me to some place I never knew existed.

"This is going to sound like some mystical experience; something esoteric. A warm brightness warmed my entire body, right down to my soul. The thought that began to run through my mind was that I was feeling God's glory and splendor. The more I looked at the sun, the more it seemed I was looking at God; not his physical face, but his essence. At that moment, I realized that God did love me, too. I wiped tears of joy from my eyes.

"But that was not the end of it. At that moment, Jack walked up to me. I didn't see her face, not at first. What I saw was the silver crucifix hanging around her neck; a symbol often taken for granted. I have never experienced anything like this before, and believe me, I have been around.

"This morning, I went to a Catholic Church and learned a great deal. As you are aware, I come from a military background, and for that reason, I know the importance of tradition. The Catholic Church is the oldest Christian church in existence. No other Christian church can make that claim. From Christ and the first pope, Peter, there has been no break in apostolic succession.

"Yesterday morning, when I saw that crucifix around Jack's neck and knew she was Catholic, I knew I had to become Catholic. I have signed up for classes and am looking forward to my baptism and confirmation."

The looks on everyone's faces was astonishing, but, the look on Jack's face was nothing short of spell-binding. She struggled to get her words out. She had not been prepared for what Frank had said. "I can't find the words to express how I feel. I had no idea that you would set your sights on Catholicism; I only had a hope for you to do so. You are beginning one of the greatest faith journeys the world has ever known.

"I would like to say something about your spiritual interaction with yesterday's sunrise. The idea that God is in nature is true. You see, God is often revealed in nature; in spirit form. You were truly in God's presence and you felt it, as you should have. You didn't hear God say anything; you felt Him. He wasn't a face looking down at you from the clouds like you see in many Christian paintings. God was in the sunrise itself. God created us and nature and when He did, He wove Himself into the fabric of everything. You were blessed by Him when you felt His presence; His essence. When we encounter God through nature, it is up to us to interpret it as part of our relationship with Him."

Jack did not mean to deliver a sermon. She was only stating an aspect of her beliefs. She was simply speaking from the heart concerning Frank's experience.

Frank had his sights set on something else. In his mind, it was every bit as important as his faith. Should things work out, he would be blending his religious journey with another journey of equal significance. He reached into his pocket and pulled out a small box and knelt down on one knee. "Jack, will you marry me?" He opened the box and presented her with a diamond ring.

"God's blessings just keep coming. Yes, I will. And I want a church wedding."

The women in the room cried and the men began slapping Frank on the back to congratulate him.

In the coming years there would be more adventures waiting on these two.